D0966323

ETERNAL SOJOURNERS

A NOVEL

DARRYL PONICSÁN

Skyhorse Publishing

First Edition

This is a work of fiction. Names, places, characters, and incidents are either the products of the author's imagination or are used fictitiously.

Skyhorse Publishing books may be purchased in bulk at special discounts for sales promotion, corporate gifts, fund-raising, or educational purposes. Special editions can also be created to specifications. For details, contact the Special Sales Department, Skyhorse Publishing, 307 West 36th Street, 11th Floor, New York, NY 10018 or info@skyhorsepublishing.com.

Skyhorse® and Skyhorse Publishing® are registered trademarks of Skyhorse Publishing, Inc.®, a Delaware corporation.

Visit our website at www.skyhorsepublishing.com.
Visit the author's website at darrylponicsan.com.

10 9 8 7 6 5 4 3 2 1

Library of Congress Cataloging-in-Publication Data is available on file.
Library of Congress Control Number: 2019946649

Cover design by Erin Seaward-Hiatt
Cover photos: © mocker_bat/Getty Images (woman); © Alex_Schmidt/Getty Images (police lights); © sdominick/Getty Images (background); © Naypong/ Getty Images (wings)

Print ISBN: 978-1-5107-4913-9
Ebook ISBN: 978-1-5107-4914-6

Printed in the United States of America

To the memory of Alvin Sargent

"The gates of Hell are locked from the inside."
—C. S. Lewis

ETERNAL
SOJOURNERS

MEMO

TO: PD
FROM: HR

Our office recently received the attached. We believe it to be the hard copy of a long email. Addressee unknown. Subject line: "As requested—."

It was discovered inside an upstairs wall of a Maragate residence made uninhabitable by "The Hundred-Year Storm" and tagged for demolition. The document of some 300-odd pages was bound by three rubber bands. An empty bottle of Sweet Briar Dragon Gin and the dried carcass of a rat were found next to it in the framing.

Findings from forensics will arrive under separate cover so as not to front-load the experience with information that would "spoil the story" and may in the final analysis make little difference.

You asked me to start at the beginning, but to this day I'm not sure when or where it began for me. I was in New York, toiling over a script with a madman producer name Gertz, who was attempting to make his first grown-up picture, having already made zillions on schlock. I'd been there for seven weeks and still had a week to go before I could go back home to LA. Walking back to my hotel from Gertz's Madison Avenue offices one night, I stopped at a café for a piece of cheesecake, my favorite thing to do in New York. I had a couple bites of the delicious cheesecake, and then with the next bite my throat seared. I immediately worried that I had been randomly poisoned—it is the world we live in—or it's possible some disgruntled kitchen worker spiked the cheesecake with tabasco, which also happens from time to time. By the time I got to my room, my heart was pounding, and my field of vision was blocked by a blue splotch with a ragged black center, which did not go away when I closed my eyes. I sat on the edge of the bed and did some deep breathing. I wrote a note naming the café in case I died during the night, and then I fell asleep. Hope's call woke me around 1 a.m. She must have forgotten the difference in time.

A week later I was shutting the front door of my new home behind me, a house I had seen for the first time only hours before. I had my shoes in hand, having walked across the living room in socks so as not to wake Carlos. It was three o'clock in the morning, not a nice hour anywhere, near the end of February, not the best of seasons, damp and foggy, colder than New York, and all I was wearing was my sports coat and the same clothes I'd had on all day. I slipped into my shoes and set out to have a look at my new hometown.

The house was close to Spanish Circle, touted as the town's heart and soul by the driver who met me at the airport, who rattled on about the town's features, including a suicide rate of zero. "Because there ain't any buildings tall enough to jump off of!"

The town was laid out like a spider's web, with Spanish Circle at its center and the major streets radiating from there to the outskirts.

My house was on Second Street Northwest (2nd St. NW on an envelope, though I am still waiting for my first letter) midway between the avenues Cherona and Minos, a coveted location, I was told.

I walked in shrouded light for what seemed too far a distance until I found Spanish Circle, abandoned at that hour.

The park was large for a small town, ten acres. Town Hall, a two-story red brick fortress, was located more or less in the center of the circle, like a bull's-eye. Walkways snaked over the lawn and under a variety of oak and cedar trees. I saw a few man-made grassy knolls, down which I imagined children rolling in play. It's what I used to do as a kid whenever I saw a knoll. (My childhood was happy, I'd like you to know.) Along the walkway were sculptural street lights with tulip-shaped shades. I stood under one of them and looked at the statue of some stalwart of local history, a thumb hooked over his belt, his other hand pointing to a prosperous future.

A spur off the walkway led to a public restroom, a squat brick bunker. A man in a black leather sports coat and jeans came out and paused long enough to look me over before disappearing into the fog. In a moment another man emerged, ferret-like, shorter, and wearing a fedora and a plastic raincoat. This one never noticed me. He scurried in the opposite direction.

It occurred to me that I might not be safe. I picked up my pace and walked toward the eastern edge of the park, to the roundabout and the circular sidewalk. Across the street were little shops and cafés and what appeared to be single-pump gas stations, too many of them to be real. More like a theme.

When Hope called me in New York I would have agreed to anything. She told me I would love Maragate. She described it as "a little slice of heaven."

"You deserve to be happy again," she said.

I did not think of myself as unhappy, only not as relentlessly cheerful as she. Yes, I lamented the sudden increase in the number of people shooting each other from their cars on the streets and freeways of Los Angeles. It was an element of life hard to ignore, though millions came to accept it, including me. You can learn to accept anything, and even thrive within it. (Which I suppose is the whole point of my story.) I did wonder aloud about the advantages of putting some distance between us and "the Industry." I admit that I had lost the ability to laugh at little things, but I would not have said I was unhappy.

Hope reasoned that what we would save on California taxes and the high cost of living in Los Angeles would pay for the new house and ensure us a comfortable retirement. (I had no plans to retire. I wouldn't know how.) Lying in my hotel room in the pain of what I thought at the time might be poison, I suggested we rent a place for a few months, to try it out. She countered that we would miss out on a wonderful opportunity if we didn't snatch up this "little jewel." I was too sick to argue. What's more, it was Valentine's Day, our favorite holiday. I told her to buy the house, sounds like a great idea.

I doubled back from Spanish Circle, following the circular side-walk that would lead me to Cherona Avenue West. From there I knew I was within two or three blocks of what was now apparently home. I turned right one street too soon, however, and lost my way.

A car was facing me, parked half a block away, foggy halos hang-ing around the headlights. I walked toward it, hoping for direc-tions. Another car, an SUV, pulled up and parked on the other side of the street. The sound of a motorcycle grew louder behind me, and when I turned I saw that it was a police bike, rolling by me like a ghost rider. The motorcycle stopped a little beyond the two cars. I was close enough now to see they were police vehicles. A man's voice said, "Stand over here behind the car." I thought he was talking to me, but he was giving the order to a tall woman in Ugg boots and a navy blue raincoat, a scarf over her head. She held a leash connected to a Rottweiler. Another cop walked from the police SUV across the street toward the woman, his hand on his holstered gun.

I crossed over and stood on the far side of that SUV, putting some protection in front of me, my line of sight over the roof. I heard the sound of running water behind me, a creek. The cops were not interested in the woman but in her house. In the dark fog, it appeared to me more like a tunnel, an industrial scarred wall making up one side of it. I could make out an open door. A cop positioned himself on one side while the other two, guns drawn, inched along the wall.

I heard, "Police. Come out with your hands up." No response came from the darkness, but then a blinding light filled the doorway and lit up the tunnel, changing from white to golden. A shot was fired. I dropped to the ground, squeezing under the SUV. Two shots, three, four. A naked woman the color of café au lait moved toward me as though gliding on air. She fell to the road next to where I had taken cover. Her face was beautiful and serene. She stared at me through dark eyes, folded her lush, charcoal gray wings, and murmured in an Irish accent, "Hope is alive."

www.whisperingworlds.com/angels

The police put me in a room painted an industrial green. I sat on one of three matching metal chairs close to a metal table wedged into the corner. It was warm in the room, which helped dry my clothes, still damp from the wet road. The fluorescent light above me made the detective look sick. He was chubby and wore corduroy pants and a V-neck sweater over a T-shirt, and he looked like he was wearing the outfit for the second day. His hair was unkempt and made his forehead appear as a triangle coming to a sharp point on the right side. His stubble beard was not a fashion statement but a negligence. Cheap glasses slid down his nose. He looked to me like a failure whose early potential was misread, and he bore a striking resemblance to Philip Seymour Hoffman, RIP. (Casting is second nature to me. Who should play me in my own biopic? I could only dream it would be Tom Hanks.)

I told him of the past twenty-four hours, relieved to be telling someone about it. I let him know that my being in town was a result of marital miscommunication and I would not be staying long. I told him I witnessed a shooting, referring to the naked woman only as "the victim," a label that made him uneasy. (I omitted the wings part and her last words. Why wouldn't Hope be alive? Unless someone was trying to convince me that she was dead, and the angel was there to tip me off with her last breath. She may have meant the concept of hope was still alive, no matter what they say, as she herself was dying, if angels can die, assuming they exist in the first place, which was an assumption I did not share. [The confusion over person or concept is something women named Hope, Joy, Faith, Prudence, or Constance have to learn to live with.])

The detective took no notes. He acted as though this were an ordinary conversation. We were two dudes, recently met, having a chat, which he turned to the weather in Miami. I couldn't understand why. I told him I had no opinion of the Miami heat. I'd been there only once, years before, to meet with Don Johnson, who was big at the time, starring in a hit TV show called *Miami Vice* and setting a fashion trend that in retrospect seems comparatively classy: brightly colored T-shirts under pastel sports coats, sleeves pushed up to the elbows. It did not feel like an American city, Miami. I was getting a similar feeling for Maragate, without the benefit of tropical weather.

It sounded like the cop was looking for things we might have in common, like two expectant fathers in a waiting room. I thought he was killing time until someone at a higher pay grade came in, and that is what happened, because another detective holding a yellow legal pad and wearing a black leather sports coat and jeans came into the room. I was sure he was the man I'd seen leaving the public restroom in the park ahead of the man with the fedora and plastic raincoat. The coincidence was unsettling.

"D. K. . . . ? How do you say your last name?"

"The *c* is silent. As in Tucson. And you?"

"Lieutenant Conventerra. You have a connection to Tucson, do you?"

"No, I use it as an example. Americans don't know how to deal with a *c* before an *s*. They feel compelled to pronounce it, which sounds awful when it's your name, so I remind them of Tucson, as an example. They can't spell it either. If I write down my name for you and ask you to copy it, you'll get it wrong." (This is true. I used to do that as a parlor trick.)

"Is this some kind of failure of Americans?"

"A small linguistic failure, I suppose."

"What about the French?"

"The French?"

"Let's say, for example, the French, they don't have that problem."

"What problem?"

"The problem with a *c* before an *s*, that you're so sensitive about."

I would have cast Heath Ledger, RIP, in the role. Something both saintly and demonic lived behind those sleepy eyes, that half-smile, hair all over the place, blondish like the other one. He was younger than his partner, though he outranked him, young enough to be my son, if I had one, which I didn't. Hope and I never had children. I never wanted to be obliged to feel proud or ashamed of anyone, including myself, if I'm to be honest about it, though one can't escape pride. (Shame is easier for most people to overcome.) Hope never voiced a reason for not wanting children. She never felt the need to explain anything. I always did, and once explained, to explain it again. And again. Maybe one more time, to be sure I was understood. Then again before going to bed, so neither of us had to sleep in doubt.

"The French are used to silent letters. And I'm not all that sensitive about it."

"So is yours a French name?"

"Hardly."

"You keen on the Frogs?"

"Sure. Only I call them the French. It's a wonderful country. Have you ever been there?"

"No way. Why would I?"

I looked at the other cop and tacitly asked the same question.

"The fuck for?" he said.

"So then what kind of name is it?"

"Hungarian."

The two cops gave that news a moment of serious thought. Something about being a Hungarian is inherently suspicious. Hungarians, for their part, feel the same way about Romanians, who feel that way about Bulgarians.

"Been there?" asked the Heath Ledger type.

"Where?"

"Hungary."

"Once, yes. You?"

"If I wouldn't go to Gay Paree, why would I go to shitty Hungary? Where were you, there?"

"Budapest. Lovely place. Sad people."

"Speak the language?"

"I don't know how anyone does, if you're not born to it. It's an impossible language to learn. That's why Hungarians are so sad. They feel isolated by their language."

(While I was in New York, I saw a woman in SoHo wearing a designer T-shirt that said: I SPEAK HUNGARIAN, WHAT'S YOUR SUPERPOWER?)

"Are you sad?" the cop asked me, a question of such intimacy I can't remember anyone ever having asked it before.

"A little, considering the circumstances."

"Isolated?"

"Kind of."

"Alienated?"

"From what?"

"Whatever. You look sad." He glanced at his partner, who nod-ded in agreement. "You look like a guy who long ago felt kind of alienated, so you chose isolation, and now you're stuck with it, which makes you sad."

It was close enough to sting, coming from a cop I'd just met, younger than I.

"I don't get why you're so interested in me and not what I witnessed."

"We're all interested in you. New in town, doesn't know where he is. *Who* he is. Where *anybody* is. Picked up dazed and confused. With an uncorroborated story we will have to do something about."

I should have realized the room was bugged. Conventerra had been the one taking notes, outside. They were probably videotaping as well. I looked for the eye of a lens. All I saw, on the wall to my right, above my head, was a calendar on which someone had been checking off the days with neat diagonal pencil lines. Whoever had that duty forgot to do it the last three days, or maybe he was out sick and no one else cared about the passing of days.

"I know who I am," I said. It is, though, a lifelong question for everybody. Don't you agree?

"How long were you there?"

"Where?"

"Budapest."

"I thought you meant under the car."

"How long were you roaming the streets of Budapest, doing whatever?"

The fluorescent lights hummed in my ears, contrapuntal to my own tinnitus. (The ringing becomes part of you.) "Six days in Budapest."

"Were you alone in Budapest? Or did you go with someone? I'm going to bet you were there alone."

"I have no idea why you would want to know, but no, I was not alone, I was with my wife."

I know, from the movies, that if you are going to talk to the cops you should never lie about anything, no matter how small, but if I told him I was alone it would only lead to more irrelevant questions.

(During one of those lonely walks I came upon a man's dead body. A crowd had already gathered. They thought he'd pitched himself off a nearby roof.)

"I stand corrected. And your wife's name is?"

"Hope."

Again, the two cops thought this was worth a moment of silent consideration, like, how could a man like me be married to a woman named Hope. (I've wondered that myself.)

"You had friends there in Hungary?"

"No. I thought I might have relatives, though."

"Looking for your roots, were you?"

"That metaphor doesn't mean much to me because I'm not a plant."

I've never benefited in real life from trying to be intellectually superior. The cop sat down on the third metal chair, with the sigh of a public servant put upon by the people he is sworn to aid and protect. "You were born in upstate New York, close to Canada?"

"Closer to Pennsylvania. Not far from Ithaca. You could have come in at the beginning and I wouldn't have to repeat myself."

"We like to have people repeat themselves, see if the story comes out the same way twice."

"Would I change where I was born?"

"You'd be surprised what people change in a story. I was in Biloxi at the time. No, it was Baltimore."

"I was at home," said the other one. "No, at the movies."

The lieutenant waited, but I had nothing to add.

"Upstate New York it is, and your father was in shoes, was he?"

"He worked for the Endicott Shoe Company."

"And your mother worked for IBM?"

"She was a bookkeeper there, yes. I thought I was making small talk with your partner here."

"Sergeant Kuggelsong," said the partner. "I told you that in the beginning. I spelled it for you."

"Sorry. I didn't know I'd be interrogated."

"You think this is an interrogation?" asked Conventerra.

"It feels like one."

"Well, put that feeling aside. I know it's hard for you, you're such a deep dude, but pretend like we're making small talk."

"Why would you think it hard for me to make small talk?"

"Body language." (I hadn't *moved*.) "So, okay, you say you have no roots. That would make you, what, rootless?"

"In a manner of speaking."

"Well, speaking in that manner, am I to believe that you don't know where you live at this point in time?"

I winced. It's automatic whenever I hear that phrase.

"You're young," I said, "so you don't know why that expression grates on the ear."

"You lost me. Now we're both lost."

"'At this point in time.' It's a phrase that was coined by H. R. Haldeman, a gentleman fascist, one of Nixon's henchmen, during Watergate. Since then, anyone with pretensions to gravitas uses it."

"Our friend here is all about language and factoids up the ass."

They needed to question me, of course, but why were they intent on making me look like a suspicious character?

"Look," I said, trying to get back on track, "as I was telling your colleague here—"

"Sergeant Kuggelsong, goddammit. How many times do I have to tell you?"

"Yes, Kuggelsong, I know." I spelled it aloud. (I've never benefited from sarcasm, either.) "I was in New York for eight weeks, working, and my wife—"

"How did you get from New York to our little slice of heaven?"

"While I was in New York, Hope called me from here and said she had found a house and wanted to buy it. We'd talked a lot about relocating, changing our lives, so I said go ahead. The job in New York was killing me, and I was ready to chuck it all and start a new life in a new town. I never heard of the place, but I guess she went on a location scout and found Maragate."

"And you never saw the house?"

"Not even pictures. She did well enough on our first house, it's appreciated crazy much, so I give my wife whatever she wants."

"Hear that, Armen? True love."

"That's his side of the story," Kuggelsong said.

"Yeah, we haven't heard her side of it. So you're like this old lovey-dovey couple? Bet you call her sweetie and she calls you her darling boy?"

(She does. Did.)

"She fell in love with this town, and I said, why not? How quickly it all happened was unexpected. But here I am."

"Relocating from where?"

"Los Angeles. Hollywood Hills."

Again, both cops looked at each other and raised their eyebrows, as though this was a piece of evidence good for them but not for me. I've seen that reaction before from people who have never been to Los Angeles. It was the city that changed my life, and I owed it gratitude. It was where I found Hope.

"And you haven't seen your house yet?" said the lieutenant.

"Well, yes, I've seen it. A driver met me at the airport and took me there."

I flew from JFK to Louisville, then raced to make the connection while speed-dialing Hope. Her phone went directly to message. I told her where I was and that I would be boarding the plane in time. I had a Bloody Mary and fell into a deep sleep on that leg of the trip. (I wasn't a drinking man back then.) I did not stir until the plane hit the tarmac. Outside, it was dark and the fog thick.

As promised, a driver was waiting for me. He held up a sign with my name misspelled. It's a family curse. (There may be others.)

"Maragate?" he said when we got into his limo. "Second Street Northwest?"

"Right." I tried to call Hope again. Now her voicemail box was full.

"Visiting," asked the driver, "or coming home?"

"I guess I'm coming home."

Lieutenant Conventerra didn't want to hear any more of my conversation with the driver.

"The driver knew what house to go to, but the owner of that house did not know and still doesn't know, *at this point in time*, where that house is. Is that what you're telling us?"

"I would recognize it if I saw it. I think. These houses look alike." Another uncomfortable silence. "The driver assured me I'd love Maragate."

"Do you?"

"Not so far."

"You're in a house you never saw, in a town you've never been to, in a country you're like ambivalent about."

"The country?"

"Well, you go on about how France is so much better. Hungary, for Pete's sake."

"Truth is," I said, "I don't much care where I live. It doesn't matter to me."

Yet again, the two cops looked at each other in that silent communication that makes everybody else an outsider. I had unnecessarily exposed myself by revealing that eccentricity. It might have sounded to them that I didn't care about anything, least of all their shit town.

"I've never heard anyone say that before," said Conventerra. "I'm stunned."

"It sounds all wrong," said Kuggelsong.

"Well, where I am, I mean, the town I'm in might matter. You have to go outside once in a while, to the movies or a restaurant, but the house itself never mattered to me. All that matters to me is that it's quiet. And warm. And the roof doesn't leak. And there aren't any rats."

"Quiet. Good roof, good furnace, no rats," said Conventerra. "That's not asking too much."

"He's easy to please, I'll give him that."

"I've never been attached to a house. All I do is work, anyway."

"Could it be you never got attached to anything?" said Kuggelsong.

"If you list them in order of annoyance, which comes first? Rats?"

"No, noise. It has to be quiet where I live."

"Interesting," said Kuggelsong. "In some cultures, noise is not seen as an intrusion. It's accepted as part of life."

"Now, you're in this house you won't become attached to, quiet house in a town you can't give a shit about, and you are not able to sleep because you are so exhausted. You take a walk, get lost, and can't find your way home."

"Yes, that's it exactly," I said, eager to get to the reason for my being there.

"It may surprise you, sir, but that is not uncommon. Just . . . when was it, Armen? . . . last Tuesday? We get a call from the 7-Eleven, there's an old guy there, wanted a lottery ticket but he didn't have any money and he didn't have any ID. In fact, he didn't have any shoes. Did he have pants?"

Kuggelsong laughed. "He had pants. Haggars. With suspenders. Only he didn't have a *shirt*." This was wildly amusing to the sergeant. He had to take out his hanky and cough into it.

"We walked him around a little, ran into somebody who recognized him, and we got him home to his old lady, who didn't realize he was gone. Small-town charm."

"My mind is as sharp as . . . well, certainly you two."

I've never benefited from snarkiness either.

"We'll see. You were saying?"

"About what?"

"About what we were talking about."

"What were we talking about?"

"You don't remember?"

"We were talking about several things," I said, "none of them relevant to the matter at hand, a police shooting."

"No, we were talking about you not caring where you are but pretty upset because you didn't know where you were."

"I wasn't upset, I was lost, until I saw three cops shoot an unarmed woman. That was pretty upsetting."

"Why didn't your wife go with you on this late-night walk? Hope. I assume she knows her way around."

"I don't know where she is."

ONE DAY AGO

(Don't you hate that? Shit way to unspool a movie, which this isn't, but I promise not to do it again anyway.)

When the limo dropped me off, I gave the driver a tip—the fare had been prepaid—and reached back inside the car for my carry-on. The car pulled away, and I saw my new home for the first time. It was a two-story frame house with what I suspected might be asbestos siding wedged between two similar houses on each side. A narrow walkway on the right side of the house led to whatever was in the back, while on the other side the space looked too small for a human to pass between my house and the neighbor's asbestos siding without risking an environmental hazard. Dim lights were on inside the house and a brighter one shone outside the front door above a concrete stoop no wider than the door itself. Smoke rose from the chimney and mated with the fog. As near as I could tell in the dark, the house itself was an unpleasant yellowish green.

A spindly hedge separated the property from the sidewalk, except for a narrow driveway that led to the smallest garage I'd ever seen. It might have been large enough to park my Porsche, which Hope promised to have shipped. Her Audi should have been in the driveway. I looked up and down the street but did not see it parked anywhere. I thought she might be off on one of her endless errands, though it seemed too late in the night for that. In the middle of a small square of lawn stood a stunted and near dead plum tree. Suffer.

I pulled my bag toward the house and tripped another exterior light. The door opened to reveal the silhouette of a short, stout

Hispanic man built like a fireplug. He wore chinos, a denim shirt and, I was surprised to notice, Gucci loafers. His curly hair was streaked with gray. He might have been forty or sixty, I couldn't guess. He stepped forward, leaving the door wide ajar.

"Doctor Kecskeméti, I presume."

He pronounced my name perfectly, with what I was later to discover was a Peruvian accent. (Most people mangle it. It's "ke-ska-MET-e.")

"Yes . . . ?"

"Carlos Cortez, at your service, señor."

"I don't understand. . . . Where's Hope? I can't get her on the phone."

"The señora hired me, sir, to get you settled and to look after the house and whatever you may need. Please, come inside and look at your new home."

The señora? Was he a houseman? A *butler*? Hope knew full well I could barely tolerate a cleaning lady coming in once a week.

Carlos pulled my carry-on and I followed. He stood to the side and gestured for me to enter, as though he were a bellhop and I a guest who had been given an upgrade.

"Please, come inside and out of this damp, unpleasant night. I am sorry the weather is not better for your arrival. It is so boring."

"I don't care about the weather."

"If you please . . ."

I went inside. Where else was I going to go? Carlos shut the door and carried the luggage to the foot of the dark stairway off the kitchen.

"Your bedroom, Doctor, is at the top of the stairs. Your office also. Would you like an aperitif? Or some coffee? Are you hungry? I can make a Spanish tortilla."

The wood in the fireplace burned and crackled. It was the only sign of comfort in the dingy living room. Two lamps, neither one bright enough to read by, were on either side of a sofa, one on an end table, the other a floor lamp with a pull chain. The sofa and cushioned chair looked like salvage. The art on the walls was early Americana, landscapes of country paths and brooks and sunsets. The floor was linoleum, except for the part covered by a hideous large carpet that I imagined was cut from a larger piece cast away by a Las Vegas casino. Its pattern was a mess of yellow and black triangles depicting whatever the eye cared to see in them.

I was repelled. We left a beautiful home in the Hollywood Hills for this? What was she thinking? Was this an elaborate joke? When would she pop up and do whatever an outrageous prankster, which Hope was not, would do?

"Do you love it?" asked Carlos.

"What's not to love?"

If he realized I was being sarcastic, he didn't show it. He was either insane or a true professional servant. "The señora spent much effort on the ambience, you see, for you. She thought you would enjoy the change."

None of this was possible. Hope had the occasional sweet tooth for kitsch, but this living room was in studied bad taste. If it were a joke, maybe about my own disinterest in "ambience," it was a bad one. If we were going to laugh about this, it ought to be soon.

"Look, Carlos, I'm a little thrown here. Can you please tell me where my wife is?"

"No, so sorry I cannot, señor, because I do not know. She left you a note."

"A note?"

"*Si*, jefe, I will retrieve it. It is in my quarters."

Carlos opened a narrow door at the far corner of the room and disappeared for a moment, returning with an envelope in hand.

"Do you live here?" I asked.

"In the downstairs casita. The señora did not want you to be alone."

The envelope had my name typed on it. The letter itself was

typed, which struck me as strange because Hope was not a keyboard sort of person. She still liked to draw her own emoticons.

I attach the letter:

My darling boy,

I'm sorry I was not here to welcome you to our new home, but if I had waited it would have been too hard to leave. I promise I will return but for now I need to be in another place and I need to be alone. I'm sure you will understand. Carlos is a gem and will look after you while I'm gone. Use this time to write something of your own, learn how to relax, meet new people, embrace new surroundings. Please don't go back to LA or anywhere else. I will come back to you. I will always love you and will hold close the memories of our good days together while I work this out.

All my love,
Your Only Hope

NOW
(Had to.)

Without quoting it, I told the cops about the letter, which was still burning a hole in my jacket pocket.

"She typed it? That's cold," said Conventerra.

"That's what I thought. It was out of character. She liked to write with a pen. We had that in common. She was proud of her penmanship."

"You can't type a Dear John. It's all wrong," said the partner.

"I don't know that it's a Dear John."

"You read it."

"Yes, and I still don't know."

"*Que será, será.*"

"We will get to what you *do* know, but for now, try to make me understand what you don't know and why you don't know it."

Say what? Since arriving at my newly purchased home, I didn't know anything. Why did Hope think I would like living in that creepy house? Why did she not wait for me? Where did she go? All of that and more before I could get my head around three uniformed cops murdering an angel. A black angel, which if I remember from mythology is supposed to be a punishing angel. With an Irish accent, and if that means something I don't know what it is. I don't know if you can even kill an angel, if angels live among us, and if they do, will unicorns eat out of your hand?

"I don't know why you're so interested in my personal story. For openers. I haven't broken any laws. I'm here of my own free will."

"Are you, now?"

I felt a chill. Wasn't I?

"They killed a black woman . . . unarmed."

"It's going around. A black person shot by the big, bad cops. A thing like that can cause a riot." Conventerra was smiling. "But not in Maragate."

"You're not taking this seriously," I said. "Look, I witnessed an odd, maybe an impossible event."

"How can you witness something that cannot be?"

"Well, yes, academically it's worth a discussion." I was not ready yet to go there, but go there I did. "The black woman had all the appearance of an angel."

"Meaning she was a real beauty?"

"No. She was beautiful, but she also had wings, and she was naked. So."

"What color were these wings?"

"Kind of charcoal gray. Her skin was café au lait."

"The French stuff again," said Kuggelsong. "Show-off."

"You think he's a Frog trying to pass?" Conventerra asked his partner.

"Got the map of Marseille all over his face."

I was not threatened by accusations of being French. (I was flattered.)

"This black angel," said Conventerra, "who decided to die right next to you, did she say anything to you?"

She said the only three words that I could not repeat, at least not there and then. Hope is alive.

"No. Only looked at me."

"I see. Go on."

"Go on where?"

"To what you don't know."

"Oh, Christ."

"Rather not bring a third party into this."

"I don't know what made Hope pick this town or that house. I can't explain it, and I can't ask her, because I don't know where she is or why she left. I don't know why two months ago I was happy in my home, my marriage, and my career, and now I'm here, God knows where or why."

"DK, I don't know you that well yet, true, but it's hard for me to picture you the most happy fella. You look like a dude who's always expecting the worst to happen, and when it does he's relieved."

"Believe me, I am not relieved."

"Then maybe the worst is yet to come. Trying to get this: she leaves a typed, unsigned note and takes it on the arfy-darfy. She could be anywhere, alone or with someone, part of a cult, in another country. She could be in Caracas."

"Caracas is a city," I informed him.

"I know what Caracas is."

"Where is it?" asked Kuggelsong.

"Venefuckinzuela."

Conventerra looked back to me. "She could be dead."

"Why would you say that?" (The angel had already called bull-shit on that.)

"Just going down the list. You didn't make a list?"

"You should always make a list," said Kuggelsong.

"She would never be part of a cult," I said. (LA has long been fertile fields for cult leaders, but my Hope would never fall for that.)

"Wherever, amigo. You got an alibi. You've been in New York for the past two months, working, all your moves accounted for."

"What the hell are you implying?"

"Don't be alarmed. Knowing you, knowing me."

"All I know about you is your name."

"You know I compare with that Haldeman dude, who I will Google before the day is over, believe me. You know I got roots, red, white, and blue. You know I'm a tenacious cop."

"He knows a ton about you, Louie, and we don't know jack shit about him."

"This is the strangest meeting I've ever taken, and I've taken some strange meetings."

"Did you 'take' a meeting before you left New York?"

"Why do you ask that?"

"Because you're dressed like you 'took' a meeting. What is that, a Hugo Boss jacket? Burberry shirt, tie. You look . . . professorial."

"When I was a student, it was rebellious to dress down. Jeans with holes in them. Dirty sneakers. One T-shirt the whole week. Now it's all the fashion to see how down you can dress. It's become ridiculous. When I get on a plane, I dress like this. It's my act of rebellion. To answer your question, yes, I did have a meeting before I went to the airport. It was brief and unpleasant and has nothing to do with why I'm here."

He looked down at his notes.

"You're a doctor?"

"PhD."

"In?"

"English lit. Emphasis on the Romantic poets."

"Not them," said Kuggelsong, rolling his eyes. "'Childe Harold' got seriously on my nerves. 'On the sea the boldest steer but where their ports invite; but there are wanderers o'er Eternity . . .'"

I finished the line with him: "Whose bark drives on and on, and anchor'd ne'er shall be."

"The fuck?" said Conventerra.

I was as shocked as Conventerra that this underachieving overweight cop even knew about Lord Byron's famous poem, let alone be able to recite lines. I never met more than five people who could. I felt bad that I'd pegged him as a cretin.

"'Childe Harold's Pilgrimage' got on a lot of people's nerves," I said, warming up to the man. "But it made Byron a rock star. In those days, a single poem could make you famous. Now, a lifetime of poems will not raise you out of obscurity."

"Selfish prick he was, your Lord Byron."

"Well, maybe, sometimes. At other times he was generous to a fault. He bailed out a lot of his contemporaries, including Shelley."

"Another asshole. Radical of the first order."

"He saw it was his duty as an artist to be radical. Without Shelley, there wouldn't have been 'Howl.' There wouldn't have been the Beat Generation."

"Oh, and that would have been such a shame."

"No poet ever had a better friend than Shelley."

"Useless bunch of perverts and liars."

"Yet you seem to have read them, and committed some of their lines to memory."

"Yeah, like a bad song that sticks in your head. Like an ear worm. Come to think of it, that one reminds me of you. No roots, no anchors, doomed to wander the seas. Neither here or there."

Conventerra listened to this with astonishment and impatience. He weighed in with, "Poetry is shit. Oh, look at me, I'm all alone and I'm walking on the beach at sunset and what's it all mean, because I'm going to die anyway."

"Poetry by its nature is going to be personal, sometimes intensely. A poet examines his own mortality for the benefit of those who don't know how, or are afraid to."

"And we should give a shit?"

"You don't have to."

"Good to know."

"Most of what you hate as poetry came long after the Romantic poets, who may have had their failings as human beings—"

"Failings? They were dangerous," said Kuggelsong.

"As poets should be," I said.

"They needed to be stopped."

"The Romantic poets could be difficult, but they had their finer natures, and when they expressed them, they were exquisite."

"So there's a lot of call for all that in LA and New York?" said Conventerra.

"Not much."

"You make enough off that to buy a house in Maragate?"

"No, I'm a screenwriter. I make money from the movies."

"Whoa."

"Took that turn so fast I fell into your lap, Louie."

"You're in the business of making stuff up, we now hear, creating illusions for gullible people. You have a vivid imagination."

"Not that vivid. I could never have imagined the last twelve hours."

Who could imagine the interrogation I was going through? I've seen interrogations before, in the movies, and on 48 *Hours*, where they interrogate one spouse who murdered the other, every week. Nothing like this.

"You make up stories about things that never happened, never could happen, doing like a scared child who never grew up, and then writing it all down for a movie."

What was I to say? In essence he was correct.

"You create the illusions and then you lure popcorn-for-brains into them so they can forget their own reality. I see an occupational hazard there. You draw yourself into your own illusions."

"You're overstating the case. It's movies after all."

"What's the process?" Conventerra asked.

"You're asking how I write a screenplay?"

"Can't be that hard. How do you start?"

Weariness leeched out of my bones. I was all but spent. I gave myself a moment, then said, "I see a dark screen. An image appears. A person, a tree, a road, the horizon, could be anything. Then I lean forward and I go to the movies. I try to keep up with it, but if I get too far ahead of the story it's no good."

"I don't get it," said Kuggelsong.

"Me neither. Give us an example."

Never far from my mind was the opening of a western I'd been obsessed with for years. Decades.

"I see a snow-capped mountain range. Dawn. Only the sound of wind. Move in closer. Something in the distance. Moving toward us. Go in closer. Two riders. On mules. Can't see their faces because their hats are pulled down. Reverse the angle. A western outpost. Who is that watching the riders come down into town? Why is he concerned? Is it some kind of trouble coming down from the mountains? And we're off."

The two cops looked at each other with expressions of mild contempt.

"Now, where were we, Louie?" said Kuggelsong.

"Beats the shit out of me. Our friend could confuse an oyster."

"Me? I'm confusing you?"

Lieutenant Conventerra checked his clipboard and said, "In New York, you were. Going to the movies?"

"I was there doing a final rewrite for a producer named Gertz. It didn't go well. 'Disappointed' was the word he used. 'Profoundly disappointed.' He blamed me, but he was trying to make a grown-up movie and it wasn't in him. I'm sure I've been fired, but he'll never tell me. I'll never hear from him again."

"You get it, though, don't you, that none of that shit means much to me or my partner?"

"I get that. It's beginning to mean less and less to me."

"Context. Context means something to us. Somebody takes a video of a cop shooting an unarmed black lady. Looks bad. Looks like murder. But without the context, you don't know what you're seeing or hearing. It could all be part of a picture too big to take in."

"Seems clear to me. Subtext is my thing," I said. "Not what's said but what lies underneath what is said. In that respect, it's like poetry."

"What's the context, what's the subtext of what went down tonight?"

"I was taking a late-night walk—you have all the context there is, you know as much as I do—and I witnessed a police shooting. Because of the victim, all context and subtext goes out the window. You start thinking, what kind of movie *is* this? Who *are* these characters? You tell me, what about the victim?"

"In due time, Doctor Screenwriter. Can you describe the cops?"

In fact, I couldn't. They wore the same uniforms. They were all overweight. That's all I remembered.

"Well, that narrows it down," Kuggelsong said.

"If you were in uniform, you'd be suspicious, at this point in time," Conventerra said to him, then turned back to me. "And what were these fat cops doing at that house?"

"I didn't say they were fat. I don't know why they were there. I don't know who the woman in the raincoat was. She had a Rottweiler. I'm guessing she called the cops. Maybe because an intruder was in her house. The cops opened fire on an unarmed black lady—"

"Three fat policemen, you say."

"—who had wings."

"You and an unnamed woman had ringside seats. That's all you saw?"

"All? It's more than I've ever seen before, out for a walk."

"Got the context, what's the subtext?"

"Anyone listening to this conversation would think you're trying to intimidate me, break my will, my grip on reality, that it's imperative that what I saw should never be revealed. That nothing about the victim should ever be uttered, or this town will never be the same."

"This town stays the same no matter what anyone says about anything," said Kuggelsong.

"I think you would you agree," said Conventerra, "and this is not subtext, this is obvious, that you are, at the moment, not yourself."

"Maybe a lesser version of myself," I admitted.

"This work you do, creating illusions and everything like that. Love it?"

Every day of my career I questioned the value of what I did and the cost to my personal life. At the end of the day, the answer was always, yes, it's worth it.

"Don't you?" I asked him.

"I'm mad for my work. But my work is to protect and serve. My work is *useful*. You make up stories for twelve-year-olds and for morons who might as well be twelve."

"I never did a comic book or a superhero. None of my movies ever needed special effects. I write for intelligent grown-ups."

"Did you write any movies we may have seen?"

Usually, that's the first question anyone asks upon learning that I am a screenwriter. I'm always embarrassed to go down the list of my credits until I name one that the person might have seen.

"My first movie was *Eternal Sojourners*. It did fairly well." (I was being modest, a trait that comes easy to me. The picture has become a classic.)

"Rings a bell," said Conventerra.

"Was that the one with the weird guy and the hot girl?"

"Yes, that was the one," I said. His thumbnail description fit lots of movies, some of them starring Nicolas Cage, a favorite of mine, as the weird guy.

Conventerra said, "I wonder if you might be angry at the turn movies took. You're getting older in a world where everybody else is getting younger."

"Nobody gets younger, but I know what you mean."

"You use any controlled substances, Doctor?"

"No."

"Years in Hollywood and you're clean."

"I didn't party. Drugs would have got in the way of my work."

"So nothing ingested tonight, then?"

"I had a Bloody Mary on the plane out of Louisville, if that counts."

"A Bloody Mary never hurt anybody. Though it could give rise to odd behavior if you're not used to it. You used to Bloody Marys, Doctor?"

"No, but I can assure you I'm sober."

"Reason I ask, when a man is in a police station with a story that includes his wife is missing, maybe after all these years things got stale. You wonder what it was all about, Alfie. Why her and not that other one? You let her buy the house but then kind of hate her for getting the one she wanted? She knows what you're gonna say when you show up so she takes it on the arfy-darfy."

Kuggelsong created a sound of resignation.

"I don't want to talk anymore about Hope, not with you."

"Back to your work, then."

"I thought we were finished with that," said Kuggelsong. I wanted to thank him for objecting.

"What is it like, making up illusions that no one wants to buy popcorn for? The audience has flipped on you. You're sweating over kitchen-sink dramas while everybody else is ordering out with head-phones on. If it comes to adapt or die, you're gonna die. Nothing wrong with that. Except you die."

"I'm dying right now. Look, I can't stay awake much longer. Can you tell me what it is you want from me, if anything? Or tell me if nothing is what you want, and I'll go home." My question had a pleading tone I never liked hearing in myself. I hear it when I talk to producers.

"I'd like you to take a deep breath and consider the possibility that you've been, like, traumatized. You're alone and afraid in a world you never made."

"Ah, so you do read poetry."

"Only if it's on a Starbucks cup."

"It's been a long hard day," I said, "What am I supposed to do with what I saw?"

"Oh, you're doing the right thing. We're here to help. You fell into a little slice of heaven. You're in a good place to work through all those mistakes of the past."

"What mistakes?"

"That's job one. Seeing them, admitting them."

"Okay, this has become harassment. I want to go home."

"Yes, you do. We can see you're exhausted, confused, knocked on your ass, okay, but it won't last forever. Nothing lasts forever, right?"

"Wrong," I said, and then that line from Keats, which is always there for the picking. "A thing of beauty is a joy forever."

The cops examined their shoes, which had military shines. Once again, I was conscious of the hum of the overhead fluorescent lights. They'd sucked all the moisture out of my eyes. "Are we done here?" I asked.

"You want to talk later, after you've had some rest, here's my card."

"You want me to come back again?"

"Only if you want to."

"Are you serious? I am out of here."

"We've got no beef with you. We might be able to help you adjust and everything like that."

"Help how?"

"We could help you accept that nobody was killed tonight, at least not in Maragate, not by three fat cops. No person, no living thing, no man, woman, or child, no demon or angel. You were hallucinating, sir, nothing to be ashamed of. You might want to see somebody about it, though."

www.policemisconduct.net/a-police-misconduct-victims-guide/

I left the police station stiff from sitting for so long on that metal chair. The morning sun had burned off the fog. I was content for a

moment to stand in its warmth. The air was permeated with the odor
of noodles, juniper, smoke, dust, and curing meat. Two leaf blowers
nearby were making a raucous noise. The operators directed the muz-
zles randomly along the ground and revved their engines, sending up
clouds of dust. I never saw anything like that back in Los Angeles.
I watched them for a moment, as you might any display of insanity, thinking it would be right up Samuel Beckett's alley. Behind me
someone shouted in an affected voice, "Excuse me, sir? Oh, sir . . .
excuse me?" It was Kuggelsong. Have Philip Seymour Hoffman come
up behind someone and say those words—"Excuse me, sir"—and you
know polite conversation is not what's going to happen next. "A
clarification, please." (You would have to hear the tone.)

"Yes?"

"'A thing of beauty is a joy forever.' Is that what you said?"

"Well, Keats said it, I only quoted it."

He punched me in the stomach. Who *does* that? I fell to my
knees, the wind knocked out of me.

"That's if the thing makes it through next Wednesday," he said.
He walked back inside as though he had only given me something
I left behind. (And he did. A sucker and a sucker punch will inevi-
tably find each other. Suffer.)

My first impulse was to dial 911. That absurdity almost equaled
two men chasing down a single leaf with the force of two opposing hurricanes. I got to my feet and bent over, my hands on my
knees, breathing deeply. Walking away would have been easier and
smarter, but I was a citizen in a free country with protections against
unprovoked attacks by the police. I went back inside.

The duty officer, a woman without makeup or a face that might
be improved by some, sat behind a window. The lobby itself was
small, no seats or anything else except a bulletin board with the customary public notices. I told the woman I had the moment before
been punched in the stomach by a detective who had for hours been
part of my interrogation. She asked for his name, which I could not
remember.

"It began with a *K*," I said. "His partner is named Conventerra. I was here a few minutes ago. You must have seen me leaving. You must have seen *him* leaving and coming back."

She did not say she was not interested, but clearly she was not.

"Are you going to do something about it?" I asked.

"What would you like me to do, sir?"

"How about arresting him for assault."

"Are you making a complaint?"

"Wouldn't you? If a policeman punched you for no reason."

She handed me a form. "Please fill this out in as much detail as possible. You can mail it in or hand-deliver it. Make a copy for your records."

I scanned the form. In the same style as my interrogation, it required far more information about me than about the event itself, implying that anyone complaining about the cops must have something to hide. One question: Are you currently taking medications for mental illness? (Technically, I was. A low dose of Wellbutrin for depression, my Hungarian birthright.)

At the end of the walkway from the station to the street was a trash barrel. I wadded up the complaint form, but before I could toss it I heard, "Excuse me, sir?" in that same affected voice. Kuggelsong again. I turned to face him. I stood my ground. I reached into my inside jacket pocket and drew my weapon of choice, a Montblanc fountain pen that I had bought years before in Munich. (I know, reaching into your pocket like that in the presence of a cop usually gets you shot.) I pointed my pen at him and demanded, "How do you spell your name?"

"Really, dude?"

"And your badge number, please."

"I've got something for you," he said. I braced myself to ward off another blow. He gave me a map of the city. "To help you find your way home, and, you know, sites of interest."

I took it from him and automatically said, "Thank you."

"No problem."

"Why did you hit me?"

"Sir?"

"Minutes ago, right here."

"Why would I do that?"

"That's what I'm asking. Apparently, you can't stand John Keats."

"That's not true, though. He was a decent chap. I was sad over his passing so young. Have a good day, sir, and welcome to Maragate."

It took me a long moment to recover from that encounter, made more difficult by the continuous blasting of leaf blowers, but with the help of the map I had no difficulty navigating my way back. The shortest route would have been to take a diagonal through Spanish Circle, but I took the longer way along the northern arc of the circle. From that walkway, I could see the shops on the other side of the street, those odd single-pump Esso stations I'd seen the night before. Each station had old-timey signs depicting different creatures: alligators, ostriches, rattlesnakes, among others. I was curious but in no mood to take a closer look. I'd been awake all night, was beat up both physically and psychologically. I needed sleep. Between the fake gas stations were places with overhanging British pub signs: Crown & Dragon, Evil Eye, Drunken Sailor, Gunga Gin. There was a shop called Jimmy Jeweler and a pottery place called Silica Treasures. One could dine at Hamburger Benny, and soon at a place called Hot Diggity Hog Dogs, still under construction. One shop was called Made in Maragate.

I saw a man with his face pressed against the window of a pub called Square on the Circle, one arm on the glass holding a fedora to block the glare of the sun. He turned, put his hat back on, and walked away. I thought he was the same man I had seen the night before coming out of the public restroom, but now without the plastic raincoat. He was wearing a suit that even from across the street looked two sizes too big. He strode away from the pub with an exaggerated sense of purpose.

The map showed that Maragate was laid out in diminishing squares, numbered and lettered, from the large outer square to the small inner square that surrounded Spanish Circle. It was a grid without imagination. From Spanish Circle the squares were divided diagonally north and south, east and west, and at their corners by "the avenues," wider streets distinguished by names that once might have referred to someone or something: Camino Oscura, Cherona, Kael, and Minos.

The only oddity in the otherwise sterile plan was the way First Street West took a dogleg instead of running a straight line, so that where it intersected with Cherona Avenue it also intersected with Second Street West, where I lived. That's how I got lost the night before.

With map in hand, I went back to where I had seen the shooting. Houses lined only half of the west side of the street, because the rest of it ran close along the Cherona River, which narrowed to a creek below. The river then passed under Minos Avenue and Munkar Bridge, wide enough for two cars to pass. One might think that it is a fine thing to have a river run through your town. You could go to it and fish or swim or idly sit and watch it roll by. This was not that kind of river. It smelled of decay, and even at its most shallow spots you could not see the bottom. The murky water seemed not to flow but to ooze.

Do angels even bleed? I saw no evidence of it. Where the shooting took place, in what I saw as a tunnel the night before, now appeared to be nothing more than an ordinary house, small, and tucked in close to the adjoining properties. I inspected the sidewalk and the walkway to the house and the grass on either side, looking for shell casings. What I had thought was a concrete wall was a dried-up hedge. I didn't find any shell casings, but I remembered from researching a police story that some cops never get over their shooting range training to pick up their casings. Occasionally it gets them killed, picking up casings while a bad guy is still around.

I hoped that someone would come out of the house and ask me what I was doing there. When no one did, I rang the bell. No one answered. I turned back and looked at the street, from the victim's perspective. It was all so ordinary by the light of day. Why was that angel in this house? It looked like any of the other houses. It looked like *my* house.

"Can I help you?"

Startled, I turned and saw a woman standing in the open doorway. She was young, hardly out of her teens, and pretty, though at my age I sometimes confuse youth with beauty.

"Yes, excuse me, I was here late last night when all that happened."

She smiled. "When all what happened?"

"You were here, walking your dog."

"I don't have a dog, sir, and I wasn't here last night. We checked in only this morning."

Inside, a young man passed behind her, glancing in my direction. "Checked in? You don't live here?"

"No, it's an Airbnb. We're on holiday."

She looked at me in an affecting way, almost as though telling me I had seen her before and having a laugh at my not remembering. I picked up an English accent and her use of the word "holiday." "Are you British?" I asked.

"Yes, of course."

Another young man inside leaned over the kitchen counter to have a look at me. I assumed he was half of another couple sharing the house.

"I'm sorry to have bothered you. Enjoy your stay." I turned to leave.

"Wait," she said, "what happened here?"

"Just something I needed to run by the owner. Do you know her name by any chance?"

"No idea, nor where she can be found."

Still another young man passed behind her, which made me wonder what was going on inside that house. It was an odd combination for a holiday. Two men and a woman, well, why not, but three men and one woman off on vacation struck me as strange, maybe unwholesome, although to be fair it was the same combination that made for my first success, *Eternal Sojourners*. Mary Shelley, her husband, and friends Keats and Byron traipsed all over England and the Mediterranean, sometimes with sisters and half-sisters and other promising poets.

"Do you live in Maragate?" she asked.

I expected she wanted some recommendations for restaurants.

"Yes and no. I have a house on the next street over, but I plan on leaving as soon as possible."

"Oh? And how do you plan doing that?"

"As I said, as soon as possible. Let me ask you a question."

"Shoot."

"Why would tourists come here?"

She laughed and said, "Thank you, kind sir, I've been asking the same question."

www.airbnb.com

My pace quickened as I neared the stoop of my house. I anticipated telling Hope all about my crazy first night in Maragate, like I used to do after some maddening Hollywood meeting, acting out all the roles. Then, like another blow to my gut, I remembered that Hope was gone, leaving me in the care of Carlos, who was waiting for me, sitting spine straight at the kitchen counter like a suspicious wife. The chill in his voice was chastising.

"Good morning, señor."

"Morning."

"How are you this fine morning?"

"Not so great."

"Oh, I am sorry to hear that, but it appears you are at least alive. I wasn't sure. I had no way to know, did I?"

He was pissing me off. I hardly knew the guy, and he was talking to me like a prissy dormitory proctor.

"And where were you all night?" he continued.

"Out."

"May I ask where?"

"Nowhere."

"I see. I was, as you might expect, worried."

"Why would I expect that? You don't even know me."

"I am responsible for you, señor. You could have called."

"I don't have your number," I said. I was not offering an excuse. I am a grown man, after all. He was not the boss of me. I was responsible for myself, regardless of whatever Hope told him.

"Your phone, please," he said. "I will put my number among your favorites."

I handed him my phone. He wanted my password and I saw no reason why I shouldn't give it to him. He could do nothing with it that would matter to me. And remember, I hadn't slept since the catnap on the plane. I'm not saying I was rendered pliable, but I had lost my defenses. I am by nature, though, pliable.

"1976."

"A good year for you, I hope. I will enter our address, too, in case you get lost again." Subtext: Only an idiot would get lost twice, but you may be that idiot. "You have no Favorites in your phone, except for the señora."

"Then you will be the second."

"Were you wandering lost all night, señor?"

"No, no, I was not."

"Maragate is a lovely place to wander, but you would enjoy it so much more during daylight hours."

I could see this conversation going on longer than I wanted it to and ending up in the same place, so I told him. (It's been said that I can't keep a secret.)

"I was detained in the police station."

"Oh, dear."

"I witnessed a shooting."

"A shooting? Here in Maragate? Are you sure? That is unheard of."

"And yet, I heard it. Saw it, too."

"I can't remember a shooting ever. . . . I take that back. The young Besterman boy shot himself through his thumb with his squirrel rifle. But that was years ago. Maragate is crime-free."

"What was he doing with his thumb on the muzzle of a rifle?"

"I have no idea."

"This was a police shooting."

"Oh, dear."

"They deny it."

"That is horrible. I cannot believe my ears. It simply doesn't happen. A plausible explanation, no doubt, will settle it. I am sure it will be in the *Herald* tomorrow." (The local paper, by journalistic standards, was a cute high school gossip sheet.)

"I doubt it."

"Were the police not pleasant to you, señor?"

"Well, let's see, they slow-grilled me all night like a pork shoulder, pulled at me, and served me up for a punch in the gut."

"Outlandish! Unacceptable, I say." His outrage lasted seconds, then, "Are you quite sure, señor?"

"It's hard to misinterpret something like that. The wind gets knocked out of you."

"With your permission, I will make a discreet inquiry."

"Yeah, you do that."

"But a shooting, you say. Who was shot?"

"A black woman."

"A woman? Black? She must have been a tourist."

"Let me put it to you: why the hell would a tourist ever come to this place?"

"Tourism is our third largest industry. Where did this shooting occur?"

"Close by, over there." I pointed in the general direction. "Not more than a few blocks away."

"Oh, dear. That is upsetting. No one in Maragate even locks his door." (Not true. He locked *our* door.) "Though you were missing all night, I had no real concerns for your safety. My only worry was that you would do something foolish, spur of the moment, like trying to leave, to go after the señora."

"Why would that be foolish?"

"Excuse my choice of words. English is my third language, you see. Counterproductive? Disloyal? Dangerous? Useless? So many words to choose from in English, it is difficult at times to express oneself with the correct one."

"You seem to have a good command of the lingo."

"This morning I brought upstairs to your room a tray of *chorizo con huevos*, rice and refried beans, and flour tortillas, your favorite breakfast, to spoil you with breakfast in bed. Imagine my surprise when I discovered you were not in your room. Well, I did not know what to think."

"That *is* my favorite breakfast," I said.

"I know. The señora briefed me on your likes and dislikes." He smiled in that way that certain people shouldn't because they have nothing to smile about. "Would you like me to do an encore breakfast?"

"No thanks. I'm not hungry. I'd like to go to bed now."

"Of course."

"And sleep forever."

"Surely not that long," he said. "A good nap and you will forget about your unfortunate first night in your new hometown. We will maintain silence down below."

I went upstairs to my room and undressed. I slid open the pocket door to the narrow closet and hung up my clothes. Hope had hung some of my clothes and fewer of her own. The room was twelve by twelve, with walls of cheap walnut-stained beaverboard. The bed was a basic double with no appeal. I fell into it and slept until late afternoon.

An amplified dentist's drill awoke me. Another one joined in. For a moment, I did not know where I was or what was causing all the racket. Leaf blowers again. I stumbled to the tiny bathroom, stuffed some toilet paper into my ears, and went back to bed. Why would any town allow leaf blowers to torture its residents? Why would blowing leaves be so important to anyone? Back in upstate New York, we would let leaves lie where they fell, until the trees were bare. Then we would rake them into piles and take running jumps into the piles.

As if the noise were not enough, a putrid smell permeated the room. I pulled my T-shirt over my nose and reread the letter from Hope. The room was already darkening.

The letter, whatever it may have lacked in details, was loving and caring, but what was with the self-help bullshit? Meet new people, embrace new surroundings, relax? Did she think I was hyper? I used to sit at my desk for hours until she reminded me to eat something. Working on a script is like being on a speeding train. I can't jump off. I have to solve the puzzle that brings it to its destination, and then I step off into either clover or shit.

I folded the letter and fell into a sorrow "too deep for tears, when all/ Is reft at once, when some surpassing Spirit,/Whose light adorned the world around it, leaves/ Those who remain behind, not sobs or groans,/ The passionate tumult of a clinging hope;/ But pale despair and cold tranquillity." Percy Bysshe Shelley. That beautiful, sad boy.

Raindrops fell upon the metal roof. Even in the rain the leaf blowers persisted, revving up and dying down, making an obnoxious racket impossible to ignore or predict. Like a dentist's drill it was sure to end, but when? And that smell. It smelled like death.

I buried my face in the pillow like an orphan. Man up, I told myself. It's an unfair expression, I know, but it got me out of bed and dressed. I sprayed some Old Spice on a hanky and held it over my nose.

The putrid smell was worse in the dark and narrow stairway to the kitchen and in the kitchen itself. Carlos had put out a bowl of homemade guacamole and tortilla chips, and a glass of *horchata*, Mexican high tea.

"Carlos, what's that smell? It's in my room too."

"Good morning, señor." (A bit of dumb sarcasm, underlining the fact that I had slept until early evening.)

"I wake up to a raucous noise and a disgusting smell? What gives?"

"Ah, we will live through this. The smell is nothing more than a dead rat. They eat the poison I put out, and sometimes they die inside the walls. It will last but a few days. I prefer for them to run over to the river to die, but you can't dictate to a dying rat."

"Please don't tell me we have rats."

"I believe I already have, señor, sorry. It is so boring, I know."

"Don't we have an exterminator?"

"*Claro*, you are looking at him. Everyone must deal with it. Nobody minds the rats, it is their choosing to die inside walls that one finds annoying. Oh, well."

I had no appetite for dipping into any guacamole with the smell of rotting rat in my nostrils.

"How long have you lived here?" I asked the man who was to have some role in my life. A walk-on, I hoped.

"In Maragate, señor?"

"In this house."

"It seems forever. I came with the house, like one of the rats." He had himself a laugh. "Fortunately for me, the señora approved the arrangement and I hope you will find my services satisfactory."

"Who lived here before?"

"I am pledged to keep private any information about my previous employer, as I will protect your own privacy. I will say only that he was a single gentleman, like——"

"Like me?"

"No, señor, I was going to say that he was, one would say, a confirmed bachelor. In that regard, he was more like me."

"Gay" was on the tip of my tongue, but if one would rather be a confirmed bachelor, let him. Live and let live. Put your face wherever it is welcomed.

"Did he die?"

"He passed on."

The euphemisms for dying are almost equal in number to slang terms for the penis. No one wants to call it what it is, no one knows why, except that it is human nature to avoid the ugly.

"Is there coffee?" I asked. I had no interest in the history of the house. I didn't plan to be in it for long.

"*Con leche?*"

"Sure, thanks."

"Coming right up! There is nothing like a good cup of joe to chase away the blues. You have been through an ordeal, this is true, but now you must put it behind you and get on with your new life. I know you can do it."

I sat at the table and wondered how two of the four things I told Lieutenant Conventerra I could not abide in any house of mine were in this one: noise and rats. I felt like someone whose car broke down in the middle of nowhere and had to stay with the only person who offered to take him in, in a house designed to make him feel even more miserable, and which in the end was his. And when I say his I mean mine. Suffer.

"Is my car in that tiny garage?" I planned to take my laptop, my meds, my carry-on luggage, and drive to Los Angeles or as close as I could get before nightfall. I do not drive well at night. I looked out the window. It would be nightfall in about twelve minutes. I decided to leave first thing in the morning. It would be easier for Hope to find me than for me to find her, because clearly, she did not want to be found. It must have been something I said, and what I said only reflected how I felt at a particular moment. I tried to remember what I might have said before leaving for New York, or on the phone while I was there, or in an email, or something years ago, decades ago, that was now bubbling up into that part of her that wanted to get even. Whatever the reason, she wanted me to live in this creepy house and wait. As a penance? Was I meant to prove myself in some way? Atone for some sin I had no knowledge of committing?

"No, señor. There is no car."

"What the hell? Hope said she would ship it. It would be here when I arrived, she said."

"In the garage, however, is a very fine bicycle, an excellent means of transportation and exercise, once your man parts become accustomed to the seat."

"I don't have a car? I've had a car since I was sixteen. I've always had a car." (The American birthright.)

"The señora had some concern about your driving, I was instructed to explain. She did not want you injuring yourself or others."

"That's ridiculous. I'm a good driver. Fine. I'll buy another one."

Carlos's lower lip jutted forward. He turned away and poured hot water into a French press. He put a cup of milk into the microwave. It was as long a moment of silence as I'd seen him in since arriving.

"Where is auto row in this town? I'm going for a test drive."

"On that matter, señor, did the señora not mention anything about finances in her letter?"

"Finances? No."

"Ah. So she has left that to Carlos."

"What about finances?"

I had a Visa card and a Mastercard in my wallet, along with about seventy dollars in cash. I had no checkbook or account numbers or even the name of our stockbroker. (I'll explain all that in a minute.) A pressure was pushing on my chest. Since getting out of that limo the night before, I was seeing my life become a cascade of loose shit. Suffer.

"A limit has been placed on your bank cards. That is, a new limit, which might be lower than that to which you were accustomed."

(On one card, it was reset at $150. On the other, zero, essentially killing it. The previous limits were $35,000 each.)

"She did that?" (It was the sort of thing an angry woman might do in the first round of a divorce fight. Or a man might do, let's be fair.)

"Now you are upset. I understand, but on a positive note, all household bills are timely paid, including my salary, and you have accounts at markets and restaurants and places of business all over town. Should you need any petty cash you can withdraw it at any ATM."

(Twenty buck limit.)

At that moment, I wanted a divorce. In the next moment, I could not imagine a life without Hope.

"The señora believed this arrangement would make life easier and less stressful for you, as when you had a business manager."

So here's the money thing and why I don't know anything about finances. When I sold my book, *Eternal Sojourners: The Restless Travels of Shelley, Keats, and Byron*, to Columbia Pictures for $150,000 I was earning $12,000 a year teaching bonehead English at a community college. The book, though I intended it to be nonfiction, was published by the University of Nebraska Press as a biographical novel because I had an ear for early nineteenth-century dialog and had constructed so many imagined conversations the book read more like a novel than a biography. Making any money from it was the least of my dreams. I would have been happy to sell five hundred copies to libraries and other readers like me. All I wanted was to beef up my publication résumé so that I might get a tenure-track teaching job at one of the University of California campuses. In a Hollywood twist of fate, Frank Pierson, an A-list screenwriter, RIP, read my book and loved it. He called his agent, pitching it as a buddies-on-the-road fish-out-of-water costumer piece with all kinds of sexual possibilities and relevance to the current generation's restless seeking. Word gets out quickly in the movie business when someone stumbles upon something different yet commercially viable. This was during the golden age of movies, when studios were all looking for the next *Easy Rider*. Pierson himself contacted me and advised me to get an agent. As much as I admired the movies he'd written, I insisted that I do the screenplay, without mentioning that I had never even seen a screenplay before and had no idea how they were written. Pierson graciously stepped aside. Now I was up to $300,000, which for a scholar who had consigned himself to a life of genteel poverty was all the money in the world. The university press was both excited and rueful. They never thought of asking for a piece of any movie money in my contract. Who the hell would ever make a movie about the Romantic poets? My new agent advised me to keep my teaching job, which I didn't, and to get a business manager, which I did. From that day on, everything remotely financial was taken care of, in exchange for 5 percent of my earnings, which were uncertain at the time but later proved substantial because *Sojourners* turned out to be a hit and, as time went on, a classic. I was nominated for an Oscar, and my date to the ceremony was the actress Karen Black, RIP, a blind date arranged by our agents. The Oscar went to someone else, I forget who, but my career was made. A few years later, I was meeting with Jack Lemmon, RIP, about a possible project and saw Hope for the first time. She was his personal assistant. I fell gaga in love. I had never met anyone so sweet in nature with such physical beauty, not to mention mad organizational skills. All that, and she was nobody's fool, though I became hers. Lemmon went on to do *Save the Tiger* instead of my script, and he *did* win the Oscar. He never forgave me for stealing away the best assistant he'd ever had.

I was not financially astute (until then, I never had any money to be astute with), but with a business manager I felt safe to remain uninvolved with money matters. I never saw a bill, never thought about taxes or investments, never negotiated for a house or car.

In time, Hope questioned why we were giving up 5 percent of my earnings for what she saw as no more than bean counting. She felt capable of doing whatever the business manager was doing. I went along with it, and my life continued as it had, with a $25 weekly allowance of cash I seldom spent and two credit cards I seldom used. I never thought I was being controlled, or punished. I never thought about it at all.

Now I sat at the table in a house smelling of dead rats, having no wheels, no money, no wife, and nowhere to go, being served coffee by a servant named Carlos who lived in the downstairs guest room and saw me as his duty to an absentee boss. I murmured, "What did I do?" It was a question I often asked Hope when I could see she was in a mood. She would snap back, "It's not always about you!" Most of the time it was, though.

"*Que*, señor?"

"Nothing. I was talking to myself."

The house had turned cold. A drop of water fell on the table. I looked up at the ceiling. A leak. Four for four. Suffer.

"I would not be surprised if tomorrow the señora walks through that door."

"When did she leave? It couldn't have been that long ago."

"You arrived last night. It was the day before that."

"Did she leave in her car?"

"*Si.*"

"What kind of car was it?" (I could not believe my wife would buy a hovel, move in, pack up, and move on.)

"Oh, they are all the same to me. I can't distinguish one car from another."

"Well, what color was it?"

"White," he said, without hesitation.

The correct answer.

www.moneything.com

Hope did not return the next day, most of which I spent sitting at the window like a dog with separation anxiety. She did not return the day after that. Nor the following day. I lived with the bad smells, the raucous noise, the leaky roof, waiting for Hope and thinking about my angel. I thought of her as my angel because no one else wanted to claim her, certainly not the police force that murdered her. In the cold damp light of the passing days, I wondered if she could have been a human with costume wings. Humans, though, don't create their own brilliant flashes of light nor glide through the air. I had to find that woman with the Rottweiler to corroborate my story or go somewhere where I might find a receptive ear.

When the rain cleared, I told Carlos I was going for a walk around Spanish Circle, which he encouraged as a cure for all ailments. Instead, toting no more than a thumb drive, my Montblanc pen, which I planned to swap for a plane ticket, my Timex—a classic but not worth beans—my wedding band, which never leaves my finger, and seventy-two dollars and change, I walked to Counterpass Avenue South, where I tried to call a taxi, but couldn't get a signal. Cell phone service is notoriously spotty in Maragate. I continued walking in what I thought was the direction out of town. Coming toward me was that same man I saw with Lieutenant Conventerra, in that sad, oversized suit and worn fedora, which he pulled lower over his eyes as he drew closer. He had the same determined stride I'd seen before. "Good morning," I said. He never slowed down, returning the greeting with a guttural sound. I stopped and watched him, until a taxi came into view. I hailed it and got inside. "To the airport, please."

"Whoa," said the driver. "That's a two-hundred-dollar ride, before the tip."

"Okay. You take plastic, right?"

"Yes, sir."

I gave him my one good card and held my breath. I had only the word of Carlos that Hope changed the limit. I was hoping to pay the driver at the airport. Or dash if I had to.

The driver sent a text and waited for a reply. He looked too old to be driving a cab. Hawkish, thin, and tall, even in the seat. I would have cast Leonard Nimoy, RIP.

"Can we go, please? I'm in a hurry to catch a flight."

"I have to clear this with the dispatcher." He looked at me in his rearview mirror. "Won't take long. What time does your flight leave?"

I looked at my watch but could not calculate a reasonable time, so I said, "I like to arrive early for a flight. You never know."

"You never *do* know, do you, and sometimes it's better that way."

"I enjoy hanging out in airports anyway. You can watch genuine displays of emotion."

He looked at me in his rearview mirror like I was a suspicious character, until his phone pinged. He read the message and said, "Dispatcher says I have to run your card before we hit the road."

"Yes, of course, go ahead, and then let's roll."

He swiped my card through his little machine and said, "No love."

I made the usual deadbeat excuses, feigning outrage that the card wasn't working.

"Do you have another card we could try, sir?"

I did, but what was the point?

"I limit myself to one card. You know how screwed up these bank cards can be."

"One card? Not advised, sir."

"Please, do this for me. I can mail you the fare, double the fare, and another hundred for you."

"Very generous, sir, but I am not allowed to extend that kind of courtesy."

I offered him my Montblanc fountain pen. "This is the big one, worth a thousand dollars," I told him, "and that's probably on the low side. I got it years ago in Germany."

"I never considered going to Germany," he said. "I don't feel I missed out."

"Okay, but you can't argue with Montblanc. It's an extraordinary pen."

"I'm sure it is, sir, but nobody uses fountain pens these days."

"I do. And people collect them. I'm offering you something worth a grand for a lousy lift to the airport. C'mon."

"How about I give you a lift home, DK, on the house, and you can rethink your getaway."

"How do you know my name?"

"It's on the card," he said, returning it to me.

"And why 'getaway'?"

"Figure of speech. Why, are you a fugitive? I can take you to Leng, no charge, if you'd like to go there."

"Where's Leng?"

"Closer than you think."

I got out of the taxi pretending to be indignant and continued walking. I'd forgotten how powerless a man is when he's short on cash and doesn't have a working credit card. While I was still in my thirties, my business manager told me I was a millionaire, in the days before kids in their twenties started showing up as billionaires from developing time-sucking apps. From my boyhood memories of the two millionaires in my town, I knew that rich men drove Cadillacs. I had my manager buy me a Cadillac, and I never thought about money again. Now here I was, the bulk of my estate represented in one Montblanc fountain pen that even a cab driver didn't want.

When I was in grad school, I was dead broke and lived hand to mouth, nourished by ramen and my studies. Back then, if I had to go somewhere, I hitchhiked. You could do that then and not worry about being murdered along the way. I stepped off the curb and stuck out my thumb, which made me laugh. I couldn't remember the last time I laughed. I must have been a sight, laughing and waving my thumb. I decided that if someone picked me up, I would go where he was going, anywhere out of Maragate. If I got no farther than the next town, Leng or wherever, I could get a job teaching bonehead English or tutoring for the SAT or even teaching screen-writing, which is now a highly marketable skill set, and with my credentials I should have no problem. I could start all over. The notion was exhilarating, what the Buddhists cherish as "beginner's mind," when everything is new again and you are a tyro, which, let's face it, is the best time of life, except that you're broke all the time, and even that can be fun if you use your imagination and know that you won't be broke forever.

I remembered there were times, back in college, when it took hours to get a ride hitchhiking. My lucky day. It was no longer than twenty minutes before a man in a Nissan Rogue stopped for me. He was fit, fair, and forthright, like a gym teacher who coached wrestling. I would have cast Richard Jaeckel, RIP. He pushed open the door and said, "Where're you headed, uncle?"

"I was going to the airport, but I'll go any—"

"Hey, you're in luck. I'm going there myself."

I could not believe my good fortune. Something was finally turning my way. I got inside, full of a sense of well-being, of newfound resourcefulness. I still had to face getting a plane ticket somehow, but I would worry about that later. I was getting out of Dodge!

"Looks like you're traveling light," said my driver.

"I know, right! Feels great!" I was jubilant. (I had a primary care doctor who once gingerly suggested I might be bipolar. Fine, but why was I getting shorted on the upside?)

"I hear you. The only way to go. Traffic'll suck till we cross the bridge, but after that, smooth sailing. Where're you flying to?"

Anywhere. First flight out. It took me too long to pick an appropriate destination.

"You don't know?" he said.

"I'm going to visit my daughter, the older one."

"Nice. What's her name?"

I took too long to select a name.

"Mary Ellen," I said, finally. I grew up in a town where most girls were named Mary Ellen or Mary Louise or Mary Ann.

"And where does Mary Ellen live?"

"Seattle." (Just to throw anyone who might be interested off the trail.)

"Fresh salmon," he said, wistfully. He opened his fist and a joint magically appeared. "Mind if I smoke?"

He toked and passed it to me. I was already on a high knowing I would soon be out of the madness of Maragate, but I accepted the offer and took a long drag. People are amazed that through my long career in Hollywood I never touched drugs, and the only times I smoked weed were in situations like this when someone passed the dutchie on the left-hand side (Musical Youth).

The smoke rose from my nostrils as I lowered the seat back. Before the bridge ever came into sight, "A slumber did my spirit seal; I had no human fears" (Wordsworth).

www.travel-hunter.org/5-reasons-why-hitchiking-
is-so-freaking-dangerous

I was shaken awake by Lieutenant Conventerra. The car's engine was still running. The wrestling coach leaned sideways with one elbow on the steering wheel, smiling like he'd qualified for regionals.

Once again, I was taken to the green interrogation room, but this time left alone with a Styrofoam cup full of bitter coffee. I used the quiet moment to have a think. Nothing that happened with the taxi driver was far enough out of the realm of possibility to induce paranoia. I had to wonder, though, how I hitched a ride so easily with a driver who happened to be going to the airport and who took it upon himself to reverse his trip and deliver me to the police station.

What was happening to me in Maragate might not have been Hope's doing alone. Logistics aside, as staggering as they had to be, why would Hope in concert with others do this to me? What did anyone have to gain? How did I deserve the torture? Who would come to my aid? I had no friends to rescue me. My professional relationships had all been short-term and the worst of them wouldn't spark any more than disparaging words confined to a producer's office. All of me was invested in one woman and my work.

Before I witnessed the murder of an angel, Hope had made three inexplicable choices: the town, the house, and her own escape. Put all that over there. Now, over here we have the police and the angel. My witnessing her murder could not possibly be part of anybody's plan. I, apparently, must be contained. Two problems: In order to deconstruct that half of it I would have to accept the existence of angels, and I would have to ignore the angel's last words: "Hope is alive." How could I? Though it all could not tie together in my mind, none of it could stand alone either.

Conventerra came into the room all falsely apologetic. Was I comfortable? More coffee? Could he call anyone?

"Yes, please, my wife."

"About that, didn't I tell you not to leave town, last time we had a talk?"

"It was not a talk, it was an interrogation, and, no, you didn't say I couldn't leave town, and what gives you the authority to stop me anyway?"

It occurred to me that if I were going to survive this mess it would help to lose the attitude. I had to learn my way around a new reality, not punch wildly through it.

"No authority at all," he said, "but it would be in your best interests. Your wife has disappeared, you're a person of interest, you've had some hallucinations. . . . Are you a danger to yourself or others? Don't know yet."

(He could find a way to lock me up, is what he was saying.)

"With all due respect," I said calmly, "you didn't know my wife was missing until I told you. I would love for you to find her. In fact, I should file a missing person's report. I can't be sure that letter from her is real."

"Frankly, my boss wouldn't take it seriously."

"Then tell me what you want me to do."

"You're a complicated dude. It's best if we stay in touch like."

Kuggelsong, the last person I wanted to see, came into the room, falsely officious. "I have only two questions: who is the President of the United States and what is today's date?"

"That's enough, Sergeant," said Conventerra. "Our man here is not in the grip of dementia."

"You could have fooled me."

"This is not a joke."

"Sorry, Louie."

I was grateful for Conventerra's meager validation, but then they talked about me as though I were not there.

"Put yourself in his place."

"Hard, but I'll try."

"Remember how it was when you first came to Maragate. Had to make new friends . . ."

"I already knew some people."

"Did your wife leave you?"

"As a matter of fact."

"You were young. This gentleman has lived a long life, yet he has no friends. No enemies either. Some professional relationships, maybe deep but all short-term." I was shaken to think that he could read my mind, unless I had earlier been talking aloud to myself. (I do that sometimes, unaware.) "Wife made some iffy choices he can't explain."

"Spoutin' poetry like a madman. That can't be good."

"Who wouldn't want to call a cab and head for the hills?"

"Only he didn't have the fare." (How did *he* know?)

"But he's resourceful, all things considered. He thumbs a ride."

"Which is illegal, by the way."

"Let's give him a pass on that. Stern warning. No more hitch-hiking."

"Lucky he got picked up by a concerned citizen."

"Slow to adapt. Maybe unwilling to adapt."

"Everybody's got to adapt. Darwin said so."

It went on like that for longer than you would expect and for more than I could tolerate. I had the sense that the conversation could go on at least as long as my previous interrogation.

"So what do we do with him?"

"Speaking for myself here," said Kuggelsong, "I'm having a hard time putting myself in Doctor Kowalowski's place." (He wasn't even close on the pronunciation.)

I looked into my empty coffee cup, placed it on the floor, and slowly got to my feet. They took no notice of me.

"Yeah, okay, but you must have some ideas."

"Not for me to say, Louie. Happy to participate, but you the man."

I sidled toward the only door.

"Try a little empathy why don't you."

"I'll give it a shot. I mean, he *is* somebody's father."

"Well, no, no, he's not."

"Somebody's son, then."

"Long ago. He's pretty much forgotten that."

"Somebody's fuckin' husband, at least."

"Not a hundred percent sure about that."

"Then what's my empathy coming from?"

"*Could* be somebody's husband, though. I wouldn't be surprised if tomorrow Hope walked through that door." (The one I was opening.)

"Why would she walk through that door, Louie?"

"Some door. A door. Not necessarily *that* door." (Which was closing behind me.)

I walked out of the station and took a circuitous route to the hovel, every few minutes looking back over my shoulder.

www.improveyoursocialskills.com/empathy

Hope did not return the next day or the day after that, or a month after that. I waited. *I promise I will return. . . .* If you can't trust your wife of nearly forty years, who can you trust? I fell back on good old Jean-Paul Sartre and the existentialists. Your circumstances do not define who you are; you can find your own purpose and happiness anywhere. Truth be told, none of that gang ever struck me as anything but miserable.

With April came the onset of seasonal allergies. For the first time in my life, like most newcomers to Maragate, I became allergic to the pollens in the air. I tried to hold the allergies at bay by popping antihistamines, without much success. I asked the pharmacist at the Rexall, where I had an account, for something stronger. She asked what meds I was on, and when I told her she said that antihistamines were contraindicated. Suffer.

Here's the funny thing: as I ran out of those meds, I simply stopped taking them. As I emptied each bottle I tossed it and forgot about it. My meds weren't keeping me alive anyway, they were just maintaining homeostasis. (Which might be another way of saying they were keeping me alive.)

In the past, they were mailed to me automatically from my online provider. I checked my account and saw that shipments were still being sent to the Hollywood Hills address. I tracked the shipments and saw that they had been delivered. Who accepted them? Was it possible Hope went back to LA without me? Or never left? Was she lounging poolside while I was trapped in Maragate?

I found a sweet spot near City Hall and was able to call my old landline number. The phone rang and rang, neither answering nor prompting me to leave a message. Were my meds piling up in a vacant house? She never told me on the phone or in the letter that our old home had in fact sold, only that she was putting it on the market. I assumed that it would sell the first day it was shown, as homes do in that neighborhood, but maybe she was asking for the moon. (Everybody in LA was asking for the moon. And getting it.)

I had no friends I could call upon to drive over to my place and have a look around. I had many acquaintances and people with whom I had had short and intense relationships during the course of making a movie, but after the first day of shooting the screenwriter is expected to make himself scarce. He can visit the set like a tourist but shouldn't make a habit of it. I didn't even have numbers for my housecleaning lady or the gardener. I didn't have *names* for them. I had been trying to call my agent, who could have sent over an underling, but it was as hard getting through to him as it was with Hope.

The blame for this set of circumstances—this lifestyle—was all mine. I needed no one in my life but Hope.

The LAPD was an option, but my recent experience with cops made me reluctant to involve the system, and it would be difficult to describe my situation should they ask too many questions. I would wind up telling them about my angel and they would hang up on me.

Then I remembered Bryan.

Before I left for New York, I was hounded by a USC student to give him a critique on his script. He gushed about what a big fan of my work he was, and how it was I who was responsible for his choosing the screenwriting life. All bullshit. I was sure he had sent out a dozen similar emails. I didn't want to read his script. If I liked it, he would never leave me alone; if I didn't like it he would tell me to go fuck myself. I explained my misgivings to Bryan, but his promises and persistence were so engaging I agreed to read his script. It was about time travel. While pursuing a fugitive, a cop discovers a portal in a Twinkie factory that can whisk him forward or backward in time in order to fight crime. The young screenwriter imagined Bruce Willis for the lead. Odds are he knew—USC film students know everything—that Willis and I had a history and he was hoping I would forward his script to the movie star. Instead, I deleted it. I did offer him some advice and encouragement, suggesting he go for something more original, maybe something based on his own life experiences. He accused me of being Old Hollywood and the reason why black writers never get nominated for Academy Awards. (He wasn't black himself.)

I went through my trashed emails until I found his, which included his phone number. It was a miracle the call went through.

"Hello, Bryan? This is D. K. Kecskeméti."

"Oh?"

I was impressed by how he was able to express such contempt in one syllable.

"How are you?"

"Awesome. I got an 'A' on *Time Was*."

"I always liked that title."

"Yeah, but you didn't like the script, did you? Well, guess who *does* like it? Guess who I've been taking meetings with?"

"Bruce Willis."

"His brother. Who finds projects for Bruce. He loves my script."

"That's great. I'm happy for you."

"We're talking about me directing my first project."

"You have proven me wrong. Good for you. Believe it or not, I'm always happy when that happens."

"Yeah, well."

His tone softened.

"Listen, Bryan. Now *I* need a favor."

"What?"

"I need you to drive over to my house."

I explained to him only that I was out of town and worried and needed him to go to the house and call me so we could have a walkaround by phone.

"I don't know, dude, you shit all over my script, why should I do anything for you? Not the way it works in the industry. You do something for me, I do something for you."

"I *did* do something for you, Bryan, I read your script, which I hardly ever do, but I did for you. I did not shit all over it. I couldn't relate to it, time travel and all that. The writing, though, was first-rate, and I'm sure I told you that. I can understand why Bruce Willis's brother is keen on it."

He grumbled something and asked, "Where are you now?"

"Maragate."

"The fuck is that?"

"Near Leng. Long story. Bryan, I would be deep in your debt."

The conversation became a classic scene from any acting class. One person tries to convince another to do something he doesn't want to do. I've written dozens of scenes like that, and acting students have improvised thousands of them. I pulled bits and pieces from some of my old scripts to convince him, finally volunteering to read his next script and to take him to dinner to discuss it, as soon as I got back to LA, at a restaurant where he could be seen with me by others who might considerate that significant.

"All right, I'll do it, but you owe me."

He never called me back. Suffer.

www.ExpressScripts.com

A professional pourer at the Gunga Gin tasting room walked me through the complexities of what I was sipping, neat, right out of the freezer.

"Linger over the alluring floral aromas. A fresh dry and crisp palate enhances the slight sting in the mouth feel. A firm structure leads you into a muscular finish of character and confidence. This will pair well with any of the teriyaki jerkies, especially the game varieties like squirrel, rabbit, or rattlesnake."

Have you ever drunk gin? Straight? Awful stuff. F. S. Fitzgerald called it the first choice of the true alcoholic, and he ought to know. Gin's only charm is the blow it delivers between your eyes that renders you resolved to whatever the next hour may bring.

The pourer looked a lot like George Sanders, RIP, tall, patrician, sophisticated, and impatient with anyone who isn't. He spoke with total confidence and crushing boredom.

I sneezed throughout his entire recitation, my eyes burning and tearing. He seemed not to notice nor care.

"Where else can you experience this?" I heard from behind me the edgy voice of Lieutenant Conventerra of the Maragate police. Did he follow me to the Gunga Gin? If not, why was he there? He wasn't tasting.

He nodded toward the dark privacy of the high cabaret tables, each with an unlit candle in an empty gin bottle. I moved with him and we sat at one of the tables.

"Adjusting to your new surroundings?" he asked.

"Like a rescued Chihuahua."

"Speaking of whipped—"

"Who, what?"

"—any news on your wife?"

Pussy-whipped is a vulgar phrase and never applicable to any relationship of mine. Most couples, as they age, move on from sex to companionship anyway. (Not a milestone to celebrate but comfortable enough to slip into when you have no place else to go.) At some unpredictable Saturday night along your way to oblivion, pussy becomes pal, which has to be startling news to any man who passes that divide and now wonders if the woman he married is the right companion for his old age. Would Hope and I have picked each other if we knew we'd be together for so long? She would have been much happier (and possibly now *is*) with a cheerful, social man, a people person like herself, who enjoys a good party and has some moves on the dance floor above and beyond the random spasms that I might risk displaying. As for me, I would have probably gone for an introverted librarian whose idea of a good time was dipping artichoke leaves in aioli while uncovering analogies in the felix culpa of John Milton's *Paradise Lost*.

I thought about lying and telling Conventerra that I'd received some emails or texts from Hope. I'd been in a daze for over a month, but was still aware enough to know that you don't lie to the police. You don't have to tell them everything—you don't have to tell them *anything*—but you don't lie or make things up. My problem is I can't keep my mouth shut. It's how I am.

"No, only the letter. Wait . . ."

I'd been carrying the letter folded in my back pocket. I gave it to him as the only evidence I had that I hadn't murdered her. He read it without any visible reaction.

"Anybody could have written and printed this."

"I know, right? What's worse, it's out of character for her to print it and not sign it."

"What about the style?"

"Sounds a little like her. Sounds like a lot of women, I guess, space and all that. Revenge in the subtext." I sneezed again, three times. "Allergies."

A ceramic bowl half full of teriyaki venison jerky was on the table. I popped a shard into my mouth. I needed the protein. I wet it with the gin. Paired perfectly, like George Sanders said it would, but the gin would have paired as well with pretzels or the misery of another night alone.

"Revenge for what?" he inquired.

"For not dancing? For raising my voice? For not being there, even when I was there? For writing about her?"

"You wrote about her, your own wife?"

"She's the only woman I know intimately. Whenever I write a woman character there's bound to be a little of her in it."

"You make it positive, though, don't you, flattering and every-thing like that."

"I can't always."

"You think she's getting even for you bad-mouthing her in your scripts?"

"I never bad-mouthed her. And even if I did draw something too close, she's sweet and forgiving. At least that's how I remember her. She's in some inner crisis, which, okay, but this is so elaborate it goes way beyond anything anyone would reasonably dream up. Making me live in a creepy hovel with a strange Mexican. How'd she come up with that?"

"What Mexican?"

"Carlos. He came with the house. She left me with a credit card with too low a limit to do anything but wait. And if I go live in the woods, what happens when she does come back? I mean, what if it *is* love and not revenge? I can't tell the difference anymore."

Why was I going on about all this? To him of all people? You tell me.

"That was my point the first time we met, Doctor K. You've got perception problems."

"I don't see it that way."

"Severe problems of perception. I mean, you don't even know where *you* are, let alone where *she* is. It's all in seeing clearly. Not many do, least of all someone like you who has been fucked up for a long time. Take solace. You're in a safe place now. Let it go. Take stock."

"Fucked up?"

"I feel you're not giving Maragate a fair chance."

"I've fallen into the habit of walking by the scene of the crime. I did on my way over here."

"Every man should have a hobby."

"I have no problem with perception, and you don't have to see four shots to know they were fired. I walk by all the time, but I never see anyone there, only once, the morning after. One girl and three men, all young."

"And did they see what you saw?"

"They were tourists, she said. The place is an Airbnb."

"Dead end. Welcome to my world."

"Can you tell from a letter like this where it was printed? I mean, what kind of printer was used?"

"You have any doubts she wrote it?" I took too long to answer. "You do. I can see why."

"There isn't a printer in the house. She might have taken her printer with her, but who would? They cost about thirty bucks."

"They get you on the ink."

"Like nobody will notice that."

"It's like razors."

"How?"

"The razor is cheap. They get you on the blades."

"Somebody is always getting you on something, hoping you're

too dumb to notice. And mostly you are. I showed her picture to the guy at the print shop."

"Henry."

"The guy who looks like Humphrey Bogart?"

"A little, I guess."

"Henry never saw her."

"You've been playing detective."

"What else do I have to do?"

"I thought you were a screenwriter."

"I am, but I need peace and quiet to write. I'm surrounded by ear-shattering leaf blowers. I've never lived in a noisier neighborhood, and I lived for a time in Hell's Kitchen, New York City. Write? I can't even read. I've never seen such hatred of leaves."

"It's kind of amusing, you, looking for clues. At this point in time what you're doing is working with me in spite of your own poetic self, helping me make deductions and such, even though nobody asked us to."

"Like something a psychotic murderer would do, to stay one step ahead of the cops."

"Like in the movies."

"Some movies."

"Not anything you would write."

"No, I wouldn't write that."

"Or it could be we're naturally curious, you and me. Something happens, we have to know why. You, because everything is a story to you. Motivations, reversals, red herrings, subtext. Me, because everything is a crime to me. Lies, cover-ups, conspiracies. That pic you showed Henry? Let me have a look at that."

I handed him my phone. I could understand casting him as the Joker if you wanted to go really dark with the whole Batman gag. (A tent pole raised far too high by film critics, who now relate more to comic books and video games than to serious cinema.)

"She's hot."

"She's old enough to be your mother."

"Recent picture?"

"About ten years old, but she hasn't changed that much."

"Younger than you."

"Not that much. She took better care of herself."

"To be frank, Doctor K, I'm bothered by the whole story."

"Me, too, but it's all I've got."

Still studying my phone, he said, "I mean, if you killed your wife before you went to New York, got rid of the body, which is not an easy thing to do but sometimes it gets done, this would be a great way to cover your tracks."

"If I had killed her, I could have simply moved here as a single man and nobody would know anything different."

"I see your point. But this is a lot for one woman to do on her own. Are you worried she has a boyfriend?"

"Of course not." (I was, a little.)

"Try this on. What if she has a girlfriend. Now, she can be in two places at the same time. They didn't want to kill you, only get shed of you."

"The problem with thrillers, which is what you're outlining now, is they all have a hole in them big enough to skate through backwards. They never reflect real life."

"When did you last speak to her?"

"You have my phone, check my Recents."

Truth is, with the exception of Valentine's Day I couldn't remember. In New York I was so up to my neck in work, three-by-five cards all over the hotel room floor, sometimes falling asleep on top of them, frazzled because it wasn't going well, worrying that I would never get another job. Sick in my stomach because of that piece of cheesecake I ate. Yes, we talked on the phone, about that house and making a big move, after I survived the night, but I couldn't remember if we spoke after that.

"You cleared all your Recents, and your voicemails. And, look, your texts, too."

"I did?"

"My, but you're tidy." (I never pay attention to that stuff.) "You're like a total blank. Almost like you were erasing your past."

"Look, I spoke to her about moving here. I gave her my okay. She was here, I was there, and you know the rest. You're shaking my chain, like you did that first night. I won't soon forget that."

"You're so sensitive. Think of that as an entry interview."

"I would like not to think about it at all."

"Or you could do that."

"You tried to prove me delusional, but guess what? I'm not."

"Maybe not as a chronic condition, but glitches occur. The brain is a complex son of a bitch. And yours has been around long enough to twist in on itself."

"If it was an 'entry interview,' why did your partner follow me outside and punch me in the gut?"

"Who?"

"Your partner, the older, fat guy."

"I don't have a partner. I don't go on patrol."

"Oh, great, now you're going to try to make me believe there was not another cop in the room that night."

"Oh, Kuggelsong."

"Kuggelsong!"

He helped himself to a shard of jerky, gnawed on it like an archeological exploration. "He punched you in the gut?"

"Unprovoked."

"Did you file a complaint?"

"Yes, in the trash can. He came out again and gave me a map of the city."

"Now, that sounds more like him."

"I think the other thing was more like him. He's crazy."

"Funny, he said the same thing about you. Why didn't you mention the punch when Biff rescued you and dropped you off that time? When we turned around and, like, where is that dude?"

"Biff, was he? Perfect. I didn't say anything because Kuggelsong came into the room and I was afraid that this time he would shoot me."

"I'll have a word with him."

"I'm sure that will settle everything."

"Did he say anything, like why he was punching you in the gut? Did you say anything, like, wrong?"

"Nothing that would ever provoke a professional to get violent. He came at me all worked up about a line from Keats. He contradicted the eternal truth of the line and punched me, like it was my fault Keats wrote it. Ironic since the whole point was, 'Beauty is truth, truth beauty, that is all ye know on earth, and all ye need to know.'"

"If that's all ye know, ye is fucked."

Conventerra laughed like a man who finds humor in things other men do not. The position of a dead body, for example. I said as much to him and wondered aloud if all cops laugh in the same inappropriate way.

"You know a lot about cops?"

"A fair amount."

"From the movies?"

"Sure, that's how we know about everything. You say you're bothered by my story. Want to know what bothers *me*?"

"By all means, in order of intensity."

"I'm bothered that in a town this size three cops can shoot down an angel—"

"Listen to you, will you."

"—and then cover it up. You're never going to do anything about it, are you?"

He picked up another shard of jerky, studied it, then studied me in the same way, before tossing the jerky back into the bowl, along with whatever germs were on his fingers, and he was a cop after all. Who knew what last those hands were spreading?

"This angel you speak of, how would you describe it?"

He took on the attitude of someone humoring a schizophrenic.

"Beautiful. Black—café au lait, actually—had a lilting Irish accent. Was naked."

"Hmmm. Erotic. A wet dream."

"In a different setting, and absent the gunfire, sure."

"An old man's fantasy."

"Why not?"

"Wings?"

"That's how I knew she was an angel."

"Large and functional, or small and rudimentary?"

"She had the wing span of a condor. Her breasts were small."

"Took notice, did you? Are you a boob dude or a butt dude?"

"I don't objectify."

"But you noticed, nonobjectively. If I asked you if her boobs were assertive or weary, you would know."

"She was androgynous, more to my point."

"Did you have a little talk with her?"

(You will understand, I'm sure, why I continued to keep her last words—Hope is alive—to myself. I was proud of myself.)

"You asked me that before."

"What did you say?"

"No."

He dropped his tone in favor of something more like a counselor paid to care but not necessarily to comfort.

"Would it be fair to say you experienced, that night, the worst night of your life?" he asked. "You'd been drinking, abandoned, in a fog, literally and the other way."

"It was a bad day."

"Can you be sure about anything? I mean, you think you know your wife intimately, but consider the possibility that you don't know her at all, you never did and you never can."

Consider that. Who can know another? You can't even know yourself. Those long interior dialogs that made up most of my life involved a woman I could only imagine. I don't know her nearly as well as the characters I created. "I'm sure of my own consciousness,"

I said. But was I? Wordsworth describes a poet as someone of "a disposition to be affected more than other men by absent things as if they were present; an ability of conjuring up in himself passions, which are indeed far from being the same as those produced by real events." I flatter myself with the comparison. Yes, when I was a kid I was a poet, before I studied the great poets, at which time I stopped thinking of myself as one, out of respect. Had I studied the great screenwriters, I might not have become one. Was I, at that moment, that night, in error about everything I was experiencing? Did I run a movie in my mind and watch it like a member of the audience? On TV news, all those witnesses to horrifying events tell the reporter: "It was surreal. It was like a movie." Did I create a surreal moment in order to retell it, like a movie? The bigger question is: Does it matter? Who cares what happened or if nothing happened? Why this quest for validation when uncertainty is the only authentic state of man?

Conventerra said, "You were bewildered in a strange town. A home that freaked you out, a Mexican servant who also freaked you out, a gone wife, which freaked you out more than anything. On that foggy night could you be any more freaked out?"

"Then how did I wind up in the police station, in an interrogation room?"

"You don't remember?"

Here is what I remembered: I'm under the SUV and my eyes locked with the angel's to her last breath. My heart pounded behind my fixed eyes. She is whisked away and thrown into the police car, which drives off, the motorcycle following, lights flashing. The remaining cop opens the door to the SUV. I reach out and tug on his pants leg. He's startled and draws his gun. I yell, "Help!" He orders me to get out from under the car, which I do. I can hardly breathe, but I have enough air to say, "What have you done?" He puts me in cuffs and pushes me into the back of his vehicle. Not another word is exchanged until I try to tell the story to Kuggelsong, who would rather talk about the heat in Miami.

"Okay, tell me your side of the story," I said.

"In the middle of a dark foggy street you waved your hands in the air like you just didn't care. You flagged down a black and white screaming like a little girl. The cop thought you were an out-of-control tweaker. You're lucky he didn't pepper spray you."

"Cops shoot you if you twitch these days and then say they thought they saw a gun. And I never screamed like a little girl."

"Who doesn't have a gun these days?"

"A naked black angel does not have a gun."

"Did you catch her name?"

He took another piece of jerky out of the bowl, examined it, and tossed it back.

"If she had a name, she didn't tell it to me. Do angels even have names? Would they need them ever?"

"There's no room under a car for a person your size."

"It was an SUV. The police force has an SUV, don't they?"

"We do. It wasn't anywhere near you that night."

"How do you know that?"

"Because I checked. The woman you saw there? Where did she come from? I mean, there was no person like that around, at the time of the whatever."

"She was as real as you or I."

But was she? A woman in a raincoat, standing calmly while cops had guns drawn, her head covered, wearing Ugg boots. Hope favored Ugg boots. She had coats galore. One of them must have been a navy Burberry. In a moment of life or death did I conjure up the one person I needed most to see? Hope never wore hats or covered her head, though. Didn't want to muss her hair. Small detail but telling.

"Did this woman witness the same thing you did?"

"Yes, she had to."

"And yet she hasn't stepped forward. Why don't you talk to her about it?"

"I told you, I go by the place every day. No one's there."

"Did you see any blood at the scene?"

"Do angels bleed?"

I extended my hand for my phone, which he had been navigating without my permission all during our conversation.

"You have the shortest contact list I've ever seen," he said.

"Long enough for me."

"I couldn't help noticing that besides Hope there is no one here with your last name. Are you alone in the world?"

I was. My sister died young, turning me into an only child, a role I did not want to assume. My parents were long dead. As were my few uncles and aunts. I may have had a cousin or two but I didn't know where. For me, there was no comfort in the shade of the family tree.

"Do you ever call who's left?" he asked.

"Yeah. They're not returning my calls."

"Maybe they don't know you at all. Maybe they exist for you, but not vicey-versey."

"Yes, my contact list of imaginary friends."

"An imaginary friend is better than no friend at all."

"Do you really think I'm insane?"

"Let's call one now."

"Why?"

"You claim to have witnessed something unique in the history of man. Don'tcha want to tell a friend?"

"Maybe later."

"I understand. Friends require emotional effort. They require personal time. They can be a distraction to someone like you who lives in his head."

"Me? I live in a little slice of heaven."

"That's the spirit. Can I have a copy of that picture?"

"What for?"

"For your file."

"I have a file? Why?"

"You made police contact. We have to make a file."

"Keep my wife out of it."

"Already in it. In your best interests to have her picture there. When she comes back, the file gets scrubbed. How's that?"

I sent the picture of Hope from my phone to his.

"If she comes back," he said.

"She promised she would."

"Yeah, in that letter."

He rose from the table.

"Lieutenant, I keep seeing this guy around town, walking the streets."

"Okay."

"He looks demented, like he's on a mission, and he wears the same clothes every day, never changes."

"Is he bothering you?"

"Yes, and I don't know why. You must have seen him, wears a brown suit too big and a fedora. What's his story?"

"You should ask him. People in Maragate are very approachable. Enjoy your gin," he said leaving. "And don't try to leave town."

"I wish."

It's possible he did not know about my second attempt. I'd squirreled away enough money for cab fare to the airport. I walked to where I had caught a taxi before, and sure enough one appeared. He pulled to the curb to pick me up. Leonard Nimoy again. He gave me a withering look and drove on. I was afraid that in the next moment or two the wrestling coach would pull up, all smiles, and say, "Need a lift?"

www.theginparlour.com

After my father died, I learned that he possessed hardly any of what we call "things." No collections, no favorite stuff, only a ruby ring his mother had given him for his eighteenth birthday, which he passed on to me. (Hope should know where it is.) My mother was not much different. She took pride in a grandfather clock everyone else thought was ugly and loud, and she had some ceramic figurines, but little more, nothing worth bequeathing to anybody. They were first generation Americans from Hungarian parents. They did not grow up surrounded by things and so did not become attached to them later in life. I grew up the same way, but when I started to make money I gathered tokens of my success, collections of like items: watches, fountain pens, handmade knives, vintage tools, memo books, sunglasses, and later all sorts of useless electronic gadgets and two of everything Apple ever made. Among my deprivations since arriving in Maragate was the company of all those things, and yet I did not miss any of them and it would have taken some effort to remember what all of them looked like or why they pleased me. All I had now was my laptop, my iPhone—nearly useless in Maragate— my Montblanc pen, my wedding ring, and a Timex.

In Maragate, the first day of spring was officially the Thursday following April 15, a day universally hated across the city. I have never been anywhere where people hated paying taxes more than those who lived in that "little slice of heaven." It was a uniting factor among them. On the fifteenth of April everyone wore black, much like the way everyone must wear green on Saint Patrick's Day. I didn't and was called on it. I had to apologize to everyone I encountered on the street by telling them I was new in town and unaware of the customs. Ignorance, apparently, was no excuse. (One old man muttered, "Communist," under his breath.) Even the dozen protestors who stood on the north side of Spanish Circle every Tuesday from 6 to 7 p.m. wore black on April 15. I asked one of them what they were about, and he told me they had been gathering at the Circle ever since the first bombs fell on Iraq. Never more than a dozen in number and often only three or four, none of them younger than sixty. Now called by many locals as The Old Fools, they were previously called The Old Frogs, a poke at both the protestors and the French, who told George Bush and Dick Cheney that they would rather not join a coalition to invade Iraq. They thought it was a stupid idea. Rather than wonder if France might have a point, many Americans carried their bottles of French wine to the streets and poured it all down the sewer. They could not, however, stop gobbling up french fries, so instead labeled them "freedom fries." In time, after thousands of American deaths, the country of France, if not forgiven by people like Lieutenant Conventerra, was at least no longer vilified. That abuse fell upon the pathetic dozen standing with their signs. (It is worth noting that none of those who defamed the French had ever visited France.)

With spring came the opening of the outdoor farmers market in Spanish Circle, every Thursday evening, a big deal in Maragate. For something to do, I attended. (There may have been other things to do but I had no enthusiasm for finding them. I did discover a vintage movie theater, The Lyric, tucked behind a gin-tasting room and was excited by that until I learned that its program never varied from animated features.) At the farmers market, I'd buy a corn dog on a stick, slathered with mustard, and mouth wrestle it as I stood listening to whatever live music was featured in the center of the circle. It might have been enjoyable if Hope were with me.

The town regarded the market as a weekly social event. Residents spread out blankets and gathered with friends and family to swill gin, sample the food, pick over the produce, listen to the music, and apparently have a good time. I cracked a smile at a few people feeling up the eggplants, which seemed to frighten them. (Frightened me a little.) Meandering among the locals one evening, I made eye contact with a woman who was sitting next to an older man in a wheelchair, a Jack Russell terrier on his lap. The woman sat on a camp chair. An ice chest between them served as a table. At their feet was a blanket to give them a bit more territory. It was not much more than eye contact, though I felt she was appraising me. The following week she smiled at me and the man nodded in my direction. A week after that she invited me with a wave to join them, and when I did she offered me a shot of gin. I readily accepted. She offered me her chair, volunteering to sit on the blanket, but I said I would stand. I can't accept a woman of any age giving up a seat for me.

"You must live here," she said, "you've been to a few of these things."

Her voice was like a window rattling in the wind, and I found it amusing.

"For now. I'm a sojourner."

"You have the look of a lost child."

"I'm sorry."

I don't know why I had to apologize for looking like a lost child.

Her name was Sandy. Coincidentally, I would have cast Sandy Dennis in the role. RIP. Remember her? Wisp of a thing, always nervous, uncomfortable in her own skin. Forever forbearing. This Sandy was maybe five-foot-two, dirty blonde hair, flat-chested, not a beauty but pleasant enough to the eye, with a sweetness in her face. I liked her right away. The man, who I thought might be her father, turned out to be her husband, a retired veterinarian she called Doc. He didn't say much at our first meeting. Speaking was an effort for him. I wondered if he had had a stroke.

They wanted to know something about me. I told them as little as I could get away with. I said I was retired, but even then I knew they'd get the whole story eventually. I can't shut up.

"From what?" she asked. "Let me guess. A radiologist. No, a professor."

"Close. I taught for a few years."

"You taught music. You were the band director."

I got a kick out of picturing myself leading a marching band. "No, I taught English. Community college."

"Do I have to watch my grammar?"

"I don't know, is she dangerous?"

I made her laugh and caused Doc to cough.

"I'm not really retired," I said. "I can't."

"Didn't save up for it?"

"It's not the kind of work you can retire from. It's more like I'm on hiatus."

"On what?"

"Hiatus. Time out. Between jobs. I'm a screenwriter."

So that's how long it took me.

"Really? I would never have guessed, but I've never seen one before."

"You've see one, you've seen them all."

"I'm sure there are some here in Maragate," she said. "There are some of everything here. They may even have a community, for all I know. I bet they do. I bet you they meet somewhere, the library, of course. There are communities for everybody, staying in their own little tribe."

"Screenwriters like to travel in packs, because of predators, you know."

"I admire people who can write. I can't imagine. I can't write for free seeds."

I braced myself for her next question: Did I write any movies she might have seen? Everyone asks that.

"Do you have a family?" she asked. I told them what little there was to say, that I had no children and my wife was currently out of town. "Oh? Too bad. Or maybe good. I don't want to pry. Are you expecting her?"

"Daily. It's a long story." Which I was sure I would tell them sooner or later.

"What's her name?"

"Hope."

"What a great name! Optimistic. Positive. Not like Sandy, which makes you feet gritty, or think someone named Sandy should be gritty."

"Or blonde."

"We take what we're given, don't we?"

I told them the whole story. It's agony for me to keep things private. (The result of having lived so long in California. In upstate

New York, we kept strangers at arm's length. In Southern California, no one was a stranger. I could meet a woman in a check-out line at Ralphs and by the time I reached the cashier I knew her husband's annual salary, the disappointments in her children, and how good she was in bed.)

I shared with them my distaste for my own house and that it came with an annoying Mexican caretaker.

"I'm not being racist. He'd be annoying if he was Dutch."

I did not say that I found their town unbearable and could not wait to see it in my rearview mirror. (If I had a car.) I told them I'd had a rocky encounter my first night in town with a couple of Maragate's Finest.

Doc and his young wife shared a look. I expected them to defend the cops in Maragate as the best in America. Sandy turned away and looked off toward the music. Doc leaned forward in his wheelchair and asked in his raspy voice, "What . . . happened?"

"Now, Doc, don't pry," said Sandy.

"I saw something I wasn't supposed to."

"Fucking . . . cops," said Doc.

"A young lieutenant named Conventerra," I told them, "and another cop who is probably a psychopath. I keep forgetting his name."

"Kuggelsong."

"That's him," I said. "He punched me in the stomach."

"Get out, that can't be true," Sandy said.

"Why I would lie?"

"Why . . . would he . . . lie?"

"Oh, no, I mean, it's unbelievable that . . ."

Sandy had a nervous, broken manner of talking, probably developed in childhood. Doc's halting speech was due to his condition.

"People in Maragate know to stay away from the cops," she said, "not that they're going to hurt you or anything, but you just do."

I stayed with them for a while longer and had some more of their gin. I sat down, but on the blanket, not on Sandy's chair. They were an odd couple, but they seemed to fit. I was curious about their story. When I tried to get up from the blanket, my knees stiffened. I needed a little boost from Sandy, who grabbed my right hand with both of hers and pulled me to my feet with all the strength she had. She surprised me with a hug, and Doc shook my hand with an unexpectedly strong grip.

"Welcome aboard . . . DK. . . . Hang in, buddy."

I took it as ordinary small talk. He was drunk. (As was I.)

Before the next farmers market, I went to K&K Hardware, a small store on Camino Oscura South, where, sure enough, I had an account. I bought an ice cooler and a folding camp chair and a table.

I became a fixture at the market, sitting with my new friends near the music, under a towering cork tree, a bottle of local gin in the cooler, a dinner of local basil citrus lamb jerky, freshly baked flatbread, and ripe red cherries on the tiny folding table. I was following Hope's suggestions: relaxing, embracing my new surroundings, meeting people. It was easier than I had imagined. I told them about the little man in the oversized suit and fedora I kept seeing around town and asked if they knew him. Sandy giggled. Doc said, "I'm surprised he hasn't come by. He usually makes the rounds. Maybe you scared him off." Sandy giggled again in her nervous manner.

www.farmersmarketla.com

The two major industries of Maragate, if you haven't already figured that out, are artisan gins and handmade jerkies, on behalf of which the residents are chauvinistic to the point of annoyance. A bit of small town charm in every shot, in every leathery bite, it's claimed. The perimeter of Spanish Circle was dotted with gin-tasting rooms, where imaginative distillers paired saffron gin with garlic chili pepper emu jerky, or ginger elderberry gin with basil citrus buffalo jerky.

The jerky joints were done in the motif of old Esso gas stations with a dummy pump at the curb. The gin rooms were made to look like intimate 1950s supper clubs, with serpentine bars and posters of Perry Como. These were the new surroundings I now embraced, because everything else in the town was more or less abhorrent: the sterile landscape of unimaginative structures set too close together, the ever-present obnoxious soundscape of leaf blowers revving, the endless maintenance of ugly little houses, the sickening smell of cured meat and juniper, the pollen-laced air that had everyone sneezing, snotting, and red-eyed from March to late October, the climate—damp and cold or humid and hot—and the drug problems, of which Maragate had more than its fair share. They were regarded as part of the small-town charm, personified by crazed and toothless tweakers who would invade Spanish Circle after dark like zombies. Given the local industry, DUIs and domestic disturbances filled most of the police blotter and were drolly reported by the *Maragate Herald* as part of the human comedy. "Police encountered one of their frequent fliers at 10:30 p.m. in Spanish Circle. The stained pants of said suspect fell around his ankles, making his attempted escape less than successful. He blew 1.8 and was charged with public drunkenness, indecent exposure, and possession of drug paraphernalia."

I never saw any mention in the folksy blotter about police gunning down a winged creature hiding in a vacation rental, the very one I was approaching now with a quickened step.

I was on my way home from a leisurely turn around Spanish Circle, taking the usual detour past the scene of the crime. As time went on I looked for, if not a seat in the "grandstand of philosophical detachment" (Eugene O'Neill), a road sign directing me to the moral path of doing nothing. In short, a way of saying, "Not my problem," and living with that decision rather than taking a Hanksian risk.

I refer to Tom Hanks in a Jimmy Stewart movie: an ordinary man is in the wrong place at the wrong time and sees something he was never meant to see and now finds himself in a place of great jeopardy. What to do? Where to turn? I didn't trust Carlos. I could not get over the feeling that he was doing an impersonation, of whom I could not say. Getting a call or an email through to Hope proved impossible on a daily basis. I was a born-again atheist, so a priest was out. The press? The local rag was mostly advertising. The news that was reported was always slanted toward the cheery and quaint. Its mission was primarily to entertain. I hadn't eliminated the idea of going public, but the *Maragate Herald* was less than I needed and I didn't know where I could find more. Also, the possibility that the editor of that poor periodical would regard me as a lunatic, since he had all the ink and I only myself, was not remote. Let's agree it was likely. I could Twitter something under a fake name and start a hashtag—#policeshootingangels—but I was not a twit, nor did I care to become one. What I've noticed is that those who do post on Twitter often need another tweet, or several, apologizing for the first one. Then they lose their jobs and/or friends, and they spend the rest of their lives regretting it.

The clock, moreover, was ticking, not like the one in the Tom Hanks movie, but the one that marked the shelf life on my eyewitness account. After talking to Conventerra over gin and jerky, my inner discourse went into basso profundo. Was it at all possible that I was in error? About what and to what extent? Did it matter what happened, or if anything happened, what I saw, or what I imagined?

I was mired in this kind of Descartian uncertainty when I spotted her on the stoop and quickened my pace. She was on the first step of a three-step ladder. She had a light bulb in one hand and was struggling to replace a dead one in the overhanging fixture. She was heroin-thin, and tall, but not tall enough for the task. I called out from the street, "Can I help you with that?" She stepped down and gave me a wary once-over. I'm a big man, with menacing eyes that I can't do anything about, so I'm often trying to put women at ease when they happen to be stuck alone with me, like in an elevator.

"Would you?" she said.

Darryl Ponicsán

I quickly went to her aid. "Happy to help, if you'd steady the ladder for me." I took the new bulb from her hand, and from the first step was able to replace the spent one.

"Hey, thanks a bunch. With my luck, I would have taken a header?"

She looked to be fifty, but some surgical work had been performed and probably not by a board-certified surgeon. The skin on her face was artificially taut.

"Where's your Rottweiler?"

Not a good opening gambit apparently. She narrowed her eyes and said, "Just behind the door."

She looked resilient, with chestnut red hair and near translucent skin. Her mouth was large and sensuous in that way large mouths can be. (Carly Simon, Mick Jagger.) I might have gone with some off-casting, Molly Parker, but Molly was still too alluring. Nothing much about this woman was alluring, and she smelled like stale smoke.

"I'm sure you don't recognize me—you might not have even seen me that night."

"What night?"

"I was here that night the police showed up, last February."

"I don't know you from Adam, dude."

Her attitude changed from mild annoyance to concern about the inevitability of one bad thing following another until a stranger emerges to make it worse.

"You were here. You wore Ugg boots and a blue coat. And you had your dog with you."

She opened the front door a crack and the dog snorted, pushing at the opening.

"Better stand back?" she said.

I did, off the stoop and several steps beyond. She backed into the house, keeping the dog at bay. She shut the door.

She knew. Everything in me sensed that she was frightened. Somehow I would have to overcome that. I went back to the stoop, folded up the ladder, and leaned it neatly off the stoop and against the house, hoping she would come out again. I waited a minute or two and debated knocking on the door or biding my time. I decided on the latter. At this point, what was the rush?

www.iep.utm.edu/descarte

Living in Maragate came at an absurdly high price. In the upscale part of town where I lived, houses that might sell for $100,000 in Kentucky and would include two horses and twenty acres started at a million and barely fit their tiny lots, accommodating no more livestock than one dog, preferably a ratter. I was informed by a local real estate agent that during the Great Meltdown and Recession, when millions of home owners found themselves in a condition analysts aptly called "underwater," with no hope of ever resurfacing to the already fished-out middle class, real estate in Maragate endured only the indignities of having to linger on the market for more than a day, of selling for no more than the asking price, and of putting up with an inspection contingency. I found out from an agent I'd met at the farmers market that the hovel Hope purchased cost $1.49 million, which she tendered in cash. The asking price was $1.4 but as the agent smugly pointed out, nobody gets a house in Maragate for the asking price.

The cash she paid had to have come from the equity in our place in LA. I had no recollection of ever signing any papers. Maybe I didn't have to. I never signed any papers for the place I was living in currently. I never knew what I was worth, nor did I care, but even I knew it was nuts to pay $1.49 million for the house in which I was now consigned to live, where the neighbors' only interest in life was pristine driveways and sidewalks, where hordes of men daily invaded with dust bazookas and performed what I saw as theater, ballet, opera, circus—take your pick—of the absurd.

I watched the blowers most of one day in utter disbelief. (It was surreal. It was like a movie.) Men with hurricanes in their backpacks attacked a dozen fallen leaves on a lawn not much bigger than a hotel room, sending them twenty feet into the air toward the street or into a neighbor's yard. Turning back, they would invariably find a leaf or two had landed back on the lawn, and they would renew their attack on a single leaf with a force nearing 300 mph of generated wind. Satisfied that no leaf remained, the men would blast away at anemic bushes, killing the odd bee and butterfly but clearing out any hidden leaves, which only put more of them back on the lawn. They would stretch upward and blast into the very trees from which leaves fall, hoping, I suppose, to finish off any that had already lost the will to live. These too would land on the lawn and had to be chased down. Then the driveway. Dirt and sand and twigs, dog shit, rat shit, and larvae, pebbles and scrapings from tires, dead birds and a variety of insects and their eggs. They blasted great clouds of toxic dust into the air, under and over parked cars, toward the street and into adjacent properties. I watched a woman leave her front door, but she could not get past the porch before she was swallowed by a poisonous cloud. Coughing and gagging, she reeled back to her house and locked herself inside. Dogs howled. Babies cried. Cyclists sped by with Army surplus gas masks on their faces. When would the curtain fall on this performance? Never, because crap blows back. Not until it got too dark to see would they cease, and that was but an intermission until it once again became light enough to blow and go. They blasted the sidewalks and the gutters, sending dried scum and old men's spit and pollen and more dog shit, more rat shit, into the already heavy air. When finally they believed they had the better of it, they blasted the dirt from their trucks and off each other's pants. At the end of the day, they held their leaf blowers above their heads and made them roar until empty of what fuel was left in the carburetor, leaving behind the sick aroma of raw gasoline.

No wonder I looked forward to the farmers market, to the peace and comfort of Spanish Circle and the companionship of my new friends, Doc Fleck and his wife Sandy. We enjoyed the diversion of the weekly market. It was the only time we spent together, but it was enough to support a friendship. I didn't know what they did with the rest of their week; they didn't know what I did with mine, which was not much of anything, besides a personal survey of small batch artisan gin and building up my courage to convince the Rottweiler woman to corroborate my story. (Though by this time I felt little moral obligation to prove anything.)

I had never gone so long without writing. The thing about writing a screenplay is you are obliged to do something with it when you are done. Otherwise, you might as well be blowing leaves. You can't hang a screenplay on the wall and feel nourished by looking at it. You can't publish a screenplay because reading one is a penance, like reading badly translated directions for assembling something made in China that you don't need. For the same reason, you can't take your screenplay to an open mic during a meetup.com gathering. All you can do with it is try to find someone capable of raising millions of dollars to kick-start its transformation into a motion picture.

I put a hand over my glass when Sandy tried to refill it with a kumquat gin from the Furioso distillery, a subtle libation lightly laced with lavender, spa-like in its qualities of relaxation, sold in a smartly designed square bottle. I preferred Sweet Briar Dragon gin, yin and yang, secure in its tradition of a quality fifth of gin for an honest fifty dollars.

Sandy, no bigger than a minute, as they say in Maragate, surprised me with the volume of gin she could handle. For that matter, so did Doc. (So did everyone.) I never thought of wheelchair-bound serious drinkers, but why not? I would drink myself silly. I did anyway, and I had two working feet.

The manager of the event always opened the festivities at precisely 5:45 p.m. by ringing a cowbell and shouting out, "Welcome to the best darn farmers market anywhere!" Everyone would cheer. "Vendors, open your counters!" At which time a local Bob Dylan knock-off or a soft rock boy-girl duet or a gray-bearded bluegrass band, or whoever was next in line would power up their outdoor amps and perform for tips. Tonight it was Rosie and the Playdates, four tough-looking twelve-year-old girls wearing makeup and fishnet stockings, on keyboard, drums, and two guitars.

"They don't . . . suck as much," observed Doc Fleck.

"As much as what?"

"As much . . . as I thought they would."

It was good to have someone to talk to once a week, which was around my limit, without dwelling on my circumstances and how I might get out of them. They assured me, as everyone else did, that there were worse places to be stuck in a holding pattern. (No one ever named any.)

It was okay to be old these days, Doc and I decided. We'd both had happy childhoods, during which our mothers were not horrified that we were playing in the dirt. We walked to and from school and wandered in the woods. Our fathers raked leaves into a pile and we jumped into the pile. We made slingshots and didn't worry about giving the appearance of violence. We breathed the air and drank the water and ate the bread. Now, the dangers were inescapable: a government that said it cared but didn't know how to show it, controlled substances out of control, well-armed psychotics, overpopulation, a corporate ethos natural to sharks, dwindling resources, climate change men cause but cannot stop, bad food, water, air, and monstrous greed. We talked about all that and whatever mass murder occurred that week, which big-city papers now put on page six, reserving page one for some cheerleader who didn't make the cut and came to school with a Glock on each chubby hip to blow away as many mean girls as she could until she had to reload, at which time the obligatory hero (gym teacher) would emerge and tackle her. On TV, however, with twenty-four hours a day in which to lure a viewership with ever shortening attention spans, a shooting can burn the daylight hours. "How did it feel?" the TV journalist asks the witness. "It was surreal. It was like a movie," she replies.

"I think," said Doc one evening, "this would . . . be a good time . . . to be a writer."

"You do? You're the only one."

Sandy had Googled me. They were both pleased to see that, though I had my share of flops, I had never written anything shameful.

"What's stopping you, mister?" Sandy asked, trying to make light of everything.

"Besides why . . . anyone should . . . bother doing anything," said Doc.

What *was* stopping me? Maybe what he said.

I told them, "Leaf blowers. Writing requires concentration. This town has sacrificed peace and quiet for an aesthetic that's, let's face it, pretty sterile. And short-lived."

"Oh, those things," she said. "They make me so nervous. I guess it's another fact of life we have to live with."

Doc said, "They scare the animals . . . and poison the children . . . rattle the aged. Almost banned them here . . . a few years ago."

"Really?"

"Yeah, there was a gal . . . started a Facebook page, did her home-work . . . presented a good argument . . . with data . . . to the council . . . that they were menaces . . . dangerous to your health . . . quality of life . . . and pretty useless to boot. They seemed to agree with her . . . but you know."

"What?"

"The landscapers showed up with their little children," said Sandy. "They were so adorable. The fathers said they would all die of starvation if they couldn't use gas blowers."

"Why? They could still do the job with rakes and brooms. It would be cheaper for everybody in the long run."

(Here I am going to stop imitating Doc's halting and breath-less way of speaking before it becomes annoying. [If it hasn't already.])

"The gal had enough people behind her," he said, "that the

council had to toss her a bone. They took some half-ass half measures and laid down some half-ass rules."

"Like what?" I asked.

"You can't go over seventy-five decibels, and you can't start till eight a.m. and you have to quit by eight p.m."

"On the west side, they start up at dawn and go till dark and I'm guessing ninety to a hundred and twenty decibels, but how would I know?"

"Bingo," said Doc. "All you know is they're too damn loud."

"The rules are hard to enforce," said Sandy. "And people don't like to call the cops."

"I can understand that."

We were tired of getting worked up over leaf blowers and the city council and the cops. We wanted, like everyone else in the park, no more than to swill gin and listen to the local brats, Rosie and the Playdates, singing an inappropriate Britney Spears lyric.

"What kind of movie would you write," Doc asked, "if you could concentrate? Could I have more ice, please?"

I dipped into the cooler and brought up some ice cubes and slid them into his plastic glass.

"My last script was about the pope."

"How can you do a movie about the pope? Isn't he infallible?" asked Sandy.

"I don't care about his infallibility, I'm questioning his culpability."

Doc asked, "Are you a Catholic?"

"Not anymore."

"So what do you care?"

"Even a lot of Catholics don't care. Mostly the young ones. The young don't seem to care about anything anymore."

"Neither do I," said Doc.

"Oh, Doc," said Sandy. "You still care about a lot of stuff."

"Then I admire the ones who don't."

"Doesn't look like the movie'll ever be made, anyway. The producer is profoundly disappointed in me."

"Let's say you were going to write something new. What would it be?" Sandy asked.

"*The New Adventures of Spiderman.*"

"Oh, you . . ."

"Maybe a cop story," said Doc.

"The world needs another one," I said.

"Now it's all about who's got the drugs. Can you do a crime story today without drugs?"

"You can't do a love story without drugs."

"What would your cop story be about?"

"A man, think Tom Hanks, witnesses some cops shoot somebody."

Doc and Sandy looked at each other the way Hope and I used to when somebody innocently slipped into our territory. Like closeted gays must feel when the talk turns to the Pride Parade. Like Jews feel whenever a gentile uses the word "Jew."

"What?" I said. (Meaning, what is that look?)

"I've seen that movie," said Doc. "The good guy has to run from the bad guys *and* the cops."

"So did I," said Sandy. "Maybe we saw it together, Doc."

"No," I said, "in this one they bring him in and try to mess with his mind. They convince him he's delusional, because he's got a lot of other unsettling things going on in his life."

"Doesn't light my fire. Why does he have to do anything?"

"And therein is the difference between life and movies. He doesn't have to do a damn thing but take what's left of his existence and make the most of it."

The double-decker tour bus, The Fizz, made its way around the Circle. The people onboard were laughing and enjoying themselves. They looked so happy in contrast to those of us in the park, many of whom seemed to resent the tourists having such a good time. Locals tend to resent tourists everywhere, I suppose, stuck with the truth that they need them. The bus was packed. I heard muffled words from its PA. Everyone turned to wave with the hand that wasn't holding a complimentary gin. They were waving at that small man wearing a fedora and a suit too large, the one who had been haunting me. He was sitting on a park bench close to the sidewalk. The bus moved on around the Circle. I could hear the fading laughter.

"That's the guy!" I practically shouted.

"What guy?"

"The one I was telling you about. He's everywhere."

"Where?"

I pointed. "Over there on the bench." But he had disappeared.

"Listen, DK, forget the cop story," said Doc. "Write something different. Like you said, you can't do a cop movie without it being about drugs."

"I think *you* said that."

"What we have to do," said Doc, "is get us some drugs."

"You're a vet. I hear horse tranquilizers are the bomb." (Not my usual lexicon, but I felt more and more at ease with Doc and Sandy.)

"Duh," said Sandy. "You both have glasses of gin. That's drugs enough for two geezers. I'm off to the hummus guy. Anybody want anything?"

"Pita chips," Doc said. "Garlic."

He sneezed three times, almost knocking himself off his chair. We had all been sneezing and wiping our eyes. (Everyone in the park. It was funny. Symphony of the sneezers.) His breathing was labored. The air was full of dust and pollen.

"Doc, I know it's personal and none of my business, but I'm curious . . ."

"I fell."

"Oh?"

I waited, but that was all he was willing to tell me.

I said, "You're a lucky man, having Sandy to look after you."

"I can stand up if I have to, take a step or two, more with someone to hang on to. I'm not that bad off. I wish I had some work. That's what I miss. If I was a writer, like you, I'd be on the job."

It made me feel guilty.

"I'm in a kind of limbo," I said. Doc cocked his head to one side, like, tell me more. "I have a script I've been working on. It's a western. Twenty-four hours in our nation's history that shows how we got this way. I plan to get back to it. Someday."

"A western? Man, you have got your finger on the pulse of the nineteenth century."

"Thirty-five years ago it wasn't that foolish."

"Wait, what?"

"That's when I started working on it."

"You've been working on a movie script for thirty-five years?"

"Longer, probably. Since just after The Golden Age of Movies, depending on how you count."

"Every day?"

"Every hour."

"Why isn't it a movie by now?"

"Damned if I know. It's brilliant."

"Somewhere you went wrong. Who's the hero? Gary Cooper?"

"I wish. This movie doesn't have a hero."

"That could be your problem."

"It's occurred to me, but in real life heroics are rare. Historically rare. Inside most heroes there remains a certain small-mindedness, a prejudice unrecognized. That's why we're so hungry for heroes all the time. You get hit in a crosswalk, you're not a victim, you're a hero."

"But it's a movie, not real life."

"I don't see them as mutually exclusive."

"What's it called?"

"*Lost Creek.*"

"Okay, see, that's your first mistake. That gives me no idea what's it about."

"You're giving me notes?"

"Unless it's about an actual lost creek. And how do you lose a creek?"

"Lost Creek is the town, in the Wyoming Territory. It grew up around an Army outpost, Fort Besterman, but they changed its name after the Army all but abandoned the post, leaving two old Indian fighters in charge, a one-armed captain and his castrated scout. It takes place in one day, during the thaw after a long brutal winter that killed off most of the cattle, so you've got a town full of idle cowboys who spend their days at the only saloon left in town. All that's left of the law is the captain, the scout, and a half-scalped judge appointed by consensus who lives above the stockade and drinks all day, looking out the window, waiting for hostiles . . . or salvation. At one time I had Bruce Willis as the judge, but I couldn't raise eight million on Bruce if he wasn't saving the world."

"I like him, all those quips, grace under pressure."

"You think he's making them up? On the spot?"

"You mean he isn't?"

"Somebody writes that. Not me, but somebody."

"Relax. I know that. How's it start? Give me the opening scene."

"Of my western?"

"No, of *Die Hard Seven*."

"Exterior, early morning, two riders come down from the mountains, after the thaw, on mules, which is already unusual."

"You ought to call it, *After the Thaw*."

"That's not bad, actually. It's gone through about six titles. Six directors, too. Hal Ashby, rest in peace, Sydney Pollack, rest in peace. Walter Hill. Martha Coolidge. I forget the other two. I'll remember tonight, middle of the night."

"Be sure to call me."

I got a kick out of Doc. He was hard to cast, a real person. Ralph Waite, RIP, would work.

"So go on," Doc said, "two riders on mules, after the thaw."

"Interior, bedroom: the captain puts a gold coin on the bureau and gets dressed, helped by the last whore in town, because he's got only one arm. Almost everybody in the movie is damaged . . ."

"Sounds like Maragate."

"They are all, each of them, the last of its kind left in town, except for the two strangers on mules. They're new. They're the future."

"But we don't know that yet."

"No, we haven't even seen their faces yet. The captain sees them off in the distance as he leaves the whore's room over the saloon, and with the instincts of an old soldier he knows there will be trouble."

"I'm hooked. Keep going."

I had drunk enough gin to fuel a pitch to a disabled veterinarian who had drunk at least as much as I. I would have happily gone through the whole story but for the appearance of that little man in the fedora. One minute he was not there, the next minute he was, coughing into a soiled hanky then looking at what he brought up. He looked sick, emaciated, thin-lipped with deep creases in a sallow face. (Doc would tell me later that he was not sick, though he appeared to be, as though a sickness from which he recovered had left its mark.)

"Ripley. You're looking prosperous."

I thought it must be a long-standing gibe. The man looked like he had been pushed out of a getaway car. Of all the people gathered at Spanish Circle, only he wore a suit, yellowish-brown so you had trouble telling where the suit ended and the man began, a ratty wrinkled gabardine too large in the shoulders and butt. It might have been thrift-store bought or something he had shrunk inward from. He wore a dingy white shirt and a blue tie stained with marinara sauce. He had on large rimless glasses that needed a cleaning. He probably couldn't see things clearly, but who am I to talk. (Ha-ha.) He looked like a deranged person attempting to appear professional, like a hand-to-mouth substitute teacher with a drinking problem. He wore tan laceless Sperry Top-Siders without socks, and his ankles were dirty. The tan fedora on his head was sweat-stained. When he doffed it, he revealed thinning gray wisps of hair far back from his translucent forehead. I thought he must be some eccentric, a local character pointed out by the tour bus driver for tourists to wave at, like a beloved village idiot. Close to his belt he held a glass like a monk's rice bowl. It had a handle and could have been a mustard jar once, now in a recycled existence.

"And what is the gin situation, most currently?" he asked Doc.

"I have Furioso. DK is drinking Sweet Briar Dragon."

"Sweet Briar is for tourists. I'll take the Furioso. The aftertaste lingers but does not wear out its welcome."

He had a droning voice, gravelly and unpleasant to the ear. It sought a tone of authority in all that he said. Doc poured a drink into his jar.

"Have you met DK? He's a newcomer, rode down from the mountains after the thaw."

The little man tucked his chin against his chest and cast a confused look at Doc.

"I do not recall having that pleasure, but I meet so many people," he said without interest.

I leaned forward in my camp chair to shake his hand, which felt like cold tripe. "Pleasure," I lied.

"How do? I find this gin pairs well," he said for my benefit and Doc's attention, "with Asian flavors."

Doc offered his bag of teriyaki emu, and the poor connoisseur helped himself to a flat jagged shard as big as his hand.

"DK's a famous screenwriter, only he can't work anymore because the leaf blowers have driven him to drink, which is good for the local economy but a shame for cinema because he's got a great new story, a mystic western."

I think he said mystic. He might have said mythic. I'd take either one.

The diminutive man, who appeared sober, but somehow I knew was not, nodded gravely. "I hate the fucking things," he said.

"Westerns?" I asked.

"Leaf blowers. But they are a fact of life, and we must all learn to live with them. They don't stay that long."

"They do in my neighborhood. I can see," I said, "how they might be useful on a parking lot, but in a residential area of small lots it's absurd. It's overkill."

"It was an issue a few years back, but most people don't give a damn . . ." His voice trailed off.

He closely resembled the famous dope fiend and paranoid writer William Burroughs, in both appearance and manner, but Burroughs, in the pictures I'd seen of him, was always clean. You could even say squeaky clean, though I recall him writing that junkies generally cannot stand the feel of water on their skin. I would have cast Burroughs to portray this guy. In the right role, a nonactor often gives a better performance, as Burroughs did, in fact, in a few movies.

www.youtube.com/watch?v=DnxweVAvE5w

Sandy returned with her purchases. She took no notice of Ripley and he none of her, as though they had agreed long before to have nothing to do with each other. She opened the hummus and put it on the table, tore open the bag of pita chips, and put that on the table as well. Then she sat down and looked over at Rosie and the Playdates with no interest. The band was doing a heavy metal riff on a song from a Pixar animated feature. (We used to call them cartoons when they were mercifully kept to no more than five minutes.)

Doc said, "Help yourself, Mayor."

Mayor? Recast! Nobody would believe William Burroughs as the elected mayor of any town in a civilized country. I couldn't believe *this* guy would be any more believable in the role.

"You're the mayor?" I tried to say it like, oh, I didn't know that, but it came out like, no way!

The mayor dipped a chip into the hummus and ate it with his head back so that anything dripping would land in his mouth or near enough to be redirected into his mouth. Sandy caught him at it and sighed sadly.

Said Doc, "Mayor Ripley Hirkill, D. K. Kecskeméti."

What town would electorally say, Oh, yeah, this is the face of our fine city. Think of us when you look at him.

"What does the *D. K.* stand for?" he asked, in a ragged voice marinated in gin.

"Don't know."

Doc laughed but His Honor was not amused. He gave me the stink eye.

"Tell me," I asked, "why didn't you choose to ban leaf blowers?"

"Bad for business."

"Whose business?"

He had to think for a moment. "The landscapers."

"Thousands of residents are made miserable so that twenty Mexican yardmen might have free rein for doing what, making noise and dust? And when it comes to that, it can't be easy lugging those things on your back, losing your hearing, poisoning your lungs. Making them use those things is a cruel punishment."

"There's more than twenty. And they're not all Mexican. A little racist to say so, don'tcha think? Then there's the roofers and the workers who blow out your rain gutters. These are hard-working people."

"I'm a hard-working person myself. Or at least I'd like to be. Let's say that every time I see a leaf blower I turn the hose on him. That's what it's like for me, trying to do *my* job."

He did not enjoy being buttonholed by a newcomer on an old issue that had already gone away.

"I would not advise a newcomer to turn the hose on anybody," a threat in his voice. "And by the way, there's more landscapers than screenwriters, and they do a lot more for the community."

"That's likely true," I said. "I know I do nothing for the community, and have no plans to, but I'm just a sojourner, not an elected official."

He gnawed his piece of jerky like a ferret, casting darting glances at me from under the brim of his frayed fedora.

This strange little man was the one I saw that first night in Maragate, leaving the public restroom right behind Lieutenant Conventerra. What were the mayor and the cop doing in a public restroom at three o'clock in the morning, moments before the murder of an angel?

He double-dipped a chip and left, walking with his head held back, like a hungry bird, the chip above his open mouth. I mimed a shudder.

"Style is an option. Clean is not," I said, quoting an old commercial slogan (Tide). Sandy stood up and gathered the chips and hummus and tossed them into a nearby trash barrel. I believe it was not the first time she'd made that sacrifice.

"You don't care for the mayor, do you?" I asked her.

"I don't think about it."

"What about you?" I asked Doc.

"Can't stand the cadaverous son of a bitch, but like the leaf blower the mayor is a fact of life."

"Why were you so nice to him?"

"My weapon. Flattery. Kiss the ring. He needs to be loved, while well aware that everyone despises him. If you talk to Hirkill, he'll tell you he's playing the long game. Well, I'm playing a *longer* game."

"That's his real name? Ripley Hirkill?"

"Believe it or not. Ripley T. Hirkill."

"What an odd duck," I said. "Usually, I like odd ducks. But this one . . ."

"He's the duck in reverse. He doesn't look like a mayor, doesn't walk like a mayor, doesn't talk like a mayor, and yet he is the mayor."

"Did you see his feet? They're filthy. And what's with the suit? And the fedora. How long's he been mayor?"

"Forever."

"People keep reelecting him?"

"They keep trying to prove that we have a sense of humor. We do, we do, honest, we do."

"Is it a paying job, full time?"

"Not much above minimum wage, but he gets by. There are perks."

"Where does he live?"

Doc nodded toward the east. "Over on Circle East, above a garage. I heard he pays a dollar a month."

"That would appear to be graft."

"It would, wouldn't it? Legally, the dollar makes it okay, I guess."

"Does he have a family?"

"He doesn't even have a history."

"He looks like William Burroughs."

"The man who wrote *Tarzan?*"

"That was Edgar Rice Burroughs. William Burroughs wrote *Naked Lunch*. He was a dope fiend writer who always wore a suit and tie, with a hat, while everyone else in the Beat Generation was wearing wrinkled khakis and dirty T-shirts. He said the cops treat you better if you're well dressed."

"Didn't help you."

As dusk approached, Rosie and the Playdates took a break, and silence fell over Spanish Circle. All eyes went to the sky, taking in the "Magenta Moment," an atmospheric phenomenon caused by the setting sun reflecting off shit in the air. All in attendance saw it as one more reason to extol Maragate, and they gave it a round of applause. I went along with the gag.

After the crowd recovered from the Magenta Moment, Sandy pushed Doc's wheelchair, with the dog trailing behind on a leash, and I lugged all their gear to their pickup. Doc had fallen asleep. I had difficulty walking a straight line. I wished her goodnight, and we shared a hug. Before leaving Spanish Circle, I took a detour to a section of the farmers market called Free Speech Alley, a line of card tables manned by people supporting or opposing one issue or another: water conservation, single use plastic bags, fluoride, too many gin-tasting rooms on Spanish Circle, dogs on the bike path, and other pressing concerns that a citizen of any small town might have, though the activists were noticeably less than active. The tables were lined up facing the donut stand, the bicycle raffle, the pulled-pork joint, and the taco stand.

The mayor sat alone at a card table. A professionally made sign was attached to it: RE-ELECT MAYOR HIRKILL. Nothing more. No motto or political catchphrase. He leaned back on his folding chair. On one side of him were opponents to the proposed McDonald's to be placed a block from Spanish Circle, and on the other side were proponents for the proposed cell phone tower on Sixth Street West. (Few proposed projects ever came to pass.)

I put down my camp chair and ice chest and held my gin bottle against the darkening sky. "Almost empty," I said. "Help me finish it off?"

"I accept the challenge."

He looked away as I poured what was left into his glass, then he turned back and happily discovered he had a drink to attend to.

"You're the only one I see campaigning," I said.

"Staying alive."

"It's only May."

"So?"

"Election day isn't until November."

"Campaigning never ends."

"You're going to sit here every Thursday? All through the summer?"

"I'd be here anyway. Where else would anyone rather be?"

I could name a few places.

"I'm new in town. Tell me why I should vote for you?"

"I'm a natural born leader." I could not help laughing. He pouted. "You'll see. I run on my long record. This is a well-run municipality. A little slice of heaven."

Some of his words were lost in the shifting gravel of his voice.

"Where do you stand on McDonald's?" I asked him, though to care less I would have to care at all.

"I'm for it. More jobs. Good food at cheap prices."

"And the cell phone tower?"

"Fine, if you don't mind AT&T knowing where you are all the time."

"I was told you've been the mayor forever."

"I've devoted my life to public service."

"Your whole life?"

"The part that counts."

"What was it that made you make that decision?"

"That decision was made for me. By the people."

"If you hadn't, though, what would you be doing?"

"I can't answer hypothetical questions."

"Just curious."

"Taking notes, are you, because you're a screenwriter?"

"Force of habit."

"Well, sir, I am a man of many talents, arts and sciences, but screenwriting ain't one of 'em, so you're safe."

"It's a warm day and you're wearing a suit. Nobody here wears a suit. Is there a reason for that?"

"Indeed there is, and you stated it. I am the only one who is." He whispered to me, confidentially. "And people treat you better if you're wearing a suit."

"Like the cops?"

"Especially the cops. Free advice. Take it or leave it."

"I can't imagine you ever had trouble with the cops."

"I was young once."

"What happens next November, if you lose?"

He tapped the side of his nose with a finger manicured by his own teeth. "I'm playing the long game," he said, as Doc said he would.

"The police in this town . . ." I started to say, swaying in place, but I hesitated because I knew I would have blown twice the limit should the police want to cite me for talking under the influence. I wanted to frame the conversation so it might lead to what a police lieutenant was doing with the mayor in a public restroom at three in the morning.

"What about them?"

"One of them, Lieutenant Conventerra. You know him?"

"Very well."

"I thought you might. What's his story?"

"Story? He's an outstanding officer, end of story."

"I met him once."

"A good friend to have."

"It was like three o'clock in the morning. Foggy morning, last February."

"I'm not surprised. He's always on the clock. As am I. There is more to running an operation like this than meets the eye, let me tell you. The lieutenant is one of the reasons we have such a low crime rate in Maragate, proud to say."

"It was at that restroom over there. The bunker."

Now, he took a much closer look at me, as though I might be a person someone once warned him about.

"It's on police rounds," he said. "We have a small tweaker problem."

"I didn't go inside, so I don't know who else was there. Maybe a tweaker, maybe someone else."

"And?"

And that was as far as I was willing to go.

He looked away. They were packing up the bicycle raffle for the night. The donut guy still had a few people waiting in line for his mini-donuts with powdered sugar. I thought he was looking at us. (He *was* looking at us.)

No official closing time was set for the outdoor market. One vendor would start to disassemble his canopy and the others would follow. At the same time, the pamphlet distributors in Free Speech Alley folded up their tables and carried them off toward waiting SUVs. The mayor folded up his chair and his card table, fit his campaign sign under it, and tucked it all under his arms.

"Hope I can count on your vote," he said in leaving.

I watched him walk away to the east. It would be a cold day in hell before I registered to vote in Maragate. I gathered up my own stuff and turned to walk home, but the donut guy was in my face. Over his shoulder, I could see his teenage girl assistant closing up shop.

"Hello?" I said. More like, can I help you?

"He's a little man . . . a little man in a big hat . . . he lies through his yellow teeth and chews with his red eyes . . . a little man . . . the bad breath behind the Maragate smile . . . the murky moment . . . a little man . . . he can walk under the door."

"Beg your pardon?"

"The less you know the better, and you don't know nuttin'. You're not part of all this . . . all I got to do is look at you . . . but no, yeah, so lay low, do your thing, find a thing, then do it, he looks harmless, sure, everybody looks harmless . . . no, yeah, everybody *is* harmless . . . until they're not."

His assistant, a girl with the look of a well-shuffled foster child, signaled me by rolling her eyes and twisting her neck, indicating her boss was deranged. He did give that appearance, in the way Dennis Hopper did in so many roles. I say that because the donut guy was a dead ringer for Hopper, both beatific and tortured, a type fascinating to watch as a projected image but not someone you wanted in your face, or in charge of a teenage girl.

"I'm on my way home."

"Well, yeah, like who isn't? A place has been prepared for you . . ." (How did the donut guy know that?) "Which doesn't mean you're gonna get it, you poor hopeless son of a bitch. Nobody else is gonna tell you . . . you don't want to listen to me, fine, why should you listen to me, I'm nobody, a donut guy . . . all I do is make donuts, that's all I do."

He turned and beckoned to the girl, who started putting some of those donuts into a small white bag. He was another odd duck, and like I said, I'm kind of drawn to the type, though finding a safe distance can sometimes be a problem with volatile ducks.

"My name is DK. What's yours?"

"You don't want to know my name. Maybe I don't have one. You can call me one-two-three, or . . ." He made a grunting sound. "You can call me that. Or call me the donut dude . . . or—"

"I'll call you Dennis because you really look like Dennis Hopper. Anybody ever tell you that?"

He began a frantic search of the ground, as though looking for something to hit me with, sputtering sounds that corresponded to no known language. I was drunk, mind you, and I was enjoying the encounter. Since one can always trust the deranged to keep a secret, I said, "Have you ever seen a black angel hereabouts, ever? Or any kind of angel?"

It was as though I beat him to the punch, landed the first and only blow. He stumbled backward, found his footing and ran a zig-zag pattern to escape any bullets that may be coming his way, almost knocking over his assistant on the way. She came over and handed me the white bag, a baker's dozen of tiny donuts. "On the house," she said. "He's a psycho. Harmless as long as he's, like, only making donuts, which is all they ever let him do, so you're good."

www.dennishopper.com

Lost Creek, the site of my western, was both an Army outpost and the town that grew up around it, now abandoned by most of the residents and by the government and God Himself. The Indian wars in the Wyoming Territory were a thing of the past, but the fort was never decommissioned. Instead it was put under the command of a war-weary captain and his scout, both of them physically and emotionally damaged by their battles. The cattle, the only other reason for the existence of Lost Creek, were all but wiped out by the most severe winter in memory. Idle cowboys drank on credit at the last saloon. Only one whore was left, and she was another victim of ennui. Everyone was waiting, waiting for something to happen, for someone to arrive and turn it all around. (Not unlike what I was doing: waiting, drinking, blaming my plight on anything but myself.)

On my long afternoon walks, my ears stuffed with toilet paper, I tried to husband the energy and determination it would take to start another run at what I was now calling *After the Thaw*. No project ever dies as long as one element in it remains steadfast, and I was the last remaining element. After all the years of different directors, producers, and actors, in a development hell of my own making, I still did not know why the story had such a hold on me, or even what it meant. That is not to say I did not know what I was doing, although I can't eliminate that possibility.

I gave up trying to call Hope every day. It had been more than two months. Her voicemail box was always full so there was no point to keep calling. Whenever I was with her, out to dinner for example, she would check her messages and voicemails after every course and then again when the bill came. What made her stop doing that?

Carlos continued to make me a Mexican breakfast every morn-ing and a Mediterranean dinner every evening, neither of which was ever particularly good, but not all that bad either. Anyway, I lost interest in food. I skipped lunch, sometimes visiting a gin tast-ing room instead, sometimes walking on the bike trail, anything to escape the noise of leaf blowers, which by some confluence of forces was louder on my block than anywhere else I walked. People simply put up with them. They were afraid of their own gardeners, I think. I lost weight, which was a good thing.

Cinco de Mayo was a raucous holiday during which everyone conspicuously gave up gin in favor of tequila. They made a big thing of it, like Sadie Hawkins Day, or Backward Day, and went about ferociously licking salt, slamming shots, and sucking limes. Spanish Circle was filled with taco and tamale booths and wandering mari-achis. Young girls in colorful costumes performed ethnic dances. A huge white tent was reserved for VIPs, though I did not know who on Cinco de Mayo would be considered a VIP, unless it was anyone willing to buy a ticket to get into the tent. Mayor Hirkill guarded the entrance, wearing a wide sombrero in place of his usual fedora. Memorial Day was also a big celebration, though somber until nightfall, full of patriotic platitudes and renewed convictions that the honored dead did not die in vain. An array of vintage armament was on display. By nightfall, that same armament propped up semi-conscious drunks. (I got part of a tank track.) Again, a white tent was pitched for VIPs, and Mayor Hirkill stood at the entrance, this time wearing an Army garrison cap.

As I walked aimlessly along the bike trail, the characters of Lost Creek distracted me from having to relive that first night in town. Otherwise I would be wondering if I had, in fact, experienced a hallucination. If so, I would not mind having another, thank you, if only to break the spirit-suffocating tedium of triviality. I never had a hallucination before. (The jury was still out on a boyhood incident, but later for that.) No question, I was beyond exhaustion that first night, back in February, after two long flights and some alcohol. I was disoriented in the town and heartsick in my unwanted hovel. I was confused and annoyed by having a stranger named Carlos as a mandatory caretaker, no matter how obsequious he was. I was annoyed *because* he was so obsequious. And as Conventerra pointed out, I was in a mental and actual fog. But who imagines something like that? My mind might have been a tad warped that night, but I was not insane. I saw what I saw. I was halfway willing to admit that the beautiful black woman I saw killed might not have been attached to a set of wings. It may have been that I thought her so beautiful I imagined her an angel, which is everybody's symbol for beauty. (If you're Keats, it's a Grecian urn.) I've never believed in demons and angels and was spared that kind of child abuse in my upbringing. That part of the event might have been, must have been, a hallucination. Angels do not exist. A naked woman, however, *was* shot, I could not deny that, and why would I make it up, even on a subconscious level? Are we not the authors of our own nightmares, the painters of our own hallucinations? Here is what I knew to be reality: the police shot a beautiful black somebody, an unarmed intruder, let's say (and naked?), and they were effectively covering it up. This in itself was not historically unique. (Including the naked part.) Police have been doing that sort of thing since the concept of policing was conceived. They get caught at it these days only because everyone over the age of eight has a camera at hand all the time. I myself had one that night but I didn't have the presence of mind to use it. I would need to find my glasses, put them on, punch in the password, and launch the camera application. By that time, the angel would have been whisked away anyway, if she was an angel, and how could she be what doesn't exist? (Rosie, lead singer of Rosie and the Playdates, after the fact, taught me how to access the camera with a single swipe, so next time, look out.)

Do I make it sound as though time dragged by slowly? That was not the case. The days sped by, which is fine if you anticipate a date when everything will change. I didn't, which meant I was falling headlong into eternity at a quickened pace.

What is time, fast or slow, without meaningful work to fill it? Not necessarily gainful employment, but good engaging work. Work that you love. A pursuit. A cause. A campaign. Or nothing more than a mundane project, something you could admire at the end of the day. I thought about taking up something healthful, like gardening. Or I could paint the house, cover up that sickly green, the color of an unwanted bodily discharge. I could restore the earth on my little patch of a yard and grow onions, open a stand at the market, and sell them. (I could be the Onion Guy.) Or I could invent something. But isn't that what I'd been doing my whole life, inventing? Though it was likely that my career would soon be over, it was *always* likely that it would soon be over, from the very beginning. That is the nature of the movie business. Career aside, I was skilled in a difficult and highly competitive art, and if I never made another dime at it or never saw my name on screen again, why should I no longer write screenplays? Who was going to stop me?

I got off the bike path at Ninth North and J, and walked home by way of Spanish Circle. I was energized to get back to work again. I would give that old western another read through and see if the magic was still there. I would accept that it might never be a movie but stay with it anyway. I could *aver* that it would never be a movie, refuse to let it become a movie, but stay with it anyway. Forever. I could make it a Zen practice, like raking sand. Crossing the Circle, I covered my face with a hankie to get past the leaf blowers. Once on Cherona Avenue, I was able to breathe again, but briefly.

By force of habit, I went by the scene of the crime. My spirits were uncharacteristically high. I decided to try again to talk to the one person who could testify that I had not gone nuts. (It's always been important to me that people don't question my sanity, even those sitting in theater seats.)

A Latino yardman was blasting the tiny bit of lawn in front of the house with a wind strong enough to roll it into sod. The leaves and twigs that had been on the lawn were landing on the drive-way of a neighbor's tiny patch of dry grass and on the overhang of the little square of stoop. I stood for a moment on the opposite side of the street, where the houses ended and the Cherona River curved under the Munkar Bridge, the hankie once again over my face. I watched the landscaper step away from the lawn to attack the driveway, blowing dust and a Butterfinger wrapper out to the street, and then repeating the process because some of what he blew landed back on the lawn. He blew the dust off the sidewalk, all over a Mini Cooper, then blew the dust off his pickup, hopped into it and drove away belching exhaust that in comparison hardly mattered.

I crossed the street, gagging on air that floated raw gasoline fumes. The woman's house was as ugly as mine and painted a similar color. I will call it yellow ochre instead of puke green. I knocked on the door and in a minute heard her talking as she approached the other side, more shouting than talking. She appeared in the open doorway, an iPhone at her ear. She held up a finger to put me on hold and punched some numbers on her keypad. She listened for a moment and angrily ended the call. "Listen carefully because *my* menu has changed, assholes. Please wait for India to answer and try to understand what the fuck they're saying." Apparently, she was talking not on but to the phone. Then she looked to me and said, "Dude, you're back here again? Why?"

The Rottweiler sidled up to her. He was the scariest dog I'd ever seen. I would have felt better had he growled at me instead of staring me down.

"Nice dog. Hi, boy, hi, buddy. What's your name, buddy?"

"I wouldn't pet him?" she said. "His name is Rufus."

I tilted my head to one side and saw that Rufus still had his testicles. Whatever aggression he might have been bred with he still possessed, as much as balls play a part in all that. My own never came under scrutiny.

"I'd like to properly introduce myself. I live on Second Street, behind and down the block from you. I'm DK. I go by my initials because my last name is bad enough. And you are?"

She raised a finger, putting me on hold again as her head went back and her mouth opened for a sneeze. Her eyes were red and watery. Finally came the blast, and then another, and still another, because like celebrity deaths sneezes always come in three. She directed them into her sleeve. I would have offered my hankie but it was already well used.

"Allergies? Sorry."

"I have them too. Never did before I came here."

"Everybody here has allergies."

"Because the air is so full of shit," I said, and she laughed. "Literally. Insect shit, rat shit, dog shit." I looked at Rufus as if to say, no offense.

"Yeah, I get it? My name is Valene."

"Pleased to meet you at last, Valene. We need to talk."

"Aw, c'mon. Gimme a break? It's my house, but I don't live here? I'm hardly ever here?"

"I know. I came here the morning after the incident and talked to the people who were staying here."

"No one was staying here that night."

"So you do remember the night I'm talking about?"

"Are you a narc?"

"Far from it. I mean you no harm." She looked cornered, which was not my intention. "I spoke to a young woman. She was here with three men. She said they were tourists."

"Fucking tweakers is what they were."

"I doubt it. She was pretty and had all her teeth."

"Really?"

"You didn't know about them?"

"I'm not at home when I can find short-term tenants? Which is a lot of the time? But I never booked three dudes and a chick?"

She went back to her phone and scrolled somewhere. Valene, you've noticed I'm sure, is an uptalker, who turns simple statements into vague interrogatives, the type of woman I could tolerate for no more than a brief superficial conversation, usually with a counter between us. She reminded me of Lauren Bacall, though Bacall had a confidence I suspected was missing in Valene. Otherwise she wouldn't be an uptalker.

"On the night in question—"

"What are you, a lawyer?"

"No, I'm a screenwriter."

"Oh, yeah, but what you really want to do is direct?"

That was an old gag line. All screenwriters were thought to be thwarted directors. "No, I never wanted to be a director. I never wanted to be a screenwriter, either. It just worked out that way."

"What's a screenwriter doing this far from La-La-Land?"

"You can be anywhere now. The Internet and all that. I liked it better when you had to be somewhere, not anywhere." I wanted nothing more than to be back in La-La-Land, but I was not going to get into all of that with her. (Then, but I would.) "I need to know what you saw that night, when I took cover behind the police car that was over there." I nodded toward the opposite side of the street. "I dove under the car, the SUV, when the shooting started." She stared at me with suspicious green eyes. "They brought me in for questioning, but they didn't want to know what I saw. They wanted to know everything about me. No one bothered to talk to you, though, right?"

"The cops here are out of control. Most people stay away from them?"

"I didn't have a choice."

"This has something to do with me how?"

"How? It happened here, at your house."

"Yeah, technically it's my house? But I told you, I don't live here? I do short-term vacation rentals, off the books, and certain people may know about that? They know when the renters leave and they know I won't show up for a day or two?"

"What people? I don't understand."

"Marginal people? Floaters and gypsies? Refugees waiting for the next train to the coast, only they can't find the station with Yelp."

"There's a train station here?" I asked hopefully.

"In your dreams. The wrong ones, they'll take everything and then shit on the floor."

"This one didn't take anything. She didn't even have clothes. She was in your house, I don't know why, but I know she wasn't looting it and she didn't deserve to be killed." Valene looked startled. I realized that although she had to be aware of the shooting that night, it was possible she did not know it was fatal. The only hook I had would have to be baited with an angel. I pointed toward the other side of the street. "You were aware, weren't you, that a murder was committed here that night and did you see the victim? Have you ever seen anything like that?"

Another leaf blower cranked up. She said something I could not hear, then raised her voice and said, "Tell me you're harmless?"

"I'm harmless." As I mentioned, other women thought I looked dangerous.

"You want a drink?"

Rufus kept a fearsome eye on me as his mistress led me to the tiny backyard, into which was squeezed a Jacuzzi, a fire pit, and a small table with four patio chairs. The little plot of lawn was freshly mown and tidy. Her phone became the third element in our conversation, like a toddler that can't be left alone and won't shut up. It never left her hand. We were halfway down our gin and tonics, and I noticed that leaves were blowing in from the neighboring yard, falling on the grass around us. I observed them for a moment, as Shelley and Mary were wont to do, and said, "Given half a chance, leaves can appear to be, well, natural."

"You have a thing about it?"

"I'm discovering I do. They don't allow them in the Hollywood Hills."

"Leaves?"

"Leaf blowers. We're fine with leaves. People here look to be at war with nature."

"Everything has to be nice for the tourists, because nature doesn't care about tourists?"

"Why do tourists even come here? There's nothing to do."

"Don't know, don't care, as long as they've got money?"

"Gin and jerky, that's all there is. Why come for that?"

"I grew up in a town where the local product was speed and porno. I landed here and thought I was in heaven?"

"When was that?"

"Seems like forever ago."

"I myself did not have that feeling."

"You're new. Anyway, I've got two couples coming in tonight for a long weekend, so I'll have Juan cranking up the blower twice a day? Sorry about that. Can't be helped. We all have to live with it?"

She checked her email and lit another cigarette, at the same time, without putting down her phone.

"So I'm told, but it's not why I'm here"

The stuff I didn't want to get into with her? (I'm sounding like her. Shoot me now.) I got into it. I told her more than I wanted to about how I came to live in the neighborhood. Once I get started I can't stop. I dislike that about myself. I told her about Carlos and the letter my wife left and how I got lost in the fog. More than she needed to know and more than I wanted to say. I can go days without talking to anyone, and then the first person I meet, I spill all the beans. I held back on any description of the victim.

About Hope, she commented, "Sounds like a lulu," at which I took offense. She was still my wife and I loved her, wherever she was.

"She's not a lulu. She's a sweet, caring woman. All of this is out of character for her. There has to be a good explanation."

"Did you ever think she might have a boyfriend? Taking him for a long test drive?"

True, that thought haunted me, but Hope's letter gave not the slightest hint of any affair, and I could not imagine after all these years she would decide to cook up such an elaborate plan in order to have one last fling. (All she had to do was ask. [I would have talked her out of it.])

"We have a strong marriage. That would never happen."

"Not many people can say that and have it be true? You might be the first, I said it once? It wasn't true."

Her delivery was annoying the hell out of me, but the gin had hit that spot behind my brow that makes all annoyances go away. I took another sip and said, "I never used to drink this early. Or this much. Or gin at all."

"In Maragate you don't need an excuse. It's your civic duty?"

"Yeah," I mumbled around the pool of gin in my mouth. "None of this matters to me much because I don't plan to be here long enough to give a damn."

"That's what they all say."

"But the thing that happened here, something's got to be done about that. The police killed someone, right in front of your house, and now they're covering it up."

"You keep saying that, and it's freaking me out?"

"Why didn't they question you?"

"Why would anyone question me? Unless somebody ratted me out about the vacation rentals?"

"You were here. You're a witness, like me. Haven't you told anybody about it?"

"Nothing to tell."

"A shooting in front of your house? You were here. You saw it too. It's one thing for the cops to deny it, it's another thing for you. What are you afraid of?"

She looked away, the equivalent of covering her ears and singing, "La, la, la, la. . . ." She took another drink. Not a sip, but a slug. I hoped that like most drinkers all she needed to lubricate the release of a secret was more gin. (Works for me.) A leaf blower on the property behind us sent a cloud of dust over the fence. She sneezed three times and gagged on the dust. She left her glass and grabbed my hand. (The phone was still in her other hand, the cigarette dangling from her lips.) She led me back into the house. Her hand was as dry and hard as salted cod. She shut the back door with her own back and leaned against it, as though we had had a narrow escape. We sat on mid-century modern bar stools at her tiled kitchen counter. The incessant revving of the leaf blower did not abate, but inside we were at least able to hear each other.

"Like your wife abandoned you? My man abandoned me. But he didn't leave everything paid for? He didn't leave me a Carlos? I'm on my own here? I have to scramble like a lizard just to stay in play. Oh, I have a boyfriend, but he's dumb as a felt boot and about as handsome. All he's good for is a place to stay when I have tenants, and some missionary sex once in a blue moon."

"Life is hard, I get it."

"No, you don't, you and your Hollywood Hills. You don't get anything. I'm under the radar?"

"Please, can you make an effort not to lift your voice at the end of a sentence? It makes you sound like an airhead."

"Okay, so we've moved on to personalities? So, fuck you?"

"Though I can see you're an intelligent woman."

It would have been easy to dislike her, but it would have been just as easy for her to dislike me. (I know I do sometimes.) I drained what was left in my glass and cared less about everything. When that happens, all I want is to go to sleep. I tried to remember what it was I had planned for that afternoon, instead of talking to this unpleasant woman. Oh, yes, work on my western. Recapture the nobility of work, the healing power of creating something out of nothing. Her anger evaporated as quickly as it arose, thanks to a video on her phone of a real cat swatting at a stuffed cat. She found it hysterical.

The doorbell rang.

"That'll be my guests? Let the orgy begin! Ta-ta. Hope your wife eats shit and dies?"

She took unsteady steps to her front door.

"It's not the shooting, is it? It's the victim. If it had been a tweaker, we'd probably know about it. They'd have no reason to hide it."

She had already opened the door to an excited foursome of millennials. I don't know if she heard me. Rufus stood two feet to my left and watched me until I excused myself to Valene and the arriving guests and went out the door.

www.rottweilerfarm.com

In June, I tried to work on my script in the public library, a one-story building that used to be an elementary school, run by elderly volunteers. Someone always seemed to be walking behind me, sneezing three times and looking over my shoulder at what I was writing on yellow legal pads with my favorite wooden pencils, Palomino

Blackwing Pearls, which I was able to find in the local stationery store, Plume 'n Parchment, where I had an account and where the woman who ran it, Millie Scanlon, knew I was a screenwriter and would ask me how it was going. (Uphill.)

Since the library offered little privacy, I left and tried a table in one of the gin tasting rooms, rotating from one room to another because they needed space for tourists. The leaf blowers usually quit around 6 p.m. so I could have worked then, but that's the hour during which I switched from gin to either beer or wine, depending upon what Carlos made for dinner. Waiting for my head to clear took until 10 p.m. I was not used to night work. I believe a writer ought to go to work after breakfast like everyone else. Still, I tried. I would write from 10 p.m. until 2 a.m. That presented a problem because I needed ten hours in bed to get seven hours of sleep. I have sleep apnea, restless leg syndrome, cramps, night sweats, occasional insomnia, and frequent nightmares, which I must say were diminishing in intensity, paling next to the real deal. To be honest, I've always dreaded going to bed, and have never been too keen about waking up either.

The blowers started up at seven every morning, sometimes earlier. I tried headphones but music was a distraction. If I'd had a car, I could have driven to a quiet place, assuming there was one somewhere. My only ride was an iXi bicycle, which was not "very fine" as Carlos described it but a silly bike with tiny wheels designed to be folded in half and put into the trunk of a car, which I didn't have. I'm a large man, and I looked foolish sitting high above those shaking miniature wheels.

One morning, as I brushed my teeth and got ready for the day, I looked for ways to overcome all the forces aligned against keeping me from the salvation of honest work. (Unless I was only making excuses, as most writers do.) I could not work in the morning, as was my routine, and I could not work at home, my preferred spot. I did not have the money to rent an office, if one were available and sound-proofed. The library lacked privacy, and the gin rooms had gin, too great a temptation. The only answer was to work at night, but with my sleep disorders and the early start for leaf blowers that was more than difficult. No matter how many forces line up against creative work, there is always room for one more.

The bathroom light was on because the house was dark by design. I noticed a large black fly lazily buzzing around the light. The fly landed on the plexiglass cover and then fell in a death swoon to the sink top. I flicked it with my forefinger, and it hit the wall. Then I saw another one staggering on the edge of the bathtub, if a fly can stagger. I flicked that one, too, and knocked it to the other side of the tub. Dead. Then another was back on the light, and above it there were five or six fat black flies clinging to the ceiling. I grabbed a towel and began flailing it at them. They had no will to escape. They fell to the floor like, well, dead flies. I picked them up with wadded toilet paper and flushed them away.

Dressed, I started down the narrow stairway, the stairs creaking under my weight. I called Carlos. He was in the kitchen, perched on a three-step folding ladder with an extension tube on the vacuum cleaner, sucking up more of the fat slow flies.

"What the hell, Carlos? I killed ten of them in my bathroom."

"*Si*, señor, it is so boring. They feed off the dead rats, are poisoned themselves, and so die in turn. One would like them to die outside, but . . ." He shrugged his shoulders. "We will live through this, señor. The vacuum is very effective. They will be out of our hair in a moment. There! Do you see any others, señor?"

I did. I fingered them, and Carlos vacuumed them up.

"How often does this happen?"

"Infrequently. Hardly at all, and the inconvenience lasts only for a day or two, never longer than a week." Suffer.

We were all but shouting, to be heard over the roar outside. I could not decide whether to admire Carlos's forbearance or to condemn it. Why do we torture ourselves when we don't have to? (We don't have to, do we?) He folded up the ladder and stowed it in the garage, along with the vacuum. When he came back into the kitchen, he poured me a cup of *café con leche*.

"Now, for *desayuno!*" he said cheerfully. "What would the señor prefer?"

"Carlos, these leaf blowers? Don't they annoy you?"

"*Claro que si.* I despise them with a passion, but one does adjust. I have become used to them, and it is their work, after all."

"But why do they have to rev them up like that?"

"Well, because those machines have triggers, señor."

"Why can't they use rakes?"

He laughed out loud. "Rakes? You are suggesting rakes?"

"And brooms, like everybody used to."

"Brooms! You are so amusing, señor. Well, of course they could, but it would slow them down."

"What's the rush?"

"Some cultures do not see making noise as an imposition on others."

I heard the echo of Kuggelsong's words. He said essentially the same thing. It seemed to me an unlikely coincidence, unless it was a sentiment widely shared in Maragate.

"That's a little racist, Carlos."

"I don't think so. I'm talking about *my* culture."

"Who does the yard work around here, you?"

"Fortunately, no. Were it I, everything would be dead."

"Everything *is* dead."

"You've not met Jaime?"

"Jaime who?"

"Like me, Jaime came with the house. He has been here . . . forever."

"We have a yardman named Jaime?"

"Now I am embarrassed. You should have met him and interviewed him by now. The fault is that you are not in the house when he makes his weekly rounds. And, señor, they prefer to be called landscapers, not yardmen. Jaime is third or fourth generation."

"A real landscaper would not hit a small garden with hurricane force wind. The whole idea of a garden is, isn't it, a haven, with birds and butterflies and flowers. I haven't seen a bird or butterfly since I arrived. Your marauding landscapers have blown them all away."

"The señora had grand plans to redo the landscaping, from the ground up, if you will, but she left before that could happen. I am sure that when she returns she will take command of the grounds and—"

"The *grounds!* Carlos, I paced it off. Our backyard is thirteen by thirteen steps, and the front yard is even smaller, and most of that is taken up by the driveway to a garage too small to house an American car. The *grounds?*"

"Señor, each of us has our own little slice of paradise here, and how big a slice does anyone need? I am confident that the señora will turn the yard into the delightful haven you envision. You could yourself, I'm sure, if you don't care to wait."

"Yeah, right." Why bother? What can you do with those "grounds"? And, besides, as soon as Hope returned, we were getting out of Maragate, if I had to tie her up with duct tape. If she returned at all. And she might not. I had no other plan than that she *would* return. She said she would, and I believed her. I waited a long time to meet her—there were other girls but she was worth the wait— and if I had to wait again, well, what else could I do? Have you ever been in love? Then you know.

"Bravo, señor!" cried Carlos. "Why wait? It will be a wonderful undertaking for you, a distraction from your loneliness and a pleasant surprise for the señora! I am excited by the prospect!"

An unpracticed ear would think it genuine enthusiasm.

I was a prisoner, but even prisoners come to appreciate having all things taken care of. It was much like being a beautiful woman, better because there was nothing sexual I had to do. If Maragate were not such a strange place, rattled by nerve-wracking noise and police shootings of unnamable victims that were covered up and a mayor who looked like William Burroughs, and if my house were not such a nightmare, cold and full of rats and fat black flies and allergies, with a leaky roof, it could be an okay place to pass the time, at least while waiting for Hope.

"I'll do it. By God, I'll turn that backyard into something nice. Jaime will earn his pay. What does he do, by the way, when he does come?"

"Blow and go, señor, blow and go. Once a week, like all the others."

"How much do I pay him?"

"Three hundred dollars a month."

"That's a little steep, for blowing up clouds of dust in a tiny barren yard."

Carlos shrugged. "It is the going rate."

"No more blowing and going. I'm taking charge."

I could not remember ever having uttered such a statement. "I'm taking charge." Me? Having lived what was by anybody's standards a successful life, I could not remember ever taking charge of anybody or anything, including myself, to be honest about it. I saw my life, if I looked at all, as one without a plan, buffeted by random events. The unexamined life is not a waste but a wonder, worth living rather than stewing over. Nobody is in charge anyway, neither God nor the universe, and the men who try to take charge end up like everyone else, usually sooner and more violently. Like a reed, I bent with the wind, but I did not break. I neither led nor followed, suppressed or supported. I had no goals. I had no bucket list, a concept I found stupid. Nothing I ever did was thought out, from my choice of college, to my major, to my ultimate career, to the places I lived, to the woman I married, and things turned out well. If you don't count the move to a house I never saw in a town I never heard about. Even that, with time, might turn out well, I thought. Until Hope returned, I had to try to make a life for myself.

My connection to my characters changed with each pass. Now I was identifying with the Tin Horn Gambler, put off the train at the spur with no resources to go any farther, marooned in a town that was itself marooned, a speck on a great expanse of what would later become known as Big Sky Country. The Tin Horn Gambler could find no takers to test his skill set, neither for profit nor pleasure, so he sat around playing solitaire, waiting for someone to buy a round. (James Woods, when he was young. The kind of actor who gets your attention but you wouldn't want him kissing your sister. Or even in the same room with her.)

Laff, the owner of the general store, is the only person who hasn't yet given up on the town. He is the last of the civic boosters. (I would cast Strother Martin, RIP.) His latest idea is to rename the town, again. Lost Creek is a sad name without promise or meaning. (Kind of what Doc Fleck implied. Kind of like Maragate. What gate?) Laff wants to change it to "Invincible." Winky, the scout, counters with "Incapable." (David Strathairn was eager to play this part, and for good reason. It could steal the show, every supporting actor's dream.) The Captain, the only one who senses that the new day dawning will bring group insanity to the town, is on the cusp of spiritual exhaustion. (The hardest part to cast. It needs Gary Cooper, RIP. It's possible that Matthew Modine is the new Gary Cooper.) Brantley's saloon is broke. Idle cowboys bang on his door, threatening to burn the place down if he doesn't open up. (Needs Eli Wallach, RIP.) Cowboys sit around the potbelly stove, spitting on it. *Hisss, hisss, hisss* . . . as the spit hits the hot iron. Elizabeth, the last remaining whore, in fingerless gloves, plays the piano, softly singing with a British accent, "Beautiful dreamer, wake unto me . . ." (At one time I had Samantha Morton.)

I knew I should write only the master shots, but I saw all their faces, heard all their voices, and knew the way they walked. I couldn't resist framing my own close-ups, describing the lighting, and laying in a soundtrack. (Tom Waits.) Directors hate that.

I rubbed my eyes, saved the changes, and went to bed.

(I never wrote a scene in which a character goes to bed, and I've never seen one I believed. In movies, a man will come into the bedroom, tell his wife a lie about where he's been, shed his clothes to his boxer shorts and go to bed. I've never done that. I shower and shave, take my evening meds, brush and floss my teeth [I start on the uppers, but sometimes when I am doing the lowers I forget if I did the uppers so I start over again], use the thing with the rubber tip to push at my gums [I have great teeth], put in my mouth guard, put moisturizer on my face, knees, and elbows, and get into my pajamas. Movies don't have time for that kind of tedious reality, I know, but it bothers me every time I see someone in the movies go to bed.)

The roar of a leaf blower woke me up five hours later. I had no sense of ever having slept. The sound was obnoxious. I could feel the bed vibrate with the revving. Unlike other street noises, the low frequency of leaf blowers permeates walls and windows and human skin. I opened the curtains and saw the racket was coming from my own backyard, from somewhere in the center of great clouds of dust.

Halfway down the stairs I yelled, "Shoot me now, Carlos."

"It is my fault, señor. I texted Jaime to come early today so that you would have a chance to instruct him in your demands."

I pulled up my pajama top to cover my nose and stepped out to the back stoop. Jaime was unapproachable, hardly visible in the cloud of his own creation.

Finally, I caught his eye. I drew my hand across my throat, the universal sign for death and please stop. He hit the kill switch and slipped the heavy backpack to the ground. He approached, his eyes downward. He was unshaven and walked slightly hunched over.

"Jaime?"

The gardener nodded.

"I'm DK." I extended my hand. Jaime looked at it for a moment, wiped his own hand on his pant leg, and shook hands.

"So Carlos told you I want to do some real landscaping out here?"

He nodded.

"I want to make this little yard a haven. Are you with me?"

He nodded again. (Not sure he knew what a haven was. Not sure I do.) "Because I can't do this alone. I need your expertise." (Not sure he knew that word either.) I was playing the boss, taking charge, pep-talking my employee. He nodded again. "Great! Let's come up with a plan." I had no suggestions since I didn't know a thing about landscaping. I felt foolish standing in my pajamas talking to a man who had been up for hours. I said, "Until then, no blowing."

"No blow?" He looked at me through narrow eyes, under the brim of his straw hat. He could not grasp the concept.

"We're going to dig this whole thing up, draw up a plan, get the stuff and make it beautiful out here. No blowing. There's nothing to blow anyway."

"It's my job," he said, a statement that usually ends all argument about whether a man should be doing what he is doing, including a lawyer trying to get an ax murderer off scot-free. A man does his job, whatever it is. Everything else is secondary, like his health and the happiness of his wife and children.

"I get that, but look at this place. It's all weeds and dead plants. It needs to be dug up and new soil brought in. It looks like it's been hit with a hurricane. Which it has. The hurricane is inside of *that*." I pointed at his leaf blower. Jaime looked at it like a man who'd been told his pit bull was vicious.

"There's leaves and twigs."

"So where are you blowing them?"

"Away."

"They come back."

"I blow them again."

"From now on let the twigs and leaves lie where they fall. If you must, use a rake or a broom."

Jaime was about to say something, but apparently words failed him, and he had nothing left to do with his head, having run out of nods.

"Go ahead, say what you want to say."

"It is not for a man, the rake or the broom."

The last thing I wanted to do was emasculate a Mexican gardener, but I had vowed to take charge. Why I had never taken charge before became a little clearer now. It involved making people unhappy.

"What did your father do for a living?" I asked, though I already knew from Carlos.

"He was a landscaper. And his father before him."

"Ah. And your father and grandfather, were they macho?"

I embarrassed myself by where I was taking this.

"*Muy* macho."

"Did they use a blower, like you?"

"My father did. But not my grandfather. That was in the old days, before."

"But I bet he did a good job. I bet he could keep a yard neat without a blower. With a rake and a broom. And at the end of the day, he was as macho as you."

Was the comparison an affront? I'm sure.

"Look at this ground," I said. I picked up a handful of fine gray particles and tossed it into the air. "All the top soil's been blown away."

I didn't know top soil from paprika, but Jaime did not disagree.

"The señora wanted me to keep the yard clean."

"Tell me what she said. Word for word, if you can remember."

He acted like I was trying to catch him in a lie, but all I wanted was to hear her words. I missed her so much. Say the word señora and there's a log jam in my heart.

"I did not talk to her," he said.

"What?"

"Carlos told me."

"You never talked to her?"

Jaime shook his head.

"You never even met her?"

Jaime shook his head.

"You never saw her, out here or out front?"

He shook his head again.

"So it was Carlos who told you to blow and go?" Now he went back to nodding. "From now on, you will take your orders from me. Not from Carlos. If you have to move anything around, use a rake."

Jaime looked down at the ground.

"Okay. When you come back next week, we'll create a garden, together, but no more blower, not ever, not on my property. Never."

www.takingcharge.csh.umn.edu/

I rode my ridiculous bike to the local nursery, another place where, like other establishments in town that I had never been inside, I had an account. I asked Gary the manager how that happened, thinking that he must have talked to Hope, but he could not remember who handled the opening of the account. He was glad to see it used. I told him I wanted to replant a barren backyard the size of a tiger cage with stuff that would attract birds and butterflies and put one's soul at ease. (Bear in mind I had never before broken ground for anything, except as a boy taking a header, a repeated consequence of daydreaming while walking.) Gary needed more information. Would I like color? Well, yes, I took for granted there would be colors. Water efficiency was a consideration, to be sure. No, I had no overall design, as such. I would be winging it with a third-generation landscaper. Yes, something to eat should be included. Things for the stomach, the eye, and the soul. Trees? Maybe a plum tree to replace the dead one out front.

Next day, a truck delivered what didn't look like that much in the nursery but in my yard looked like wretched excess. No matter. Carlos and I celebrated this first step with a cold *horchata*. Included in the shipment were bags and bags of mulch and organic gardening soil, fertilizer and nutrients, and some basic tools. Even before Jaime arrived, I got down there in the dirt on my hands and knees and broke a sweat turning over the desiccated earth and mixing it with rich mulch and soil. I watered it and almost expected something to pop up and bloom in gratitude.

In the morning, I ached in all of my hinges, but I had a sense of well-being. Jaime showed up and I took charge. While he pulled out the dead plum tree in front and replaced it with a live one, I laid down two short rows of onions and radishes.

Later, still on my knees, patting lovingly the soil around my newly planted seeds and sets, I said over my shoulder, "Jaime, get the marigolds, please, and let's plant them so they surround the vegetables." (I was making an artistic statement in a medium I knew nothing about, though I may have known a tad more than Jaime.)

When no marigolds appeared, I turned and saw my landscaper staring down at three different flats with no clue which were the marigolds. "Or the geraniums," I said, "if you think they will look better." He looked over his shoulder at me, then back at the flats. It was not a language problem. I could tell he did not know one flower from another. What did catch his attention was something he did know: five errant leaves where they should not have been, which for him was anywhere he was standing. He watched them aggressively.

Apart from that loss of confidence in my gardener, it was a long and satisfying morning, after which I could look at something wonderful that I made, unlike a morning spent writing a script when I never knew what I had. I took in my new garden, breathing deeply and smelling the new soil and feeling a kind of gratitude—Jaime had already motored, not given to such reflections—and I wondered if everyone who works in the soil feels what I was feeling then. A sense of basic purpose, of belonging in a way that could not be disputed. I was impatient to see my garden grow. I watered it daily, not too much, and spread around some fertilizer. I gave thought to the outlandish idea that even if Hope should return tomorrow, we would have to wait until the garden was in full bloom before bugging out of Maragate. We would both want to see how it turned out, and sit there for a while, holding hands across a patio table, in front of a sweating pitcher of iced tea.

That scenario hardly had time to be properly lit before disaster struck.

I get it that tillers of the land survive at the whim of nature: drought or flood, pestilence or plague, heat or cold, but how often do they wake up to the horrible sound of a leaf blower obliterating their dream of verdancy? I witnessed this crime from my upstairs window, Jaime barely discernible in a whirlwind of marigold, geranium, and zinnia petals, their colors swirling in the spray of dark, newly constituted soil.

Still in my pajamas, I rushed downstairs and out to the yard. I swear that along with my outburst I heard the screams of my massacred flowers and veggies.

I covered my nose and mouth with my PJ top and pulled the dust bazooka from his hand, but it was attached to his backpack and the backpack to his back. It did not stop running until he hit the kill switch.

"You're fired! Take this piece of junk and get off my property. Don't ever come back!"

"*Que?*"

www.burpee.com/flowers/marigolds/

Fiddler Jones, the heavy in my western, is a bully of the old west, and not all that unlike a bully of the new west. His prejudices extend to anyone who isn't like him, and that would include people of intelligence or those with manners and morals. He articulates twisted logic to his own advantage. He has no ethics of his own and doesn't tolerate those who do. He chooses to lie no matter how obvious the truth may be. He has affection for no one but himself and has never experienced empathy or even understood why such an emotion exists. (I am not above some gag casting, and for Fiddler I liked Michael Richards in his first dramatic role. The character is rangy, hawkish, and with outrageous hair, which is pivotal to the plot. Richards was a hard sell from the beginning, impossible after he went on his rant about black people. A dozen other good actors could play the role, but to raise eight million dollars even independent filmmakers must answer the investor's first question: Who's in it? I insisted, for reasons that would be obvious, that The Kid be played by a total unknown, which is always a risk. I wanted the deaf mute to be a true African at least six and a half feet tall, someone whose mere presence quiets the room. At one time, I thought I could use Shaq O'Neal, but that would be the worst kind of gag casting and the role is far too demanding. Anyway, to answer the question, I told the investors I had Bruce Willis, James Woods, David Strathairn, and Samantha Morton. Love the script, but we need a bigger name.)

I was at the dining room table in a moment of relative quiet, thinking about Fiddler Jones, when I remembered that although Carlos and I had had a disagreeable conversation about Jaime (he didn't want him fired, I said he was, period), I never called him out on the other matter.

"Carlos?"

"*Si*, señor? What is it now?"

The more time we spent together, the more he lost the obsequiousness that so annoyed me in the beginning. Now he felt free to be impatient with me, and at times sarcastic.

"Well, what it is now is, why didn't you ever tell me that Jaime took his orders from you?"

"Who else would he take his orders from, if not me?"

"Well, Hope, for instance."

"When the señora was here, she was busy with getting the house ready for you, though she never told me she was leaving. She had no time for the grounds, and so I continued to give orders to Jaime as I had been. He will be hard to replace, believe you me."

"I don't want to replace him. It's a wasteland back there. I don't give a damn how many leaves pile up."

"Everyone has a landscaper. Our house will be the only one without one."

Our house?

"So Hope was much too busy readying the house to deal with Jaime, because it was such an enormous undertaking to bring *la maison* to its full glory. It fell on you to give Jaime his orders. Blow and go?"

"In three words you are correct, señor. As always."

"What possible good does it do to blow shit up into the air?"

"The question is rhetorical?"

"Let's say it's not."

"*Bueno*. Then to blow caca into the air provides employment for those who can do little besides blow caca into the air."

"I see. In any case, Hope would have introduced herself to Jaime. She is outgoing, and she speaks a little Spanish and likes to practice it."

"*Si*, she practiced with me."

"What's more, Hope was sensitive to the feelings of anyone she paid to provide a service. She would not snub a gardener."

"And yet, she did, as did you until you had unreasonable complaints."

"What state are we in?" I asked, out of the blue.

(I know, it sounds stupid that I would not know even that much about the town. Maybe Hope told me and I forgot. I had assumed it was somewhere in northern California.)

"Ah, señor, can you tell me today's date?" (I could, within a few days.) "Or perhaps, who is the president?" (I could, but I didn't want to think about that.)

"I am not senile! Where the fuck am I, you . . . you . . ." (Words are my tools, and yet I had none with which to hammer him.)

"Of course you are not. You are deliberately unaware. Wear it with pride. And señor, there are laws that address screaming profanities to employees like that."

I suspected when I stormed away from him that Carlos was making faces and mimicking me behind my back. At times, I worried about the food he was making for me. Suffer.

www.labor.ca.gov/laboriawreg.htm

I stood on the back stoop and looked at my wretched yard, "the grounds," a mini-swath of destruction. I was mourning the loss of my garden, which I believed would have turned out beautiful and nourishing in ways I'd never taken the time to appreciate.

Something along the fences would have fortified the boundary between me and the five noisy neighbors whose properties bordered mine on two forward sides, two aft sides, and a single in the rear. I had introduced myself to a few of them, on advice from Sandy Fleck, who subscribed to the belief that all things can be worked out neighbor to neighbor. (Where do people *get* that idea?) I asked if they might please ask their gardeners to use rakes. I explained that I was a screenwriter and could not work when the trigger-happy blowers started their symphony of the insane. Not in those exact words, but I suppose I could have been more diplomatic. I did say that I fired my own landscaper and did not miss him, so I myself was no longer part of the problem.

The first neighbor I approached was an old lady, frail and frightened. She opened the door a crack. As pleasantly as I could, I explained my predicament vis-à-vis the torture of leaf blowers.

"Why, that's terrible," she said. "Mind you, it doesn't bother me much, I'm officially deaf, but I can understand your concern."

I raised my voice and said, "Thank you. It's become more than just a concern." I was pleased and grateful. Maybe this talking to your neighbors stuff isn't all that bad a gambit.

"People who work with their minds at a desk," she said, "deserve some peace and quiet. They *need* it."

"I know I do. And what about people like yourself, who spend their time at home? And sick people trying to recover. And babies, though I haven't seen any of those in this town."

"I could not agree with you more, young man."

It had been a couple of decades since anyone called me a young man.

"Then you'll ask your guy not to use one?"

"Goodness, no, I haven't said a word to him in years. I don't think he speaks English." Her voice dropped to a whisper. "I'm afraid of him."

I knocked on another door. This one was answered by a shaggy-headed bearded man, all hair and oversized sunglasses, wearing cargo shorts and a T-shirt that said: REQUIRES ADULT SUPERVISION.

"Excuse me," I said, "sorry to bother you. I'm DK, your new neighbor from over there." I pointed but he didn't bother to look. "I was wondering, do you ever talk to your landscaper?"

He had a booming voice that shot across Second Street like a pirate ship cannon.

"Do I ever what? Why the hell wouldn't I? Is this some kind of stupid poll? Are you from Immigration? I don't know his status, don't care. He blows, he goes, and he's cheap. Done."

I repeated to him the details of my situation, in effect begging him to let me do my job, too.

"Not my problem," he boomed, and slammed the door in my face. I've noticed that this attitude—not my problem—is more prevalent than it used to be, maybe because there are many more problems to disavow, or maybe because people have become uncaring about anybody else's discomfort. I'd never heard the phrase until the twenty-first century.

I pressed on to my third neighbor, a man of at least eighty-five, a long life of anger etched all over his face. He wore mommy jeans held up by both belt and suspenders, a man who would never be caught with his pants down. As soon as I said "leaf blowers," he shouted upward into my face, "Fuck off before I give you something to complain about." He was all of five foot two. I backed away, and he yelled, "There are more important things to worry about."

"Well, I'm not asking you to ignore those other things. I'm just asking you to be a good neighbor."

"Do the garbage trucks bother you, too, you fruit?"

"No," I said, "but you do, you old runt."

He spit out—I mean, saliva was spraying, "Go back where you came from! We don't want your kind around here!"

My kind? Screenwriters?

"Sir," I said, "I would like nothing more than to go back where I came from. I apologize for calling you an old runt."

"Fuck you!"

"And you, too, sir. I withdraw my apology."

That door was also slammed, though by that time my face was some distance from it. I was going to give up, but I was curious about how the last two neighbors would react. Odds were fifty-fifty one of them would be reasonable. (Anywhere else.) I had gone from cordial denial to abrupt indifference to outright hostility. Would the next neighbor shoot me? I didn't care. I could use the sleep. As it turned out, the last two were not at home. Both houses looked vacant, though landscaping trucks were pulling up as I made my getaway.

Given my experience with Jaime, I didn't want to think too much about my lost garden, but I looked again and tried to envision how I could shield myself, if not from the noise of my neighbors then from the thought of them. Bamboo. Fast growing, thick. They make and shed leaves at an alarming rate and I would welcome every one of those leaves. I would let the yard go a foot deep in leaves. In a way, I identified with bamboo—the bending in the wind thing. I imagined a narrow walkway of stepping stones to a wicker table and chair in the far corner of the yard, where I might put my head back and see the moon when it was directly overhead, or have a cup of coffee during the odd moment when no leaf blower was in operation, and once more punch my way through Wordsworth's "Prelude." A blower started up at that moment, breaking my reverie. Suffer.

I felt the cell phone vibrate in my pants pocket. I tore at it, sure that this time it had to be the love of my life, at long last. Who else would be calling? Nobody calls me. I would beg her to come back and get us out of this place. I would ask for forgiveness, whatever it was I said or did or didn't say or didn't do.

My spirits deflated when I saw that it was Teddy, my agent, who'd been ducking my calls ever since I left New York.

"Hey, DK, how're you doing?"

"Living the dream."

"Good, good, good."

All of our conversations began that way.

"I left a ton of voicemails for you, Teddy," I told him.

"You did?"

I had one finger in my ear to block out the roar of the blower. I told him to hang on. I went inside and closed myself into the downstairs "powder room," a tight little amenity where the actual release of any powder would suffocate whoever might be locked inside. The noise was still loud but bearable, a life adjustment I'd been told by everyone that we all must make. "Can you hear me?"

"Some major buzz in the b.g., but I can hear you. So, DK, here's the story, and there's no easy way to say it. You crashed and burned in New York."

"I expected."

"You're off the project."

"I expected that, too."

"Gertz hates you and never wants to see your face again. He wishes you luck in your future pursuits."

"Am I dead to everybody?"

"Not to me. You're still a rock star in this office." (I did not respond.) "I believe in you, you know that."

I knew nothing of the kind. He seemed to take pleasure in telling me I had crashed and burned.

"The good news is, I've got something for you. It's a stretch, but also a chance to reboot. I want you to think about it before you say anything. Okay?"

"I'm thinking."

"It's a comedy."

"Everything I do is comedy."

"I did not know that. I will pass that on. Why do people say the D in DK stands for Downer?"

"Bad rap."

"You know the director Roger Smythe, the Englishman?"

"What's he done?"

"He had a sleeper hit with *Middle School Mischief*."

"Never saw it."

"About three middle-schoolers who rob a bank. A Jewish American princess, a pseudo-ghetto black kid, and an Asian geek. It was hilarious. No names. The diversity was the star. He's great with kids. Asked for you specifically, he's a huge fan."

I've always wanted the approval of people I've never met. "What's the project?"

"Ready for this? *Girl Scout Confidential*. Wall Street meets the Girl Scouts of America."

"The hell?"

"It's a send up of the cookies competition. You've seen these little Girl Scouts selling cookies."

"Sure. They're all over the place."

"Work their little butts off, pushed by moms and scoutmasters, but in the end the money goes to the corporation that runs the scam. So it's a whacky comedy with a social justice angle. Roger says he can find a dozen Harvard writers who know sophisticated comedy, but when it comes to social justice, not so much. That's why he wants you. He believes he can make you be funny."

"I am funny. He doesn't have to make me anything."

"They have to do this at a price so I won't be able to get your quote. I'll pin 'em for the back end."

My career had come to this, a Girl Scout comedy at fire sale prices. Okay, maybe I no longer held the hot hand, but I was still in the game, I still had a seat at the table.

"DK? Talk to me."

"I've gone back to my western."

"Please, say it isn't so."

"New title. *After the Thaw*. What do you think?"

"Better, but nobody wants to see a western, no matter what you call it. Unless you call it *Spider-Man* and it *is* Spider-Man. Which isn't all that bad an idea. Spider-Man on a horse. You have to seriously think about making some money and salting it away. This recession could go on for years."

"We're in a recession?"

"Believe me, this Girl Scout thing could be huge, a franchise. An annuity for life."

"Teddy, I'm in a bit of a predicament here." I went on to tell him of my arrival in Maragate, my wife's disappearance, and how horrible the town was.

"Really? I heard it was nice there."

"You've heard of the place?"

"Never been, but it's supposed to be nice. Kind of hasn't been discovered yet."

"Do you know anyone who's ever been here?"

He took a minute to think about it. "Not personally. I think it was in *Condé Nast*."

"Yeah, well, they didn't see what I saw. First night in town, I saw three cops shoot somebody."

"Are you serious now? Are you fucking with me?"

"I had to dive under an SUV. They took me back to the station and a psycho lieutenant and his partner grilled me for hours. The partner quoted poetry and punched me in the gut. They tried to convince me I was delusional." (I'd forgotten until that moment that Shelley had visions and heard, if not voices in his head, inappropriate sounds, making him jump up and spin around. Bipolar most likely.) "They even made it look like I could be involved in Hope's disappearance."

"She'll be fine. Women. They do that sometimes. But those cops, outrageous. Terrible for you, but you know what? I see a good story here. What's the second act?"

"Teddy, this is not a pitch. This is my life now. There is no second act, at least I can't see one. Or a third act. It's not a drama, it's what happened. Here's the thing . . ." I took a deep breath.

"What's the thing?"

"Who they shot wasn't really a human being. More like an, a creature of some sort."

"A creature? What kind of creature? Don't say vampire because vampires are over."

"I'm serious, Teddy."

"Me, too. Zombies, still bankable if the slant is fresh."

"Nothing like that. Nobody believes in vampires or zombies. This was something you could believe in. Some people do. Others hold out hope."

"The hell. What."

"A beautiful black woman, with big feathery wings."

"Hello?"

"Yeah."

"An angel?"

"I think so. Who else has big wings?"

"I'm not going to question, like, your sanity, DK? And what you think you saw? But I have to tell you, I love what I'm hearing. I'm getting hard. Halle Berry? Or, better, skew younger, Kerry Washington. Who else is in this?"

"I'll tell you, but don't cast, okay? This is not a movie. This is what happened my first night here. A woman, another witness, the owner of the house, she was there, too. I went back when the cops let me go, but I couldn't find her. I did make contact some weeks later, but she was not cooperative."

"Sexy woman? Dangerous?"

"Maybe, in an offbeat way, if you like that type. I found her annoying as hell."

"You can clean her up."

"She denies everything."

"Jennifer Lawrence."

"Way too young, and too beautiful." After years in the business, it's impossible to resist spontaneous casting. "I was thinking a little more like Molly Parker."

"Wonderful actress, but not big enough."

"Or Lauren Bacall."

"Too old."

"She's dead, Teddy."

"Missed that."

"Forget all that and listen to me. This is real. I'm desperate. I don't know where to turn. This town is freaky, the town and everybody in it. It's surreal. Like a movie."

"That's what I'm saying."

"*Like* a movie. Only this happened. I saw it."

"Could be a vehicle for Tom Hanks. He wouldn't mind another Oscar. You gotta give this some thought, flesh it out. Think Hanks."

"I thought of him from the beginning."

"We're on the same page, brother! Look, you're fast. You could knock this out in a few weeks."

"I've been working on the western for thirty-five years, that's how fast I am."

"I don't want to hear about that western! I want to trample it with its own longhorns."

"You didn't read the script, did you? The cattle are wiped out. And longhorns are a Texas thing."

"Are there six-shooters in it?"

"Of course. It's a western."

"I want to shoot it six times with its own six-shooters."

"I thought about Hanks but only as a role model. For me. Not for any movie."

"We could go younger there, too," he went on. "Bradley Cooper. Now you got Jennifer. They love working together. What's the arc?"

"I'm not talking about a character, it's *me*. I've got no arc. My fucking arc landed me *here*." (I am not given to profanity, and I dislike it more as I grow older. It's a sign of impotence in the face of language, a metaphorical limp dangling participle.)

"Write me a treatment, DK," my agent said. "Please. Do a treatment. If it's shit, we'll forget we ever had this conversation."

"It's not a movie, Teddy."

"You said it was."

"I said it was *like* a movie."

"If it's like a movie it *is* a movie. You said it was surreal."

"It's worse than surreal. I need to get the hell out of here, but I'm afraid of losing Hope forever. I'm stuck, is what I'm saying with all of this. Somehow I have to make the most of it."

"Hope would never leave you. Yours is the marriage everyone wishes they had. Women do this, they come back better than ever."

"Not all of them."

"I can see the poster: *The Dark Angel*. Bradley Cooper and Jennifer, with an angel looming behind them, big black wings. Kerry Washington."

"She had an Irish accent."

"Ruth Negga! She's Irish."

"Good actress."

"Maybe you hold back the reveal that it's an angel. Make it the turning point, say page fifty. You see her first as a human, get to know her, and then you see her as an angel."

"You're giving me notes on a script I'm never going to write."

"I have an idea. Great idea. Take a breath." (I did.) "You started out writing books. Write this as a book. We'll sell the rights, package it with Bradley, Jennifer, Ruth, and any damn director we want, you attached for the adaptation."

"I wrote *one* book. A fluke. I don't think I can write another. I don't think I can write anything anymore." That's a confession no screenwriter should ever make to anyone but his wife, if he can locate her. Certainly not his agent or anyone else in the industry. It's like revealing you have cancer.

"First of all, never say that. That's exactly why you should do the Girl Scout project. It would be a breeze for you, get you back in the action. A warm-up for the real deal, the black angel story. Have some fun, make some money."

It did make sense. I was always confident enough to tackle any subject and pull a good story out of it. My God, I made a great story out of the Romantic Poets, which was impossible or it would have been done already. Hope would know where to find me, if she wanted to. Where's the betrayal? *I* was the one who should feel betrayed. Girl Scouts. Why not?

"Can I sleep on it?"

"If you snooze you lose. Can I at least tell Roger you're interested?"

It would be my ticket out of Maragate. I could leave my explanation with Carlos. See ya. When Hope returned, he could present *her* with a letter. I'll write mine in longhand, in ink, with my Montblanc. (The flow of ink into words on a white page is forever a sensual experience. At least for me.)

Why did I not say yes immediately? It's not like I couldn't put aside the western if it meant getting out of Maragate.

"If I do it, I'm going to need first-class transportation to LA, a furnished apartment, and per diem. I'll want to hit the ground running."

"Now that's the DK. I know. We'll get you out of that shithole and back on the A list."

"I'm off the A list?"

"Have to take this call. Stay in touch, bro."

www.girlscoutcookies.org

I walked along the bike trail, my reverie broken only by voices behind me saying breathlessly, "On your left," as another cyclist in tight concept pants sped past.

The two most worrisome times in a screenwriter's life are when he does not have a job and as soon as he gets a job. Once he is into the first draft he is fine, but upon agreeing to an assignment he is beset with anxieties: Can he make it happen, is it right for him, might it fail because of something beyond his control? (Like casting or the marketing department saying, "We don't know how to market this," as they often say and get away with.) Once the screenwriter commits, a hundred people will be counting on him. Millions of dollars are at stake. Jobs will be created. He will have to work hard and fast and cleverly, and give it his heart and soul, and at the end of it he might prove profoundly disappointing to everyone involved and be fired.

The studio will want Adam Sandler as the CEO of the corporation exploiting the Girl Scouts. By the end of the movie the CEO will see the error of his greedy ways, as no real CEO ever has in the history of corporations, not counting the Japanese whose CEOs have the integrity to kill themselves, and he will adopt one of the little girls, setting up the sequel. (Annie joins the Girl Scouts.) The director, Roger Whatshisname, would have to defend me as his choice. He would have to convince the studio that I can be funny. Pushback over not hiring a woman to write about Girl Scouts could poison the project.

I could get behind the gag casting of Alec Baldwin playing the same character he played in *Glengarry Glen Ross*. Cameron Diaz could be the scoutmaster. Her ass is still highly marketable. (I would argue.) Put her in Girl Scout shorts and knee socks and try to resist *that* when you see the trailer. Or go in the other direction, Melissa McCarthy, and now it's all about accepting yourself. There's too much of that going on anyway. (I considered Cameron *and* Melissa. Dueling scoutmasters.)

I could fill in the rainbow with little girls of every conceivable ethnicity, and for the core group: an obnoxious little scout and a sweet one, a brainy girl and a dumb one, a cutie face and a homely mug. With corresponding moms and dads: the helicopter mom, one who drinks too much, a nerdy dad, a creepy dad. What was it about, I asked myself, a question the writer should not dwell upon because there will be a world of people telling him what it is about, after he finishes the first draft. It has to be funny but not mindless, sophisticated but not inaccessible, ironic but only a little off the sides, sexy but safe. Don't use the F-word, everybody keeps their clothes on, and you've won a PG-13 rating.

All of this mental meandering, second-guessing, projecting—in the Hollywood sense of the word—made me sad with its cynicism. Who's to say it wouldn't be an intelligent picture with Tom Hanks and Meryl Streep and kids you could love, and fully fleshed out parents? It could be the kind of wonderful picture you'll want to see every Christmas.

At the moment, however, the most important thing about the movie was that it would get the screenwriter back to Los Angeles and the life he used to lead. Stuck in Maragate, all that was me was disappearing from my memory, including Hope, who had been with me more than half my life. What kind of loyalty did I owe her now, after what she did? It's not like she had Alzheimer's and wandered off. It's not like I was getting on with my own life while she was sinking into oblivion. Time had lost its meaning, if ever it had any.

I had no saved voicemails or emails from Hope, no letters but that one, which wasn't much like her. I did have pictures on my phone and computer, and I would sit for hours looking at them. It was much like grieving, without the solace of having seen the body. Look at that face. The beauty that once was in my life was gone. In the pain of missing her, I was at risk of forgetting her. I needed someone to tell me something about her, to see her again, if only through another's eyes.

Carlos, through his own filter, reconstructed the short conversations they had, all related to moving into the house. Some of them sounded like the woman I knew and loved and lived with for years. Some of them did not.

I dropped into the office of a real estate agent I had met at the farmers market, the one who knew what Hope paid for the house. She gave me the name of the selling agent. That office, Advanced Realty, was a short walk away. Most of the real estate offices were a short walk away.

Felicity bore a strong resemblance to the agent I'd just left. It struck me that both women looked a lot like the agent who sold us the house in the Hollywood Hills so many years before. They were all over fifty but under sixty, and would be for the rest of their lives, with highlighted and sculpted blonde hair, decent figures but harried miens, and driving Range Rovers. Felicity's was silver and luxurious. I know because when I caught her at the door to her shop she was on the way to meet a couple to show them a house for the second time, to close the deal. She swept me along because she "simply adored" Hope and was thrilled to meet her husband, in whom she didn't seem profoundly disappointed. No burden was put upon me to tell her why I was there, which was fortunate because I wouldn't know how to explain it. (Tell me about my wife.)

"She is the sweetest woman, and gorgeous. You're such a lucky man."

"I've heard that."

We were not a block into the east side before I regretted whatever it was I was doing.

Her memory of Hope: "What a tough negotiator!"

I found that hard to believe. Hope was a cream puff. Not as soft as I, but with the same reluctance to make anyone uneasy.

"How she managed to get that place at only ninety K above the asking price was a feat to behold. I believe the owners knew they could do better, but they loved Hope and her story and it was a clean deal, no contingencies."

"Her story? What was her story?"

"Well, really, all about you. She wanted a place for her husband to escape the pressures of Hollywood, to relax and enjoy some good old small-town charm, to get involved with a caring community, make new friends, start a whole new routine. To write in peace and quiet."

Now, that *did* sound like Hope. Sometimes she wore her concern for my state of mind like a hijab.

"Ah, about that . . ." I started, then hesitated.

"Yes?"

"About writing in peace and quiet . . ."

"Yes?"

"There was a disclosure section in the contract, right?"

"Absolutely. Everything, no matter how minor, that might affect the value of the property is disclosed. Was there a problem?"

"Was and is." Her eyes narrowed. "Was it disclosed that leaf blower noise makes the neighborhood uninhabitable for anyone who works at home? Or lives at home during daylight hours."

She burst out laughing, a horsey guffaw, a brassy girl laugh.

"You're kidding, right?"

"I can't work at home. That's no joke. That, like, defeats the whole purpose of everything my wife wanted to do for me."

"Leaf blowers? They're everywhere. Try to buy a house where you don't hear leaf blowers."

"I never heard any in the Hollywood Hills, where I used to live."

"It's not like they're running all the time. Really, there are more important things to worry about."

"Yes, I'm sure there are. But that doesn't mean we can't worry about loud noise and bad air, too."

"Really?"

"You never know when they will be running, or how many of them, or when they will stop, or when the revving will go high or low. It's the worst sound there is for anyone trying to concentrate."

"They don't bother *me*."

"You're never home."

She couldn't deny it. Real estate agents are seldom at home. If you are not there (wherever) leaf blowers are not a problem.

"If the seller didn't disclose leaf blower noise, I want my money back. You can have the house."

"You can't be serious."

Was I? Was it possible? Could I be refunded all that cash? I could go back to LA, find a nice apartment, work on my western, and get my life back, some of it. Hope could find me, she was far more resourceful than I. For that matter, I would be free to change everything, go anywhere. I could go alone to Paris, a beautiful city in a civilized country, and live well there until the house money ran out, and then I could kill myself, in a city that has always understood existentialism. I was feeling all tingly at the prospect, until I remembered I left my passport with Hope. I could get another one. How did I get the first one? I would go to the post office. The post office knows everything.

"I'm serious," I said. "I hate it here."

From a forced smile her jaw fell to a disbelieving gape, as though I were the first person ever to say that aloud. (I may have been.)

"May I call you DK?"

"Please do."

"DK, trust me on this, you are going to fall in love with this town. I'll bet anything."

"It's a bet."

That someone did not have it in them to love Maragate was incomprehensible to her, not to mention insulting.

"DK, if you don't appreciate living in the best zip code in America—"

"I'd rather live in the worst arrondissement in Paris."

"Then I have a simple solution."

"Yes?"

"Put the house up for sale. I could sell it for you in a Maragate minute and you will probably make a tidy profit."

"I've thought about that."

"Hold that thought."

She pulled to the curb in front of a cottage that would have been right for somebody's grandma. Newly painted in puke-yellow ochre, only one step up to the front door, a window on each side of the door, no garage, no carport. The front of the house was about fifteen feet wide. A couple in their seventies stood waiting for her. A leaf blower worked on each end of the block, slowly converging on Grandma's cottage. This was on Seventh Street East, the low rent area of Maragate.

Had she left the keys in the car I would have been able to steal it and hit the road.

A plexiglass box was affixed to a white stake at the sidewalk. I got out of the car and took a flyer out of the box.

This is what it said: "Storybook home on the coveted east side of Maragate, minutes from Spanish Circle. (All sides of Maragate were coveted, I was learning, and every piece of property in the town was minutes from Spanish Circle.) Beautifully landscaped grounds. (The front yard consisted of two small squares of lawn turning brown on either side of the pebbled walkway.) This quaint residence has two bedrooms and one bath. The kitchen overlooks a backyard perfect for outdoor entertaining. Hurry on this one. It won't last long. Priced to move at $899,000."

In fifteen minutes Felicity and her clients came out of the cottage all smiles. Hugs were traded before one last cherished look back at the gem about to go into escrow.

Felicity got into the car, started it up, and said, "Ka-ching! Gotta get back to the office and crank out a contract. Where can I drop you?"

"Don't tell me you sold that place for eight hundred and ninety-nine thousand dollars."

"No, I'm gonna tell you I sold it for nine twenty."

I thought there had to be something morally wrong with what had transpired before my eyes, but I could not say what. It's the sacred Free Market, after all. Capitalism, fair and square. Those that got it get more of it; those that don't, play the Lotto. Before I left for New York, a contractor was finishing up a spec house in Beverly Hills that would be listed for $200 million. A tour of the house would cost a prospective buyer $50,000, refundable only upon purchase.

"You know how long it took me to get that place off the market?" I didn't care. "Three days!"

This was the only time I ever shared a moment alone with a realtor who had just sold a house. It was embarrassing, like catching someone masturbating.

"We've got a few minutes," she said. "Let's deal with you. You want me to sell that house for you? Like tomorrow? If not tonight?"

"I'd love it. But you'd need my wife's signature, wouldn't you?"

"And Hope does not want to sell? I can understand that. It's *hard* getting into this town."

"Hope is gone."

"Gone? What do you mean . . . God, she isn't—?"

"If she were dead, I wouldn't need her signature, would I? She's gone and I don't know where and I don't know when she'll come back. She promised she would."

"I don't get it."

"Neither do I."

"Don't you talk to her on the phone?"

"To her picture. Not to her."

I turned my phone toward Felicity. The picture of Hope. She looked so beautiful. She hadn't changed in years.

The agent took her eyes off the road to look at the picture, then back to the road. She reached over to stop me from turning the phone away. She leaned toward me and looked at the picture again.

"Careful," I said. "Watch the road."

She turned her eyes back to the road and fell silent.

"Something wrong?" I asked.

"No, nothing. Why?"

"You stopped talking."

"I don't talk *all* the time."

She tried to smile. I held out my phone to her.

"This is Hope, the woman who bought the house from you, right?"

"Of course it is. Don't you know your own wife?"

She pulled into a parking place with her name on it and bolted from the car. I got out and held my phone over the open door of her Range Rover calling, "Wait, are you sure? You didn't seem to recognize her."

She juggled her bag and portfolio and loose papers. She dropped her water bottle and left it bouncing on the ground. "What is your problem?" she answered, then ran into her office.

www.entrepreneur.com/article/222558

Lieutenant Conventerra agreed to meet me behind City Hall and to come alone, which made me believe that to some degree he took me seriously. I made my way diagonally across Spanish Circle. Along the way, I walked past two panhandlers, unusual in Maragate. They were sitting on the ground like unfortunate brothers, their cardboard signs propped against their knees. I glanced sideways at the hand-scrawled pleas. One said: ANYTHING HELPS. The other: NOTHING HELPS.

Another big white tent had been set up next to City Hall, with a guard at the entrance. I sat on a park bench not far from the street, facing the tent. I was ambivalent at best about meeting with Conventerra again. I'd diagnosed him that first night as a high-functioning psychotic, in the way that cops often are. Still, in my last go-around with him in the gin mill he showed signs of helpfulness, like a volunteer guide whose job it was to lead me around hazards of which I might not be aware. He also planted a notion in my head that I wanted to be rid of, though my encounter with Felicity the real estate agent only made it loom as one more dark possibility. Maybe Hope had a girlfriend. It happens.

He was behind me before I knew he was there, then sitting next to me, brushing the remnants of crumbs from his pants. It looked like he'd been detained by a doughnut.

"What can I do for you, Doctor K?"

"Are you in a rush?"

"Not at the moment. At the moment, I'm all yours. Would have been more convenient at the station."

"I didn't want to bump into Kuggelsong."

"So what's on your mind?"

"Something you said, which at the time I thought was ridiculous. You said what if my wife had a girlfriend? I think I'd know. I'd know. But if that happened, you said, she could be in two places at the same time."

"In a way. She'd have a workable shadow if she needed one. Why would she need one?"

"I told you that first night that this whole thing was far out of character for her. I can't imagine she could conceive of it. Since then a couple of encounters are messing with my head. It has me thinking she *didn't*. At least not alone."

"Go on."

"I had a landscaper named Jaime. Came with the house. Hope was the jefa, but he told me he never laid eyes on her. Then recently I met the agent who sold Hope the house. She went on about her, how sweet she was, which she is, and what a savvy negotiator she is, which she isn't, obviously. She paid a fortune for a hovel. Here's the thing, though. When I showed her Hope's picture, the one on my phone, the same one I showed you, she didn't recognize her. She became all flustered and couldn't get away from me fast enough. If Hope didn't buy that place, who did?"

"And why, would be your next question."

"It would be. Why else but to put me in a trap. Safe, looked after, but out of the way."

"Why's it a trap? Why isn't it what you said you wanted, a new chapter in your life?"

"Let me count the ways."

I quoted the Browning line, as everyone does, whether they know it or not, but Conventerra waited patiently for me to count the ways.

"Because this place is shit, and she would have seen that, if she'd ever been here," I said.

I was afraid he might think I was acting all French and would go back to his psycho side. Instead, he said, with some sympathy, "I'm sad to hear you say that. Most people who land here count their blessings."

"I'm not one of them. I want to go home."

"But you are home."

"No, no, I'm not. Home is with Hope. God save me, I could live in Maragate, if only she were here with me."

"Well, she will be, in time, I'm sure. Unless, of course, you—"

"Killed her?"

"I was going to say drove her away. Unless you became impossible to live with and she chose a whole new thing."

"Obviously, I did drive her away, but I don't know how or why, and she's not talking. Maybe I wasn't easy to live with but I wasn't impossible. I'm not mean or abusive. You'd hardly know I was there."

"Not a good recommendation, Doctor K."

"She didn't have to set me up here."

"Thought you said it didn't matter where you lived."

"You misinterpreted that."

"If you don't like it here, go. Maragate's not for everyone. But once they go, they can't come back."

"You told me not to leave town." (Lame, I know.)

"That's the only reason you're staying?"

Devotion? Fear? Ennui? A set of psychic chains?

"Can you give me a lift to the airport?" I asked him.

"Not a taxi service."

"Lieutenant, what do you make of what I told you?"

"This Jaime dude? He came with the house?"

"That's what Carlos said."

"Then he knows the routine, knew his duties."

"Blow and go."

"She's busy with other things, she lets him blow and go. She'll get to know him later. At the time, she didn't have to talk to him and vice versa."

"Hope is outgoing and warm. She would not have a man working for her without meeting him, saying hello at least. I would, but not her."

"She might have changed. People do. Some of them should. Some of them damn well better. You spend some time here, you start thinking about the things you've done, and how you'd do them different, if you had a chance."

"What about Felicity, the real estate agent?"

"Felicity Brainard? From Advanced Realty?"

"That's the one."

"She's been here forever, successful, pillar of the community."

"Fine, but she didn't recognize Hope, after she went on and on about her."

"She said she couldn't recognize the picture?"

"No, but I could see it on her face."

"You told me it was an old picture."

"I also said she hasn't changed since then. Felicity was rattled. I pressed her and she said, yes, it's Hope and then ran away flustered."

"She's always flustered, always in a rush. She's a real estate agent."

"Are you playing the devil's advocate or do you really believe—"

"The devil can speak for himself," said Conventerra.

"Now you're saying nothing is amiss, yet not long ago you thought I might have murdered my wife."

"Does that mean you're under arrest? Under suspicion? It doesn't work that way. Without evidence, it doesn't matter what I think. Now you're trying to make the case that Hope never existed, at least not here in Maragate, that her girlfriend fronted for her. You've got no more evidence that way than I have my way. In the meantime,

I'm here to protect and serve, so we're back to my original question: What can I do for you, Doctor K?"

A group of four young people, three boys and a girl, stopped at the entrance to the white tent. I could not be sure, but I thought the girl was the same one I talked to at Valene's house, the one who told me she and her three friends were renting the place, which Valene denied in our short meeting. That was some time back. If they were tourists, why would they still be in town? Seeing them again was more than coincidental.

The boys looked my way as the girl had a word with the guard. I had the sense she was trying to distract him. I turned to see what might have attracted their attention and then thought maybe they were looking out for a cop and unfortunately finding one. Or I could have been their object of interest. (The curse, one of them, of the screenwriter is that possible scenarios are sparked by the most mundane of occurrences. In my case they are usually grim, and I say to myself, why do you *do* that?) In a moment, the four young people were allowed inside.

"What's with the tent today?" I asked Conventerra.

"Sustainability Commission, brainstorming over a nosh."

"What are they sustaining?"

"Our little slice of heaven."

"They need a tent? How many are on the commission?"

"Twelve, and two alternates." (The tent had a capacity of at least one hundred.) "Their job is to keep things in balance."

"I thought that was your job."

"You want to apply? They're always looking for new blood."

"I don't get involved."

www.rulesofevidence.org

After the Thaw is an ensemble piece, and every actor in it can claim that the movie is about him. The Captain, however, will carry the sentiments of the audience. As I say this, I can see that it ain't necessarily so. It could be The Kid. (The original title, which suggests that the movie is about "The Kid.") Or the African, Ham, and all that he represents, both then and now.

Each actor will have his notebook in which he jots down all his observations about his character, details beyond what is in the script, beyond what he looks like and how he walks and talks and dresses. He will make lists of the character's favorites, his peeves, his fears, his desires, his quirks, and his habits. The actor will compliment himself on his painstaking preparation and talk about his process during interviews, but the screenwriter does this for *all* of the characters, and no one expects less. The screenwriter will come to know his characters better than the people in his own life. The starting point for me about any character is: What does he want? (Without desire there is no conflict, without conflict no drama. There is mostly sitting on a cushion on the floor waiting for enlightenment.) What does the Captain want, on this defining day and for the long run? It is not a simple thing to discover, not for me, not for the Captain. What he appears to want may not be what he truly wants, and what he wants by the end of the movie may not be what he wanted at the beginning. It may be the opposite of what he wanted. The Captain may want no more than common decency. (Which, let's face it, evolves through time, so one must look for it in himself.) He wants the rule of law, surely. But he is in a land where law is scarce and most people like it that way. He wants a purpose in life. He wants love. Does he understand that in his time, 1887, in this place, the Wyoming Territory, none of what he wants will he get? He probably understands that better than I.

I stood at the bar of the Deer Park tasting room, making notes. I am never far from a pen and a three-by-five card. In the pauses, I sampled Radish Gastrique gin paired with squid jerky.

I was sluggish to realize that my best chance now to get *After the Thaw* made would be to take the Girl Scout job and show my western, in its 116th draft, to each of the twelve producers who would inevitably be attached to *Girl Scout Confidential*. One phone call to Teddy, and within the week I could have a stretch pull up to my hovel and whisk me back to Los Angeles, land that I love, City of Angels (What angel?), where a luxury short-term furnished apartment would be ready for me, with Chopin on my playlist and in the freezer, and an Epson printer on the desk next to a ream of all-purpose paper. Why was I stalling? Hope had my number and my email address. She could contact me at any time. Or not. At times I wondered if she, like my murdered angel, ever existed at all. (Ask me to prove it—I couldn't.) The job would be a hard four to six months of making Girl Scouts cute and funny and smart without making them annoying. Who knows, I might have a good time of it. Despite all opinions to the contrary, including my own agent's, I always thought of myself as a writer capable of making people laugh.

I took my phone out of my back pocket and called Teddy. The call would not go through. Maragate was notoriously bad for cell phone reception. I walked around looking for a sweet spot. In a dark corner of the place near the emergency exit was a lone table. I sat at it and was able to connect, if I kept the phone within a twelve-inch radius.

"Hello, DK, how are you doing?"

"Living the dream."

"Good, good, good."

"Okay, Teddy, I'm in."

"Pardon?"

"The Girl Scout gig. I'll take it."

The silence sucked the mixed aromas of gin, radishes, and dried fish out of the room, along with my self-worth.

"DK . . . you never called."

"I laid out my terms. I said I was interested. I'm calling now."

"I'm sorry, bro, they're going in a different direction."

The dreaded "different direction." No one ever asks what direction because everyone knows the answer: Away from you. I was bummed that my escape was foiled once again.

"Can you find me something else, in a hurry?"

"Let me talk to you like a Dutch uncle here, DK." He was too young to play uncle to me, Dutch or otherwise. "This is a business of relationships. You get to know people, establish rapport, go to their parties, their kids' bar mitzvahs, you support their charities. You attend a wedding, a funeral. You take a lunch just for a bite to eat. You call them up, ask them how they're feeling and what they're working on. If you're nominated for an award, you go, and you go to the after-party, win or lose. You wouldn't do any of that."

"I did, in the beginning."

I loved all that, but it got in the way of the work. I learned back then that working only when I had nothing on the social calendar put me in a hole. I had to work *all* of the time, and allow nothing else to go on the calendar. That, by the way, was Shelley's dilemma: Does the artist need companionship or isolation to create? He posed the question of whether great art required the support of others or the rejection of society. (The artist's rejection of society, not the other way around, which is a given.) It was a dilemma for me as well, putting aside the question of whether or not screenwriting is an art. Shelley never answered his own question, and so he wavered from one extreme to the other, traveling with Mary and her sister and sometimes Byron or Keats from one ideal spot, sure they would all live there together forever creating great poetry, to another ideal spot where they would be lucky to stay out of each other's way. Shelley never had to ponder if movies were art. (Paddy Chayefsky never had to ponder if video games were art.)

"People don't know you, on a personal level," my agent told me. "They think you're aloof."

"I'm socially awkward, you know that."

"Bullshit. When you smile, it lights up the room."

"When was that?"

"You choose to be alone."

"I kind of have to."

"No one talks about you because they never see you. The younger execs, when your name comes up, they think you're dead."

"I feel like I am." Well, that sounded full of self-pity, which Shelley might agree was every poet's character flaw. (And fuel.) "You don't know, after all, do you, when you are dead. Even as I talk to you, how would I know?"

"You're bringing me down, bro."

"So, if somehow I came back, would I be on the ash heap?"

"They admire what you've done. I could get you into meetings all day long—everybody would like to meet you—but nobody is going to call you back. It is what it is."

"What else could it be?"

"Exactly."

"Spec scripts."

"What about them?"

"The life blood of the industry. I have one, a good one, maybe a great one, if you pay attention."

"That western? Stop it, please."

"It can stand with *High Noon*."

"With what, now?"

I was out of the game and would never be let back into it. My seat had already been taken by someone else.

"I always thought the work would be enough," I said, like a rejected husband, a role I no longer needed to research.

"They loved you long time, but on top of everything else you made the mistake of getting old."

"How do I correct that?"

"I've got a call waiting. Gotta take it. Listen, we can talk tomorrow. Sorry?"

We never spoke again. Suffer.

One morning I negotiated the narrow dark stairway to the kitchen shining a penlight on the steps below me. A few days before I had encountered a rat on the stairway and almost stepped on it before it scurried downstairs to a hiding spot unknown.

Carlos was busy in the kitchen, as usual, preparing what looked like a picnic basket.

"What are you up to today?"

"*Buenos días*, señor."

"Yeah, good morning. You going on a picnic?"

"No, you are. I am preparing a basket for the fireworks. Everyone will gather tonight at the soccer field with food and gin to share. It is a grand annual event, and you must be a part of it."

"Must not. Fireworks are stupid."

"Then you are the only person in the good old US of A who believes so."

"It is a ritual long past its ability to glorify anything, especially war. It makes no sense."

"Not everything has to make sense, señor. You must give yourself over to having some senseless fun every now and then."

"People love to see things blow up, I get it, but every Fourth of July children lose fingers, old horses drop dead, frightened dogs leap fences."

"None of that ever happens in Maragate. Try it, you may like it. Everyone does."

"Take it yourself. Don't you ever get a day off?"

"If you can resist the wonderful things in this basket, then I may indeed take them myself and find someone more appreciative."

"That would be anyone."

"I'm sure."

I poured myself a *café con leche*. He still made coffee every morning but he had stopped serving it to me.

Lieutenant Conventerra's indifference to what I thought was salient evidence in the matter of my wife pre- and post-Maragate colored my mood. In July, "Here I sit, altogether Novemberish."

Since showing her picture to Felicity the real estate agent, and after
learning that Jaime the gardener had never even met her, I could not
refrain from playing grim scenarios in my mind. As I told you, for the
screenwriter the internal projector is always running and often over-
heating. The plotter in me saw the twists, though I like to believe my
scripts were character-driven. I *did* speak to her from New York and I
knew the sound of her voice. She talked to me at length about wanting to buy this house. She was under no duress, no hint of any crisis.
She was as cheerful as ever, and excited by the pending change in our
lives. Never a mention of any compelling urge to sleep with another
woman. At the time, I believed myself poisoned by a piece of New
York cheesecake and though I listened and tried to match her enthusiasm I wanted nothing more than to lie down. In hindsight, I could
find no purpose in any elaborate scheme to isolate me in a remote
and corrupt town, consigned to a rat-infested, fly-specked, cold, dark,
leaky, noisy house with neither money nor wheels nor now the will to
escape. Then why was I here, and where was she? Each scenario faded
in with that v. o. question, played on my inner screen, and then faded
out with Tom Waits singing the title song called, "Suffer."

I said to Carlos, "I have a question about the señora." I had to
shout because the leaf blowers outside were in full force, as though
deliberately trying to drown out any inquiries I might have.

"As Minnesota Fats would say, shoot, señor."

"Okay, simple question: What did you think of her?"

"The señora is a fine lady, and I enjoyed her company. She was
pleasant to be around." He gave me the stink eye which said, unlike
some people. "She was appreciative of my cooking and all of the
things I did to make her comfortable, as I have tried to do for you."
Again with the eye. "I so look forward to her return."

"Tell me, what did she look like?"

"Señor? Have you forgotten what your own wife looked like? I
find that cause for alarm. Old timer's disease might be one diagno-
sis," he said, with an annoying chuckle I was hearing more often
these days. "Tell me, please, if you can, what is today's date?"

I sneezed three times, first sequence of the day. My eyes were burning. Carlos never seemed to be bothered by allergies. Nothing seemed to bother him. I wiped my eyes and blew my nose.

"Let's say we're comparing perceptions. What did she look like to you?"

"Perceptions, oh . . . perceptions, señor, are instilled by demons." (Wait, what?)

"Is that some Mexican superstition? You don't trust what you see? Your own perceptions are the work of demons?"

"*Claro que si.* What you see is one thing, what you perceive another. Your eyes are the demons' remote cameras."

I knew nothing about Carlos, nothing about his upbringing, his superstitions, his religious beliefs. Not that I cared to, you understand, but I would be lying if I said I never thought about perception along those lines.

"Okay, but when you see a person, any person, you kind of know what they look like. They're tall, short, black, white, fat, skinny."

"Different strokes for different folks."

"Right. What did the señora look like?"

"*Bueno.* I saw a radiant smile and full sensuous lips, if I may say so. Eyes of blue, and her hair was, ash blonde? Is that the word?"

"That's the word. What else?"

"Her skin was fair and without blemish. She protected herself from the harmful rays of the sun. She looked younger than her age."

"Which was?"

"Oh, I have no idea, but she must be quite a bit younger than you."

I let that pass. His description was accurate. It also matched the picture on my phone.

"Anything else?"

"In short, a beautiful woman, but what is more, gracious and considerate. A fine figure, if again I may say so. One only hopes that she is appreciated by all who know her."

"Did she wear glasses?"

He hesitated, looked to the ceiling.

"At times, when she had to read something."

"How tall was she?"

"Señor, all kidding aside, I am beginning to worry about you."

"Please, tell me how tall she was."

"Of medium height."

"So what would that be?"

"Actually, she was my height."

"And what is that?"

"Five feet and five inches."

Hope was five-six. She wore glasses for reading anything of length, like one of my screenplays, and she looked adorable in them. (Also gave good notes.)

"Did she have any friends here?" I asked.

"I would like to think that I was a friend, as well as an employee."

"Any others?"

"She was here so short a time before she felt it necessary to escape."

"Escape?"

"My apologies on my choice of words, but it did have the appearance of an escape. From what, I have no idea. She seemed in a hurry. She was in no danger, that I am aware of, and nowhere is one more free than in Maragate. People escape from elsewhere to come *here*."

"Did she ever go out, to a bar, a restaurant, anywhere?"

"I wouldn't know, señor. She was so busy arranging things for you."

"You would know if she went out. She wouldn't be here. You always know when I go out."

"On occasion, I might look for her and not find her, but never for long, before she would appear again. I never asked her where she had been. That would be impertinent."

"You ask me, all the time."

"*Si*, but that is my job, you see."

"What things?"

"Señor?"

"What things kept her so busy?

"The house, for one."

"Arranging this house had to take a day."

"A house is an undertaking, like a ship. Coming aboard, you are not aware of all that went into making it shipshape. And then she had to arrange, in point of fact, a life for you, free from any obligation but to write. She wanted to make it like heaven for you, where all things are taken care of, so that you could write the Great American Movie." (A soupçon of sarcasm?) "She would be profoundly disappointed to see how you fritter away your time."

"She makes friends easily. I'd be surprised if she didn't have at least one in Maragate."

"She may have, but she did not introduce me. From my observation, she simply did not have enough time for friends, and the neighbors, as you've noticed, can be standoffish until they get to know you. Tell me what is on your mind, señor, truly?"

"Isn't it obvious? I can't understand why she would do all this and then disappear, leaving nothing more than a typed letter."

"On that I have no idea, señor, but I am sure she will return."

"Sometimes I can't believe it was Hope that was here."

"Then who else could it have been? Another woman who looked like your wife with the same name? If you are concerned for her safety, you should perhaps contact the police."

We'd had a hatch of ugly black moths. I spied one of the outliers and stalked it from the dim kitchen to the dark living room, a place I found depressing and usually avoided, not that my upstairs room was any more cheerful. I made a couple of sweeps with my hand but the moth was able to avoid me. Carlos had no idea where they were coming from, though he told me this was not the first time they appeared. "We will live through this," he said, which was his approach to all problems. (Not a bad one, actually.) He regarded the moths as harmless seasonal visitors. They gave me the creeps, like the black flies. Suffer.

In pursuit of the moth I noticed a wire running two feet along a section of that hideous Las Vegas carpet, from the wall to the sofa, an area where no one ever passed, except for Carlos should he want to start a fire in the fireplace, which hadn't happened since that first foggy night in February. I looked closer, flashed my penlight on the floor and found a telephone, a landline.

I had never noticed it before, due I'm sure to the insane illusions created by the carpet. For that matter, I'd never noticed the absence of a telephone or that one hadn't rung all the time I'd been in the house. It sat on the floor on the far side of the sofa, its wire connected to a wall jack.

"Carlos?"

"*Si*, señor?"

"I found a phone in the living room!"

Carlos leaned over the counter and smiled at me. That chuckle again. "Imagine that!"

In ways like this he had become overtly sarcastic, swinging from servile to cynical.

"I don't even know the number."

"It is printed there, right on the body of the instrument, you see."

I didn't bother to look. "But it never rings."

"I believe the señor takes calls on his cellular phone."

Not since my agent called. I patted my pockets. "Where *is* my cell phone?"

"On the dining room table, where you left it last night. You were *mucho borracho*."

The dining room was where an egg would drop if it rolled off the kitchen counter. A qualified contractor would recommend surgically excising it and expanding the kitchen into its space. No one but I ever sat at the dining room table, which was handmade and not in a good way. I retrieved my phone and as usual checked for any voicemails or texts. Nothing.

"What about telemarketers?" I asked. "Back in LA we would get ten calls a day."

(From mortgage companies, AT&T, Time Warner, ADT home protection, offers of free cruises.)

"Oh, we are not bothered by such things in Maragate. The city council was able to put the entire town on the Do Not Call list."

"I was on that list. And I told anybody who called me to put me on that list and never call again. It seemed only to increase the number of calls."

"Ah, but you were not then in a little slice of heaven. Here, you will not be disturbed."

He was oblivious to the irony that we were shouting to each other because of another onslaught of leaf blowers. Like Carlos they took no holidays. He turned back to his kitchen preparations. I sneezed three times more and wiped my burning eyes.

Even in my interior dialogs, I could not call Carlos a servant. He was more a paid companion booked by a concerned wife who withdrew her own companionship. Would that she had hired a nice Mexican woman instead, with deep brown eyes and olive skin . . . I sometimes slipped into fantasy, believing my real sex life was over. (We die in increments. Suffer.)

I returned to the living room. Neither end of the sofa provided a comfortable place to sit for any longer than a moment. I risked it, reaching down for the phone. I heard a dial tone. I tried to remember how to call back the last number that called. Was it pound-ninety-nine, star-sixty-five . . . no, star-sixty-nine. I punched it in and got the number. A recorded message sent me to the voicemail for Lieutenant Conventerra of the MPD. I hung up.

"Carlos?"

Once again, he leaned over the counter, put out by my interruptions. I shouted across the room, "When did this phone ring last?"

He thought about it. "Oh, señor, it's been forever. Nobody uses landlines anymore. If you like I can discontinue the service."

He looked back at me impassively, comfortable in his lie. The din from outside had no effect on him.

"I have spears of jicama in lime juice and tortas to die for, should you change your mind," he said, and turned back to his preparations.

www.cdbaby.com/as-chaos-unfolds

The Fourth of July parade made a loop around Spanish Circle and was known as, "The best darn parade in America," sometimes amended to, "for a town this size," and further amended to, "in a circular route." Everyone went to see the parade, arriving before dawn to stake out favorite spots and to set up folding lawn chairs and coolers full of gin and some beer as well because of the heat. Sidewalks were jammed, and some chairs had to be set up behind the crowds at the front line and into the park itself. I had to walk in the middle of the street to make forward progress. The parade hadn't started so others were doing the same thing.

I enjoy parades if they have drum and bugle corps, preferably playing Beatles songs, and if they have majorettes. And tubas, the more tubas the better.

If I could find some vantage point I was prepared to watch at least some of the parade. If not, I would keep on walking, maybe until I dropped. A woman called my name. I looked along the mass of people. Sandy Fleck darted out of the crowd toward me. "Happy Fourth of July!" she cried with childlike enthusiasm.

"Same to you, and many more." (The only holidays I recognize are Valentine's Day and Thanksgiving. Love and gratitude.)

She grabbed my arm and pulled me out of the crowd and to a canopied spot she had claimed the night before. "You have to sit with us," she said. Doc was under the canopy sitting next to a young black man who was also in a wheel chair. Young to me. He looked to be in his mid-forties. A folding table held fruit and bagels, gin and sparkling water, and a blender rigged to a battery.

"Hey, DK, your first Maragate Fourth," Doc said.

"Yes, but my fourth Maragate first."

Doc looked at the man sitting next to him and cocked his head as if to say, that's the way he is. (Though I've tried to change, Lord knows.)

"DK, this is Terry, my homie from rehab. Welcome to the Crips and the Bloods."

Terry grinned. I bent forward and shook his hand. In another minute, I had a Ramos Fizz cocktail in that hand. Fleck and Terry had already had a few.

"The best parade in America," said Terry.

"For a town this size," said Doc.

"I can't wait," I said.

"Look at all these people," said Sandy.

"I know, right?"

"Relax, DK, you might have a good time."

People spend so much effort, time, and money trying to have a good time. I've never understood it.

The theme was Salute to the Arts, and after a ragtag squad of old soldiers in bits and pieces of vintage uniforms carried the flag to open the parade, the Grand Marshall, a watercolorist wearing too much makeup, rode in an open 1955 Cadillac. She waved to the crowd with the talented hand that had five times won the Jerky Festival poster contest.

Mayor Hirkill and the town council followed in other classic convertibles, and after them came the Boy Scouts, a surly looking troop of miniature thugs, and the Girl Scouts, tarts in training. (I had more than a twinge of regret that I hadn't said yes immediately to that Girl Scout idea.) Came then the Rotarians, some Hispanic horsemen twirling lariats, yoga schools, karate dojos, and plumbers in their trucks. Anyone with a van and a logo was in the parade: electricians, pest control, and cable TV, frozen yogurt shops and hamburger joints, and of course one distillery after another and artisan jerky curers throwing samples to children who risked falling under truck wheels to get them. Two big favorites were a pack of dachshunds called Weiner Wonders and someone in a chicken cos-tume. It was staged to look like the little dogs were chasing the giant chicken, though all the poor dogs wanted was to get out of the heat and lie down. (Dogs are innately smarter than their masters.) Came then unsteadily an Uncle Sam stilt walker and Mayor Hirkill, again, this time on foot and carrying his campaign sign promoting his own reelection, looking like William Burroughs on a bad day. (I've read a couple biographies. I don't believe Burroughs ever had a *good* day.)

"Didn't we already see him?" I asked.

"He always jumps out of the car near the end of the parade and cuts across the park so he can make a campaign loop," said Sandy.

"He does it every year," said Doc, "whether there's an election or not. He's the village idiot the village has to take seriously."

A man with a garbage can on wheels and a wide shovel scooped up horse droppings and received a major ovation. More classic cars. Kids on unicycles. I kept waiting for a marching band but none arrived. Instead there were more floats extolling collectively and individually the art of distilling gin and curing meats. Besides the Grand Marshall watercolorist, this was the only other art being saluted. Came then, at long last, the fire trucks that marked the end of the cherished parade.

By that time, I was on my third or fourth cocktail and raising my voice with the others, declaring it the best darn parade yet and how life didn't get any better than this. (I shuddered to realize that might be true.)

We sat under the canopy for another half hour or so, waiting for the crowd to thin out. Terry fell asleep in his chair, a thin line of drool lazily leaving the corner of his mouth. Doc nodded off, too.

"You put in a lot of work to set this up," I said to Sandy. "Thanks."

"Oh, it's not that hard, I got it pretty well down. I do it every year. The boys seem to enjoy it."

"I admire you."

"Me? Why?"

"For not coming apart, I guess."

"Well, I admire you, too."

She put up her hand for a high five, and I delivered. I can count on that same hand how many times I've ever done that.

"But I *have* come apart," I confessed.

Her nervous laugh was on the edge of hysteria. "Oh, get over yourself, mister, you'll be fine."

"When?"

"If, not when."

"If what?"

"If you become *of* the town instead of just *in* it."

"Shoot me then. Shoot me now."

"You're gonna come to love this town, betcha anything."

"I already have a bet down that I won't."

I guess we were having a good time. I might have smiled.

She put her hand on mine and said, "What's your wife's name again?"

"Hope." I liked the comforting touch of her hand. It had been six months, more or less.

"Don't think I haven't come close to pulling a Hope." She patted my hand. "I've often thought how wonderful it would be to go off and not care about anything anymore. I would set things up so that Doc would have everything he needed. Everything except me, which I would reclaim for myself. But there is that promise, not the one I made to him but one I made to myself."

"And what was that?"

"I promised myself I would be the one person who never let him down."

"If Hope made that kind of promise, she's broken it."

"Not yet. She said she'd come back. She'll show up."

"How would you leave? If you left."

"I'm not leaving ever. That's all fantasy. I've got it pretty cool here."

"I would take care of Doc, if you did."

"Really? I could save two birds with one stone."

"Whoa. That's like a koan," I said. She giggled in her ragged way.

Whoever brought Terry to the parade failed to return and take him back, which upset Sandy.

"A little irresponsible, if you ask me," she said. "Forgetting a person isn't like forgetting a bag of groceries in the parking lot of the supermarket."

"I've done that."

"Who hasn't? But have you ever left a disabled person in the park?"

She and I took down the canopy and packed up the picnic. She asked me to load up the gear and take Doc home while she tended to Terry. Before I was clear on what was expected of me she was wheeling Terry, still fast asleep, across Spanish Circle.

I walked the three blocks to find their pickup, then returned to load up. By that time Doc was half awake, looking like the parade had passed him by, which it had. A generous drink was left in the pitcher. We divided it evenly and drank up.

"Where's Sandy?"

"Taking Terry home. Somebody was irresponsible. I'm going to drive you home. Ready for that?"

I hadn't been behind the wheel of a car since I left LA. We inched along in traffic on the roundabout, stopping every twenty feet to avoid running into dazed pedestrians jaywalking.

Doc lived on Minos, SE, on the edge of town in an area known as Bonny Falls, behind what used to be his animal hospital, now leased to a younger vet. Once away from the Circle we were able to move along at a brisk twenty miles per hour. I was careful, intent on the road before me. Doc Fleck unleashed a torrent of bad language. I glanced to my side and saw the object of his anger was his own cell phone.

"Slice of heaven but you can't even make a fucking phone call. AT&T wants to put up a cell tower, but Hirkill and the rest of them assholes won't let 'em. You ever see one? You can't tell what it is.

It could be a tree. But, noooo, it's a quality of life issue. Aesthetics. Magnetic forces. Property values. Assholes."

I took my own phone out of my pocket and passed it to him.

"Fuck, yours doesn't work either."

"Who are you trying to call?"

If he knew, he'd forgotten. He stared ahead for a few moments and then said, "Taxi?"

"You don't need a taxi, Doc. We're in your truck."

"Where're we going?"

"Taking you home."

"Where's Sandy?"

"Had to take Terry home."

"Poor Terry. As fucked up as me. More."

"How'd that happen, Doc? To Terry? Doc?"

"Turn next right. There's my place."

www.dark-chronicle.co.uk/az/turel.php

Doc walked into his house, one arm over my shoulders as I gripped his hand so he wouldn't slide off. I settled him and went back and unloaded his wheelchair. A strong wind was pelting me with heavy dust. I ran inside to get away from it and was worn out by the effort. Doc asked me to pull in his shutters. We could still hear the wind, which always puts me on edge. It wasn't easy getting Doc into bed. I thought Sandy was too small to have to do all this, and too young to spend her time this way. Doc fell asleep, the terrier at his side. I was able to catch a nap myself on his sofa. When I woke up, I saw Sandy half-reclined in the easy chair, her feet up.

"I fell asleep," I said.

"That's going around."

"The sun, gin fizzes, overstimulation."

"No explanation necessary."

She gave me some water, a couple aspirins, and then some coffee. The wind was still blowing.

"Is it always so windy out here?"

"Always."

"How did you get home?"

"I caught a ride."

"How do I get home?"

At six, inside the animal hospital, the vet's assistant puts the pets into their crates where they stay until six the next morning. Sandy told me I could get a ride with him.

"Did you like our little parade?" she asked.

"More than I thought I would, considering there wasn't much about it that reminded me of an actual parade. The horses, I guess."

"Maragate is not an easy place to get used to. You're still adjusting. Some people never do. But you really should make an effort, or at least don't fight it."

"What about Doc, has he adjusted?"

"Not really."

"You?"

"As you see."

"Is Doc happy?"

"Kinda like you."

"Sorry to hear it. You weren't born in Maragate, were you?"

"Nobody was born in Maragate. I came from a place you never heard about."

"I never heard of *this* place. What brought you here?"

"Sex, drugs, and rock 'n roll." I laughed, a good feeling. I remembered it from before. "No, really," she said.

"I thought you were a librarian or something."

"I've changed, which is the whole idea. But never enough. I'm here for you, if you need to sort it out. When you need to."

In the past, I accepted the friends Hope made as my friends too, but I seldom had that feeling of affection, like I had for Sandy and

Doc, friends I had made on my own. I wondered if I could confide in her. At least she made the offer, more than most people would do.

"I don't tell everybody all that," she said.

"All what?"

She smiled. "Which is easy because people in Maragate tend to withhold. It's part of their nature. They tell you only what they think you should know, not a bit more. And they might think you shouldn't know a damn thing."

"Charming. LA is the opposite. Everybody tells you everything, even things you don't want to know."

"You'll get used to the change."

"My head's been spinning since I got here."

"The gin is designed to keep it spinning."

"I don't even like the stuff. Beach plum gin? I mean, c'mon, farm-to-bar organic gin?"

At six o'clock, I had to go home. Maybe I could write, if the fireworks weren't too bad.

"Sandy, I asked Doc how it happened. He said he fell."

"Yeah, he won't talk about it."

"Like you said. Withholding."

"Like I said."

"When someone lies about an injury, he's either ashamed or afraid."

(That wasn't anything I'd ever thought about before, but it seemed true.)

"Or he doesn't want to relive it," she said. "There's nothing he can do about it, why talk about it? He's put it behind him."

"Has he?"

Her head came up. I had opened the gate to a restricted space.

"What's he been saying?"

"Nothing. The Maragate trait."

"He came from Philadelphia. He'll tell you. Nobody's shutting you out."

The vet's assistant knocked on the door and called out that

he was leaving. I said good night to Sandy and we embraced for a moment.

An embrace can do wonders, can't it? Comfort, heal, calm. I wasn't raised all huggy, so I never got into the practice, except with Hope because I loved her. Before Sandy, I don't think I ever hugged anyone I didn't love a little. Hope, and before her Mary Ellen in high school, the smell of talc on her shoulders, and Anita, my university professor of Grammatical Analysis.

elalp.cbalwiki.ets.org

I found Carlos in one of his snits. I wondered when if ever I would step into that house and not feel despair. Waiting for Hope was like waiting for Quinn the Eskimo. (Or Godot. Or Lefty.)

"Good evening, señor."

"And to you, trusted servant."

"Did you enjoy the parade, señor?" he asked, in his most supercilious way.

"The Ramos Fizzes helped."

"Oh, we had Ramos Fizzes, did we?"

"Yes, we did, which is why I am so cheerful now." (I wasn't all that cheerful.)

"*Que bueno*, because that will be short-lived."

"What now? Locusts?"

"The parade has been over for hours."

"So?"

I headed for the powder room.

"Where were you all that time?" Carlos asked through the door.

I hate having to talk to someone through a bathroom door, especially when I am attending to a bodily need.

"I beg your pardon? Since when do I have to tell you?"

"The señora called and she was very upset."

"She called! Hope called!" In my excitement, I sprayed the wall. I was thrilled and at the same time bereft I had missed the call. I cannot describe my state of mind on hearing this long-awaited news. "She called here?" She lives! She's coming to get me! Everybody's gonna jump for joy!

"Yes, after she tried to get you on your cell phone."

"There's no reception! There's never any reception." I washed my hands and came out. "Goddammit! That's the call I've been waiting for, dreaming of. Son of a bitch! What did she say?"

"I told her that I did not know your whereabouts. She was quite cross."

(Who says *cross* anymore?)

"She expected you to know where I was?"

"No, señor, she expected you to *tell* me where you would be. She was not upset with me, but with you."

"With me? Pissed at me? What did she expect, that I would always be available?"

"Yes, and isn't that the definition of true love?"

I wanted to strangle him.

"But what did she *say*? Did she say when she'd be back? Did she leave a number?" As I spoke, I was calling her. No room was left for me to squeeze into her voicemail box. "What did she say, goddammit!"

"If you will please calm down, I will tell you. Hysteria will not help the situation."

I did my best.

"Okay, okay. Now tell me what she said, exactly."

"*Mejor. Gracias.* It seems she is not in a position to call at any particular point in time."

"What does that mean? And don't interpret, tell me her exact words."

"Her words were, 'I'm not in a position to call at any particular time.'"

"What the hell does that mean?"

"I don't understand the confusion."

"*Why* was she in that position? Or not in that position?"

"She did not say. She did say that she will call back."

"When?"

"At first opportunity."

"What does that *mean*? It sounds like she's being held hostage."

"Oh, I'm sure that is not the case. It is possible she is likewise somewhere where reception is suboptimal, for reasons different than here, where we reject eyesores and intrusions on our privacy. Not for us. She is hiking perhaps. Camping, possibly. At sea. On a retreat. The important thing, I should think, is that she sounded fine. Her only stress was in failing to find you."

"She was stressed?"

"As I say."

"What did *you* say?"

"I said that you went to the parade, or at least in that direction, that you don't like parades or fireworks or any of the other things that most people enjoy, and I haven't seen or heard from you since. That is what I told her because that is the truth."

"Goddammit, that makes it sound like *I* disappeared."

"Well, during the period in question I suppose you did. I still have no idea."

"Where is it written that you have to know everything I do and everywhere I go?"

"It would be helpful for the next time the señora calls."

"Tell me what else she said?"

"She asked how I was?"

"How *you* were?"

"Polite conversation. You might try it sometime. She also asked how you were doing."

"Well, wonderful, I'm grateful she asked about me. What did you say?"

"I said you were adjusting, but slowly."

"Adjusting! I am fucking sick of hearing about adjusting."

"Do you kiss the señora with that mouth? I could not say you were thriving."

"And why 'slowly'?"

"It has been months. The unfortunates living on the streets have adjusted to homelessness in less time, and here you are, in a beautiful home, all things taken care of, in a little slice of heaven."

"Stop it! Don't ever say that again! I'm sick of hearing that."

I wanted to smack him but at the moment he was my sole link to the woman I loved, the only person in the world I did love, or who loved me.

"What else?"

"That was the sum and substance. The call was brief."

He folded a light jacket and put it on top of the picnic basket and headed for the door.

"Where are you going?"

"To the fireworks, of course. Since you refuse to join in on the festivities, I am taking your advice and going myself. I am giving myself a night off."

"Was that all of it? That's all she said?"

"She seemed in a hurry. As I am now, señor. Fireworks."

With that he was gone, and I was alone in the house for the first time. It was at last silent, except for the creaks overhead, the knocks below, the hums within, the house sounds for which you have no explanation. Flexing. Contracting.

I hoped Carlos would never come back. I wanted a bottle rocket to land on his head.

Could she have gone to Esalen, or someplace like that, a bucolic retreat? We had been there together a few times. It was a beautiful place to get away, perched on a cliff overlooking the Pacific. Clothing was optional, but we had good bodies then and did not mind displaying them. (Though the Esalen philosophy was that all bodies are beautiful, my own observation was that some are treats to the eyes and others not so much, and at some point in life one should try to recognize the difference.) Back then I enjoyed the freedom of walking around the lush setting naked and soaking in the hot springs. The last time we were there we spent five days. I took a gestalt workshop to work out some problems not in my own life but in the life of one of my characters. (The others in the workshop were moved to tears by my coming face to face with the troubles I devised for my character, so I knew I was on the right track. It was like previewing.) Hope took ecstatic dancing, a better choice. Afterward, I was spent and thought that a stay of five days in intense gestalt therapy was overkill. She had had a much better time and felt rejuvenated. She said she would love to spend a whole summer there, with no television or phones.

Esalen had an office, and a landline. I went to my own land-line to call. I got the number and put in a call, but it was after hours on the Fourth of July. I stood on the disgusting carpet I would like to burn and told myself I should calm down and call again the next day. What if she is using an alias? Why would she, though? Ordinary people don't use aliases. They have credit cards they must use at places they visit. Another thought occurred to me, late, I admit, because I was still feeling the effects of drinking all during the parade. I punched in star-sixty-nine to get the last number call-ing in. I assumed she called on the landline, not to Carlos's cell phone. Nothing. Not Hope, not Lieutenant Conventerra. The phone's memory had been cleared. Suffer.

I hurried out of the house. I didn't bother to lock the door behind me. Burglars, have at it. Arsonists? Please. I walked to Spanish Circle and joined the throngs moving across the park and toward the soccer field. The Hope I knew would have sent a clear message with concrete information. At the very least, she would have said that she loved me, and maybe she did. Carlos was an unreliable messenger.

The field was covered with blankets. People lolled about eating jerky and drinking gin, waiting for the first blast. I moved along the periphery to the restriction line, where a firetruck was at the ready and some cops were posted to keep kids from getting too close. I caught sight of Lieutenant Conventerra, leaning against the cinderblock restrooms. Did he have an affinity for public restrooms or were they known crime scenes? He was smoking an e-cigarette.

I backed away, but he caught sight of me. I didn't care for the man, nor did I have any real reason to talk to him, but I approached him anyway because I did not want to appear rude.

"Lieutenant Conventerra."

"Doctor."

He said it in the way you might say, not a doctor.

"Glad to see you out with the people," he said, "enjoying a fine old tradition."

"I could say the same about you, but you're probably on duty. This outhouse looks suspicious."

"I'm always on duty, but this is just a good place to watch the fun. Here, there's room for you."

I stood next to him and said, "I heard from my wife."

"Oh?"

"You told me you wanted to know."

"Where is she?"

"She didn't say."

"How did you hear from her?"

"By phone."

"And she wouldn't tell you her location?"

"She talked to Carlos. She couldn't reach me directly because cell service in Maragate sucks."

"Carlos?"

"My houseman, my caretaker, my chief cook and bottle washer. You know Carlos."

"I don't think so."

"You talked to him on the phone. My phone. My landline."

"What number is that?" Of course I didn't know. "A world of things you don't seem to know," he said.

The first midair explosion cracked the night and almost knocked me off my feet.

"Son of a bitch! Why does this still exist? Why would anyone still want to see fireworks?"

"You're here."

"I was looking for you."

Which wasn't true. I was looking for Carlos. I wasn't done with him.

Conventerra looked to the explosion in the sky and said, "Chrysanthemum. Nice. And why were you looking for me?"

"To tell you this and ask why you called my house and spoke to Carlos."

"You should ask Carlos. He could tell us both."

I knew I should, but Carlos was a liar and a manipulator, and I didn't want to have to point that out and continue living under the same decomposing roof. He probably lied about Hope calling. But why would he? Control? Messing with my head?

The music accompanying the fireworks was Katy Perry's "Firework." (Why not?)

I checked my cell for recent calls. The last one was from my agent, when he told me about the Girl Scout job. I must have sighed.

"No love?" asked the cop.

"I was checking for recent calls. If you miss a call, if it doesn't go through, does it appear under Recents?"

"I don't have that kind of phone."

He looked up and said, "Crossette." A star splattering against the sky in four different directions. We talked between artillery blasts.

"Anyhow, you can call Carlos again and ask him about the conversation he had with my wife."

"I'll take your word for it."

"Wow, we're making progress."

"How are you adjusting to life here?"

"Why do people keep asking me that? It's driving me crazy."

"Are you able to write your little movie stories and everything like that?"

A shrill nerve-wracking, drawn out whistle had some veterans covering their heads with blankets.

"God! Who pays for this stupid display?"

"All donations. Not a cent of taxpayer's money. People love fireworks." Still looking up he added, "Horsetail. Beaut."

"Not all people. Not everywhere."

"We like a good time here. I heard you're writing a new movie."

"Who told you that?"

"You've been seen working on it, at the library, the tasting rooms, Hamburger Benny."

"Someone reported that to you?"

"I heard it's all about Maragate."

"Trust me, this is the last place in the world I would want to write about."

"You're like a lurker, you are, or a troll. I can't remember the difference. You stand outside, watching, never mixing in."

An unkind characterization, but I was unable to object.

"You look at people, in their town and customs, chance occurrences and the weather and you massage everything into a story meant to titillate and distract Diet Coke-for-brains from their shit lives."

"Don't buy a ticket."

"I heard you're making fun of the town. You made it an abandoned outpost run by a one-armed cop. Would that be me? What would be the symbolism of that one arm?" Looking up: "Willow."

Anyone reading over my shoulder in public places where I wrote could not come away with an accurate description of what I was doing. The only other person with any knowledge of my script was Doc Fleck. And probably Carlos. Carlos seemed to have knowledge of everything. Neither would know details.

"Who *does* run this town? If not you. Mayor Hirkill?"

"You make a movie about Maragate and make fun of it, you'll be the fool. Everybody wants to come here. Everybody loves it here."

"I would never write about Maragate. Nobody would believe it."

"I'm all about freedom of speech, express yourself, etcetera. But don't be dumb. These are real people here. Don't turn them into something they wouldn't recognize."

"Then why would it matter?"

Crackling bolts of light tore across the sky. I turned and walked away. His flat voice: "Kamuro."

I found Carlos in the center of a sea of blankets and camp chairs. He was sitting with Mayor Hirkill, who was face deep into one of Carlos's tortas. I stepped over and on blankets and between the littered drunks to get to him. I had to contort my steps and at one point almost fell, saved by two obese women who caught me, one at the shoulders and one at my butt. They thought it was hysterical. I changed my plans and looked for the shortest route away from the mob and the infernal display of useless explosions.

www.esalen.org

Now, with your forbearance, I will tell you about my wedding anniversary and an episode of which I am not proud, but an episode that confirms, if you still have any doubt, that I was a prisoner.

I celebrated alone with a dinner of fish 'n chips, after a couple gin 'n tonics, sitting at the bar of Square on the Circle. (We were married one hot August evening at Jack Lemmon's house by Thomas Bradley, mayor of Los Angeles.) I had taken to having my dinner there two nights a week, alone at the bar, Tuesdays and Fridays usually, to get away from Carlos and to play the lottery. (Should I win, I intended to hire a stretch, charter a jet, and fly to Paris with no more than bad memories and the clothes on my back. Without Hope, I would be miserable, but I was already miserable. I'd rather be miserable in Paris.) Our anniversary that year fell on a Saturday, always risky at the Square on the Circle because of the Yeow Girls.

The bar was L-shaped. I preferred sitting at the short section, the big window with a view of Spanish Circle at my back. I was enjoying my fish 'n chips along with a pint of Pliny the Elder when I heard a few of the regulars guffaw and shout insults to someone at the window behind me. When I turned, I saw Mayor Hirkill. His face was pressed against the window, his hands cupped around his eyes. He peered inside like an orphan left out in the cold. He saw me, too, I was sure, before he went his way.

I learned from the regulars that this was a common occurrence, the mayor showing up at the window and peering inside. He could not come inside himself because he had long ago been eighty-sixed for life by the owner-bartender, a tough little nut named McGraw. I found this fascinating and asked what a man had to do to be eighty-sixed for life. (I wasn't even sure what eighty-sixed meant.) The mayor, it seemed, was at one time a regular at the bar, cadging drinks from tourists by regaling them with stories of his life at sea. He claimed to have been a captain in the US Navy, in command of a mighty warship, the USS *Begonia*.

The regulars knew he was full of shit and seldom engaged him for longer than a moment, mostly to complain about poor cell phone reception and noisy leaf blowers. It did not take all that long for tourists to grow tired of him as well.

"And that's what got him eighty-sixed?" I asked. (I came to love the expression. I wished that I could eighty-six somebody, that I had a place from which I could eighty-six people who offended the social order.)

"No, I could put up with that," said McGraw. "Let's say it was inappropriate behavior."

Maragate was a favorite destination for young sturdy-legged blondes in short skirts to throw a bachelorette party for one of their own about to step up to matrimony. This usually occurred on a Saturday afternoon or evening, at which time the regulars, men over fifty-five, would go home because they couldn't handle the trilling, followed by the weeping, concluding in the foul language and the fighting. As McGraw told me, "It can get ugly, but they spend well."

Hirkill, back when he was allowed, looked forward to the arrival of what they called the Yeow Girls, which led to his never being permitted entry again.

"He's an influential man," I said. "Aren't you worried he'll find some way to make trouble for you?"

"No, he loves the place. Once a week he begs me to be let back in, but I tell him never, not ever. He's convinced he can turn me around."

No Yeow Girls were in attendance that night, so I did not have the opportunity to observe the sort of behavior for which they were feared. I lingered after dinner, drinking the local version of a Pimm's Cup cocktail, garnished with a small triangle of bison jerky. I spent the moment reliving in my mind the happiest day of my life, the day I married Hope. Later, I played dice poker with some of the regulars for drinks. I had beginner's luck and told McGraw to reserve my last drink for next time or I would not be able to walk home. I was melancholy when I left but not defeated, having won at dice, engaged in friendly conversation, and avoided being eighty-sixed.

The shops on the Circle were closed. Maragate shuts down early, except for gin rooms and restaurants. (And The Lyric, a vintage movie theater. Oh, if only they showed vintage films. The Lyric ran animated features and nothing else. I asked the manager why. "People go to the movies to escape," he told me. I've heard this theory many times, mostly from producers trying to get me to write schlock.) I walked home by the light of a full moon, swatting bloodthirsty mosquitos. I passed First Street and looked to see if any lights were on in Valene's house. I had no intention of trying to persuade her again, but I hoped that she might have a change of heart or an attack of conscience, if she had either to work with. It seemed to matter less as time went on. If no one else cared, why should I?

When I turned down Second Street I noticed a battered pickup truck parked in front of my house. At first I thought it was Doc's and

I worried that something might have happened to him and Sandy needed my help. That sobered me up somewhat and quickened my step. It wasn't Doc's truck, though. He had a Ford. This one was a Toyota, the vehicle of choice for radical Islamic terrorists.

The outside light in my front yard was off, which struck me as strange. It was a photocell light and came on when darkness fell and stayed on all night. I stopped and backed up a few steps, taking cover behind a blue weeping juniper bush, a foreboding shrub I had to look at whenever I left the house. I saw movement in the shadows and then in the light of the moon, Carlos and Hirkill carrying the rolled-up Las Vegas carpet that had been covering the linoleum in my living room, tied in the middle by a long white extension cord. I understood then why Hirkill had been peering into the window of the Square on the Circle that particular night. He wanted to make sure the coast was clear.

What do you think of when you see two men carrying a rolled-up carpet? That there is a body inside, of course. Everyone does. We have all seen countless movies and television shows during which such a scene was played. (None that I ever wrote.) In fact, the scene has been played so often dramatically that the only way to use it now is to play it for laughs. Watching these two small men, a Mexican built like a fireplug and a wiry politician in an oversized secondhand suit and fedora, struggling under the weight of a carpet that I would otherwise be happy to be rid of had the makings of a comedy, but I did not laugh.

The thought that my wife's body might be inside that rolled up carpet may have been irrational, but inescapable.

Carlos and Hirkill lifted the carpet into the bed of the truck and dropped it. Some of it hung out over the tailgate. They stopped to catch their breath. I dialed 911 and put the phone close to my lips so that I might whisper my call for help without being heard by the two criminals across the street. Of course, the call failed to go through and they drove away.

Nothing appeared amiss inside the house. If anything, the hovel was improved by the absence of that sick carpet. Still, I felt violated knowing that Hirkill had been inside my home.

I have to make note and assure you that I am an advocate of privacy, mine and others. I was never on Facebook, LinkedIn, or Twitter, and I didn't even know of the existence of other similar apps, though I am sure there must be many. To me, one of the greatest transgressions one person can commit against another is to read his mail. That's to give you some idea of how difficult it was for me to decide to search the "casita." I tried the door, half hoping it would be locked. It wasn't.

The casita was no more than an ordinary guest room, and not even much of that. More like a monk's cell. Cheerless. A small bed, a desk hardly big enough for a computer, if there were to be one, which there was not. A chest of three drawers containing socks and underwear and folded shirts. A closet smaller than a phone booth— remember those?—stored nothing more than a change of clothes and shoes. A bathroom slightly larger than the closet housed a set of towels and the usual toiletries. It was hard to believe that a man could live with so little. I went back to the desk, which had a locked drawer. The walls were painted a pleasant blue. I saw nothing in the way of decoration with the exception of one small framed print of eight-by-five inches depicting some poor soul tormented by birds of prey. I looked at it more closely. The light in the casita was as dim as the light throughout the rest of the house, but I could see that the miniature painting was not a print but an original, in oils. It was reminiscent of a Goya. It had that sensibility. It was a good reproduction or homage, probably by some Oaxacan imitator.

And so begins the episode.

www.reviewjournal.com/knowing-vegas-match-the-carpet

I sat in a dark corner of the living room and waited for Carlos to return. I was in a proper snit, this time our roles reversed. (The first snit in which I've ever been.) I did not turn on the outside light or any other. As I waited, I thought about how many times I had seen this scene in movies and television. (None that I would ever have written.) Someone comes home, turns on the light, and is startled to see a man sitting in his chair, maybe drinking his whiskey, having a cigarette. It's a staple of film noir. "Who are you?" asks the someone surprised, if he doesn't know him, or if he does, "How did you get in here?" The intruder waves off the question as nonsense—he can get into any place he wants to. None of this should apply in the scenario I was setting, and yet it did.

Carlos was startled when he opened the door and turned on the light. "What are you doing here, señor?"

"I live here." (A painful thing to admit.)

"Are you *un poco borracho*, señor?"

"Beside the point. Sit down, Carlos. We have to talk."

Two badly reupholstered chairs were arranged behind the sofa. I don't know why. I sat in one and upon my order Carlos sat in the other. If he were at all concerned, he did not show it.

"It occurs to me I don't know much about you."

That is when I learned he was Peruvian, not Mexican.

"Are you illegal?" I asked.

"That is such an unkind word."

"Is it? It's accurate, though. Immigration is either legal or illegal. There is no gray area."

"And you call yourself a poet," he said, which stung. (At one time, I did call myself a poet, and not only to get girls, which never worked for me anyway, though Shelley, Byron, and Keats had to beat them off with sticks.) "I am a refugee."

"From what?"

"From the things that try men's souls."

"Like what, for example."

"From paranoia." (He was killing me.) "Language is important. We are all guilty of using at times the easier word. Immigrants are not illegal, they are either documented or undocumented, and who doesn't hate official papers? In my case, however, I do have the proper documents, señor."

"At some point, I may need to see them."

"At that point, I will be obliged to show them to you."

"Do you have a family?"

"At one time, I did, like most people. Now, it is only me."

"What are your plans for the future?"

"I live in the now, señor."

"But where do you see yourself five years from now?" I asked, like someone from HR doing a quarterly evaluation.

"I see myself here, having a conversation with you that is more pleasant than this one."

Where did I see myself five years hence? Dead, would be one possibility. Another? What he said. Which brought on a shudder.

These preliminaries were meant to impress upon Carlos that we were at a serious juncture. He either did not notice or did not care.

"Would you like a cup of coffee, señor?"

His offer disarmed me. Lately, his attitude and my suspicions had put a wall between us. (A higher wall.) We would never be friends, but at least we could be cordial.

"Yes, please."

He went to the kitchen where we have one of those instant-hot attachments to the faucet, perhaps the only amenity in the joint, so with his French press the coffee took no more than a few minutes. He poured a cup for me, and I asked him to pour a cup for himself. In six months under the same roof, we had never had a cup of coffee together.

"Señor, I can see that you have more on your mind that my place of birth, my familial history, and my legal status." He came back with two cups and gave me one. "Please, tell me what it is."

I saw him trying to take control of my interview, which I would not allow. I learned that from the cops. (Even though I had pretty much lost control when I accepted his offer of coffee and then invited him to have one with me and sit down together like pals.)

"In a moment," I said. I sipped the coffee, and that quickly it *was* the moment. "Let's start with the telephone."

"The telephone?"

"The landline. You told me no one ever calls, but somebody did call."

"Who, señor?"

"You damn well know who? Lieutenant Conventerra."

"I know of no such person."

"Well, he knows of you because he called you on that very phone." I pointed to it on the floor, next to the sofa.

"When?"

"I don't know."

"Why?"

"I don't know that either."

"Please, remain calm, señor. If someone called, this lieutenant you speak of—this soldier or sailor—it is possible that the señora took the call." I hadn't thought of that. I assumed Conventerra had called to check up on me with his confidential informant. "He might even have been calling you, señor, at a time when no one was here to answer the call."

"You're always here."

"Not always. Not twenty-four seven, as they say. I do the marketing. I shower twice a day. And you must have noticed tonight, sometime before I opened the door, that I was not here." (All of what he said was reasonable and made me appear paranoid.)

"Lieutenant Conventerra is with the Maragate police."

"Ah, then that explains it. You did have an encounter with the police, did you not?"

He suppressed a giggle. I got up and kicked a magazine rack I had never seen before. Copies of *Us* went flying. ("Celebrities: They're Just Like Us!")

"You are overwrought over nothing, señor."

"Oh, I'm overwrought, all right, over *something*. And stop calling me *señor*, for shit's sake."

(I imagined myself for a moment as the protagonist in one of my own movies. What would the audience think during this long scene? *The guy's turning into a dick.* It gets worse.)

"Very well, but I honestly have no idea what you are so upset about."

"Listen to me. Jaime the gardener never saw Hope. Your description of her was a little sketchy."

"But I—"

"Hold on. I'm talking. She left me a typewritten note. The real estate agent did not recognize her picture, I don't think."

"Real estate agent?"

"And I have doubts she ever tried to call me and got you instead, on the Fourth of July. I think you've been telling me lies from the first night I arrived."

Now it was his turn to sip his coffee, and he took longer at it than I did. The face of confusion he showed me a moment before had now changed to something like pity.

"Doctor, why would I do that? You are here in the house that your wife bought for you, for you to start a new life. I know it has been difficult. I realize that you resent me and yet need me at the same time. It puts you in an uncomfortable position. I am no more or less than a humble servant. You are imagining a plot that is not possible and has no reason. Someday the señora will return and it will all make sense. I will make a gentleman's bet with you that you will come to love your new hometown."

All over Maragate people were making book that I would fall in love with the shithole.

"I don't even know if my wife is alive," I said. "For all I know, somebody rolled her up in that carpet and . . ." I did a bit, a double take, looking for the carpet. (You've seen it in a hundred movies, mostly comedies. None that I would have written, though I maintain that I can be funny.) If I could catch him in one lie, I would catch him in all his lies. "And where is that carpet, by the way?"

"Are you just now noticing it is gone, or are you doing, as they call it in your business, a bit?"

"Please tell me where it is."

"I got rid of it after all your complaints, even though the señora thought you would be amused by it. I disposed of it and you will never have to see it again. I hope that will make you happy."

"And how did you do that?"

"I gave it to an acquaintance who had need of one that size. He was happy to get it and I thought you would be happy to see it gone."

"Who is this acquaintance?"

"He is the mayor of Maragate, as a matter of fact, and I met him at the Fourth of July fireworks display. He admired my picnic basket, so I invited him to share it with me, the picnic I had prepared for you, which you rudely rejected. He loved it and thanked me profusely. Later in our conversation he mentioned his need for a carpet. I told him I might have the solution."

"And it took you another month, without asking me?"

"I forgot about the conversation, until he showed up tonight with a pickup truck he had borrowed from his landlord. You weren't here, but since you hated the carpet I was sure you wouldn't mind. So we loaded it into the truck and installed it in his quarters."

"How did he know where you lived?"

"I must have mentioned it."

"Did you mention me as well?"

"Very likely. We are a part of each other's lives, like it or not."

"Why did you turn off the outside light?

"Did I?"

"Yes. I was across the street."

"Spying on me?"

"Happening to see you."

"But the outside light is on."

"Now it is."

"And always was, Doctor. It is automatic."

What was the point of going any further? I would become only more frustrated with him.

"You are eighty-sixed, sir," I declared. "Effective immediately."

(I did enjoy saying it. I've grown to enjoy the modern custom of using nouns as verbs, as in, "He referenced Paragraph III, Item B." Most of all it was fun to use a number as a verb, as in "high-fiving.")

"Eighty-sixed? I don't understand."

"Eighty-sixed. I eighty-six you forever. You have to go now and never come back."

"And how does this translate from 'eighty-six,' Doctor?"

It was no fun if the other person didn't know what it meant, and I not able to define it any better.

"You're fired, okay? Pack up your things and leave."

"Oh, I couldn't possibly do that, señor."

www.urbandictionary.com/define.php?term=eighty-sixed

It was a Mexican standoff, so to speak. Carlos informed me that I could not fire him because I did not hire him. Though I had a longer reach, he was younger than I and had a lower center of gravity, so I had little chance of physically removing him from the house. Instead, I dialed 911, this time on the landline.

I whispered breathlessly, "There's an intruder in my house," and hung up. I sat down and silently finished my coffee, believing I was in control of the situation. Carlos went into the casita. I imagined him packing a bag, but he came out with a brown envelope and sat down. He held the envelope on his lap. The door to the casita was ajar.

"I must tell you something," I said, "and I include an apology, even though it is my house, after all. When I saw you were not here, I went into the casita."

"But you knew that I was not here. You saw me go with the mayor and the carpet."

"Yes, yes, but it is the one room in the house I have never seen and I was curious."

"Doctor, it may be your house, but it is my casita, and like you I value my privacy. If you had waited a few moments and asked me, I would have been happy to show you my quarters."

"We can let the police sort it out."

"As you wish."

The silence lay back upon itself. "And the silken, sad, uncertain rustling of each purple curtain/Thrilled me—filled me with fantastic terrors never felt before" (Edgar Allan Poe). The longer we waited, the closer I came to apologizing for my own paranoia. (Except that I am not paranoid.)

"I noticed a miniature oil painting," I said. He sat quietly and oozed contempt. "You can't miss it, so . . . I was there for no more than a minute."

"To appreciate a painting like that requires far more time than a minute. It is a world in a teacup. It can take a lifetime."

(Which is the way I feel about some poems.)

"It's an excellent imitation of a Goya."

"Because how could a lowly servant such as I come into the possession of an original Goya?"

"I wouldn't know. That's your business." Again, the silence, expanding from its own center. "An original would be worth a fortune."

He looked at me with contempt. We sat in that ballooning silence until two uniformed cops with guns drawn came to the door. I saw them through the window as they approached. It brought back memories of that terrible first night in town. I considered that they might bust in guns blazing so I called out, "Come on it, it's open. And nobody in here is armed."

They came in cautiously, looked at us both sitting there, and asked which one was the intruder.

I explained the situation, and shortly arrived Lieutenant Conventerra who said, pleased with himself, "When I saw the name and address on the call, I wasn't going to miss this. What's up?"

The cops had by then holstered their guns, and one of them told Conventerra, "Looks like a domestic dispute, Lieutenant."

"Hardly," I offered.

"This one is the owner, wants to fire that one who's the employee and get him out of the house, like now."

"You remember Carlos?" I said to Conventerra.

He looked at Carlos with no sign of recognition.

"Hold on," he said. "This is a domestic thing? Is that why an armed response was necessary?"

"It is not a domestic dispute. This man is in my house against my will. I want him put out. I did not ask for or expect an armed response."

"And what's your story?" he asked Carlos.

"My story is simple, sir. I have a contract." He took a few sheets from the envelope on his lap and handed them to Conventerra. "It is a lifetime contract, signed by the titled owner of the house, to manage all affairs of the house, financial and physical, and to man-age as best I can the welfare of the current occupant of the house, the distraught man you see before you, whether he likes it or not."

(I did not like it one bit.)

The lieutenant perused the papers. He showed the signature sheet to me. "That your wife's signature?"

"I don't know."

"You don't know?"

"Do you know your wife's signature?" I asked him.

"I'm not married, but I think I would."

"I can't be sure."

"It looks like a valid contract."

"I'm sure it does," I said. WTF? What was she thinking? Why would Hope give Carlos so much power? For life? His or mine. Or was the contract a forgery, like the Goya on his wall?

Conventerra sent the other two cops back to their patrol, telling them he would handle it. He took the few steps toward the kitchen and said, "Nice place." I thought he was being ironic. He flicked on the outside light and looked out to the backyard. "Nice big yard to relax in," he said, like a real estate agent working a new listing. I was nonplussed. The backyard was a vest pocket wasteland. Was it that my perception was pathologically compromised by demons or was everyone else dreaming?

"So tell me," said Conventerra, coming back into the living room, "what was the straw that broke the camel's back here?"

Since I did not respond, Carlos said, "A carpet that used to be right here, if you can believe it. He found it in poor taste. He told me repeatedly that he wanted it disposed of."

I resented his side of the story, because he was correct.

"I saw him and the mayor carry the carpet out of here and load it onto a truck," I said. "They were struggling with the weight. Something might have been rolled up inside of it. A body, maybe."

"Whose body?"

"I would expect you to find out."

"A body in a rolled up carpet? Like in the movies?" (See?)

"It could happen."

"Let me get the picture here. You witnessed your employee and the mayor carrying out a rolled-up carpet to a truck, and you're worried there might be a body in it?"

"They were struggling under the weight of it."

"Carlos," he said, turning toward him, "was there a body in that rolled up carpet?"

"No, sir, there was not."

Carlos told him the same story he told me, about meeting the mayor, who needed a carpet, and having the mayor show up with a truck.

"And you're sure that nobody was rolled up in the carpet?" the cop asked.

"Quite sure," replied Carlos, with a chuckle. "It is a big thick carpet. It was heavy and unwieldy, and neither the mayor nor I is what you might call a spring chicken. That is why we struggled with it."

"Okay, I want you two to go to neutral corners. I'm going to go to the mayor's place and get his side of the story."

"I want to come with you," I said.

"Not happening."

"He's seen my home, why shouldn't I see his?"

I hated the petulant sound of my own voice. Telling you the story now makes me feel beyond redemption. But no one is beyond redemption, not even the dick I'd turned into.

"You stay," Conventerra told me. "I'll be in touch. You want the carpet returned?"

"God, no," I said.

"You're happy Carlos got rid of it?"

"Well, okay, that part."

"Was anything else taken?" he asked Carlos.

"No, sir. Wait, yes, we wrapped the carpet with an extension cord, which the mayor promised to return. I told him we have a drawer full of them, but he insisted he would return it."

"So it's all about if a body went along with the carpet?"

As I mentioned before, in connection to movie scripts, the screenwriter should not answer what it's all about, so I didn't.

Conventerra left, looking far too amused.

Surprise! The mayor backed up Carlos's story.

Carlos and I continued to live under the same roof, staying out of each other's way, like an old dysfunctional couple, each afraid of what the other might be capable of doing. (I was capable of doing nothing. He, on the other hand, might possess the power to commit me.)

I was permitted to examine his contract. It described no circumstances under which he could be fired. None at all. It was what you might call ironclad. Suffer.

You will agree, I am sure, that even if you could not believe it before, you can no longer assume that I was not a prisoner, nor that Hope had nothing to do with it.

"And the whole earth would henceforth be/A wider prison unto me: No child—no sire—no kin had I,/No partner in my misery;/I thought of this, and I was glad,/For thought of her had made me mad." Byron, again.

https://answers.yahoo.com/question
/index?qid=20090412123647AAOblgc

The tree-tall African mule rider, Ham, sits outside while The Kid goes into the saloon and tries to get a room for the night. Bradley: "No rooms for niggers." The Kid politely informs Bradley that Ham is, in fact, an African with magical powers. Bradley doesn't care what powers he has. But when The Kid buys a round for the house with gold that he and Ham brought back from the mountains, Bradley abruptly changes his mind. Winky runs back to report to the Captain, who knows in his bones that this is the start of something bad. If they can keep Fiddler Jones away from this, they may yet avert mayhem.

I was working on my laptop at a table in Starbucks, relieved from the late August heat by their intermittent air-conditioning. My hovel had no central AC, just a window unit in my bedroom that worked only sometimes and gave off a foul odor. Starbucks coffee was over-roasted and bitter, but they had free Wi-Fi, mostly reliable, and I could back my chair against a wall to keep away curious eyes. Other screenwriters who had crashed and burned were able to come back with a good spec script, why not me? My western had been shopped, to be sure, but not yet to death. It was still evolving under my fingertips. As my first agent used to tell me after a rejection, it takes only one to say yes. Which was true in those days, but now it takes a village. For an executive at the studio level to cover her ass, she must say no until she can't anymore, when the project has attached to it an A-list director and a fail-safe cast. Even then she must build consensus. It is possible that my script was snakebit from the beginning by the invisible specter of political correctness. Even in the context of nineteenth-century Wyoming Territory, I should not allow Bradley to call Ham the N-word. Any euphemism, however, would be phony, and I don't roll that way. Equally as politically incorrect was the suggestion that Native Americans once scalped their enemies. It didn't help its commercial chances that the story, which takes place during one day, covers issues of race, gender, violence, gay rights, law, politics, and economics, either dramatizing how America got to be this way or revealing that it had always been this way. The movie was not, however, issue-driven, and the audience would not even take note of the issues until they gathered afterward for coffee and conversation. (Do people still do that?) All that aside, conventional wisdom dictated that I "open it up" or make it "a bigger canvas" or "lose the arias." I should not, would not, could not, but after all these years I didn't know what else to do with it. I faced the fact that I might never be able to return to my career, but one thing I could do, and no one could stop me: I could write a western. I grew up loving westerns and grew old working on one, and now that I had reached old age I wondered if working on it was all that was keeping me alive.

I used an application called Final Draft, which made life much easier for screenwriters. No more scissors or scotch tape, no more carbon paper and whiteout. Saved hours.

At that particular moment in Starbucks I was Googling Mayor Hirkill. (I tried to Google Maragate shortly after my disastrous arrival and got, "Did you mean Maritime Law, did you mean Marilyn Gately, did you mean marzipan," until I soon forgot what I meant.) When I entered Hirkill's name I got, "Did you mean major turtle?"

I bounced in my seat when I heard the ding of an email arriving, which usually I ignored because all my emails in the past were spam promising to enlarge my penis or sell me Viagra at ninety-nine cents a pop. (The last time I bought nine of them from Costco, forever ago, they were sixty dollars a pop and I still had four of them left.) The little window at the upper right corner of my screen that comes on with the ding showed Hope's email address. I held my breath and went to my inbox.

Subject line: Are you all right?

My Darling boy, I expected you would call or email me by now. I keep trying to call you but your voicemail box is always full. What's wrong? I'm not in a position where I can call at any time, but why wouldn't you be able to call me? Are you settled in? Don't you love it there! I know the house needs work but the possibilities are endless and as soon as I return we will start remodeling. I love you and miss you desperately. I'm making great progress and expect to come home a new person, and SOON! Please, please, please, get back to me and tell me how you're doing. If you're not there, I'll die. Sorry this is so short but I have to run. I love you. Forever, Hope.

I was encouraged by her words. They led me to believe no third party of either gender was involved. I saved my changes and quit Final Draft. I took a sip of what was now cold latte. A pressure on my chest sang out, go to the ER. Instead I clicked on Reply.

My dear sweetheart, what the fuck is going on? Settled in? I've been here for over five months. And, no, I don't love it. The house doesn't need remodeling, it needs to be burned down. The town is horrible. I have suffered abuse from the night of my arrival, which I will not go into here. I have been calling you and emailing you every day, until I gave up in total frustration. You did not mention that you somehow managed to get through to Carlos. You would think you could get through to me. And what's the story with Carlos? I don't trust him, and I don't like having him around, but at this point I have to depend on him while at the same time worrying that he will put me away. Apparently, you gave him the power to do that. Thanks to you, I'm a prisoner here. I know I was not the most attentive husband in the world, but what did I do to deserve this? I don't know where you are or what you are doing. I spend my days drinking gin and torturing myself with my western, which is now called, *After the Thaw*, BTW. You have to come back NOW, and let's find a way to reconnect and put this all behind us. I love you.

I proofread it, ignoring the syntax—it's email, after all (which also applies to this, so excuse me for any lapses)—and focused on its tone. Yes, it was angry, something she had long accused me of having as my default reaction to everything, which was not true. Who wouldn't be angry? She had to know that I loved her. Did I have to prove it every blessed day? If she was keeping score, how did she tally the last five months? Most importantly, we'd made contact. We could work through this. I'd like to say we've worked through worse, but nothing was ever this bad.

I hit Send and waited for the whoosh sound. And waited. And waited. A window finally came up telling me that my mail account was unable to connect with my server. Would I like to try another account or try later? I tried another account. Same message. I told it to try later. The email went into my Outbox and stayed there. (It is still there.)

I took my phone out of my pocket and, without much hope, thought I would try one more time to call her. It occurred to me then that I could send an email on my phone. My server could go fuck itself.

What happened next would crush even Tom Hanks. My phone would not accept my password. My password is 1976. It's always been 1976, from the first time I needed a password, and I use it for everything—though they say you're not supposed to do that—and it had always worked before. My phone, like a living thing (one *more* living thing), was rejecting me. Suffer.

I turned back to my laptop and signed on to an iPhone forum and searched to see if anyone had dealt with the issue of the phone rejecting a long-established password. No matches. I posted the question. That is, I went through the process of posting the question, but I could never find the question itself posted.

I looked around Starbucks at all the people drinking coffee, working on their own laptops, or amusing themselves with their tablets, or nose deep into their phones. They were mostly older people tentatively navigating the web with two fingers, but I caught sight of a millennial Asian kid in line to place an order, his head in a perpetual subservient bow to his lord and master. I cradled my own phone like a sick puppy and stood next to him.

"Excuse me, I wonder if you could help me with a phone problem."

He looked around as if to ask, why me, but he knew why. He was young and Asian, his burden in a hi-tech world.

"Yeah, all right."

I turned the screen to him and punched in my password.

"You forgot your password?"

"No, it's the right password."

I demonstrated again and again, as we inched forward toward the counter.

"That doesn't happen," he said. "Are you sure you're not confusing it with another password?"

He might have added, as older people are prone to do.

"I've had this phone for four years and it's always had the same password."

"Your phone's an antique. Maybe it died."

He wasn't trying to be funny. "Thanks anyway," I said.

"No, wait a minute." He placed his order for a caramel latte and paid for it via his phone, something I could never do, and why should I? He said his name was Keith. "What you have to do is plug it into your laptop. Go to iTunes and it'll recognize your phone and then you have to clear it entirely. You can set a new password but you'll have to rebuild your content."

"I don't have any content."

He looked at me in disbelief.

"Well, it might not work anyhow."

"What do I do then?"

"You're screwed."

I hurried back to my table, but of course I didn't have the cable for my phone. I rushed home and did as Keith instructed. It didn't work. I was screwed.

I used the landline to call Apple. I put a finger into my uncovered ear to block the noise from leaf blowers outside, and after half an hour of navigating an automatic menu I connected with a technician who stopped me in the middle of my question. He took my personal information and told me that my membership in AppleCare had unfortunately expired, long, long ago.

"I could not help overhearing," said Carlos from the kitchen. "Can I help?"

We barely spoke to each other those days. After my attempt to eighty-six him and his refusal to leave, I had to make peace with the devil, so to speak. The only control I had over him was dependent upon his willingness to play the role of servant. Two days after "the episode," I was publicly ridiculed in the pages of the *Maragate Herald*, in the police blotter section, everyone's favorite: "Maragate's Finest were summoned to investigate the theft of a large carpet from a West Side residence. The homeowner, an eyewitness to the caper, expressed his concerns that a body may have been inside the rolled-up carpet. Investigators found the purloined article but no cadaver was secreted within. The owner of said carpet not only refused to press charges but declined to accept the return of the evidence after it was brought to his attention that he, in fact, authorized the removal of the carpet because it did not match his decor."

Though no names were mentioned, everyone knew that I was the subject of the farce.

Yes, it made me the fool of the week. I could see Carlos's fine hand in my slander. I was suspicious of any help from him, but I couldn't keep this to myself. (My tragic flaw. Another one.)

"I had an email from the señora today."

"Bravo! Is she returning?"

"I don't know. I can't answer it and I can't make a call from my phone."

"I myself do not own a computer, so I have no idea—"

"Then why ask?" I snapped. "I can't send her an email because my server or something won't let me, and I can't call because my phone won't recognize my password. I'm screwed."

"I believe you can use somebody else's computer to send an email. And though you need a password to make a call, I do not believe you need one to answer a call, and how many calls have you made since you've been here, besides those unanswered by the señora?" (One, to my agent and one to the kid from USC.) "Luckily, I have not discontinued service on our landline. You can call her on that one. Or you could ride your bicycle over to the Verizon store, where you have an account, and buy a nice new mobile phone."

I felt like an idiot, and Carlos by his grin let me know that I was one. I started to dial Hope's number on the landline, but I had never committed it to memory. It was on speed dial on my now useless cell phone. Later that day, I reconstructed my email on a library computer and that one gave me the satisfying whoosh. It was the first time I was able to make contact with Hope since I left New York. (If I *did* make contact. I have no way of knowing because she never responded.)

Complete the following sentence: "Hope did not reply to DK because . . ."

A. The message did not go through.

B. The tone of his message put her off.

C. She was constructing a zinger of her own.

D. Her original email to DK was a hoax.

The answer: None of the above. Or all of the above. It doesn't matter. To be young and in love is the best your life will ever offer you, when chemistry is compatibility and passion is loyalty.

I took my petrified phone to the Verizon store on my ridiculous bicycle, as Carlos suggested. I looked like a performing bear. Cars honked their horns at me as they passed, coming as close as they could without committing manslaughter. Once there, I had to wait forty-five minutes until an overweight man with a permanent curled upper lip, kind of like Elvis, RIP, took my phone.

"Can you fix it?"

He wouldn't hear of it. He showed me what I should have instead. I knew nothing about my account, which had been set up by Hope, nothing about passwords, nothing about what he needed to know in order to get us through the labyrinth Verizon believes is necessary before allowing you to buy a phone. In the end, I had to give up my previous existence as an iPhone owner and Verizon customer and be born again.

"Put it on my account," I said.

"Thank you, thank you very much."

I insisted on having my old number. It was a matter of life or death, given that my wife was missing and that was the only number she had for me. One would think nothing could be easier, but it was a feat of such skillful maneuverings that the clerk demanded a high five for accomplishing it. He set my password to 1935 (He said it was his own d.o.b., but that would have made him older than I.) and handed me the phone. He punched my number into his own phone, singing, "It's now or never . . ." My phone rang! I was back in business! The ringtone, a techno mix of echoes, feedback, and chimes, gave me the heebie-jeebies. I made him set it to what a telephone ring has sounded like for generations. By the time I left the store, I was like the father he never knew.

www.digitaltrends.com

I invited Doc on one of my aimless walks, both to give Sandy a break and to enjoy his company. I pushed his chair along the bike path, grateful for the distraction. I could not work beyond musing. (Now that I think of it, musing is pretty much what my work *is*. Or was. My use of tense may waver here. You receive me unedited in notions of time.) Fear, suspicion, and anger had turned into simple ennui. Except for the circumstances in which it left me, it was not complicated. It was rejection. After so many years as a writer and husband, I should have been used to it. Used to it? I was an authority on it.

"Look at this place," Doc said. "A pleasant sterile landscape." He was angry because his dog was not allowed to walk next to him on the bike path. "This town sucks out whatever joy is left in a peach pit."

"I thought you were as chauvinistic about the place as everybody else I run into."

"A fake harmony is how we abide. How's your western coming along?"

"Slow going."

Apart from the rejection, assuming that's not enough for a writer to want to jump off the Eiffel Tower, what was it that would push me toward my next best choice? To be honest with you, the passage of time made witnessing the murder of an angel seem not all that traumatic, violence aside, no more than discovering that what you believed was not true *was* indeed true, if I were to believe my own eyes. My psychological and physical abuse at the hands of the police was a new experience for me, but hardly new in the culture. In American society, there are fourteen-year-olds who might find it banal. It was not pleasant to be stuck under the thumb of a Peruvian servant, but he *did* cook for me and he did his best to make the hovel a home. Leaf blowers? An unnecessary torture for no good purpose. A daily theater of the absurd that would have made Genet and Ionesco froth at the mouth. A leaf blower is not only an assault on reason but also a battery upon the lungs and ears. Why would people treat each other that way? Why does one neighbor drive another to close himself in his house and turn up the TV and wait out the ungodly disturbance? I suppose it is to save even a few more pennies on cheap labor. But why this mania to move leaves in the first place. Let them alone and they will return to fertilizer, like the rest of us, leaving a nicer aroma.

"I could maybe live in this place if there were no leaf blowers," I said to Doc.

"News flash: You're already living here. Anyway, I doubt you'll find out. Leaf blowers are here to stay. Part of the deal. Practice patience. It comes easier than you think in Maragate."

"I'll give it a try."

"You ought to get more involved. Or involved at all."

"Why?"

"You're going to be here a while."

"Only until Hope returns."

"Yeah. Well, till then."

I like doing someone a favor when it requires no more than showing up. I was more used to the other kind: someone asking me to read a script or a producer asking for a free rewrite. The first was always an invitation to discord and resentment, the second against Writers Guild rules. All Doc Fleck wanted was that I fill a chair at the city council meeting, and only if I believed dogs should be allowed on the bike trail, from which they were prohibited.

My opinion was that grown men in any combination of cargo shorts, shower shoes, tank tops, and baseball caps should not be allowed on airplanes, in restaurants, or at parties where mature people are in attendance, but I had no problem with dogs being allowed everywhere, including those places. I agreed to fill a seat between Sandy and Doc on the pro-dog side of the room. I believed it was Doc's means of tricking me into civic involvement. Did he have any idea where it would lead? I know I didn't. I was doing no more than granting an easy favor by occupying a seat. That night at the council meeting, however, sent my career careening in another direction.

Before the meeting began, Doc whispered into my ear, briefing me on each council member, two on either side of Mayor Hirkill, who had removed his hat for the occasion. Florescent lights reflected off his waxy scalp and wispy hair. The council members had name-plates before them. (Spelling is correct.)

"Lucian Soggarrdd, heir to Quartermaster Gin. Libertarian. His family made a fortune during Prohibition and the two world wars. Rabid Catholic. Pro-life. Wants abortion doctors executed. Mongo Cisterno, environmentalist. Has a Ford Expedition and a Chevy Suburban and has them both washed every day. Eddie Bausker, founder and CEO of Sol Tace Jerky. Known around town as Special Ed. Has an opinion on everything but not until his wife tells him what it is. Tim Mucken, successful merchandiser—I don't have a clue what that is—votes the way the chamber of commerce wants him to. And then there's our municipal embarrassment."

Twice during this rundown Sandy told him to hush.

"We're counting on the mayor's vote. I've been filling that prick's bowl for weeks, but Hirkill is an unpredictable shit heel. Mongo is solidly in our camp. All we need is one of the other three. We're hoping Special Ed's wife told him to let the dogs in."

Sitting at a long table to the side of the council were the city attorney and the city manager and some woman recording the min-utes. I settled in for what I expected would be two hours of boredom, but I had nothing better to do. I had always had a rich interior life and seldom found myself bored, until Maragate. Now I was bored all the time. The last act of any significance that I undertook was to call Esalen and find out that Hope was not registered and hadn't been during the previous two months. Aware that people use aliases that match their initials, I prevailed upon the receptionist to check for any guest with the initials H. K. She wasn't thrilled with the request but Esalen is all about fulfillment.

As Doc described them to me, I looked at the council members and gave a moment's thought to small-town government in general. I was sure council members took abuse for many of their decisions, but they should not be underestimated. They were volunteers after all, unpaid, giving up their free time and sitting through long boring meetings in the service of the people, doing their best to provide for the health and safety and quality of life for the residents of the town in which they decided to stake their futures. Often, I imagined, municipalities were ahead of the curve on those matters vis-à-vis the state and federal governments. Good things start at the neighborhood level, spread to the state, and finally to Washington. Bad things too, I suppose.

The meeting began with the Pledge of Allegiance to the Flag. When everyone sat down, Hirkill explained that the first item on every agenda was an opportunity for members of the public to speak for three minutes on any subject not otherwise up for later discussion. In the silent pause that followed, I looked for someone to rise and go to the microphone. It seemed to me that the offer of three minutes of attention from a town council was something not to be wasted, an opportunity for anyone in a state of despair. And that ought to be everybody in Maragate. When nobody stood up, I did, which changed everything, and for a long time.

People were surprised to see me rise, no one more than I. From the reaction of the crowd, one would think that few ever used their three minutes. (Afterward, Doc Fleck told me hardly anyone ever did, unless it was to express gratitude.) I spoke my name and address and the fact that I was a newcomer to Maragate.

"I understand the issue of gas-powered leaf blowers has come before the council before, and at that time some half measures were enacted," I said. I had never even considered dealing with the nuisance in this way, by pleading before the city council. But once on my feet it made sense. I'd never been to a city council meeting anywhere, nor knew anyone who had. (Remember, I lived in LA and worked in the movies.) "It was determined, as I understand it, that leaf blowers would continue to be allowed to pollute the air and shatter the peace but only for twelve hours a day, and not above a specified decibel rate. You do realize that that's not working? Half measures can't work. Only by banning these destructive tools can you achieve any relief from the havoc they create. There is no responsible way to use a gas-powered blower."

Hirkill rolled his eyes.

"If you use one, you are committing an assault upon your neighbors' health and well-being, upon their children and their pets and upon the air itself. You are responsible for blasting toxic dust into the air at hurricane force. Use one of these things and you make yourself responsible for unrelenting, deafening noise. You make yourself responsible for preventing people like me from working at home. Now, someone might look at the police reports and think it is not a problem. Who's complaining? But the truth is that most people do not like to call the police. They don't like exposing themselves in that way and they believe, correctly, that it won't do any good anyway. I am not going to call the police every time a leaf blower disturbs the peace. I'd be on the phone all day. And I have had some experience with the MPD. I don't care to have any more."

As soon as I said that, I wished I hadn't. It sparked a muted gasp from the audience. It would get back to Lieutenant Conventerra in about three minutes and he would track me down to grill me about the time I spent in Hungary.

"The only argument for these dust bazookas is that they save time and time is money. But if your yard guy works an hour on your place and twenty minutes of that time is blowing and you pay him twenty dollars an hour, that means six dollars and sixty-six cents goes toward blowing debris into the air. If it takes ten percent more time to rake and broom, the cost goes up to seven-thirty-three." (Always good at math, I did a quick calculation in my head.) "An increase of sixty-seven cents. Even if it took fifty percent more time, which is unlikely, it would cost you . . . three dollars and thirty-three cents more to have a quiet neighborhood and clean air. So, if it's all about cheap labor, factoring in the human costs, how cheap do you want to go?"

The room erupted into applause, stunning the council. Hirkill rapped his gavel and said that my time was up. The applause fell into an embarrassed silence, which was followed by Hirkill saying, "Thank you, Doctor Cakeskimtree."

Most people mangle my name and I give them a pass. It is a difficult name for an English speaker. Hirkill, however, took pleasure in it.

I sat down. Doc Fleck whispered in my ear: "Why did he call you 'Doctor'?"

"I have a PhD."

"You never told me that."

"I never told him either."

Until I told Lieutenant Conventerra and his partner whatshisname, the only one who knew was Carlos.

A short man, thin, and wearing creased blue jeans and a clean white shirt tucked in, and with a military style crew cut going gray, stood up from our side of the room and took the microphone. He looked over his glasses at the councilmen and identified himself as Al Myra. He looked like a man who could get in and out of confined spaces. He gave an address on the east side.

"I was not going to say anything tonight—I'm here for the dog thing—but listening to the previous gentleman, I have to speak up, and I haven't told this to Jesus. I was a door gunner on a Huey in Vietnam, mowing down people whenever I saw them moving below. All these years later, every morning when I hear a leaf blower I jump out of bed and hit the deck because they sound like the M-60 I used to spray hellfire with. I break into a sweat. Pause and repeat throughout the day. I use a rake around my place, and it works fine. For dirt and dust, I use a broom. Support our troops."

A council accustomed to (and appreciative of) an apathetic electorate never using their allotted three minutes now had two in a row, and they didn't know what to make of it. They looked apprehensive, wondering perhaps if one or both of the speakers might be deranged. Hirkill asked if anyone else felt the pressing need to speak, as though asking how much more of this shit must he endure. A woman from the anti-dog side of the room went up to the mic and introduced herself as Harmony Meadows. She was forty, maybe younger, slight, and shy, uncomfortable to be the center of attention.

"Like that gentleman—thank you for your service—I'm here on the dog issue, but I have a story to tell about leaf blowers. My neighbor lady came down with a mysterious illness, high fever, trouble breathing. The doctors saw something in the X-ray of her lungs and had to do exploratory surgery. They found in her lung a few tiny pieces of twigs. Actual twigs in her lungs. She told the doctor she had the neighbor from hell who was always blowing his yard into hers. The doctor said she must have inhaled the twigs when he was blowing, but there was no way to prove it. Look, I don't like to ban anything, but when there's a cheap alternative, and you've got a public health and safety issue, why not? Why not do something for a better quality of life if you can? You don't let cell phone towers in town. People say the sound waves cause brain tumors, or that the government would use them to trace our whereabouts and that would threaten our quality of life. You control vacation rentals to keep down rowdy parties. So what about the daily noise and air pollution caused by leaf blowers?"

With that she sat down, amid another round of applause, this time unsure and brief. The council looked cornered, then relieved when no one else stood up to speak.

I expected them to have some response to what was said by three diverse citizens, but as I said, I had never been to a city council meeting before, not in any city. Why would I? Things were fine until Maragate. Instead of acknowledging the three speakers, each council member related in turn what he had done over the weekend, as it applied to municipal business. Mongo had been to the Blessing of the Junipers; Bausker had open-air office hours Sunday afternoon at Spanish Circle and listened to the concerns of several of his constituents, though he did not say what those concerns were; Lucian Soggarrdd and Tim Mucken together toured the Soggarrdd Memorial Reservoir with the head of the water department, who showed them that the water level was continuing to drop despite the recent rain. They urged citizens to conserve water.

When it was the mayor's turn, he said, "Well, it's appropriate that since tonight's *hot* issue is *dogs* to tell you that I officiated at the ribbon cutting and the grand opening of Hot Diggity Hot Dogs. I know the whole town has been on the edge of their seats waiting for Kenny to open his hot dog shop, and let me tell you, it's worth the wait. I sampled the Chicago dog, with melted cheese, the Polish dog with sauerkraut, and the classic chili dog, with onions."

Doc whispered, "All comped, of course."

"Don't ask me which was the best, they were all delicious, and I washed 'em down with a bottle of Moxie. Let me tell you, it brought back memories of my youth."

I whispered to Doc, "Where would that have been?" I thought he might have been raised by wolves.

"No one knows," he answered.

"So let's support this new business," the mayor went on, "and enjoy hot dogs the way they're supposed to be. And just in time for the start of the new school year."

The rest of the meeting crawled on tortoise feet. First, a proclamation honoring the Grand Marshall of the Fourth of July parade, the best darn parade in America, read by the mayor with the same enthusiasm he afforded hot dogs. Then, approval of minutes and dispensing of old business, followed by a discussion on the practice of fracking. Even though the closest threat of any fracking was a world away, the mayor believed they should take a stand and pass a resolution condemning the practice. The debate took longer than I expected and became heated at times. The consensus was that the anticipated number of jobs gained by the pipeline was inflated, and at the end of the day only Canada would reap the benefits while America would run all the environmental risks. A vote was called, and the mayor prevailed, with the support of Mongo, Tim Mucken, and the man with no opinions. Lucian Soggarrdd thought they had no business voting on the issue in the first place.

All that was followed by a much-needed break. I stood up to stretch. A few people came to me and said that if I were to circulate a petition opposing leaf blowers, they would sign it, because they hated the fucking things.

When the meeting resumed, the controversial local issue was finally faced.

Long lines of people waited behind the microphone to speak for or against. Since I had already argued on a different issue, and since I had no dog in this fight, so to speak, I chose to sit quietly. From time to time I made eye contact with the mayor, who looked away. I tried to figure him out. His resemblance to William Burroughs was uncanny, which troubled me because I had enjoyed reading of the dope fiend's exploits, a fugitive wastrel in a suit and tie, while Hirkill seemed to represent no more than small town orthodoxy.

At the end of what I worried might be endless arguments for and against dogs on the bike path, the members of the council had their say, each beginning with either, "I'm a dog lover, and . . ." or "I'm a dog lover, but . . ."

Mongo and Soggarrdd were approving of allowing leashed dogs on the bike trail, Bausker and Mucken against it. The deciding vote was the mayor's.

Doc Fleck squeezed my arm.

"I had a dog once, Rover, a pit bull," said the mayor. "Rover did all his business on the carpet. You should have seen that carpet. You should have *smelled* that carpet. Oh, what a carpet. I had to throw that carpet out."

Each time he said the word "carpet," people sniggered.

Hirkill said, "So I'm a dog lover, but—"

Doc's hand released my arm. "The son of a bitch flipped again," he whispered.

"—the problem is with the owners who let their dogs poop anywhere, don't clean it up, and let them walk twelve feet ahead on those extending leashes, endangering cyclists and senior citizens.

I'll be voting to maintain the prohibition of dogs on the bike trail. No dogs mean more bikes, more exercise."

Mayor Hirkill arrived at the next farmers market riding a bright new Trek bicycle, the Earl style, rigged with a clever trailer on which he could display his RE-ELECT MAYOR HIRKILL sign.

www.alternet.org/modern-pestilence-leaf-blowers-generate
-infuriating-noise-toxic-gas

Labor Day in Maragate is not celebrated. Unions are despised. The only interest in labor held by the citizens of Maragate is that it be cheap. The prevailing attitude is that anybody with a job ought to shut up and be happy. After Labor Day, the breezes were cooler and the days shorter, sad reminders that the farmers market would soon be over for the season and that I would have passed both a spring and summer in that shithole.

Sandy was off getting her hummus and pita chips when Mayor Hirkill pedaled up to our spot under the cork tree for his usual shot of gin and shard of jerky.

"Nice bike," Doc said.

"I won the raffle," the mayor explained. "I've always been lucky."

"Did you buy a ticket?"

"Some people are lucky, and I was lucky enough to be one of the lucky ones."

"Luck runs out," said Doc, pouring him a second shot, which the mayor drank while still astraddle his new bike. "That's a six-hundred-dollar bike if it's a dime. Ed's Cyclery must have liked your vote."

"I am at peace with my decision," said the mayor, and pedaled on.

We drank and listened to the Gin Blossoms, three old guys on guitar, bass, and mandolin playing a Pat Boone cover of a Fats Domino original.

"You two seem to enjoy hating each other," I said.

"Can't speak for him."

"Are you at peace with his decision?" I asked.

"The dogs don't know, so they don't care," he said. "This isn't the first time Hirkill flipped at the last minute."

"And people are all right with that?"

"Most won't be aware that it happened. That's life in Maragate."

"Sandy told me you came here from Philly."

"Long, long ago."

"What made you come here?"

"One day I was up a tree trying to rescue a cat, which is a stupid thing to do. Leave a cat alone, he'll come down eventually. But I had a way with felines and the poor thing was making a terrible fuss. I was up there, looking him in the eye and thinking, who isn't up a tree, one way or the other? And then I fell."

"That's how you wound up in the chair?"

He looked off as though trying to remember.

"Sure," he said.

"So what brought you here?"

"New start."

"But why here?"

"Why not here?"

"Because you don't seem all that happy here."

"Neither do you."

"Only I can't leave. Why don't you leave, I wonder?"

"No place else to go, and too hard to get there, so I try to make it better where I am. Good job, by the way, on the leaf blower rant. Everybody knows you're right, but leaf blowers are here to stay. Sometimes I think they were invented just for Maragate."

"Doc, why do people move here? And what convinces them to stay?"

"The gin and jerky are famous."

"There's no history to the place, no coastline, no lakes, no mountains."

"You haven't been around. There are vistas—views, at least."

"Views of what? Twisted trees, fields of weeds or junipers? I admit the gin and jerky are pretty good, but other than that . . . I never heard of this town before I found out I had a house here."

Doc said, "Probably lots of places you never heard of."

"Doc . . . ?"

"Yeah?"

"What state are we in? And don't ask me today's date, just tell me."

"You don't know what state you're in?"

"I never get any mail."

"You take the fuckin' cake."

"Yeah, I know."

"You bought a ticket."

"I never bought a ticket. Hope did that. It was all prearranged. I slept most of the way. Carlos tells me I'm deliberately unaware."

"Good on you. Teach me."

Sandy returned with some big white onions and a mix of peppers. Doc liked them with his scrambled eggs. She broke out the bag of chips and opened the hummus.

"DK wants to know what state he's in," Doc told her.

"Maybe an analyst can help him with that."

"The geographical state."

"Utah, for goodness sake. You didn't know that? How could you not know that?" she said, arranging our snack.

Yes, I agree, how could I not know that? Or not care? Or never ask until then? Hope must have mentioned it, but I would have vetoed Utah. Nothing good ever came out of Utah. Breakthroughs come from California. I had assumed I was somewhere in Northern California, near Redding, say.

"I've never been in Utah. I had a picture once in Sundance, but I didn't want to make the trip. Where are all the Mormons?"

"You know how you hear about Utah that it's a different world? This is kind of what they mean." Doc released the brake on his chair and started to wheel himself away. "I gotta go take a piss. Want me to take one for you?"

"Please. I can't get out of my chair."

Utah?

"I'd better go with him," said Sandy.

I watched her push Doc to the same public restroom where I'd seen Conventerra and Hirkill that first night, which seemed so long ago and was still inexplicable.

I began a little interior dialog, about the known unknowns and the unknown unknowns and this spot in Utah. A cell phone rang, and I twisted in my seat frantically looking for mine. (You know why.) But it was Sandy's phone that was ringing. She had left it behind. I reached over to her chair and didn't think much about the etiquette of it before I answered.

"Hello?"

Silence. I thought it might be a telemarketer and was about to shut it off. Then a man's voice said, "Who is this?"

"Not my phone," I said. "I'm answering for a friend."

"Who's the friend?"

"Sandy Fleck. Who are you calling?"

He hung up. Anyone would think it was a misdial, right? I would have, too, except for the near certainty that the voice I heard belonged to Lieutenant Conventerra.

www.mysteryofutahhistory.blogspot.com

Why would Conventerra be calling Sandy, if it was Conventerra? It could have been anyone. Pretty sure it was Conventerra. I was ill at ease, creating on my interior screen an unsavory scenario, as usual.

Three young people approached me tentatively. The girl had dark hair, parted in the middle, and wore a tank top over breasts too

small to collaborate on any appreciable cleavage. One flawless bare
knee came through a hole in her jeans. (Not a designed hole, but
the genuine article.) Her feet were bare, delicate, long, and narrow
with high insteps and toenails neatly pedicured but unpolished. She
was sure of herself, unlike her two friends, who appeared doubtful
and were dressed in T-shirts with logos I didn't understand, draw-
string cotton pants, and old white tennis sneakers. I recognized the
girl right away and assumed the men were two of the three I saw
with her at Valene's house.

The thin one said, "Hey. 'sup?" in a somewhat effeminate voice.
The other boy did a slow turn, like a soldier checking the periphery,
then stopped to make eye contact with another young man a hundred feet away. This one was eating what from my distance looked
like a corn dog. The girl looked dreamily up to the trees and beyond.

"Hello again," I said.

"You remembered. Sorry we had to drop out of sight."

"Not entirely. I saw you go into the big white tent."

"Hidden in plain sight."

"And why sorry? I never expected to see you again."

"You never expected to see us in the first place."

"True. I was looking for the lady of the house."

"Please don't bother," she said.

"She can do you no good," said the thin boy.

"And you can?"

"That is why we are here."

"What were you all doing in Valene's house?"

"We thought it was yours."

Imagine. What would you think? I tried to keep a calm exterior,
but inside I was roiling, in both fear and anticipation. Who were
these kids? Was it possible they could help me in this quagmire? In
the scenario I was living, was this the reversal I'd been waiting for?
It felt that way, but it was more than I could grasp at the moment.

"What were you all doing at the Sustainability Commission
meeting?"

"Looking for you, but you were with that cop. You're seldom alone."

"I'm usually alone."

"We went in so we wouldn't look too conspicuous."

"I don't understand."

The boy said, "But I did want to know what they meant by 'sustainability.' Fascinating. They expect to run out of things and then destroy what's left."

She asked, "Ever imagine you'd wind up here?"

"Do I know you?" I asked. They looked familiar in a way hard to pin down, as though I'd heard about them and halfway knew what they looked like but had never met them before. I didn't know many young people, unless you count studio executives blocking the production of my western. (A uniquely American genre of which the young are all but unaware.)

"We know you," said the girl. She was talking to the trees, which had most of her attention.

"How do you know me?"

She took a moment to frame her answer, but before she could say anything, the boy jumped in.

"You stood up at council and spoke," he said, before she might offer a different answer. They spoke with unusual accents, like Italians who went to school in England and were still not at ease with the American idiom.

"You were there?"

"And you never saw us," she said.

"Was that such a big deal? All I did was state an opinion."

"A contrary opinion, in a place where it is better kept to oneself."

"True that," I said. (It's a favorite phrase I don't get to use often enough.)

"Standing up and spouting contrary views used to be what we were all about," said the thin boy. (Boy, man, man-boy, they were grown-ups but not exactly somehow.)

"We don't have that much left to say anyway," said the other boy, saying his first words. He had been scanning the area, stopping to make eye contact with the boy in the distance. "It's time for action. Words won't even get you to the gate."

"What kind of action is it time for?" I asked.

"Would it be impolite to ask your name?" His voice, unlike his friend's, was low and mellifluous. His simple question, stated so formally, took on a gravitas. "For the record."

"What record? I thought you knew me."

"Cough up a name, will you?" said the girl, playing tough, as though she already knew me but wanted to make sure I was not an imposter trying to infiltrate her gang.

"You first."

"I'm Mary."

"They call me PB," the tall boy said. "And this is Jack."

Jack said, "Yo," which sounded like a word new to his lexicon. He continued to scan the people coming and going around us. We had our own little space staked out beneath the cork tree, but people were naturally milling about nearby.

"Who is that boy eating a corn dog that you're so interested in?" I asked.

Mary said, "You're not all that drunk."

"That's Georgie," said PB. "He is in grief, you see."

"Over what?"

"Everything, it seems."

"Are you guys in some kind of trouble?"

"I expect we might be," said PB.

"Let's say we're travelers, and we are not always welcomed," said Jack.

"Not here anyway," said Mary, with another of those smiles in which I could lose myself.

"Simple sojourners," PB added.

"Travelers like gypsies, or sojourners like you know where you're going next."

"We share everything," the girl said, "including the same disease." Then she turned her attention back to the treetops.

"What are you looking for up there?" I asked.

"Falling leaves," she said, in all seriousness.

"Again, your name, if you would be so kind?" said Jack.

"I also go by my initials, DK." Jack nodded, as though approving.

PB said in a whisper, "You know the mayor is dirty."

It did not surprise me that anyone would think so—the whole town accepted it—but why these three, who would be expected to have no stake in local government? Besides, how dirty can a small-town mayor be? (Free gin, cheap rent, a new bicycle.) I played dumb. "I know, right? It's an embarrassment. When did he last have a shower?" I looked past them for Doc and Sandy. He seemed to be taking a long time for a pee, but then old men do. The important thing is that you still can.

"Hark, DK, be aware, they have put a tail on the mayor. They are going to get him."

The conversation had taken an ominous turn. The three young sojourners were giving me cloak and dagger dialog. And *hark*?

"Who? Why? I mean, he's visible as hell. You can't escape him. He's all over the place."

Georgie, off in the distance, signaled with what was left of his corn dog. I could see Sandy pushing Doc away from the restrooms.

"Hie away," said Jack.

"Wait, what?"

PB whispered, "Beware of the mayor. And the coppers. They'll put a tail on you, too."

"I can't imagine why," I said, though I believed that Lieutenant Conventerra had been tailing me ever since that first interrogation. "Who *are* you kids? How do you know me? Where did you come from and why are you here?"

"It's where we're going that matters," said Mary, at the same time coy and impatient.

Yes, I was drunk, but as Mary said, not that drunk. I believe I was one hundred percent lucid and dreaming anyway. Those kids were not of this age, but I knew the age from which they traveled, the Romantic. PB? Percy Bysshe? Mary, his teenage mistress and intellectual equal? Jack? John Keats? Georgie? Lord Byron? Was the gang all here? Or did I assemble them in my own special delirium? *Hie away?*

"Mayhaps, at a later time, but soon," said PB.

Mayhaps! Well, that sealed it.

"We need to get you out of here," said Mary

"God, yes! You can do that? But how?"

"We will meet again," said Mary. "Be ready."

They scanned the area and silently agreed on a direction out of Spanish Circle, to my right.

"Hold on. You can't drop that on me and disappear. It's because I saw something, back in February, right? Is this about that?" They didn't answer, but they didn't have to. I could sense they knew. They moved farther away. "The shooting . . . who was it that got killed. *What* was it? Why?"

They were already far enough away for two children to run between us. The children gave no indication that they heard me, but it kept me from shouting out anything more about shooting and killing.

Mary let the other two go ahead of her and turned back to me. "Do you know why angels can fly?"

"Then it *was* an angel!"

She twisted her face in a comical way and said, "It is because they take themselves so lightly."

Like a little girl, she skipped after her two friends. I called out, "Was the angel real? Tell me, if you know!"

She stopped again, still smiling, and answered: "The angel was not real."

"But I saw her!"

"Nor was she unreal."

With that, she skipped away, hardly touching the ground. The casual intensity of her words knotted me at the knees.

https://en.wikiquote.org/wiki/Angels

I suspect you are saying right now, "He may not be on the spectrum, he may not be schizophrenic, but how stupid can one person be?" No one has ever accused me of being stupid. Naive, yes, childlike, sometimes, deliberately unaware, I hope so, because these personal deficiencies have served me well, and in the end have proven themselves to be blessings.

I heard my name and turned to my left. Doc and Sandy had returned from the restrooms. The four young people were out of sight. The encounter had made me dizzy, but I acted as normally as I could under the circumstances.

"DK, you all right?"

"You look like you've seen a ghost," said Sandy.

"Did you see those three kids I was talking to?"

"Didn't see anybody."

"They thought they knew me. You didn't see them?"

"No, but I wasn't looking."

"They were right here, moving in that direction."

"It's pretty crowded," said Sandy. "What about them?"

"Sitting here, you can meet all kinds of people," said Doc.

"Not these kinds of people."

"What did they have to say?" asked Sandy.

"They said they were travelers."

"Probably tweakers," said Doc.

"Tourists?"

"No, more like sojourners."

"Probably squatters," she said. "They'll hide out in vacation rentals that aren't booked."

"Hide out from whom?"

"The cops, of course."

"What happens when they get caught?"

"I wouldn't know. Somebody kicks their asses."

"They reminded me of people I used to know."

Of all the characters I could have conjured up, the Romantic poets would be obvious choices, right? The Romantic poets had a profound effect upon my youth and subsequent life. In the depths of my dilemma, sitting alone in a crowd, having all but given up on any kind of lifeline, I summoned up the poets. Why not? If I were getting around to conjuring now, however, why would I have seen them days before, off in the distance entering an oversized white tent, or before that, occupying a house they thought was mine?

I had another gin and splashed it with tonic. We sat and listened to the Gin Blossoms sing still one more song made famous by Pat Boone covering Fats Domino.

I turned to Sandy and said, "You forgot your phone when you took Doc to the men's room."

"Not the first time," she said. "Nobody calls me anyway."

"But somebody did."

"Really?"

"Hope you don't mind, I answered it. Thought it might be important."

"Was it?" she said, in a guarded way.

"Hung up. Could have been a wrong number."

"A butt dial," she said, and giggled in her nervous way.

"Is that a real thing?"

"Is what a real thing?" asked Doc.

"Butt dials."

"Not with me 'cause I'm always on my butt."

I was looking for a way to say that I vaguely recognized the voice calling Sandy, to see her reaction, but I had other things on my mind. Somehow the poets, if I understood them at all, were going to get me out of Maragate. A woman approached us. I recognized her from the council meeting. She repeated her name for me, Harmony Meadows.

"I wanted to thank you again for bringing up the leaf blower thing at council."

"Thank you for joining in. That was a scary story about your friend, inhaling twig fragments."

"Quality of life issues always lose to commercial interests around here." She looked at Doc and Sandy. "I mean, we're all lucky to be here, it is our little slice of heaven, but . . . anyway, you were brave to stand up like that."

"It didn't seem that risky but thanks. Can I ask you a personal question?"

Sandy shifted nervously on her seat when Harmony said tentatively, "I suppose so."

"How long have you lived in Maragate?"

"Seems like forever."

"How did you get here?"

"Well, that is a little personal. I'm embarrassed to say, even though it's hardly a secret. I followed after a lover. When I got here, he was gone."

"That's almost my story. I came to join a wife, but she was gone."

We may have talked a bit more about the coincidence without revealing any more details. Sandy was relieved when Harmony finally moved on, and for the first time she made a chastising remark. "In Maragate, people don't ask such personal questions."

"I'm from Southern California where there are no other kind."

"Well, this isn't Los Angeles."

"I've noticed."

"It's a little slice of heaven," said Doc. This time you could pick up the sarcasm all the way to the mini-donut stand.

I said, "Then I think it was a slice off the ass end."

I got a laugh out of Sandy. She went back to being her lovable ditzy self.

"Could be we got an end cut from a deficient heaven," said Doc.

The phrase stuck me. I was sure I'd heard it before, somewhere in a poem, but I couldn't recall which one. It was an apt description—deficient heaven—because every reason existed for having a good life in Maragate, stacked against every reason for assuring you wouldn't enjoy it.

"Maybe a deficient hell," I suggested. "Our little slice of hell, minus the fire and brimstone, but welcome to all the rest."

"Don't we have more pleasant things to talk about?" said Sandy.

We dipped pita chips into hummus and washed them down with gin.

"Like a bus station," I said. "Somewhere in the midst of nowhere. Neither here nor there. A whole other place. With worse coffee."

"Well, I guess we are going to talk about it. Boring."

"Who says heaven and hell have to be separate metaphors?" Doc said.

"Or metaphors at all," I said. "Jean-Paul Sartre said hell was other people."

"The simple explanation."

"That's it for me, thank you," said Sandy. "You boys have fun being miserable. I'm going for mushrooms."

I watched her walk away. She reached into her bag and took out her phone. It was at her ear before she blended into the crowd.

With no other choice, we leaned back and listened to the music.

Doc said, "It was wrong of Pat Boone to record that song, but Fats Domino, if he was here, would never say it. That's why he's not here."

"Doc, there's something I have to tell you."

"Sounds serious."

"When I answered Sandy's phone, it was a man calling."

"Okay."

"He hung up, but I think I recognized the voice."

"I don't want to hear about it."

"All right. I had to mention it. We're friends."

We didn't say anything after that until more people stopped by, people who were not at the city council meeting but had heard about my performance and wanted to offer words of support and express a little anger and frustration, as much over the mayor as the leaf blowers. He was a flip-flopper, a mooch, an embarrassment, totally unqualified for the job. They told me all this in hushed tones.

"See what's happening here," said Doc.

"Discontent. Easy to spot."

"I'm sensing a groundswell."

I was sensing dizziness and a malaise fueled by a diet of exotic jerky and artisanal gin, triggered by my conversation with the subjects of my doctoral dissertation, not to mention that odd call on Sandy's phone, or the brief discussion of heaven and hell and the deficient versions thereof.

"You may be the one we've all been waiting for," Doc said.

"Well, that's biblical, speaking of heaven and hell."

"You could run against Hirkill and unseat his sorry ass."

"It will be a cold day in metaphorical hell when I even vote for mayor. And why run anyway, since the mayor has been elected time and time again? Forever, you said."

"It's like Bush the younger? Did you know anyone who voted for him?" (Not personally.) "There are about five thousand registered voters in this town," he said, "and I think I know most of them, but I never ran into anybody who would admit he voted for Hirkill."

"Doc, I'm going to sum this up as crisply as I can." I waited a moment for his full attention, then said, "I don't care."

"You don't have to. If it's your destiny, you'll come to care."

As though on cue, the Magenta Moment did its uncanny magic and people applauded, a ritual response copied from desirable places like Key West that actually have beautiful sunsets. I applauded with the rest of them, because I thought that if I didn't, someone might notice and use it against me.

www.forbes.com/your-best-defense-against-butt-dials

In Lost Creek, back in the Wyoming Territory, there was no mayor. The Judge, who sat at the window in his upstairs room above the stockade, a bottle of whiskey on the floor beside him, his holstered Colt pistol hanging from the back of his chair, came the closest. The Captain, appointed by the Army, was obliged to make arrests and throw miscreants into the stockade until they sobered up and apologized, but when it came to real crimes he believed in an impartial trial before the Judge, who had read the law. He had shown himself to be a fair man, and so by acclamation the people named him judge, and subsequent hangings were considered by all to be fair and square.

Anyone of even average intelligence and social awareness must believe that he could do a better job than those representatives currently in office, and he is probably right. (Of course, anyone of lesser intelligence feels the same way, believing his opinions are as good as anyone else's data.) Everyone knows what is wrong with government, but why can't they fix it? In my fantasies, I've imagined myself a senator or a governor solving long-standing problems and heading off crises before they occur with simple logic and the desire to do the right thing. All any city, or country, needs is a leader of dignity and integrity, and positive results will follow. This fantasy would, of course, bypass the bother of a campaign and raising the money to wage it, and the corruption likely to follow. Should I take Doc's advice to run, and should I win, I might be able to make Maragate a more hospitable place in which to live, for them, and to sojourn, for me. I could expose the jingoism that gives rise to the chauvinism that fools people into believing they are in the best of all places when they are demonstrably not. But why try? I had no attachment to Maragate. Let them stew in their own juices. I was there waiting only for Hope to return. (Or for the Romantic poets to whisk me away, because my angel made a mistake, my angel who was real and not real and was murdered for it.) I wanted no involvements beyond the Thursday night farmers market with Doc and Sandy. Strangers, however, were now stopping me on the street to express appreciation for my standing up against the torture of land-scapers and their leaf blowers. They urged me to run for mayor, all the while pretending to be asking me the time of day, in case any-one was watching.

I mulled over the possibilities at a table in Thai-O-Thai waiting for my date, thinking about *After the Thaw* and politics (which is what my western is all about, which is what all westerns are about) and the moral question of should I even be here waiting for a woman who was not my wife, an issue that Shelley or Lord Byron would never have raised but in hindsight should have. I thought about the angel's last words, "Hope is alive." I would never know if she meant Hope or hope.

It would be my first dinner in months not eaten alone. Although we were domiciled together, Carlos and I were not what you would call close. He dined on his feet eating bits and pieces as he prepared dinner for me, then retreated to the casita. I don't mind eating alone. In fact, I prefer it to eating in a crowd (which for me would be three or more), but after all that time I found myself longing for the company of a woman at an intimate dinner for two. Not this woman, who I didn't even like.

Often, I pinch the bridge of my nose and close my eyes when I'm writing. It helps me, though I don't know how. I had been doing that in Starbucks when I sensed a presence at my table, or rather below my table. I opened my eyes to Rufus, the menacing Rottweiler, and his paralyzing stare. I looked up and saw his mistress, Valene, the disagreeable off-the-books landlady, the only other witness to a police crime I was trying to forget. She stood next to me, scrolling her iPhone for the latest, and in a moment smiled down at me. I said nothing. I closed my laptop and leaned back. She lowered the phone like an armed victim unwilling to shoot to defend her-self. (You've seen that scene in movies. None that I would have written.)

"Okay, so I'm sure I was, like, rude to you?" she said in her annoy-ing upspeak. Who the hell started that, and why do women, in the

majority, believe it makes them sound nonjudgmental instead of
goofy? (Linguists say it started with Valley Girl–speak, born out of
the deep insecurities of postpuberty, then mutated into a vocal virus
that spread to Canada as a tonal means of asking, "Am I agreeable?,"
a question of existential significance to all Canadians, and soon
returned south again, stronger and cure-resistant, sweeping the US,
until even Terry Gross and the women of NPR were infected.)

"You might say that," I said.

"It's been on my mind. I'm not that girl?"

She wore high heels and skinny jeans, which made her appear
to be six feet tall. Objectively speaking, she wasn't bad, personality
aside. She offered to buy me a scone, but the pastries at Starbucks
suck.

"A refill, then?"

"I'm already over-coffeeed. Thanks anyway."

"I try not to regret stuff? But I was cunty with you, so please
accept my apology. The only one I ever handed out, I think. And I
wasn't exactly honest either?"

"Would you like to sit down and talk about it?" I asked her.

"I would?" she said, "But not now, not here?"

That is how I came to be waiting in a Thai restaurant, doing
what I always do while I'm waiting, unspooling my western movie,
sidestepping into unlikely fantasies like becoming mayor of a town
I hated, comparing my life to those of the Romantic poets. (Mine
was twice as long, so there.) The restaurant was on Spanish Circle.
All the restaurants, except for the fast food joints and taco wagons,
were on Spanish Circle. She breezed in fifteen minutes late, lay-
ered with flowing wraps because the weather was turning chilly,
Rufus on a leash, which was off-putting in a Thai restaurant. (In
any restaurant, I mean. I apologize in advance.) She air-kissed the
Asian hostess, only the second Asian I'd seen in Maragate. I rose as
she made her way toward the table. She tightened her hold on the
dog's leash and gave me a warm hug. I'm not a huggy person, but
one can go for only so long without becoming noticeably needy.

We sat down, the beast on the far side of us. I tried to get right down to issues, but she said, "Let's relax for a moment? Let's have some food first? Good food promotes good feelings?"

It would have to be extraordinary food to overcome my bad feelings for her, but she was the only person who could, if she would, back up my story. Honestly, why did I care? Mary already told me all there was to know about the angel. (Almost all.)

Valene ordered two Thai gin and tonics, and when they arrived in large round glasses I thought I was looking at an underwater garden: lemon, lime, and orange peels, juniper berries and cardamom pods, a pinch of cassia bark, a few coriander seeds, a sprig of rosemary, and about six ounces of gin and tonic in equal proportions. She drank hers through a straw. I've never liked that, so I took out the straw and drank it like a man, picking botanicals out of my teeth after each sip.

I told her she looked good, which she did. She told me I smelled nice. (Old Spice.)

We had the special: jerky of marinated flank steak in soy, coconut juice, palm sugar, and roasted coriander, served with Burmese garlic sticky rice and sweet and spicy sauces. She took a picture of the plates and posted it. (Somewhere.)

"What do you think, five stars?"

"Pretty exotic," was my review. "Now, Valene, can I call you Valene?"

"In high school, they used to call me Valene, Valene, the blow job queen."

"That couldn't have been very pleasant," I said.

"I got used to it. I've been called worse?"

"Children can be so cruel."

"No one to blame but myself."

"Well, I'm not going to call you that."

"What did they call you in high school?"

"Slim."

"That had to be long ago."

"I stopped playing basketball and took up the sedentary life of a writer."

"Were you any good?"

"I got rich."

"As a basketball player?"

"First string. Pretty good. I was a guard. I didn't score much, but I had a lot of assists. Lost interest after high school, turned to poetry."

"I was a cheerleader for a while? Valene, Valene, the blow job queen shakes her ass." (She made me so uncomfortable.) "I was a Girl Scout, too, but I had to quit. I got knocked up?"

"I'll call you Valene, if that's okay."

"I'm not the sensitive type about shit from the past? The past is past, and that's why they call it the past. Otherwise they wouldn't call it anything? What's your sin?"

"Pardon?"

"Everybody's got one."

"Nobody ever asked before. I'll get back to you. What's yours?"

"If I see it, I have to suck it?"

"Why is that a sin?"

"I know, right?"

"If we can get to that night in the fog outside your house, last February. I saw something otherworldly."

"Sweetie, we are going to get to the bottom of everything? I'm going to tell you what I know? I'll do the right thing. It takes me a while, but I do get there."

For dessert, we had chocolate beef jerky cheesecake with horse-radish meringue. She took a picture of it and posted it. She told me she would be sleeping in her own house that night because she had no current guests. "Unless a better offer comes along?" (If it did, it would not come from me.)

We left the restaurant and walked toward her house, Rufus on her safe side, away from me. I slowed the pace.

"You were in Ugg boots and a blue raincoat. A cop was talking to you. He told you to stand by his car, which you did."

"That cop's name? Cairo Blackair." She paused, but I had nothing to say. "I don't know either."

"Don't know what?"

"That name."

"Blackair is an unusual name, but so is mine, in a different way."

"No, why his mother named him Cairo? Probably something funny happened with the syrup?"

"Do you know him?"

"More like I know *of* him. He's a bad dude?"

We were on the right track, but before I could ask another question the dog, who seemed to know the way, pulled us into the Oso Grande. We would be having a nightcap. Her idea of a nightcap was a Long Island Iced Tea. I try not to drink after dinner but that night I had an Irish coffee, ordering a second when she ordered her second. It was too noisy to talk. We sat at the bar. The phone was back in her left hand. Her right hand was on my knee. I could not remember the last time a woman came on to me, and that includes my own wife. I had a few Viagras somewhere (not on me), all that was left from a prescription of nine filled forever ago.

We left the Oso Grande, our gait less steady, and as we walked she prattled on about how lucky we were to have the best Thai restaurant in America? maybe in the world? and how the Oso was the "funnest" bar anywhere? and how everything was awesome?

"The other day," I said, "I gave the fro-yo guy exact change and he said, 'Awesome.'"

We passed along the oozing creek (the Cherona River), and I said, "This is where the SUV was parked. I stood right here and looked over at your house. Then the shots. I dropped down and rolled under the car."

"Right before that, I'm behind my car? I heard this *whoosh* over my head? I looked up, nothing but fog?"

"You heard a *whoosh*?"

"I don't know how else to describe it?"

"Like the whoosh you hear when you send an email?"

"Like that, only way louder and up above my head?"

"I saw a glow of light, flashes from the guns, the victim falling right here, next to me. I looked into her eyes."

"Honestly, I didn't realize that anybody was shot? Not until you mentioned it that time? I thought it was the door slamming. Sometimes that happens when the back door is open."

"It would have had to slam four times."

"I only heard the one, because I was hoofing it behind Rufus."

We reached her house.

"Home at last. Come on in."

As I mentioned, her house had no more curb appeal than my own and they could easily have been confused, one with the other. Her interior, however, was staged for tourists and pleasant in that temporary way, like an upgraded hotel suite, an aspect I must have missed the first time I passed through her living room. A red leather sofa and matching easy chairs were grouped around a wall-mounted flat screen television set with soundbar attached. Rufus settled into his beanbag bed. She turned on the gas and flames rose through a bed of bits of blue glass in the fireplace, creating gold and blue dancing light. She turned down the other lights and invited me to sit on the sofa. I worried she would sit too close to me. Instead, she pulled up a hassock and sat in front of me, her hands on my knees. Given her confession (or boast) on her high school proclivity, I held my breath for her next move.

"I have to tell you something?" she said. "It would have been all right, you know, my favorite thing, my reputation and all? What happened around that time, though, and I wasn't the first girl ever? I took some money for it. Why not, I was gonna do it anyway? Only then I went ahead and said okay to the birdie— which was serious money, for a teenager." (As in, smile for the birdie, but you may be too young.) "One thing led to another, you know, multiples, gang stuff, and ATM." (I later Googled it . . . ["Do you mean atom?"] . . . and kind of wished I hadn't.) "That crossed the line, I mean, even I could see that? I tell you this because it's in the past? I'm not that girl anymore? So, don't get any bright ideas?"

"No bright ideas. Let's start at the beginning."

www.xnxx.porn.com/atm

The following morning, we sat side by side on a wooden bench in the lobby of City Hall, waiting to talk to Mayor Hirkill, who routinely held a daily office hour from eleven to noon, allotting fifteen minutes to each of four lucky citizens, first come, first served. At noon, City Hall closes for the lunch hour. We arrived at five after eleven. Someone was already with him. No one else was waiting. The receptionist called it a busy day.

Our stop for coffee at Starbucks and my nagging misgivings about what we were about to do made us late. As we sat waiting, Valene surfed the web on her phone. "Valene? Can we please stow the phone during this meeting?" I asked her like a patient teacher talking to a disinterested pupil whose cooperation was sorely needed.

"Sure," she said and continued to surf until then.

Hirkill was no more than a misfit, an unlikely cheerleader for a losing team that keeps cheering, "We're number one!" That didn't mean I could trust him. It could easily have meant I shouldn't trust him. Valene and I debated through the night before I deferred to her judgment. I agreed because I couldn't come up with a better idea. I couldn't come up with *any* idea. That boy (Shelley's avatar?) warned me to beware of the mayor, that he was under surveillance, but I could not reveal that to Valene or to anyone else because adding my encounter with the Romantic poets and the brilliant author of *Frankenstein* 150 years after the last of them had died to what I was already claiming to have seen would do little to convince anyone I was rational. No matter. I needed no warning to beware of Hirkill. Some people you do, instinctively. Valene, however, knew him better than I, and she knew the town much better than I could ever hope to, which would be not at all. She convinced me that, short of calling in the FBI, Mayor Hirkill was the only person we could take into our confidence. Let *him* call in the FBI. On our own the FBI would think we were a couple of aging drunks who had gone off the rails, which might not have been too far from true.

In Valene's home, having got out of the way—her way at least—a dark passage through pornography and a return to chastity, which hadn't existed for her since age twelve, we got down to the details. To wit: she came back to her house that foggy night two days after the latest guests had left, as was her routine, to clean up and check the damage. She found her front door ajar and called the police. She was fearful that tweakers had broken in and were squatting. She was even more afraid when the cops drew their guns, but she understood the precautions. ("Tweakers have zero control? And mad strength?") That strange glow filled the front door. She heard a *whoosh* above her head. With the first shot, Rufus pulled the leash out of her hand and went running into the fog. She ran after him and missed everything that followed. It took several blocks before Rufus stopped to take a dump on somebody's dying lawn. She stepped on his leash and had him under control again. By the time she returned, everyone was gone. She went into her house and checked it. Nothing was trashed or stolen. She never saw the victim, and she never saw me. She did not know either of us existed until I showed up at her door. Up until then she was content for the sake of her clandestine business to let it all slide.

Her value to me as a corroborator was dicey, but one thing was clear: the cops fired a number of shots that night at something that glowed in the dark, and as citizens we needed them to explain themselves.

Again and again I asked her if she had caught even the slightest glance of the victim. She searched her memory, but all she could remember was that whoosh and the strange glow. Almost like a magic act. Whoosh, glow, shot, and gone.

"It could have been E. T. with a flamethrower, for all I know, that glow thing?"

"It was an angel," I told her.

She pushed at both my knees. "Get out!"

"I saw the wings. The creature was black, more café au lait, a woman, but androgynous."

"Okay, and that means?"

"Neither male nor female, but like both."

"Awesome!"

"The chances are better we'd be believed if we did claim it was an E.T. people believe in E.T.s."

"A fucking angel!"

"Beautiful features. Small perfect breasts, but it was those eyes, those wings, thick, dark."

"Definitely dead?"

"No doubt."

"Can angels die? I mean, didn't they used to be like these terrific human beings who died and got to be angels instead of, you know, just getting through the day like the rest of us?"

"I don't know about angels, about the recruitment details or standard operating procedures. You know why?"

"Why?"

"Because I don't believe in angels! Or demons outside of one-self." (That long-held belief had become tenuous at best. That I could not believe in angels did not mean they could not exist.)

She made a pot of green tea with local honey, which people believed held at bay the dreaded allergies rampant in Maragate. (It didn't.) We drank the tea at the counter in her kitchen. She had a George Foreman grill. A small Sharp TV was mounted on the wall, on an extending metal rack.

"Valene, how long have you been in Maragate?"

"Too long. Like, forever?"

"Where did you come from?"

"I'm trying to forget."

"Why here?"

"I had a job offer, a legit job? At a distillery? But my car was totaled by this semi carrying sides of beef, on the bridge? The job fell through, and I've been scrambling ever since."

"How did you get this house?"

"Insurance settlement. The house is all that supports me now?"

"Are you worried?"

"About what?"

"About revealing what I told you."

"Well, maybe, but you got to do what's right?"

"If you even know what's right. Sometimes it's hard to tell."

"Could have been a tweaker," she said. "That angel? Tweakers look weird and dress funny sometimes? And you can't tell the boys from the girls, they're all so fucking ugly."

"This creature was beautiful. Beyond words. The cops would like me to believe I was hallucinating, and frankly I can't bet my life that I wasn't. Lieutenant Conventerra . . . you know him?"

"Kind of?"

"He denies that there ever was any shooting. That there was ever an SUV cop vehicle in the area."

"Well, we know that's not true. They're covering up? We have to tell somebody?"

"Thank you." I felt a renewed sense of Tom Hanks, a second wind for climbing to the moral high ground. I was even beginning to feel a bit of affection for that edgy airhead. "Any ideas?"

We went through a process of elimination, concluding that the mayor was our best bet. "In this town? There are very few chances for the mayor to look heroic? He'll be over this like flies on shit."

During the ten minutes we waited in the lobby of City Hall, the phone never rang, no one else came in to transact any business, and no one got in line to talk to the mayor. It had been a long night, and I was nodding off on the hard wooden bench. The sound of footsteps coming down the stairs from the second floor kept me from falling into a well-deserved stupor. I looked up to see a familiar face.

"Carlos, what the hell are you doing here?"

He was as surprised as I. He studied the two of us sitting side by side on the bench as though we were taking a break along the long walk of shame, which could not have been further from the truth.

"Good morning, señor. And how are you this morning?"

Hispanics and the French and probably every other culture in the civilized world begin a conversation with the offering of some friendly greeting and a brief inquiry into your state of being, forcing Americans to do likewise, though it is ingrained in us to get to the point. (Time is money.) "Good morning," I said. "How are you? That's nice. Why are you here?"

"I might ask the same thing of you, señor, but that would not be my place."

I did not disagree with him.

"What are you cooking up with the mayor now? I hope it's legal, at least."

Carlos gave me his smug smile, descended the last few steps, and went out the door.

"Who was that?" Valene asked.

"The infamous Carlos, my houseman, and apparently a little too tight with the mayor. He's the enemy within. We should rethink this."

I took her hand, about to drag her out of City Hall, but the old receptionist, who looked a lot like Ruth Gordon, RIP, said, "The mayor will see you now."

Seeing no reasonable way out, I followed Valene up the stairs. As a gentleman, I should have adverted my eyes, but she did have a good butt, which was kind of my thing in my youth, and where is the harm, after all, in a furtive yet appreciative glance from a reasonable distance? Anyway, you can sue me if you want to. I have no job to lose.

The mayor's office was stark. There were no family pictures in his office, no coffee cups declaring him the Best Dad in the World. His only memento was a silver-plated apple on a walnut base. An

American flag and the city seal (*Juniperus Communis*) made up the entire office decor. I shook his hand, which felt like uncooked liver. Valene and I took the two seats on the visitors' side of his desk.

"Are you here to get married?" he asked, a smirk on his gaunt face. "I can do that, by the powers vested in me. Where's the ring?"

The mayor displayed a sense of inappropriate humor not unlike Richard Nixon's. I wondered if he might not be, like our late president, a tad autistic. (But at times I've wondered about my own place on the spectrum.)

"We've met a couple times in the park," I said, "DK."

"The screenwriter, friend of Fleck's. Foe of the leaf blowers. Here with Valene, Valene . . ."

"That's right," she cut in, with an attitude. "We have heavy shit to deal with and only fifteen minutes?"

"Strange bedfellows," he said, still smirking.

"Ripley, we've got something important to tell you?" Valene said. "I mean, really important? Earth shattering important?"

He leaned back in his chair, touched all of his fingertips together under his chin, and said, "I'm listening."

"You go, DK?"

I told him the circumstances of my arrival in Maragate, leading up to my late-night walk in the fog. I alluded again to my seeing Lieutenant Conventerra and another man leaving the public restroom, one after the other without implying that the mayor was that other man.

"I was lost," I said, "and came upon two police cars and a motorcycle cop in front of what I later learned was Valene's house." I turned my head to her and saw that she was thumbing her phone. "Valene." (Like that teacher, losing patience.) She put the phone back into her purse.

"I was there too?" she said, "Standing behind a police car?"

"And why was all of this happening?" he asked.

"I came home to an open front door, and I called the cops. I was afraid some maniac was still inside?"

"And was someone?"

"As it turns out, yes," I said. "I was standing behind the police SUV."

"Why?"

"I was curious. Police drama, happening right there."

"I understand. Some people are so thirsty for drama that if none occurs they will create some. Anything for a distraction."

"We are not those people," I said.

"We ain't creating shit," added Valene.

He took off his glasses and wiped them with his hideous tie.

"Go on."

"Someone ran out of the house and the cops started firing. I dove under the SUV, and a body fell right next to me. A woman. A black woman."

"Are you claiming . . . was this person armed?"

"Not in the way we commonly think of it."

"So you are claiming that an unarmed black woman was shot by . . . I assume the cops were white?"

"They were."

"An unarmed black woman shot . . ." He put his head in his hands. I did not fully appreciate that what he imagined was every mayor's worst nightmare. "How many times?" he asked.

"Four, I think."

"By three white cops?"

"I didn't say there were three." I expected a dramatic pause, like in the movies. (I might have written something like that. Sometimes the pauses are the best parts. And the hardest to write.)

"You said two cars and a motorcycle." (Damn.) "That's a serious allegation."

"I know. Somebody has to do something about it."

"And that's the whole story?"

I would let it be.

"I spent the rest of the night being interrogated by Lieutenant Conventerra and Sergeant Kuggelsomething."

"Kuggelsong," said the mayor.

"They kept me there until morning, asking questions, mostly about me, strange questions that had nothing to do with what I had witnessed. You already know more in these last few minutes than they would let me tell them in hours of interrogation. They told me I was hallucinating. They made veiled threats. Kuggelsong punched me in the stomach."

"Now, that's another serious accusation."

"They didn't think so."

"Ripley, the cops are covering this up?"

"Now, Valene, let's not jump to conclusions before all the facts are in. You say this happened in February? That was over six months ago. Why did it take you so long to bring this to my attention?"

"It became clear that the police weren't going to do anything. No accusations, but I thought they were covering it up. I tried to locate Valene for corroboration. For some time, I couldn't find her, and when I did—"

"I dummied up?" she said. "I didn't want to get involved?"

"And now, six months later, what do you want of me?"

"To do something about it. What do you think we want?"

"What would you like me to do about it?"

"I don't know, call in the FBI?"

"You have evidence?"

"Yeah, him and me? That's why we're here?" said Valene.

She was coming through for me, that flinty uptalker. My feelings for her were changing, though they started at such a low bar they had nowhere to go but up.

"I didn't know where to turn," I told Hirkill. "I was sure no one would believe me. Conventerra's position was that I was a raving lunatic, subject to hallucinations. When Valene finally backed me up, she convinced me that we should reach out to you."

"I must tell you, Doctor Kecksmeckski, and Valene already knows this, I'm sure, that Maragate has long been considered by many to be the magnetic center of the universe."

"I've not heard that."

"It's true," she said.

"Quite often," the mayor went on, "until they adjust to it, new-comers are prone to visions. Over the years, countless people have called the police reporting all manner of things they have seen, while the old-timers smile and accept them for what they are: visions."

"Lieutenant Conventerra never told you about me, about what I saw, and the interrogation?"

"Why would he? He reports to the chief. The chief never reported a police shooting to me. My goodness."

"Well, there was one," I said. "It wasn't a figment of my imagination. It wasn't a vision. And I do have another witness. Valene."

"Valene," said the mayor, as though speaking to a child, "why did you, as you put it, dummy up when Doctor Keckskimetric first approached you?"

"Okay, I've been letting my house out, okay, as a vacation rental? I wanted to stay below the radar? No but yeah, my conscience got the best of me?"

"Skipping out on the T.O.T., were you?"

She looked at me and explained: "Transient occupancy tax?"

"That, too, is a serious matter, but we will put that aside for the moment. Tell me, Valene, did you ever see this black woman before? Before you saw her shot."

Valene hesitated. I did not want her to lie, but the truth would not help us.

"I never actually saw her? I mean, when they shot, it spooked Rufus and he ran like hell, and me after him, and it was foggy as fuck?"

"So am I to understand Doctor Cruskamenski was the only one to see this victim?"

"No," I said, "the police saw her, and they saw who she was."

"Who was she?"

"That's the hell of it, Ripley. Go ahead, DK, tell him the rest of it, the best part?"

The mayor leaned forward in his chair. I was reluctant to go on, but where else could I go?

"The cops shot an angel," I said. "Yes, you heard me correctly. An angel. She fell right in front of my face."

For a long moment, no one moved or made a sound. Then Hirkill picked up his phone and said, "Ruthie, anybody waiting down there? Good. Nobody else today. Lock up when you go to lunch."

https://www.quora.com
/Are-wrong-decisions-better-than-indecision

We left the meeting cheerful and encouraged that the miscast mayor was going to stand up, jump in, and expose what happened that night. Though he looked for more credible explanations—and who wouldn't?—the story of angels among us was not dismissed. We joined him in trying to find some other possibility. It could have been a traveler, one of a tribe that plagued the town, young people with no purpose in life, squatting in vacant homes, sometimes wearing costumes. (Like the Romantic poets who came back into my life.) But what of the glow? Maybe from the TV or the fireplace or a camera flash. And the wings, were they even real?

"You're sure you saw wings?" asked Mayor Hirkill.

"Hard to miss."

"But maybe it could have been something else?"

"Like what?"

"A white shirt billowing out behind. The kids wear these oversized shirts, untucked and sometimes unbuttoned."

"Her wings were charcoal grayish."

I considered all of what he said, to keep him on our side. "I don't think it was a shirt, black or otherwise, but I suppose the wings could have been fake," I said.

"Exactly! A costume."

"But why? Who wears fake wings, sitting in a house alone? Naked."

"Oh, you'd be surprised what people do when they think they're alone."

"I didn't see any means of attachment," I said. "For the wings. No straps or anything like that. They were coming out of her skin, and . . . and she . . ."

"Go on, Doctor Krossacessi."

"She folded them as she died."

"Well, now wait a minute," said the mayor. "We've been so wrapped up in the drama we've forgotten the most important thing. We can all agree, can't we, that angels don't die."

"If we can do that, then we're also agreeing that they do exist."

"We would be, wouldn't we?" he said, deflated. "But if we suspend our disbelief and agree they exist, we don't have to accept that they die."

"I think we do," I said. "All things that live will die. Unless they're immortal."

"Which angels are, I believe."

"But things we believe are immortal may not be, including God. He might have left the building before the last set."

"Instead of dying they might just transform," said the mayor.

"Which is the deal with all of us?" stated Valene equivocally.

"Technically, I don't know that she died or was taken prisoner or that she transformed into something else. All I know is that she was shot, by police, and she looked dead."

"Have you ever seen a dead person?"

"Yes, but I've never seen one die violently."

"It is disturbing. Traumatic to most observers. Never sure how it happened, who's to blame, and takes forever to forget, and then it still comes back at you. I have another question. This angel, if that's what it was, why did she choose Valene's house? Did she have a reason, or was it a random choice?"

No way was I going to tell him what Mary told me, that the angel

made a mistake. She was supposed to be in my house. I have a theory but let's hold off on that for the moment. She was obviously a
winged messenger, but with no skill at reading a topographical map.
Fortunately, Valene had a credible explanation:

"Shit is always happening to me?"

"We have to find out who or what was shot that night," I said.
"That will answer all other questions. Are you with us, Your Honor?
It's going to take a thorough investigation."

"I'm in," he said. "We've already started the investigation, right
here, the three of us. I will contact the chief—"

"We can't allow the police to investigate themselves," I said.

"Why not?"

"That's a traditional practice proven dicey at the least, especially
when it comes to cops shooting black people."

"Isn't the racial issue superseded by the species issue?"

"One may outweigh the other, but the police must not be allowed
to investigate themselves for anything. You can't expect *anyone* to
investigate himself."

"It's what we all do, though. That's why we're here," said the
mayor, in what I saw then as a reasonable philosophical posit, applicable to all realms.

"You're talking about taking moral stock, but we didn't commit
the crime. It's a legal investigation, not a moral one. The cops are
going to say she had a weapon and they feared for their lives, even
though she was naked. They're always fearing for their lives, so
everything looks like a weapon."

In the time we spent with the mayor his spirits rose and tumbled.
He defended the local police, all of whom he knew personally, but
he agreed finally that an independent investigation was called for in
this case. He would head it and keep it on the "down-low."

Naturally, I said nothing about the three kids who cautioned me
against the mayor, calling him and the cops dirty, or that he himself was the subject of surveillance by persons unknown. (You see,
when necessary I can keep a secret.) I would not make the mistake

of claiming a conversation with Shelley, his wife Mary, John Keats. and Lord Byron. ("If I should meet thee/After many long years/How should I greet thee?/With silence and tears.") I made a mistake like that back when I was a thirteen-year-old freshman in Owego Free Academy. After having been forced to read Scott's epic poem for an English assignment, I had a vision of the Lady of the Lake. We may have been the last class in the history of American education required to endure that particular assignment, but I admit the poem had a powerful effect upon my young psyche and may have set me on my life's course. During a classroom discussion, Mr. McGregor asked us to imagine what the Lady of the Lake looked like. We could draw a picture for extra credit, a useless exercise but one that he hoped might spark some creativity in a class that would much rather participate in a good game of hangman. I volunteered that I didn't have to imagine what the Lady of the Lake looked like because I saw her the weekend before, standing on a skiff just off the shore of Cayuga Lake, and if I had had a camera at the time I could have taken her picture, because she wasn't all that shy. She was not much taller than I, I told Mr. McGregor and the class. (I was five foot two at the time. I grew twelve inches in the next three years.) She had long chestnut colored hair in ringlets and was draped in flowing silks from neck to ankles. Her feet were bare and pale and perfect. She smiled but said not a word. Her smile made birds sing. (It probably sounded like I had a boyish crush on her. [I *did*!]) Mr. McGregor called me a smart-ass, and all the kids laughed because they were always primed for me to say something goofy. (I may not have been the one who invented the stunt of holding your tongue while saying, "Molasses on the table," but in my school I was the one who perpetuated it.) Mr. McGregor ordered a sit-down with Miss Cunningham, the counselor. I assured her that I had never seen any other characters of fiction come alive. (I swallowed back my sighting of Silas Marner, who was driving a yellow Buick at the time, because that would not support my vision, it would only confirm my original smart-assness.) Miss Cunningham had a word with my parents and suggested I be made to apologize to the whole class for being such a wiseguy. I did, an apology memorized by rote, then I sat down in shame. When Mr. McGregor stepped out of the classroom with Miss Cunningham, I stood up again and announced to my classmates, "Fuck you all, I *did* see the Lady of the Lake, and I hope I see her again."

But I never did.

www.walterscott.lib.ed

A load was lifted off my chest. Valene and I had done the right thing, at some risk to ourselves, and she was confident that Hirkill would get to the bottom of it. "He'll come off as a crusader for justice?" It would be advantageous to his reelection. Though that was already in the bag, he liked to remind the voters how necessary he was to their own well-being.

We waited to hear back from him, and during that time I looked everywhere for the poets, hope fading that they were, one, real, and, two, going to do what they said. After three days, we called the mayor's office for an update. Ruthie said he was unavailable. We waited a week and called again. Two days after that we each received official letters, mine from the city attorney, Valene's from the city clerk. My letter ominously outlined the legal consequences of false accusations and fanciful tales, citing precedents in law concerning, among other dire consequences, involuntary commitments for exhibiting dangerous behavior. The letter also raised rumors of the disappearance of my wife and the possibilities of foul play, and if any investigations were to commence, perhaps that would be a good starting point. Valene received a letter including indecipherable forms demanding payment of back T.O.T. in the amount of five times what she actually skimmed, or she would be subject to a $100,000 fine and three years in prison. Both letters were strident in tone and threatened draconian punishments that I knew could not be levied in a democratic society. But does one ever really know? Some felons are growing old in Texas prisons for using controlled substances back in the sixties that are no longer controlled, except in Texas. Even so, I felt sorry for Valene—she had much more to lose than I—but she took it in good stride. She wasn't going to let that little weasel push her around? I thought we might become friends, with or without benefits, if I could ever get her to speak like an adult.

Rain had been falling off and on since the morning after we spoke to Hirkill. I had cabin fever. One day I called Valene and asked her to meet for coffee at Starbucks, a reasonable walk from both our houses. (A reasonable walk from anywhere in America gets you to a Starbucks.)

"Like a date?"

"Sure," I said.

We each brought our threatening letter to read together and to plot our next move, if there was to be one. Valene's suggestion was, "You could write a press release? For all the wire services?"

"I don't know how to write a press release or how to disseminate it, and I would rather not have my vision of a black angel become the focus of the story."

"Duh?"

"The focus should be the police and political corruption in Maragate."

"There's always the *Herald?*" she said half-heartedly.

"They already dislike me."

"I know . . . but you're not *un*likeable?"

The rain was heavier now. Valene checked her weather app. "Flood warning. I mean, like, serious warnings?"

We decided to table it, stick a pin in it, put it on the back burner, roll it up in a sock, sleep on it, pray on it (her idea), put it in the pending tray for a rainy day—which this one was already—and get home before the rain got any worse. (Too late.)

The sky turned black, and the rain, after going sideways, cascaded, creating the sensation of walking through Niagara Falls. (Which I'd done for years in nightmares, after having been forced by my parents to ride under it on a tourist boat.) We had umbrellas, but within a block of Munkar Bridge we were soaked. The puddles we jumped over on the way to Starbucks had grown to water traps. Street gutters were awash, floating leaves the blowers had removed the day before, spilling over the sidewalks. I looked more closely. Raw sewerage was floating in the water.

"Where does all this shit go?" I shouted.

"Cherona River. Maragate's not big on drainage?"

"Does this mean the drought is over?"

"The drought will, like, never be over?"

Which meant that the epidemic could now begin. Suffer.

We crossed the bridge. I stopped to look down. The river was rising before my eyes. It reached to the top of the low bank across the street from Valene's house and gained momentum down First Street. Valene held on to my sleeve. I did the gentlemanly thing and helped her to get home. At her door she said, "You'd better stay with me? This is another one of those hundred-year storms. It's going to get dangerous, I mean fast?"

"*Another*? When did you have the last hundred-year storm?"

"Three years ago. Seven people disappeared?"

"The town didn't do anything about drainage after that?"

"They said it was a hundred-year storm? We'd never see one like that again, they said. But they said that the time before the last one?"

I waited until she was safely inside and then made my way to my hovel, slogging through the disgusting water, which was rising. The river, made fierce by the deluge, reached Second Street. On the sidewalk, I slogged through sewage mid-calf high.

By the time I got home, the front yard was under water, which was threatening to rise above the stoop and into the house itself.

I took off my shoes and my drenched pants outside on the stoop.

Inside, I called for Carlos. The house was cold and dark. The power was off. The roof was leaking in several spots, dripping into pots Carlos had placed under them.

"Carlos!"

He came down from my room with a flashlight and a bucketful of water.

"I replaced the bucket under your leak," he said. "It is so boring."

"My leak?"

He opened the door to the cellar, asked me to hold the flashlight, and emptied the bucket into the water that had already flooded the space. It had risen high enough to take out the hot water heater and furnace. A rat was clinging to a short length of two-by-four.

"Can I make you a quesadilla, señor?"

"Is this really the time for a quesadilla? We're experiencing a hundred-year storm."

"Si, señor. We will live through this. I'm afraid the water heater and furnace will have to be replaced. Also, the drywall in the basement. Mold, you know."

He went to the fireplace and started a fire. I stood in my underwear with no thought of doing anything to protect hearth and home.

"I am sure," Carlos said, "the water in the crawl space has taken out the duct system." He noticed I was immobile in my spot. "Have no fear, señor, I have already called the proper repairmen and we are high on their schedule. We are insured, it will all be taken care of. You can go on with your writing or whatever. In a few weeks, we will be as good as new."

Carlos's disinterest had nothing to do with the calm that came over me. Let it rain. Let it flood. Let the deluge carry everything away.

"On the positive side," said Carlos, as he returned to the kitchen, "let the feast begin! I must cook all the food in the fridge and the food in the freezer as it thaws. After the thaw (he laughed: my title), comes the feasting. Good news! We are cooking with gas!"

I laughed, too. "Sometimes," I said, "you just have to say, fuck it all."

"*Que bueno!* That's the spirit!"

"Let's have that quesadilla."

By the time I finished my snack, the noise of the rain pounding on the roof diminished. I took a look outside. A small river of shit still ran down the street, but the rain had stopped and the flood waters were receding. In the backyard, I stood to the side while Carlos opened the outside door to the cellar. All of the water from inside gushed out, carrying with it bits and pieces of whatever had been borne on it, including that rat on his raft.

www.water.usgs.gov/edu/100yearflood.html

Nine people disappeared in that storm's flood, never to be seen again. The mayor extended thoughts and prayers. He was surprised that the number wasn't higher, as if to say, maybe next time. Felicity and the other agents scrambled to get the listing on nine newly available houses. The reason each storm was classified as a "hundred-year storm" was to put off any attempt at engineering municipal drainage, a costly undertaking. The fantasy of unseating Hirkill had some righteous appeal for me. All that might be required would be awakening the electorate to issues they had long ago accepted as what they had to live with, including leaf blowers, which came out in unprecedented numbers following the storm. Most of the debris was blown from one property to another. And back again.

Doc Fleck ignored my earlier rebuke and on his own gathered an "exploratory committee." They summoned me to a meeting. Harmony Meadows and Al Myra, my allies from the last council meeting, were there, along with two people who were introduced to me as Learned Cropp, director of the local community center, and Chrissy Nayler, founder of an LGBTQ group called I Yam. Valene was there with a winning smile, proud of herself for keeping the secret. Sandy appointed herself official photographer of the event and took scores of pictures with her iPhone, which struck me as odd because by all appearances the meeting was clandestine.

It was held in a back room of the King's Arms pub. Everyone but I turned his head to the wall when the wench came into the room with a pitcher of Guinness, a carafe of pistachio gin, and a bowl of smoky rabbit jerky.

"Everyone knows why we're here," Doc said, after she left, in his halting manner, fighting for each breath.

"Everyone but I," I said, my tone too arch by half.

"DK, I'll get right to the point. We want you to run for mayor."

"Maybe next time," I said, which was supremely sarcastic. Next time, I would be far, far away, having lunch at either La Coupole in Montparnasse or Pink's on La Brea.

"A decision has to be made tonight. Tomorrow is the last day to file."

Doc handed a folder to Valene, who still smiling conspiratorially, opened it on a table. I saw scattered sheets of signatures. "The only requirement is that a candidate has to get thirty signatures in support of his candidacy," Doc said. "We have two hundred and nineteen, all gathered within the last forty-eight hours."

"Are they real?"

"Of course they're real."

"Because I don't know more than a few people in town. Even the people it this room, it seems, don't want anyone knowing they're here."

"Second nature," said Chrissy. "We're hoping to sandbag Hirkill."

"Hirkill has infiltrated my board," said Learned Cropp. "I'm walking a tightrope."

The community center was housed in an abandoned distillery and survived on grants and donations in a town where donating was seen as assuaging some hidden guilt or, worse, perpetuating a dependence on the kindness of strangers. Hirkill had managed over the years to cut the center's share of city grants to near zero while still publicly expressing great support for the work it was doing. I learned that night that another one of his long games was to tear down the community center and turn the site over to developers for retail, office spaces, and condos, one of which he would snag for himself at a deep discount with an interest-free mortgage. His fallback plan was that legislation would go through allowing small tribes to lease land in order to build and run casinos away from their own reservations, clearing the way to tear down the community center and lease the land to the Cattawissas, a tribe of sixteen, more like an extended family, living on an acre and a half on the east edge of town. It would necessitate a rezoning, but Hirkill would have no trouble with that. Four of the members of the planning commission were in his pocket. How he might benefit from a casino in the middle of town could be imagined.

"And then there's the leaf blower shit storm," said Al, the Vietnam vet. "Since Harmony and me spoke up, the landscapers are unloading on our houses big time. I'm a freakin' wreck, man."

"I'm afraid to leave the house," said Harmony.

The noise was already so unbearable where I lived that I thought it could not become any worse. (A truism: no matter how miserable you may be, it can always get worse. Suffer.)

"He's been campaigning for months, so there has to be someone running against him."

"Oh, sure," said Doc. "Chester Manfred is running against him."

"Then throw your support behind Chester Manfred."

"Chester Manfred is the mayor's protégé, his hand-picked opponent. He runs against him every election and gets about thirty-five percent of the vote. Hirkill gets forty-five percent and the rest go to Kim Kardashian, The Situation, and Donald Trump. That's on a turnout of about thirty percent, unless there's a hot initiative on the ballot."

"And there seldom is," said Chrissy.

"Then why does he campaign so hard?"

"It's who he is and all that he is. He loves campaigning."

"Why do people vote for him?"

"Force of habit. Fear. Quid pro quo. A grudge against the town. Some might actually like him."

I accepted a shot and a beer from Al, who appointed himself the designated bartender, which did not require that he himself stay sober.

"What the hell is going on in this town?" I said, and not for the first time. How could a town turn itself over to Hirkill, a flip-flopper and double-crosser? A man with no family, without visible means of support, unclean, inarticulate, who looked so much like William Burroughs it gave me the creeps. (In his office, I looked at his hands. Burroughs had cut off his little finger to impress some man over whom he became obsessed. I couldn't tell if Hirkill was missing a digit. And that silver apple. Burroughs was playing William Tell when he killed his wife.)

I sucked up the shot of gin and swirled it around the leftover mouthfeel of the shard of rabbit jerky I'd just eaten.

Chrissy might be the strongest of the group, I thought, with the most energy, certainly the youngest. She had short hair, severely groomed with lots of product, a navy blue vest over a short-sleeved blouse, and blue jeans. I could not tell if she was lesbian, gay, bi, transgender, queer, or some combination. (Just curious. Didn't matter. Don't sue me.)

"He publicly expresses great support for our group," she said, "then works in the shadows to deny us any permits for fundraisers or consciousness-raising demonstrations. We tried to hold a Transgender Day of Visibility in a quarter of the Circle. He said he preferred invisibility."

"Think about it, DK," Doc said, "from this room alone you can get the community center vote, the gay vote, the anti–leaf blower vote, the dog owner's vote . . . and the votes from everybody who's sick of Hirkill."

"That would be just about everybody," said Al Myra. "A landslide."

"Look, I'm a newcomer. Don't you have to live in town for a year or something?"

"No! That's how Hirkill became mayor in the first place. Just six months, and you qualify."

The reminder that I'd been a prisoner for over six months deepened the funk I was already in. Would another six months pass by in much the same way? Suffer.

"I have zero history of public service or even volunteering. I don't know the local issues."

"The council avoids local issues! They make proclamations, they pass resolutions on pipelines and bailouts and wars. Doesn't mean shit, but they feel good about taking a stand."

"It's a wild idea, me of all people."

I took a moment. My disaffection for Maragate ran counter to any kind of public service.

Finally, it was Al Myra who spoke up.

"After 'Nam I thought all the fight was knocked out of me, but by God I'm ready to muster one more time, one more search-and-destroy mission, ready to toss myself on the rotating gears of the machine and bring it to a halt."

He was echoing lines from some of the young activist orators of the sixties, when a generation fought against injustice, risked their futures, and put it all on the line. Nothing is so stirring as newfound commitment to an impossible cause.

"Please do this, sweetie," Valene pleaded. "What have you got to lose?"

"Win, and all you got to do is serve one term," said Doc. "You'll have an office, a quiet place where you can work on your western. You can push through a ban on blowers and make it quiet enough for you to write at home after your term is over."

"Say yes," pleaded Learned Cropp.

I loved the idea of having a quiet office. I remembered how pleased I was when Paramount gave me an office on the lot. I would get up every morning and make the short commute drinking coffee and listening to NPR. I would put in a good long day's work, and then I would drive home, like I had a real job. Often, I would have Cobb salad at the commissary with Ridley Scott or Barry Levinson, talking projects, or with Linda Fiorentino or Raquel Welch, flirting. Good times. Maybe I could duplicate that in Maragate. I could go to my office at City Hall every day, have lunch at Hot Diggity Hot Dogs with Al Myra or Learned Cropp, talking local issues, or with Chrissy Nayler or Harmony Meadows, not even flirting. Maybe I could make a difference, if not for the town, for myself. I could find at last some purpose in the torture of waiting for Hope.

"Does the mayor have any power over the police?" I asked.

Doc broke into a wide smile. "He's the chief executive. If he wants someone fired he can do that. He can influence protocol and procedures."

"Or get a cop to break somebody's jaw," added Chrissy.

"Could he demand an investigation into police activity?"

"For sure."

"That's what I'm talking about!" trilled Valene.

Hirkill, that little weasel, went running to the city attorney. He couldn't wait to be part of the cover-up.

"I'm in," I said.

(The next day the weather would turn out to be unseasonably cold. The irony was not lost on me. In skullcap, gloves, and a Patagonia windbreaker I pushed Doc in his chair to City Hall where he showed me how to register to vote and to file papers to run for office.)

A muted cheer went up, hugs and handshakes all around, and what began as an exploration turned into a celebration, subdued but wet. Sandy and I found ourselves alone in a corner of the room. I don't know how we got there. I believe she led me there by the elbow. She wasn't at all drunk.

"You don't have to do this," she said.

"It *is* a little nuts."

"People are always looking for the Messiah."

"Not me."

"Or a hero at least. Someone to get out in front."

"Not me either."

I selfishly imagined having influence over the police. I could find out once and for all what happened that first night in February. Best of all, I would be the boss of Conventerra and Kuggelsong. Sandy moved closer to me, leaning her body into mine. Over her shoulder, I saw Valene looking at us and doing a slow burn. Doc was raising his glass with the others.

"Tell me something you've never told anyone," Sandy whispered.

Where did *that* come from? It brought back memories of parties when I was a hot young screenwriter, and some actress on the come would start something up with me.

"You first," I said. (Which is what I used to say back then.)

"Okay, I will. I'm having an affair."

"Whoa. I expected you to say you dye your hair."

"Why would I dye my hair?"

"Why would you have an affair?"

"DK, look at me. I'm still young, and Doc . . . you know. I still have needs."

"Does he know?"

"No, and you're not going to tell him."

I did not want the burden of that secret, especially since I had already dropped the hint to Doc and he chose to step on it. She cornered me like that for the sole purpose of confessing. Why me? (I say that a lot, don't I?)

"Don't you want to know who with?" she asked.

"Lieutenant Conventerra," I said, deadpan.

"Wow. You're good."

"A cop? *That* cop?"

It always makes a difference, doesn't it? The affair is one thing, the person with whom you're having it is often a bigger thing. Lying about it is the worst thing. (I'm told.)

"Now it's your turn," she said.

The party game I thought this might be was already over, as the party itself was winding down. It was no longer entertaining. She looked up at me, waiting. I could have walked away. But, okay, if you're going to lay something like that on me, I'll see your affair and raise you one murder. And, like an affair, *who* is a bigger thing than *what*.

"Back in February I witnessed a murder. I saw the cops shoot somebody." Her reaction was a widening of the eyes. "Don't you want to know who?" She nodded. "I saw them murder an angel, a beautiful black angel. I told Conventerra. He didn't believe me."

I was more upset by her affair than she was by my angel. "What will you do with what I told you?" I asked.

"What will you do?"

"I've already done all I can. Unless I can win this election."

On the walk home Valene wanted to know what Sandy and I were so chummy about.

"I told her about the angel."

"Was that a good idea?"

"Don't know."

"Did she freak out?"

"Not at all."

"She probably thinks you're crazy."

"Probably."

"I think it's time to escalate our relationship?"

"And what would that escalator be rising to?" I asked.

"Something sexual."

Now, you must remember, I had always been true to my wife. But it had been over six months, and I had serious doubts I would ever see her again, to the point of hoping I wouldn't, at least not in this place. I made it clear that the ride up the escalator she was proposing would be strictly recreational.

"Spend the night," she said. "You won't regret it."

As I mentioned, she was in her own way attractive and she did have a self-professed skill set I wouldn't mind seeing demonstrated.

Best of all, she had put together two sentences that avoided upspeak. A turn-on.

"I'll make you feel better all over than anywhere else."

Another declarative sentence, though something of a head-scratcher. Anyway, I was halfway there.

Still, I begged off. Let's say I'd been overserved at the celebration. In heels, she was as tall as I, and our faces were right there, close to each other, so, yes, I'll confess to some kissing and incidental groping, but it went no further than that. It wasn't exactly innocent, but it was not enough to break up a long marriage, if ever I had to review my time in Maragate. (Which I am doing now.)

www.innocenceproject.org/causes/false-confessions

As always, Carlos was waiting up for me. As soon as I came inside, he turned off the living room light and made for his casita. I stopped him.

"Carlos?"

"*Si*, señor."

"Remember that morning I saw you come out of a meeting with the mayor?"

"The day I saw you waiting to see him, with that woman, yes."

"I'd like to know why you were seeing him."

"As would I like to know why you were with that woman, but I would never ask."

"Thank you, but I have to ask. How close are you with Hirkill?"

"Then I would have to ask you the same question, in regard to the young lady who is not your wife."

Do you get the feeling I was no match for him?

"We are no more than associates working on a common cause," I said. "That day we were in City Hall on an issue of local government."

"As was I."

"I didn't know you were interested in local government."

"And why wouldn't I be? Maragate is my home, my permanent home."

"You never mentioned anything about local government except to praise it."

"I find your new interest far more surprising, since you express your contempt for the community openly. But if you must know, the mayor was interviewing me for an appointment to the planning commission, which is an important position in Maragate, a stepping-stone to the council, which is unrepresented in the Hispanic community. That is to say, there has never been a Latino on the council, or on the commission for that matter."

"You? You never leave the house."

"It is a problem, yes. I told the mayor that my looking after you gives me little free time."

"I see you at breakfast and dinner. If you're looking after me, you're doing it from a distance."

"I do it all the same. I pledged to the señora that I would take care of you."

I was too tired to argue that I could take care of myself.

"If you do want to get on that commission, you'd better hurry. I'm running for mayor, and I doubt I would appoint you to anything."

I meant for that to cap the conversation in my favor, and I suppose it did, except for his giggling at the notion that I could unseat Hirkill.

www.plannersweb.com/topics/being

The unexpected influence of the newcomer is always interesting whenever or wherever it occurs. It is in the cherished tradition of the American western. A lone rider comes into town. He has no stake in the place, but when trouble arises, he risks his life to do the right thing. Triumphant, refusing any other reward besides a kiss from the schoolmarm, he rides off into the sunset. My western had none of that. When The Kid and Ham the African came down from the mountain on their mules, after the thaw (I really liked the new title), they were treated first with scorn, then with enthusiastic acceptance when it was learned they possessed gold dust. These two odd companions had, however, a vision for the future in a town that was mired in the past. The Captain knew it would lead to trouble.

Two weeks after announcing my candidacy for mayor at a press conference for the staff, all three of them, of the *Maragate Herald*, I was named by a "select committee" as the city's honorary alcalde. I had no idea what an alcalde was, honorary or otherwise. (Do you?) I'd been honored by a town that evoked in me only dread. Doc Fleck, now my campaign manager, was on fire. I'd never seen him happy before.

The appointment of honorary alcalde was made yearly, he told me, and up until then given to someone with decades of local service and conspicuous boosterism. Presenting the award to a newcomer was unprecedented. (And not too unlike naming the lone stranger in town as sheriff.)

"This is huge," said Doc, when he read me the announcement. "Huge!" Alcalde, he explained, is either a Portuguese or Spanish or Italian word, used in this context as recognition for someone who has risen high, or in my case subliminally, in the esteem of his fellow citizens, a kind of honorary mayor.

"Wait, I'm running for actual mayor," I said. "Is this a way of tossing me a bone?"

"The opposite. They want you to crush Hirkill."

Elsewhere in the paper was a public statement from Hirkill objecting, not as the mayor, mind you, but as an ordinary citizen. Any number of more deserving people, he said, could have been honored. I did not disagree.

"The 'they' that want me to crush him. Who are they?"

"The select committee."

"And who are they?"

"No one knows. Membership rotates, and the names are kept secret."

"Someone must know."

"Well, yeah, there is a chairman, but that rotates too."

"And his name is kept secret."

"Naturally."

I read the article in dizzy disbelief. My name was misspelled and the misspelling was inconsistent. It described me as a famous screenwriter who fell in love with Maragate and moved here several months ago after buying a home, sight unseen. Since then, it went on, I've had a positive effect upon my adopted hometown, volunteering for the community center, Take Some Paws Animal Rescue, and a variety of other local organizations. The article described me as having a lifetime membership in The Friends of the Library and being a true friend to the Hispanic, Asian, African American, and LGBTQ communities. (Apart from Terry and Benny at Hamburger Benny, I didn't know there *was* an African American community, and the only Asians I ever saw were the boy who helped me with my iPhone at Starbucks and the hostess at Thai-O-Thai.) I was an unrelenting activist for the quality of life in Maragate, I learned, and a great supporter of the arts and of the local gin and jerky industries—that much was true—and a valued member of B'nai B'rith. (I'm not Jewish.) Most outrageously, I was a close friend and confidant of Al Pacino. (I worked with him briefly, but we were hardly good friends. I had never mentioned Pacino to anybody, though most people know how to use imdb.com.) What's more, the article went on, I was in the process of writing a screenplay for a feature film set in Maragate in which Pacino would star. (He *would* be an interesting choice for the Captain, that world-weariness thing.) The production would use local talent for the smaller roles, provide jobs, and give national attention to our fair city. I was liberally quoted: "I've found my little slice of heaven, and I want to share it with the world. Everybody bet me that I would fall in love with Maragate, and I guess they win. The small-town charm I've encountered here has warmed my heart and has inspired me artistically, profession-ally, and personally. I plan never to leave."

I almost puked. (My least favorite scene in any movie. The next would be the shrink/patient scene, followed by the two guys stand-ing at urinals scene.)

In a footnote, the select committee acknowledged that Dr. Kescekmétis (sic) is currently running for mayor but his being named alcalde should not be construed as an endorsement.

"It's an endorsement," said Doc.

"How is this possible?"

"In Maragate, all things are possible. It's like the Army."

https://en.wikipedia.org/wiki/Alcalde

The first evil, and apparently a necessary one, of any democracy is that before you can run for public office you have to come up with the money for your campaign. Without enough money, you cannot even run for senior class president. In my case, however, money was not a problem. Shortly after my last conversation with my agent, I began withdrawing twenty dollars a day, my maximum, from the ATM (the ATM in the proximity of which we do not necessarily gag), squirreling it away for that special day I would take my leave. I had around $2,500 and I contributed all of it to my own cam-paign, said investment cutting off my only plan for escape. No rules were in place against self-financing. Hirkill got his money from the chamber of commerce.

(An interesting aside: I needed a place to stash my cash without Carlos discovering it, so one night at the farmers market I bought an eighteen-by-twenty-four inch painting from one of the artists who sold their dreadful stuff there, a wolf baying at the moon, done in acrylics. The artist was thrilled with the thirty dollars I gave her.

I took it home, *un poco borracho*, and showed it to Carlos, who commented, "The señor has found a find." He volunteered to hang it for me, in my closet perhaps. I informed him that I was capable enough to hang a painting, and I would give it a place of honor. But then I had to ask him where I could find the proper tools. I worried that he would suspect I was hiding something behind that painting, which was indeed my intention, so I hung it on my bedroom wall. But I then removed my cork board, now filled with notes I'd made on *After the Thaw*. It looked like someone had already cut out a hole in the wall behind it. A crude patch covered it. I opened the space and discovered an empty gin bottle standing in the framing. The bottle was old and dusty with a label I did not recognize, and inside of it was it a note. I wrapped the bottle in a towel so that Carlos would not hear anything when I hit it with my hammer. I unfolded the note: "Give up Hope." I reeled and fell back on the bed. I lay there numb and dumb. Recovered from the initial shock, I reasoned, again, that everything was not always about me. Some long ago lush, probably predating Carlos, put it there, some tenant who decided to replace his old and moldy drywall with cheap beaverboard. He knew that someday a subsequent tenant would tear down the hovel or at least trash his handiwork, and he wanted to give that unfortunate individual the benefit of what he'd learned in Maragate. The note had nothing to do with me. I think I was rattled so much because he capitalized "Hope.")

At the Bank of Maragate ATM, I finished my transaction—getting another twenty bucks—and turned to see that the next person in line was Mary Shelley, as I was calling her. (Though she could have been Mary Mary quite contrary for all I knew.)

"You show up now?" I said. "I've been looking all over for you and your gang. You kind of weirdly dangled some hope and then vanished."

"Pray, do you know what you are doing?" she whispered, as though I were doing something inappropriate. She stepped out of line and pulled me by the elbow. "Come with me."

"Where are we going?"

"You may have to tell me."

She wore a black felt hat with a wide brim, and sunglasses. She had on the same jeans I saw her in the first time, with a hole in the knee. "I've got a lot going on right now," I said, I'm running for mayor you might have heard."

"Who has not? Everyone's talking about it."

I felt jerked around, but it's not as though I had a pressing appointment.

We walked east away from Spanish Circle and into Nu4U, a thrift shop, where a few tourists pawed over the used goods. We went past bric-a-brac, gin memorabilia, and women's wear until we reached the men's corner, where Shelley, Byron, and Keats, as I called them (again, they could have been the Bowery Boys), were trying on sport coats long out of fashion and old-guy caps that made them look ridiculous.

"Behold the candidate," said Mary dryly.

"What is this cloak and dagger stuff? What do you want from me?"

"Do you know what you're doing?" PB asked.

"You're not the first to ask me that. What am I supposed to be doing? Is it about my running for mayor?"

"Do you not find it strange that you have become the man of the hour?"

"I do. What could be stranger, and how would it be any business of yours? I assume you're not registered to vote."

"Listen to yourself," said Mary, "you're enlisting into the harmony."

"What does that mean?"

"You've been enticed out of nothing else to do," said Georgie. "Your idleness undoes you."

"Not cool," said Mary. Her odd accent was killing me.

"Soon you will be powerless to escape," said Georgie.

"That happened long ago. I'm trying to make the most of it."

"Soon you too will think this is a little slice of heaven," said PB.

"Hardly, but it doesn't have to be hell on a cracker either. That's why I'm running for mayor."

In truth, I was no longer so eager for them to "hie" me away. They never said where, they never said why, and for all I knew they shared the same delusions.

"A window will open, but it will close again in a trice."

"A trice? Who *are* you people?"

"Consider us fixers, in personae not unfamiliar to you. From here you can go in only one of two directions. Either way you will need a pull or a push. We're the pull. Take the pull, my friend. The bell tolls no clearer."

"Really? It's clearer now, is it? Why are you so interested in me?"

"Honestly, we're not," she said, "but we pay our debts."

"Is there any way we can parse this to its essentials, or at least state it a tad less obliquely?"

"You are a mistake," said Jack, like a mad scientist.

"I knew it."

"And now you are looking to make eternity trivial," cautioned Mary.

"I am not. My movies are not trivial. My life is not trivial. Where did you come from? Are you even of this world?"

"What world?" said PB, which caught me off guard. Truth be told, I always believed there was more than one, but could not fathom how or where it might exist outside of my own mind.

"Some things," Mary said, and finished in a singsong, "that happened for the first time, seem to be happening again."

"But I have to know where and when," I hissed, frustrated, my purchase on reality slipping away. "Please tell me, in plain English, what it is you want of me, and then I can respond. Make it clear, in sentences I can understand."

They all smiled. An irony I was missing was obvious to them. (Maybe that, as poets, simple clarity was anathema to them, and I should know that.)

Said Jack: "E'en like the passage of an angel's tear/That falls through the clear ether silently." (Keats. Talking about time.)

Mary added, "Angels seek but the sad. The happy can take care of themselves."

I felt as though I were defending a dissertation with a terrible hangover, after which my committee would tell me to come back in a year.

Georgie took a knitted scarf off a rack and wrapped it around his neck in the Parisian fashion. He found a mismatched geezer cap, put it on, and sauntered out of the shop without paying. In a moment, Jack said, before leaving the shop, "We will meet once again, but not after that."

The other two lingered, as though sorting out what they might say to me before they rejoined their friends. I had become impatient with them and their sense of foreboding, which at long last I was finally overcoming in myself.

"You saw an angel," said PB. (In fact, until Jack hit me with the angel's tear thing and Mary with the angel of the sad thing, I'd forgotten about that, and didn't care to be reminded.)

"And she saw you," said Mary, "too late. She was supposed to be the push."

They both hurried out of the shop. I started to chase after them, but why try?

The money I hid in that wall, where I discovered a note in a gin bottle advising the finder to give up Hope, was spent on yard signs: KECSKEMÉTI FOR MAYOR—A NEW VISION. The slogan came from Allison Waxweather, the only paid staff member of my campaign, a tireless twenty-two-year-old recent graduate of an online university with a double major in public relations and social media. She never told me what the new vision was, besides getting rid of Hirkill, but we were all impressed with her enthusiasm. We paid her eight dollars an hour.

After I was named alcalde, donations rolled in, all anonymously. We were able to host lunches at the senior center, where we promised the old and infirm rides to the polling places. We bought ads in the *Maragate Herald*, and as a result got the lion's share of free ink and photo ops. We staged a cocktail party at the community center and filled the place with starving artists agreeable to trading their votes for saffron gin and sweet chipotle jerky.

We took our signs to the farmers market, where we set up a card table near Hirkill's. Doc Fleck stopped giving him free gin. This was war. We stayed sober ourselves for a change.

That first night people warily circled my table but were fearful of approaching. Hirkill looked on smugly. Nice try, he seemed to say. Finally, I got up and mingled, introducing myself and shaking hands. This was so out of character for me that I became light-headed. When I went back to my table, people followed me in twos and threes, tentatively at first, then taking courage. Soon I had a small crowd around me, wishing me luck and asking me my agenda in guarded whispers. I told them my agenda was predicated on being a one-term mayor. That political position seemed to delight them. No town should have the same mayor forever, I said, loud enough for Hirkill to hear me.

In the days that followed, I stood and carried a No More War sign with The Old Fools, protesting two endless wars—or was it three now? I had always held my ego in check, but once the campaign began, it raged out of the closet. (Not a pretty picture.) I made the rounds of art galleries and studios during First Tuesday Art Walk and stroked my chin while taking in canvases of every conceivable view of Spanish Circle and every variety of single stem flower, lecturing to all within hearing distance on the subject of postmodernism. (I made it sound far more complicated than it needs to be. Simply put: fuck anything modern. [There I go again, sorry.] Postmodernism is here to stay, I told my audience, but of course nothing is here to stay. Postmodernism demands a high profile. Anonymity is the ultimate failure of our time. I was stealing from Lionel Trilling when I told them that the Romantic Age was characterized by serenity, the Modern Age by authenticity, and the Postmodern Age by visibility, which accounted for the phenomenon of people being famous for being famous, people like Paris Hilton and the whole Kardashian clan. One might be anti-Kardashian in this age but not non-Kardashian.) I went to local amateur theatricals, reprisals of old chestnuts like *Our Town* and *Bell, Book and Candle*, and regaled the audience during intermission with inside stories of Brad Pitt and Angelina Jolie, or Pitolie, as I decided to call them. My critics (Hirkill and Chester Manfred) said I was a Hollywood hack, out of touch with small town ordinary life. Taking a page from Karl Rove, I agreed, claiming that is exactly why I should be elected mayor, without providing details of why one should follow the other. No one asked. My forthrightness counted for more than logic.

As you might expect, I felt like a whore, a fake, a shameless opportunist. In short, like a narcissistic politician. Guess what? It worked, and isn't that all that really matters? Two weeks before election day a poll conducted by a company called Miscellaneous Soundings with a website but no other proof of existence showed Hirkill with 34 percent of the vote, Chester Manfred with 19 percent, and yours truly with a whopping 40 percent. Five percent were still undecided, and likely always would be, while 2 percent did not know an election was in the offing.

What is most astonishing is that during my frequent visits to the gin and jerky rooms, instead of sitting alone morosely getting soused on gin and belly sick on cured meats, instead of agonizing over why Hope abandoned me as she did, or how finally to write "Fade Out" at the end of my western, I was sipping spirits like a connoisseur, nibbling the jerky like a bon vivant, and declaring to the crowd clustered around me: "One must not confuse culantro with cilantro, this *culantro* infused gin would pair beautifully with a papaya salad over fried shallots and dressed with a soy-based vinaigrette."

I know, it sounds like everything I'm not, but maybe that was what I needed all along. To be not me. (Or not to be not me, that is the question.) I'm sure you know what tinnitus is. Long-time sufferers, of which I am one, want to kill themselves. But then they learn to live with it, so that should it stop, and that happens sometimes, they don't notice for days that it's gone. Similarly, days would pass without a thought of the love of my life or the wards of my imagination in the Wyoming Territory or that once I saw a dark angel murdered by the police. Times were, on the campaign trail, when I would laugh out loud at something said or seen that a month before I wouldn't have found amusing at all. Up until then, laughing out loud was something I could not get the hang of, and I was envious of those who could. In the beginning, I would force a laugh to seem like a good guy you would want to have a beer with and then elect to high office, but soon the laugh became genuine. Fake it till you make it. If you can't let it go, let it in. Steal it till you feel it.

An alcoholic doesn't know how to say goodnight, but I was hardly drinking at all. I was simply having a good time. A party? I'll be there. An after party? Lead the way.

My transformation began at the farmers market when I plunged into the crowd and said, "Hello, I'm D. K. Kecskeméti, and I'm running for mayor. Come by my table and we'll chat." By the time the market shut down for the night, the smile was no longer forced. Win or lose, at least I had a purpose. Without one you're only waiting for the day to end.

One night, after my staff took away the card table and chairs, I turned to walk home. Hirkill was staying until the last voter left the Circle.

"Do you even know what you're doing?" he asked me.

"You're not the first to ask me that, so there must be something confusing about it."

"You're an amateur."

"So was Muhammad Ali, once."

"You're in over your head."

"Then it's fortunate I can swim."

"Do you even know where you are?"

"'If you don't know where you're going, you might wind up some-place else.' Yogi Berra."

It was the first and only time I ever saw Hirkill laugh. I never saw William Burroughs laughing, in pictures of him. Laughing was an unlikely extension of an obvious resemblance, and it made me queasy. Like watching Virginia Woolf dance the Locomotion.

"Do you know how long I've been mayor here?"

"Forever is what I hear."

"And you're going to unseat me? Who do you think you are?"

"The newcomer, riding on a mule, down from the mountains, after the thaw."

He squinted his eyes. "Yeah, well, that's going to go over big." I turned to one side and saw Dennis the donut guy in the dying light pantomime jerking off.

"I had a wife once," the mayor said. I had no response to that non sequitur, and I was still trying to figure out the donut guy. Hirkill turned to see what I was looking at. Dennis quickly became engaged in tearing down his stall. "Someone shot her."

"That's terrible."

"Through the head."

"Somehow even worse."

"Yeah, you know who did it?"

"You?"

"The me I used to be. It was an accident, but, hey, I was responsible. So."

"Why are you telling me this?"

"To atone for that sin, I've devoted myself to public service. I took a dying town, a broke-down outpost away from everything, and I made it a great place to live, I put it in the black. People come here, they don't want to leave. Like you."

To be painfully honest, I was not spending as much time think-ing about leaving, and my getaway money was already spent on my campaign.

www.allaboutphilosophy.org/postmodernism.htm

Another Tuesday night, dinner alone at Square on the Circle, I bought a lottery ticket. "I probably won't win," I told McGraw. "Probably not," he agreed. My fantasies no longer included how I might make good use of millions of dollars. (I already had millions of dollars, no idea where.) After dinner we shook out dice from the leather cup for drinks and I couldn't lose. The mayor pressed his face against the outside window and was hooted by the regulars within, now including me. I was accepted, more or less, as a regular. More, because I shared my won drinks; less, because those guys were serious drinkers with histories of colorful confrontations with wives and other people they didn't like, and I was a neophyte to the haze of booze, promising but not yet in their league. None of them knew that I was running for mayor, and I doubt they would have cared. I intended to buy a round for the house closer to election day and make an announcement. I hoped no one would treat me differently. I would not be surprised to learn no one there ever cast a vote. They trashed the town in their own way, refusing to drink gin. (Jerky was okay.) They drank bourbon and beer. When I asked why no one in that bar supported the local product, I was told, "Fuck that shit," which revealed a vein of anti-Maragate anger I had heretofore believed I alone possessed, that is, before the hints that Doc and my cadre of supporters had similar misgivings but never admitted them aloud. When others think they are in heaven, why point out the lack of resemblance.

I walked home remembering bits and pieces of conversations I had with Doc about the mayor. The "exploratory committee," now my campaign staff, acted as though they were entering into a dark conspiracy rather than a free election. I stopped for a moment at the bridge and looked at the foul water oozing downriver. I thought of youthful days spent lolling alone on the banks of the Susquehanna River, an anthology in my hand, comforted and inspired by the rolling water. Thus preoccupied, I was distracted by a stirring in the wild juniper bushes on the far side of the creek in the triangular piece of land too small to build upon. When I did take notice that the bushes were shaking, I stepped back from the curb, concerned that I might have spooked some wildlife. Imagine my utter shock—I mean shock so bad I should have been given some chocolate and wrapped in a blanket—when a head popped up from the bushes and an assertive Hoboken voice familiar to me hissed, "Cashewmetti? The fuck?"

"Gertz?"

I was eyeball to eyeball with Gertz, the New York producer who fired me. (Most recently.) The producer who never wanted to see me again, who was profoundly disappointed in me because my script about collusion to deny sins and crimes at the upper strata of the Catholic Church lacked pizazz. Gertz was so successful he went by only one name. At his zenith, he had one Bentley for daytime and another for night. He owned a hockey team and a jet and was rumored to be a sexual predator of both genders. Then, like many before him, he rose to his level of incompetence—running a major studio—and did himself (like me) crash and burn but with a golden parachute rich enough to do anything he wanted or nothing at all. Like many before him, he went into indy-prodding, adapting comic book characters still not bled dry. Our sorry collaboration was the first time a superhero was out of his mix. (I maintain that writing poetry is a superpower and that the Romantic poets should be as popular as the X-Men.)

"Get in here, quick!"

He jumped out of the bushes, grabbed my arm, and pulled me after him, pushing my head out of sight. I was pricked by the thorny bushes.

"What are you doing here?" I asked.

"Keep it down."

"And hiding in the bushes?"

"Shut the fuck up for two minutes."

I had to know what he was doing in Maragate, but it is prudent not to question the insane in real time. I squatted in silence.

The beams of headlights passed over us. A battered van screeched to a stop at the curb. The driver, a panting chubby young man with reddish-yellow hair blowing like a burning bush, jumped out, ran around the back of the vehicle, and slid open the side door. "Mr. Gertz?" he called in a stage whisper. Gertz grabbed me and pulled me to the van. You've seen this scene in many movies. (None that I would have written.) Your basic kidnapping gag: car skids to a stop, bewildered man is thrown inside. Hardly ever happens in real life, but I suppose once would be more than enough if you happened to be the man.

Why would Gertz and this other wild one want to kidnap me? The answer was, they didn't. Their victim was already on the floor of the van, bound in duct tape, blindfolded and gagged.

Gertz pushed me into the van and jumped in after me. The driver shut the door and ran back to sit behind the wheel.

"Go! Go! Go!" said Gertz. (Again, you've seen and heard that in the movies. Not from me.)

The reckless ride had us rolling in the back from one wall of the van to the other. You can picture me shouting disjointed expressions of fear and wonder, none of which were acknowledged by Gertz. We made it to a straight and quiet street, and the van slowed down. The young driver asked, "Who's the new guy?"

"This is D. K. Cashewmetti back here."

"Really? Big fan, man. I loved *Ordinary People*." (Wasn't mine.) "I'm Tommy Boy, Mr. Gertz's assistant."

Tommy Boy was a movie from the mid-nineties and starred Chris Farley, RIP. This Tommy Boy could have been his twin.

"I produced DK's first movie," said Gertz, "gave him his big break. Remember, DK? Good times."

I never worked with Gertz before our ill-fated venture.

Once out of what they perceived as a danger zone, I was able to take a look at the unfortunate other passenger, the presumptive kidnappee. He wore navy blue sweat pants pulled high over his stomach, the way some old men do, and a white sweatshirt with the logo: PALM SPRINGS, 1938. He wore a watch cap pulled down to the blindfold that covered his eyes.

The van entered an alley and Tommy Boy cut the headlights. We came to a stop and got out. I stood in the dark alley with no idea where I was. They yanked the groaning old man out of the van and got him to his feet.

Gertz put his finger to his lips for silence. I followed them through a gate in a high wooden fence to a small backyard, and then over a path of stepping stones. I could have bolted before that. I would have found my way back home. But I had already seen something I shouldn't have (again), and I had enough interest in this strange turn of events to play it out to the next step. Once across the yard, they helped the kidnapped gentleman up three steps and into the back door of a house.

"Turn on the light, Tommy Boy."

In a movie (not one that I would have written) this would be the moment when the audience realizes they've been watching a dream sequence and are either delighted or pissed off. (I personally abhor dream sequences.) The room in all respects, with the exception of the Goya imitation, was Carlos's casita. (A faded square was where the small painting should have been.) Now you might think, maybe it's not a dream sequence, maybe they really are in DK's own hovel, having crossed his own yard, which I must allow is what I myself thought. Though the bridge is only a couple blocks from where I lived, they could have driven around the town to make it seem they were going to a distant house, to an alley I did not know about, through a gate I never noticed, over a yard I did my best to forget, and into a private entrance that I didn't know was there, if this were, in fact, my house, for a purpose of which I could not conceive.

Or it's possible none of this was about me. (Everything doesn't have to be about me.)

They sat the hostage on the bed and undid the duct tape, the blindfold, and the gag. He was a frail man well into his eighties with wispy white hair.

I asked in a calm conversational way, "Gertz, who is this man? And what are we doing here with him?"

"A caper, buddy, just like in the movies. I'll show those assholes you can't fuck with the Gertz."

"Where are we?" I gave no hint that I thought we might be in my own servant's quarters.

"Don't worry about it."

Tommy Boy took a bottle of water from a craft services table, like on a movie set, complete with fruit and snacks and soft drinks, and gave it to the old man, who said, "Bless you, my son," in a barely audible voice, with a thick accent I could not pin down. They ignored him, and for his part he seemed unperturbed by what was happening to him. He serenely lay back on the bed and shut his eyes.

"Walk me through this, Gertz?"

"DK, you're a helluva writer, but you can't find your ass with both hands. You, like, need someone to manage you." (I once had Hope.)

"It may be obvious to you, but to me it's, well, inappropriate behavior. How did you even find this town?"

Gertz told me he was on a location scout for the rom-com of Plastic Man and Wonder Woman, and through a series of misfortunes found himself marooned in Maragate with no one to help him but his local contact, Tommy Boy, who had been given to him by the film commission, and whose room this was. Unlike me, Gertz had a plan. He was going to ransom the old guy for safe passage out of Maragate.

"Are you in?" he asked.

"In what? Leaving? I tried that."

"It's happening, and I don't care who has to get fucked up in the process."

I assumed that included me.

"A month ago, I would have said yes. A week ago. But now I'm running for mayor, and people are counting on me."

"You're fucking kidding me. Counting on *you?*"

"I like my chances."

"I don't know how you ever got as far as you did."

"I don't either."

I looked at the old man now peacefully sleeping on the bed and wondered aloud what made him so valuable as a hostage.

"He's the jackpot, buddy boy."

Gertz dropped several old issues of the fan magazine *US* on the unoccupied side of the bed and withdrew a pair of scissors from his Tumi shoulder bag. "Make yourself useful," he said, giving them to me. It would be my job to scan the magazines for a list of words he compiled and to cut them out. Gertz himself would paste them into a ransom note. (A scene you might have seen in twenty-three movies. None that I would have written.) The words were the standard fare of ransom notes (it's not rocket science), and it was easy going, except for the key word: pope. Nowhere in the pages of *US* could we find the word *pope*, as in, "We have the pope. If you do not meet our demands . . ."

I looked more closely at the old man, then turned to Gertz, who nodded and smiled.

"Gertz, he's not our pope."

"But he's *a* pope. Works for me."

"He doesn't even look like a pope."

"You don't look like a writer. Trust me, he's a pope, and he's not the only one."

"What do you expect to do with him?"

"Safe passage and trebled damages. You don't fuck with the Gertz."

It seemed the right moment to bolt. I shot out of the door, across the yard, through the gate, down the alley in the light of a full moon, dialing 911. I could not outrun a two-toed sloth, so I anticipated Gertz or the younger Tommy Boy tackling me and including me as part of the package, or making me the incidental body from which you cut pieces to send as a message that you mean business, but no one followed me. Bewildered I found my way home.

Item from the police blotter of the *Maragate Herald*: "Officers were called to an address on the south side late Tuesday night to a hostage situation in progress. An anonymous tipster had called in to report that the pope was being held for ransom by two desperate characters. The caller, a hysterical man possibly under the influence, gave detailed descriptions of the pope and his abductors, who used the aliases 'Tommy Gun' and 'Guts.' Officers debated putting through a call to the Vatican and inquiring after the whereabouts of the pope. The debate, it is reported, is ongoing and provides an amusing break from the stress of police work."

www.thecatholictraveler.com/papal-calendar

My previous explorations of Maragate had been limited by and large to walking from my hovel to the gin rooms of Spanish Circle and along the bike path that ran through the north of town. Now that I was campaigning I discovered that Maragate had well-defined neighborhoods, characterized as much by the personalities of the people who lived there as by their terrain and whatever swirled around them.

Our political person-to-person push lasted a week and started in the Bonny Falls neighborhood, where Doc and Sandy lived. Bonny Falls was flat as Kansas and as windswept. No one knew where or how any waterfalls could have ever existed, so maybe the area was named for some clumsy woman who kept tripping over herself. Doc's neighbors opened their doors to us and listened to my spiel.

Since in the past he had treated all their pets, and now vouched for me, they promised me their votes. I had the sense it didn't matter to them and they might forget by election day. We told them we'd give them a call and a ride to the polling place if they needed it. We were serious about unseating Hirkill at long last and taking Maragate in a new direction. (We still didn't know what that direction was, but anywhere away from where it was and had always been would do.) The wind picked up and we had to cover our faces with hankies to avoid breathing in all the dust. Sandy held on to one handle of Doc's chair, I to the other. Despite the wind already blowing crap everywhere, leaf blowers abounded, not to be outdone by Mother Nature herself.

Though Valene was not a volunteer by nature and had no interest in politics, she stumped by my side, primarily because she knew I could grant her amnesty for her T.O.T. problem if I won. And lately she wanted to be by my side anyway. She thought she had a future with me. I now have to confess that I did succumb to her charms one evening in the Jacuzzi and experienced her queenly skill set, spontaneously and with no need of pharmaceuticals. It rendered me guilt-ridden, but not for long and not enough to put the brakes on what became an intimate relationship, one that I knew wouldn't last and that I would end and disclose to Hope as soon as she returned, if ever she did.

I promised Valene only that I would let her off the hook for her delinquent T.O.T., provided she register and make timely payments in the future. Her reaction? "Awesome!" Everything to her was either awesome or hella or lame.

The political plan was to work our way from the outskirts of town in toward Spanish Circle, from the outer Ninth Street square, ending in my own neighborhood, which I learned was called Circle West. After Bonny Falls, we went to the Cherona neighborhood, the low rent district, comparatively speaking. (Rents were high everywhere, and the vacancy rate low.) Al Myra, the shell-shocked veteran, lived in this neighborhood, in a neat, well-cared-for cottage.

He lived alone on a dead-end road littered with abandoned cars, which represented another kind of landscaping, I suppose, because two leaf blowers were stirring up a cyclone around the mangled hardware. Al did the door knocking and introductions, and though not all of the residents knew him, they knew of him, had seen him around, and could say that he never bothered anybody. Sure, they would vote for me. Why not?

Ninth Street North was known as the CO Flats, for Camino Obscura, a dry, almost desert-like terrain subject to brief but violent lightning storms whenever the weather came in from the north. Within the environs of Maragate, I learned, was a surprising number of microclimates. In large part that accounted for the quality and variety of the local gin. This neighborhood was Chrissy Nayler's neck of the woods, and it was plagued by wasps and their human counterparts. She warned me in advance that folks on the Flats didn't have filters.

The first man to open his door had drooping eyes and needed a shave. "Fuckin'-A I'll vote for you. Cocksuckin' Hirkill has been mayor long enough." The older I get, the harder it is for me to listen to language like that, but in my new role as a man of the people I leaned forward and out of the range of imaginary microphones whispered, "I'm fucking counting on you, man." He high fived me. Variations of this conversation, with the same foul language, occurred at every door that opened to us in that neighborhood.

We went then to True West, where packs of stray dogs—they might have included some coyotes and dingoes—wandered freely, foraging for food. We picked up sticks and stones and huddled together on our rounds. The people I met there seemed fearful, and why wouldn't they be, surrounded by packs of feral dogs. I promised them I would round up the critters and find homes for them. Fortunately, they didn't ask how. The town had an animal rescue organization, but it was woefully underfunded. (Most people seemed to be waiting for someone to rescue *them* and give them a forever home.) Honestly, I *did* want to make things better for them. They were miserable. (By comparison, I had nothing to complain about. This was a helpful insight but still short of comforting.)

We hit Circle East confident we had racked up a lot of votes from people who were either pissed off or didn't give a damn. Circle East was a middle-class neighborhood of fences and gates, which opened to us with hesitation. We stood on freshly painted but seldom used porches and engaged in polite but noncommittal and brief conversation shouted over the sound of nearby leaf blowers. These people were unwilling to express an opinion on any subject other than landscaping and property values. It was an area that got sun in the morning but fell early into shade and darkness, when bats filled the evening skies. I didn't do as well there, but I remembered that it was Hirkill's neighborhood, where he lived above somebody's garage and walked on my old carpet in his crusty bare feet.

At last we got to my own neighborhood, and Valene's. The places we'd visited, each with a personality, much like the red and blue districts into which cable news had separated the country long ago, were subject to one or another pest or weather abnormality. My own neighborhood, Circle West, considered the best part of town, had rats and the fat black flies that fed off the dead ones, hatches of moths, and the most raucous leaf blower noise. It was populated with greedy developers, lawyers, day traders, con men, and hustlers of various stripes. That might have included Valene, I thought, but what was I doing there? I should mention that all of the neighborhoods have in common the curse of allergies, and both campaigners and voters sneezed continually in clouds of juniper, ash, and mulberry pollen.

"But where else would you rather be?" Valene asked me, in all seriousness, slipping her hand into my empty back pocket.

Our neighborhood, as I said but it bears repeating, was the noisiest area of Maragate. People there cared more about clean driveways than anyone's peace and quiet, not to mention respiratory health. I wish I could say that they were merely standoffish, but they were aggressive and confrontational. Nothing mattered more to them than cheap labor, their own convenience, and curbside appeal. They didn't like newcomers, and they especially didn't like me, because they heard that I wanted to take away their leaf blowers and leave them with brooms and rakes, like in the olden days. They told me to go back where I came from.

"I'm going to lose my own district," I told my crew. "That's tantamount to a public stoning for a politician."

(A role for which I thought I had good preparation. Political movies as a genre are generally insightful, and I had seen them all. I was even personally responsible for perpetuating some of the illusions surrounding politics. I was in Washington for the Robert Bork hearings, in the room with a director coming off a big success with a mockumentary [the first dozen mockumentaries were funny, the last twenty not so much] and an actor notorious for researching the hell out of a role before backing out of the project. I met with a political strategist in Washington and asked him a question he had never been asked before: "In all the movies you've seen about politics, what was the one thing missing?" He thought about it and said, "The hustle for money. The time and energy that all politicians have to put in begging for contributions." I didn't put the hustle for money into my script either. It would have slowed down the story.)

"Wait till the next poll comes out," said Doc Fleck.

"I'm optimistic," said Al Myra, which put on me an odd sense of obligation. I had the feeling the old soldier was saying those words for the first time ever.

Pushing stakes bearing my campaign signs into dried-up front lawns was like slaying vampires. It was an arduous task but one we all thought would in the end be worth it. It was the nitty-gritty of retail politics, eye to eye, yard sign to yard sign. While we were thus engaged, hard at work, Hirkill put in a single call to the mackerel wrapper, and the lead story the next day was about my missing wife and the suspicions surrounding my possible role in her disappearance. The article stated that an investigation was under way and an arrest was imminent. The picture they ran of Hope was the one on my cell phone. Only Carlos and Conventerra ever had access to that.

It killed me in the new poll: Hirkill, 37; Manfred, 23; Kecskeméti, 30; Undecided, 8; What election? 2.

www.politicalcampaigningtips.com

Doc Fleck's inner pit bull barked repetitive profanities. (There are only so many.) He blamed himself for not anticipating Hirkill's treachery, but who could imagine a blatant smear campaign in a small town where no one wanted to be mayor anyway, with the exception of Hirkill and now me. Others neither wanted to be mayor nor cared much about who became mayor.

Allison Waxweather, our young media expert, was far from defeated. Her motto, she kept telling us, was "Never give up." (Curiously, that was also the motto of every film producer with whom I ever teamed on my western, all of whom eventually gave up.) The rest of the campaign crew moped around in Charlotte Grumm's tasting room swilling ginger gin. I pretended to be more affected by the turn of events than I was. I had no reputation to uphold, and I knew there would be no investigation into my wife's disappearance or the murder of my angel or the kidnapping of the former pope.

Al Myra, silent all night, took a deep breath and said, "Listen up, I'll be the one to ask it. DK, man to man. Did you do something bad to your wife?"

"No, Al, she did something bad to me."

"Fine, we got that out of the way."

Allison had already posted denials on Facebook and Twitter and wanted to call a press conference and air out the whole mess. I had nothing to deny. I didn't want to talk about it. For long enough it was *all* I wanted to talk about.

My campaign staff and I went to the next meeting of the city council. I had been going to all of their meetings and taking my three minutes to urge them to have a serious discussion on the rights of one man with a leaf blower to scatter debris randomly versus the rights of another man to enjoy peace and quiet and healthy air. No one on the council or in the audience was surprised to see me again. They expected my usual mini-lecture presented in my customary academic fashion.

The house was full because of a hot item on the agenda, the dissatisfaction with Time Warner cable service and why there should be only one alternative, DirecTV, which reminded older people of the antenna days and ignored the fact that when you punch holes in your roof you're just asking for leaks. After the Pledge of Allegiance, I stepped to the microphone and said, "My wife is missing." Some in the audience gasped. The council members were made uncomfortable, but it was my three minutes and I could use them as I pleased. "I don't know where she is or why she left. I have faith that she will come back."

I gave them an abbreviated account of how I came to town and why I had to stay even though I once preferred not to, omitting the angel incident.

"I can't work at home in Maragate. I can't even enjoy a cup of coffee in my own backyard. Is that asking too much of the neighborhood in which you live? Trigger-happy landscapers wreak havoc where I live." I told them of the lack of basic amenities in the other neighborhoods, of rats, wasps, and stray dogs and bad or no cell phone service. And on the subject of dogs, I questioned why a dog on a leash cannot be allowed on the bike path. "Is it because Mayor Hirkill has a shiny new bike?" The mayor scowled. "And why is the community center, which should be a city treasure, crumbling for lack of municipal grants? Look, I like gin and jerky as much as the next guy, maybe more." That got a laugh. "But why should we turn ourselves into a theme park? Why have you, under the leadership of Mayor Hirkill, taken Spanish Circle, the heart and soul of Maragate, and turned the perimeter into kitsch for the tourists? Yes, we have a stake in tourism, but the feather merchants who come here to get shit-face have no stake in us." (Feather merchants? Subconscious recall of a favorite boyhood author, Max Shulman. Shit-face? Old college days.) "Who are more vital to the community, any community," I hammered at them, "the visitors or the residents? It's a simple question." I was getting applause now. "Why are some residents excluded and hindered and considered freaks because they were born with different preferences?" Five hardened lesbian fists shot skyward. "And why are some people beyond scrutiny because they have a badge? Why are we so afraid of the MPD? Because we've seen them in action?" People were told to quiet down or be removed. I was told by the mayor that my time was up, but I pressed on. "All that is foul about Maragate can be laid at the dirty feet of one person, a person without dignity or decency, who unfortunately is the face of Maragate. The fault is with an apathetic and cynical electorate, because in a small town like this we have allowed a misfit to cement his position and go unchallenged. Gentlemen, let me remind you that you are not career politicians. You are beholden to no one. You don't have to spend every waking moment worrying about your own reelection. You are volunteers taking on a hard assignment. In the morning, you will wake up and go to your real careers. All but one of you. You aren't hoping to get a job in a casino when you finally leave office. You do not seek to benefit financially from your position. Do you?"

"I said your time is up, Doctor Keckskimento," said the mayor.

"Little slice of heaven? Really?"

"What's wrong with liking the town you live in?" said Hirkill, raising his voice. This was unprecedented. Protocol dictated that no council member may respond to anyone during public comments.

"Nothing," I answered, "if you know why, and if it's true."

"Your time is up!"

"And so is yours, Mayor Hirkill."

My crew stood up and cheered, emboldening others to do likewise.

I chose to leave during the break, after pretending to be concerned over the quixotic service provided by a cable company that enjoyed a virtual monopoly. Personally, I hadn't watched a minute of television since arriving in Maragate. (No TV in my house.)

As I made my way to the exit, I got pats on the back and grateful handshakes. Outside, I ran into the city attorney smoking an e-cigarette.

"You know I'm running for mayor," I said.

"Good luck with that," he said with lawyerly disinterest.

Besides Hirkill, the city attorney was the only one at the meeting wearing a suit and tie. The difference was that his suit was in style, unwrinkled, and clean. I stood a head taller than he. I stepped closer to underscore the difference.

"Have you been city attorney long?"

"Forever. I have my own practice, but—"

I finished his sentence, "It's a nice way to bill some night hours."

"I don't mind."

"When I become mayor, I plan to launch an investigation." His head came up, and a vapor rolled over my face. I stepped back. "And that letter you sent me will become part of it." I was feeling tough, though I knew he had far more power to make my life miserable than I had to disrupt his. After my performance inside, however, I was up to calling him out.

"What letter?" he said.

"The threatening one you sent me."

He took a long slow drag on his device and lengthened the pause by the languid release of whatever it was he sucked in.

"Could I please have a copy of this letter?" he asked.

In an instant I understood that he never wrote that letter. For a long moment we looked at each other, neither one of us risking saying anything that might incriminate our libelous selves.

(One rule of screenwriting is to leave a scene before it is over. And . . . scene.)

I told no one of my suspicions that Hirkill forged the letter to me on the city attorney's letterhead. I reread the letter Valene had received. It had the appearance of validity but the same hyperbole of threats. I was sure Hirkill wrote both of them. The chance existed that the city attorney had suckered me and both letters were legitimate, but I knew a cornered weasel when I saw one. (Literally, I didn't. I've never seen a cornered weasel, though I've often wandered the woods of Tompkins County as a boy. What I did see was the Lady of the Lake. I did, dammit.)

I had picked up some support after my performance before the city council and later picked up a lot more when a number of my yard signs were stolen or defaced by persons unknown but largely suspected to be from Hirkill's camp. Hirkill himself publicly denied any knowledge of such acts and condemned the perpetrators, in the manner of a politician who knew who did it and was covering his own collusion. My motto, "A New Vision," had been spray-painted to read, "A Newcomer's Vision" or "A New Vision Up His Ass," or "Fuck the Polack," displaying the vandal's ignorance of the difference between Polish and Hungarian surnames. The *Maragate Herald* editorialized on the shameful behavior of some partisans and how it did not reflect the majority of Maragatians, who were salt of the earth. A few letters to the editor dismissed it as part of the rough and tumble of politics, but most were outraged by this new and ugly turn in what had always been boring campaigns. People who normally wouldn't notice now became interested in following the campaign events and subsequent polls. (I can only imagine the consequences had the vandal been apprehended in the dark of night defacing his own campaign signs. I'm not proud of this particular strategy, but to quote any number of political advisors who are wont to justify their basest behavior, "It worked." Going into the Meet the Candidates Forum, Hirkill and I were in a dead heat, with Chester Manfred trailing far behind.)

The American Legion hall, where the Candidates Forum was to be held, was located on Counterpass Avenue South and Ninth Street, a good hike from my house. I walked as fast as I could, not to be late. I had not thought to ask anyone for a ride, nor had anyone thought to offer me one. No matter. I was drinking far less and getting back into shape. The walk would do me good. I carried a flashlight because night had already fallen.

I passed the high school, where rumor had it that only the strong survive. Behind me I heard the sound of skateboards. I stepped to the curb and gripped my Maglite like a weapon. Four kids rolled to a stop beside me.

"What-ho!" one of them shouted. That would be Shelley. Lord Byron brought up the rear.

"You guys again," I said.

They were as furtive as before and Mary as adorable.

"We meet again," she said.

"I'm still trying to make sense of our meeting *before*."

Shelley said, and I'm not making this up, "Have you heard those duets, Sinatra and Barbra?"

"Look, kids, I'm in a hurry. It's the Candidates Forum and I'm—"

"Yes, but have you?"

"Everyone has. Best voices ever. National treasures."

"They diddle with the lyrics. They slip about because they can, in little ways the poet never would have wanted, or he would have written them that way. Utter rot. Don't you agree?"

"You have a point, but—"

Mary added, "Like actors who think dialog is merely a suggestion."

Some actors are like that. Maybe most. They want to make the dialog more in tune with what they themselves would naturally say, instead of what the character would say, instead of what a trained actor (like the Brits who win more than their fair share of Oscars) would say, which is exactly what the writer put down. I'd forgotten. I never liked singers doing that to classic songs, either, no matter how famous they were. It showed a lack of respect in favor of self-adoration. I'd never given it much thought until then. Why would these four be brooding over it? And now making *me* brood over it. Were they trying to remind me of who I once was? (Don't remind me.)

"Look, guys, I kind of get that something is going on, and I should be involved, you think, and for some reason you can't tell me all about it. Apparently, don't know why, you can only make oblique remarks that are enough to get me worked up but finally leave me confused. Things are starting to turn my way here, so—"

Said Mary, not having heard a word, "It is not enough to adjust to your circumstances. You have to *like* them."

"Says who?" said I.

"You know Huxley?" asked PB.

"Which one?"

"Aldous."

"A little. I'm no expert."

"I'm paraphrasing. Huxley said the secret of happiness is liking what you have to do. All conditioning aims at that: making people like their inescapable destiny. Or making yourself like it."

"Sounds like Huxley," I said.

"Aye, and here's the rub: *you* don't have to make yourself like it. This is *not* your destiny."

"Then what is?"

"Come with us and find out," said Mary.

Keats, the downer of the bunch, which is saying a lot since none of them was the life of the party, said, "Or go on with your shadow show, please your audience until they find someone else."

Georgie, Lord Byron, said in his silky voice: "A war is waged, in a silent game, unseen, unheard, but suffered all the same."

He'd written better lines in his prime, but still, winded from the skateboard and everything, as ad-libbed rhymes go, it wasn't bad. Some of what they were saying made sense to me but only as theory. I had my own boogie now, so to speak.

"Come with us, sojourner," said Shelley. "Your existence has gone out of compass."

Three Romantic poets and their muse were, if not protecting me, at least warning me and enticing me away to . . . what? Better the misery you are in—which by the way I was overcoming, thank you—than the unknown, which may prove even worse. Still, these were the immortal geniuses who made me who I was. I owed them, to be sure, though they could show a little gratitude to me for bringing them to a mass audience, well beyond the sinus-infected lit majors and bespectacled librarians who doted on them in musty carrels. I made their names and stories familiar to millions, who met them for the first time on the silver screen while munching popcorn and drinking Coke.

As though reading my mind—and why wouldn't they be able to do that—Byron, still riffing, said, "What you did in life is settled and weighed. What you failed to do is eternal and saved."

Pure doggerel, a forced rhyme colored with new age spiritual crap. I was profoundly disappointed, and I chalked it up to his dying short of full maturity. They stared at me, imploring me to make a move, which I did. I looked at my watch. Wrong move. Our shadows, which had been visible in the light of the moon, disappeared. I heard a *whoosh* overhead. I looked up to the sky. A dark form passed over the moon and was gone. When I lowered my eyes again, I saw that the poets and Mary were gone as well, their skateboards abandoned on the sidewalk.

www.hellopoetry.com/words/skateboard/

The Meet the Candidates Forum was sponsored by the chamber of commerce. It was late in the game to be meeting the candidates, but Hirkill had set the schedule when only he and Chester Manfred would be candidates and the customary twelve people could be expected to show up. This time, over two hundred voters packed the American Legion hall. More folding chairs had to be brought in, and many people were forced to stand.

The three candidates shook hands before the commencement of the forum. Hirkill had the hand of a leftover ham bone and Manfred the spongy hand of a fat milk maid. We stood behind three plywood podiums, with His Honor in the center.

The presidency of the chamber of commerce was another position no one wanted, long seen as a stepping stone to a seat on the city council, one more position no one wanted. The current president, Bill Buddusky, an ornamental-iron merchant, introduced us with false enthusiasm, reading from notes. As candidates, we were not allowed to refer to notes, which was fine by me. Oratory on the fly was a skill I'd developed as a teacher. Each of us was to introduce himself and make a brief statement before taking questions from the moderator and the public.

Chester Manfred made it clear that his reason for living was Spanish Circle. It was a community treasure, he said, but a vulnerable gem that needed constant "TLC." From Spanish Circle all blessings flowed, and he would be a stalwart steward of the heart of Maragate. That was his whole platform and had been forever.

Now that the weather had turned colder, the mayor wore a quilted jacket, maroon, under his suit jacket. He was congenial and joked that he didn't need to introduce himself. "Unless there is anybody here new in town. Oh, wait a minute, there is, and he's standing right next to me." He scored a few laughs. "Mr. Katzsakowski is a fine man, I'm sure, but—"

I corrected him. "It's Kecskeméti. Doctor Kecskeméti."

I've always thought it overbearing for a PhD to call himself "doctor" off-campus, and in Hollywood it counted for nothing anyway. It was only in Maragate, beginning with Carlos, that people took to using the title.

"Whatever," said the mayor, like some teenager, but in a gin-soaked gravelly voice. "Newcomers come into town and fall in love with it. They want to burn the bridge behind them. Then they set about trying to change our little slice of heaven by bringing some of what they left behind in Los Angeles and New York. Toronto, Miami, Seattle, St. Louis . . . but we like it just the way it is. You don't like it, you should go back where you came from."

A number of people applauded that sentiment. I thought it one of the uglier retorts of a civilized man. "My advice to everybody is, don't rock the boat. We've got a good thing going here. Tourism is up. Our gin and jerky industries are booming. Our economy is on the up while others struggle. Detroit, anyone?"

He got another laugh.

"Look, I know I'm an oddball. But I'm *your* oddball. Okay, I don't own a pair of socks, but I've been leading this town for . . . like, for-ever, steering the ship through calm and storm. I've been accused of being a career politician. Would you rather have an amateur?" The applause grew louder. Even I was beginning to admire his chops. He stood hunched over his podium, put out on everyone's behalf for having to go through this Kabuki dance. "You all know how I live. I'm not rich or famous." He directed toward me his well-honed stink eye. "I'm just a poor servant of the people, proud to be. I, too, have a vision for the future. It may not be a 'new' vision"—he used air quotes—"but just because something is new doesn't mean it's good. I see myself as a prophet, and I predict this little burg will continue to be the best darn place anyone could hope to put his feet up, lean back, and let the rest of the world go by."

The moderator called time. Hirkill got a good round of applause. When it was my turn, I introduced myself as a newcomer with a fresh set of eyes. I told them that if I was rich I didn't know it and you couldn't see it. I didn't own a car or a shiny new bicycle. Yes, I owned some socks and enough of a wardrobe to make myself present-able as the face of Maragate, something every community deserves at a minimum from its mayor. I knew I wasn't famous because no one could pronounce or spell my name, and most movie fans could not name more than two screenwriters anyway. (Aaron Sorkin and that creepy guy who keeps finding new ways to make violence hilarious.) Now I had them laughing with me. (Self-effacement works every time.) I proposed that it would not be the worst thing to happen to Maragate if a few new ideas filtered in from Los Angeles, New York, and the other cities Hirkill was so xenophobic about. Then I cut into the red meat.

"Rationally, statistically, by any metric you choose, apart from gin and jerky, Maragate is *not* a little slice of heaven." A chorus of gasps upended the room. It was an assumption unanimously accepted and sung aloud until I had the temerity to say otherwise. "It is a tyranny of harmony." (Something I gleaned from the poets.) Now folks looked about for someone to explain that to them. "And the harmony itself is a lie. What better place to be, you are told. But chanting, 'We're number one!' does not make you number one. There *is* no number one. That is all jingoism, the refuge of exploiters and the misinformed." I was making them uncomfortable, my forte in social situations. "Do any of you work at home? I would if I could. Can you have a cup of coffee in your own backyard in the morning? Or a gin 'n tonic in the evening? Can you take a nap on a hot afternoon? Or do you have to set your schedule around the intrusion of leaf blowers? Good luck with that because you never know when they will start or when they will go away. You know only that they will return the next day. Is it so important to the quality of life here that every last leaf must be blown from where it is to where it is not? And why does the town have no drainage? It has plenty of rain, though we are always in a drought it seems. Why is it all but impossible to make or receive a phone call? Why do trash collectors miss your house? Why are our sidewalks buckling? Why do packs of stray dogs and swarms of wasps plague your neighborhood? Or rats infest your homes? When did methamphetamine become a joke instead of a social problem? Why are the police not held to account for their actions?"

A breathlessness put the room in a bear hug. Though I was used to creating drama, it had always been on paper and then on film. This was live, off the cuff, and I was loving it.

"Is it my imagination, or does a sense of fear and anxiety pervade this community? Is there an unnamed invader, an Ugly Spirit, a force of evil in our midst?" (That one I stole from William Burroughs himself, who claimed that an Ugly Spirit took him over after he shot and killed his wife, and his only refuge was to write, as Hirkill's only refuge was "public service." If PB was Shelley reincarnated, and it sure felt that way, why, I wondered, couldn't Hirkill *be* Burroughs? You could say that it was all a game of spontaneous casting, the screenwriter's favorite pastime. [When he isn't constructing speeches for his inevitable Oscar win.] But what if the donut guy really was Dennis Hopper and the Verizon guy was once Elvis? And Sandy was the one true Sandy Dennis? Because I bring it up here does not mean I wasn't aware of the possibility long before. Just saying.)

Like a revolutionary at the barricades, I exhorted, "Break ranks! Free yourselves! Call a halt to the lockstep march and start the ecstatic dance!"

The audience looked at me blankly, then turned to each other with the same uncomprehending expression. What's he saying? Do I like him?

The mayor spoke out of turn and the moderator did not stop him. "You asked if it was your imagination. Yeah, it is. You're in the imagining business. You should stick to that."

"You had your turn, mayor, now let me have mine. I didn't interrupt you."

It was embarrassing to hear those words come out of my mouth, as they do out of the mouths of the talking heads on Fox News over a cheesy political debate, which of course this was.

"Doctor Kosowalshiti is making us sound like a totalitarian slum. Let me remind you that while other towns are facing bankruptcy, Maragate is in the black."

"Because perks are cheap and infrastructure expensive."

"I resent the implications of that remark!"

Now the moderator tried to restore order. (He didn't have a

gavel. He had to jump in front of us.) The audience got woked, though I'm not at ease using that word. They were getting more woke than they had ever expected. They were at last—dare I say it?—aware.

"May I ask the mayor what he thinks are the implications of my remark?" It was time to aim away from my foot and pull the trigger.

"Well, the implication is scandalous, that I am dishonest, and everybody knows I have been a tireless public servant for more years than I can count."

"It's been forever, which is much too long."

The moderator said, "Gentlemen, you will have a chance to interact with each other later in the program, but I would like to get to the issues now and have you answer some questions."

"If any issue is more important than the mayor's honesty," I said, "and the chokehold he has had, forever, on this strange deluded town, I'd like to know what it is."

"This is an outrage!" screamed Hirkill. (Though he was unable to raise his voice far above the gravel quarry in his throat.)

I took two letters from my inside jacket pocket and held them above my head like semaphore flags, one in each hand. "I have here two letters, forged by the mayor, using the signatures of the city attorney and the city clerk, full of serious threats designed to keep two errant citizens of Maragate under his control. I don't know whether they are enough to put Hirkill into jail, but I do believe they are enough to kick him out of City Hall."

In bad movies when the heavy is shot between the eyes (not a scene I would ever write), he often takes a second or two to register total astonishment before he falls. Hirkill looked like that.

The forum fell out of control. People stood and tightly gripped the seats in front of them or shook their fists, shouted, poked fingers into chests, or covered their ears and wept. No matter how furiously the moderator waved his hands, he could not settle down the energized crowd. Chester Manfred, of all people, accomplished that when he waved his hands and yelled, "I've got something to say! I've got something to say here!" Since he never said anything that didn't involve protecting Spanish Circle against unnamed and unknown forces, people were curious to hear what it was. "I am going to withdraw from this race, effective immediately. I am ending my campaign and I ask all my supporters to vote for Mayor Hirkill."

Came then a week of nothing else in the *Maragate Herald* but my dramatic waving of two letters and the chaos that ensued. The letters themselves were reprinted. The city attorney was quoted as having no recollection of writing the one attributed to him. Likewise, the city clerk could not remember writing hers, nor did she have a copy on file.

Everyone understood the threat against Valene and most sympathized. She was not the only one renting vacation rooms or houses off the books. The meaning of the threatening letter sent to me, however, was a mystery, one that I chose not to clear up. I was not at liberty to discuss details, I claimed, because of the investigation that would begin on Day One when I was elected mayor. (Though candidates always promise it, nothing ever gets done on Day One.)

www.aauw.org/resource/how-to-candidate-forum

Our campaign, which never possessed a headquarters, set up shop at the King's Arms, the same pub where it all began. We drank tarragon gin and waited for the election returns. The scandal that followed my dramatic accusations against the mayor went a long way toward turning me into the Tom Hanks I always wanted to be. Hirkill denied all charges, calling it a political stunt, before he dropped out of sight, which in itself got a lot of attention because he had always been omnipresent. The town was divided and saw the election as a choice between two oddball characters, one of whom they were used to but was now toxic, the other of whom was hoity-toity but friends with Al Pacino.

Chrissy had one of her lesbians posted at City Hall, where early returns were announced as they were counted. Since her calls could never get through to us, she had to run back and forth across Spanish Circle and relay the current count. As expected, I lost my own neighborhood by a wide margin and the east side by a closer margin, but by 10 p.m. I had won the election by some seven hundred votes, a landslide.

The drinks were on what was left of the campaign fund. We partied until after midnight. I honored my new position by remaining sober. I walked home under my own power, with Valene hanging onto my arm. She had no obligation to stay sober. We turned the corner toward her house and stopped for a moment to share memories of the horror of my first night in town, now fading, and farewell to all of that. We kissed, and she pressed her nose against my face to show me how cold it was. I put my mouth over her nose to thaw it, and at that moment my phone rang. My new phone hadn't rung since it was tested by Elvis in the Verizon store. It had to be Hope. What would she think of my becoming mayor of the town within which she had isolated me for over six months?

"Hello? Hope?"

Alas, it was not Hope. Nothing ever *has* to be what you think it will be. What might be might not be, and the reverse is also true.

"It's Lieutenant Conventerra."

One of the things I looked forward to as the new mayor was being this guy's boss. Why was it *he* never had trouble placing a cell phone call?

"Yes?"

"Where are you right now?"

Every conversation I ever had with that man had been circuitous. Now all of a sudden he was direct.

"Walking home. It's been a long day."

"Yeah, and it's not over yet. Something you ought to see . . ."

Before I could ask what, he added, "Mr. Mayor." I must admit, I loved hearing that.

"What, where, and why?" I asked.

"The playground, Spanish Circle. Your first mayoral crisis. I can have a car pick you up."

"All right. I'm seeing Valene to her door. That would be the place where three of your cops shot a winged creature. Pretty sure it was an angel."

By the time I eased Valene into her house, telling her that there would be plenty of time later for the two of us to celebrate in our own special way, a police SUV pulled up to the curb. It might have been the same one I scrambled underneath that first night, only this time Sergeant Kuggeleong was driving.

I was wary about getting inside. It became the kind of moment (not one that I would ever write) in a lot of bad moves when the audience is saying, "Don't get in that car!" I got inside the car. What was he going to do, take me to the edge of town and shoot me? It was one thing to sucker punch a screenwriter; it was a whole other thing to shoot a mayor.

"Congratulations are in order," said Kuggelsong.

"And apologies," said I.

"From who to who?"

"From you to me."

"For what?"

"For punching me in the stomach for no reason."

"Why would I do that?"

"For no reason, as I said, except that you could and then say you didn't. But guess what? You won't be doing that again."

"Okay," he said, not only without fear or guilt but without interest.

The ride to Spanish Circle took only a moment, so I did not have time enough to play grim scenarios in my mind, which had always been my custom. (No longer, thank you. I've come a long way.)

Kuggelsong got on the roundabout and took me to the north side of the Circle, where he jumped the curb and drove over the grass. The playground area was a circle of sand containing the usual equipment: a jungle gym, merry-go-round, climbing towers with slides, and a swing set. During the weekly farmers market, the playground was full of kids dropped there by parents while they shopped. On that night, a white tent covered the swing set, a smaller version of the tents that were set up for exclusive parties during gin and jerky events. The walls of the tent were luminescent because of the lighting that had been set up inside. I could see shadows moving about.

"The lieutenant's in the tent," said my driver.

I got out of the SUV and walked around to his side. I motioned for him to lower the window. When he did, I punched him hard on his left ear.

"Son of a bitch!" he yelled.

He covered his ear, which I sincerely hoped was ringing like the hammers of hell. At the same time he fumbled to open the door. I pushed it back on him and punched again, hitting the back of the hand that was covering his ear. I hurried to the tent, prepared to deny everything. I was mayor now.

I heard the crackling of a police radio from within the tent. Conventerra, in his usual leather jacket and jeans, this time with a wool turtleneck to ward off the cold, emerged to greet me. "Mayor K," he said, and ever after I was known as Mayor K, since my last name seemed overly challenging to my constituents. He was not exactly laughing, more like trying not to laugh.

"What's so funny?"

"Sorry. Sometimes you can't help it."

"Inside?"

"Yeah. You have to see this before we break it down."

He held open a flap, and I walked ahead of him into the tent, passing a photographer and a uniformed cop on the way out, who were also suppressing laughter.

The swing set was constructed of four inverted steel V's supporting a sturdy bar from which hung six swings and the naked body of

Ripley Hirkill. He had fashioned a noose out of a white extension cord and apparently stood on one of the swings, then stepped off and became his own executioner.

"We're investigating," said Conventerra, "but it is what it is."

He and I and the deceased were alone inside the tent. At the moment, I felt nothing except a sense of disbelief, a state I had become used to in Maragate, and the irony that this thing happened while my campaign staff and I were across the street swilling gin, and with the extension cord Hirkill never returned after the carpet caper. I stood with Conventerra about twenty feet away from the body, which had turned a shade of blue found nowhere else in nature, and as the lieutenant moved toward it I followed him. A rain of unpleasant emotions chilled me: shock, embarrassment, revulsion. In a bad movie, this would be the scene (not one that I would ever write) where Tom Hanks throws up. (Puking scenes in modern movies are as repetitious as pissing scenes.) I'll admit to gagging, but I shook it off and steadied myself. Hirkill was hanging naked, with an erection on one side of him and a tail on the other, of about the same length.

"We have to talk," Conventerra said.

"What will we say?"

"I'm going to have to start the paperwork on this first. How about three o'clock?"

"I'm tired. I want to go to bed."

"Better I brief you sooner than later. You won't be able to sleep, anyway."

"You're probably right."

"We will keep it private. Meet me at the men's restroom in the Circle."

www.io9.com/5967742/the-science-of-human-tails

The fog crawled over Maragate as it did that first night I arrived in town. Fog is never cute, but this was as foreboding as fog can be.

By three o'clock it was thick as snot and similar in color. Inside the men's room, Conventerra told me what I'd already come to suspect (I'm not stupid) but had no facility for believing. The briefing took an hour, but it will take me forever to process.

We stood in the freezing tiled men's room in the inescapable odor of urine. I kept interrupting him with my babbled, "What about . . . ? How could it . . . ? When I . . . ? Why would . . . ? But where was . . . ?"

He held up a hand and said, "All things are possible in heaven and hell, and, like, in between."

I wanted to sit down, but that would have to be on a filthy toilet, so I stood and listened to him much as he had listened to me when I told him I saw the police murder a black angel with an Irish accent. What he said was equally as preposterous. He described a situation of events put into motion that cannot be stopped but often can be steered.

From Day One, as it's called, I asked myself, why am I here? In the meeting with Lieutenant Conventerra, I asked the same question.

"You're supposed to, you know, figure that out for yourself."

So figure I must, or try. Time is on my side.

Remember Tommy Boy? He was nobody's assistant, at least not Gertz's. Carlos was not a servant. Sandy was not having an affair with Conventerra. The Fizz *was* a tour bus, but nobody ever rode it twice. As for Valene, she was the genuine article, a lost soul like me, though Rufus the Rottweiler was more than her pet. My angel? I must stop thinking of her in the possessive. She was never mine, I was to be hers, and the truth is I would have followed her anywhere. It pains me to know I would have and pleases me to know I didn't have to, no more that I had to follow Mary and the poets. I had been the unknowing object of a tug-of-war. I don't ask why. I accept that the game was scratched for lack of participants. Will it ever resume? Who knows?

Mary Shelley, you see, was correct. The angel was not real; neither was she unreal. Stay with me here. All things in order to exist must meet some basic criteria: they must occupy space and have a place in time, have matter, be affected by those forces with the capability of affecting something that exists. By those criteria, and nobody's come up with any contradictory ones, that beautiful black messenger did not exist, which is not to say she was not real. She was, in the way that other things do not exist and yet are real. Like love. Like hope. Hope is not hollow. It is not unjustified anywhere it happens to exist, however dark the day and long the night.

But let us keep all that to ourselves, play the long game, and soldier on.

Conventerra outlined my duties and responsibilities as mayor. They were not onerous. They were not even necessary.

About the time I sensed the lieutenant had done his duty, a man opened the door and breezed inside. His sudden appearance rattled me. I mean, it was now four o'clock in the morning. Conventerra was expecting him. He was a large man with pent-up energy and slick black hair. When he spoke, I heard Eurogibberish mixed with words out of his own officialdom. He was the justice of the peace, there to swear me in. I suppressed my laughter. (Think Sid Caesar, RIP.)

Conventerra shook my hand after the shithouse ceremony, wished me luck, and said something about patience.

I know all this sounds like too much to absorb, but the effect upon me was a click or two short of overwhelming. Inklings denied became truths accepted . . . but still denied. I had only one more question.

"Where is Hope?"

"Wouldn't know. Where it's always been, I guess. Like, springing eternal."

He left a moment before me. I washed my hands under a push faucet timed to quit in five seconds. I splashed some water up onto my dry eyes and wiped them with my sleeve. When I stepped outside, I noticed a man who appeared lost. He stood under one of the Circle's tulip-shaped light poles. He seemed to be watching me, cautiously, as though I were watching him. In fact, I was. What was a stranger doing in Spanish Circle at four o'clock in the morning? He looked suspicious.

In answer to your original question, I am neither here nor there. Not because of some devilish plan or outlandish conspiracy. That's on me. I made the argument—to myself—that the elaborate prank I first thought myself to be the butt of is close enough to the truth. Now, fortunately, I was an individual of more than passing significance. Maragate is a community focused on its own survival. It needs to keep the best and lose the rest. Its residents are numbed by gin and puffed up by false civic pride. They are motivated to protect their own property values, which are always appreciating and ever worthless. They are soothed by a cunning harmony they willingly join. Everyone is in play, marked by his own particular fears and foibles. In short, it's much like any other small town in America.

With all that I've learned and experienced, I choose to believe I live in a small town somewhere in Utah, a little slice of heaven. Who is to say how long I will sojourn here? I could be gone tomorrow. (Probably not.)

www.youtube.com/watch?v=MOpWEjAnLUQ

If any mourning for Hirkill took place, I was not aware of it. He had no family and no friends other than the quid pro quo sort. I sometimes think that Hirkill was a fugitive from a crime beyond the power of God to forgive. Disgraced and defeated, he hung himself (though that was still under investigation) and revealed a rare but not unheard of anatomical condition.

To be sure, the words of Shelley came back to me: "They've put a tail on Hirkill. Be careful or they'll put a tail on you." I took it to mean that someone was following the mayor and might soon be following me. As it turned out, Hirkill had an actual tail, but no one has claimed responsibility. Medical science has only theories.

Until I started writing one, I had never seen a screenplay. Film was not a major, minor, or even an offered course in any university outside of Los Angeles. I turned out to be a quick study. Now, as then, I picked up the arcane lingo of city proclamations with no difficulty. My first proclamation honored my late predecessor.

WHEREAS, city government is the bulwark of our democratic system; and

WHEREAS, city public servants are the first line of defense in protecting our democracy; and

WHEREAS, the mayor of any city bears the greatest burden in the future of that city; and

WHEREAS, the City of Maragate is known as "A little slice of heaven"; and

WHEREAS, the City of Maragate is renowned for its artisan gin and jerky industries, its Spanish Circle, its farmers market, and its friendly people; and

WHEREAS, the late Mayor Ripley Hirkill was a tireless supporter of the city; and

WHEREAS, Mayor Hirkill served with distinction for many years;

NOW, THEREFORE, I, D. K. Kecskeméti, PhD, Mayor of the City of Maragate, by virtue of the authority vested in me by the codes of the City of Maragate, do

hereby proclaim the month of January during five consecutive years as

RIPLEY HIRKILL MONTH

in the City of Maragate and call upon the people of the City of Maragate to observe said month with appropriate activities and ceremonies befitting this recognition.

IN WITNESS WHEREOF . . .

Etcetera, etcetera, signed by yours truly.

During my public reading of this proclamation, I noticed Gertz, the mad producer, in the audience. He flipped me the bird for ratting him out, pretending to pick his nose. I extended my middle finger against the back of the framed proclamation.

After five years passed, no one made any public recognition that the sixth January was Hirkill-free, because no one had paid any attention to the previous five.

I won reelection in another landslide, this time running against Doc Fleck, Roosevelt-like in his wheelchair. We agreed he should be my opponent every election cycle. People seemed to like it that way. Though political opponents, Doc and I and Sandy still spent time together at the farmers market under our favorite cork tree, drinking basil citrus gin and gnawing on black cherry squirrel jerky, but as mayor I felt obliged to devote some time to wandering the Circle and pressing the flesh, accepting shots of gin along the way. I always made a stop near the playground where the Hoagg family set up their picnic. Tall and Cindy Hoagg were a nice young couple who kept a close eye on their three children playing in the sand. (Tall had been a hobbyist pilot, with his own small plane. The family used to enjoy outings in the air.) I looked forward to the snack Cindy always offered me: a tuna fish salad sandwich and macaroni salad, exotic fare for me.

Once, leaving the Hoaggs with sandwich in hand, I overheard a newcomer ask them how long I had been their mayor. Cindy said, "Forever." Everyone knew me, though most had long forgotten that I was once a screenwriter. I would walk the perimeter of Spanish Circle and wave at The Fizz whenever it passed by. (How do I explain tourism in Maragate? It is what it is. Which pretty much explains everything these days.)

Our proclamations, always supported, were a big hit. We issued one to Thai-O-Thai, where Valene and I often had dinner, comped, declaring a week in May as Thai Food Week. The yellow-bellied sapsucker, under our leadership, became the city bird.

Proclamations of a more serious nature were not avoided, I should say. We presented a proclamation to solar power, though few houses had roofs large enough or angled correctly to create solar power, and the owners of those that did would not allow holes to be drilled into them, which was just asking for leaks. (We didn't get much sun anyway.) We honored The Old Fools for steadfastly protesting two unnecessary and endless wars. Or was it three? And we honored our troops who fought in those unnecessary wars.

Under our leadership, we opened up the bike path to dogs on leashes, one of our most controversial decisions, which also neutralized the one issue of my perennial opponent, Doc Fleck. Since Chester Manfred had a new purpose in life, finding out who murdered his mentor (www.whokilledripley.com), Doc Fleck took up preserving Spanish Circle as his new cause. #savethecircle.

No matter your circumstances, life can always be made a bit more pleasant. The worse it is, the less it takes.

Look at Chrissy and her LGBTQs, for example. I made sure their application for a "Lipstick Lesbian" float in the Fourth of July parade was approved. They were delirious. They named me an Honorary Queer.

Harmony Meadows and Al Myra reawakened the grassroots effort to ban leaf blowers. (And, I am informed, a May-December romance ensued.) The debate was heated at times. I remained neutral on the subject. Since becoming mayor, I spent all my days at City Hall. I discovered that if you are not where leaf blowers are being used, they are not a problem, to you. Two council members were in favor of a ban, calling it a no-brainer with overnight benefits to residents in terms of cleaner air and quieter neighborhoods. The other two were opposed. (One was renting a high-end house at a below-market rate. His landlord made it clear he would evict him if he voted to ban what was legally sold on the open market. The other was having an affair with the wife of a landscaper and didn't want to make waves.) I cast the deciding vote, to ban. The town enjoyed a hitherto unfamiliar peace and quiet.

Valene and I remained a couple, of sorts. I could never repair her speech patterns, which used to annoy me no end, so I talked myself into believing that her uptalking was charming? What's more, I forgave her her sordid former life. (Everyone is entitled to a false start?) She enjoyed dropping by my office with Rufus and squeezing under my desk, like a scene in a bad movie (one that I wouldn't have written). She pressured me to declare Hope legally dead so that we could marry. I told her, let's wait a year. (It's been forever.)

Valene would stay with me whenever she had tourists renting her house? Which was almost always? (Carlos disapproved.) We slept together, entwined, always close to falling off my narrow bed. In the morning, we would lie together and spoon and talk a little. "I had the weirdest dream? We had a baby? But I couldn't see its face? I kept trying? And trying?" I would wrap her in my arms and coo, "It was only a dream? Don't be frightened."

The duties of my office were not demanding. I had a lot of free time. I had time, for example, to take art classes at the community center. Free of charge.

One evening in August, stifling, humid, and without even a hint of breeze, I sat on a bench at the edge of the Circle, sketching in walnut ink the frontage of Le Centre du Gin. The farmers market was underway behind me. The Fizz came by and momentarily blocked my view when it had to stop for a pedestrian jaywalking. The driver announced on the PA, "Hey, folks, it's our lucky day. On our left, a sighting of His Honor, Mayor K, expressing himself through his drawings. The mayor recently won the poster contest for the Battle of the Gins Festival. Congratulations, Your Honor!"

I waved back to the passengers. My eyes locked with those of a woman sitting in the last row. She stopped waving and stared at me, leaning over the back of her seat. She smiled, a smile I would recognize in a dark room. She had let her hair go gray, but she was still as beautiful as the first day I saw her, at Jack Lemmon's house.

The bus picked up speed as it rounded the upper arc of Spanish Circle. I left my art bag and sketchbook on the bench and ran after